680 MILES AWAY

TARA J. STONE

ISBN: 1-7349142-6-2
ISBN-13: 978-1-7349142-6-9

For my siblings.

"Father of the fatherless and protector of widows is God in his holy habitation. God gives the desolate a home to dwell in; he leads out the prisoners to prosperity; but the rebellious dwell in a parched land."

Psalms 68:5–6

The Doppelgänger

January 16, 2016

"ID?"

Evie raised her eyebrows in surprise, but she complied, taking out her driver's license and sliding it under the box office window. The young man on the other side of the window checked her license, and his fingers dexterously flipped through a box of envelopes until he found the one with her name on it.

"Evelyn Vincent," the young man said, handing her license and the envelope to her, "enjoy the show."

"Thanks."

"It was nice of them to comp your tickets, at least," Regina said as Evie turned to her and gave her one of the tickets from the envelope.

"It would've been nicer if they'd given me the job," Evie replied with a smirk. She'd never really expected to land a full-time spot in a professional orchestra at eighteen years old, but the audition was good experience anyway. And like Regina said, at least they'd given her free tickets to their concert. It made the money she'd spent on gas and the hotel almost worthwhile. Speaking of... "Thanks for coming all the way out here with me."

Regina flapped her lips. "Girl, you know I'm always up for an adventure."

"Yeah, except if I'm involved, it's usually a misadventure," Evie responded.

Regina snorted. "Fair."

Evie smiled. Even though Regina was a class ahead of Evie, the tall soprano was her oldest and closest friend. She knew all Evie's secrets, all her flaws and weaknesses. When Evie had been at her lowest, most desperate bottom, Regina had been the one to help her resurface and start over again. And somehow, Regina still put up with her after all these years.

An usher scanned their tickets, and Regina headed immediately for the bar. She wasn't twenty-one, but Evie knew that wouldn't stop her. If Regina's fake ID didn't work, her flirting surely would.

As they shuffled forward in the line at the bar, Evie absently fingered along with the lobby music, using her right forearm as a stand-in for the neck of her violin, her thumb covering a quarter rest tattoo on the inside of her wrist. Her left wrist sported a matching eighth rest. The fingering was an unconscious habit, one she didn't remember forming, almost like a tick.

Her mind wandered back to the audition. It had only taken them an hour afterwards to call her and deliver the unfortunate results. She'd played remarkably well, they'd said, but she lacked experience. Evie snorted to herself. It was a tactful way of saying they believed she was too young, too immature to be a full-time professional. But she'd done just fine taking care of herself for more than a year already. Well, maybe **fine** *was a stretch—*

Regina interrupted Evie's thoughts with a colorful expletive and shook her arm. "Look! Look at that girl over there."

It took Evie a moment to figure out which girl Regina meant, but when her eyes found the right target, her breath caught.

"Freaky, right?" Regina said.

It was freaky. The girl had Evie's face. She was obviously much younger than Evie—twelve, thirteen at most—but the resemblance was uncanny. She had Evie's chin and mouth and distinctive nose. The cheekbones and brow. The slight build and short stature. They were just far enough away that it was impossible to see the color of the girl's eyes—Evie's were gray. The only clear difference was the girl's hair, which was long and wavy and a shade darker than Evie's straight, light brown bob.

"Your doppelgänger," Regina said. "They say everyone has one. You should go introduce yourself. See her reaction."

Evie didn't care to see her own reaction to such a meeting, let alone her Doppelgänger's. She wanted to stop staring at the girl, but she couldn't. It was just so weird. The Doppelgänger walked hand-in-hand with a boy a little older and more than a head taller than her. Evie's eyes searched the faces of all the adults near the pair, not daring to hope... But the young couple appeared to be unchaperoned. They must be on a date. Evie couldn't decide whether it was cute or nerdy for kids their age to go to the symphony for a date. The two exchanged a few words, and the Doppelgänger smiled. No dimples—Evie had dimples, just below the corners of her mouth.

"You don't suppose—"

"No," Evie cut Regina off. "Don't even think it." But it was too late. The forbidden thought had already crossed Evie's mind.

"I'm just sayin'," Regina ventured. "It's possible."

"Are you gonna order something or what?" A middle-aged woman behind them gestured toward the bar—and the waiting bartender. There was no longer anyone in front of them.

"Sorry," Evie mumbled, forcing herself to stop playing this strange game of spot the difference with the Doppelgänger and concentrate on ordering a soda. She insisted on paying for Regina's drink, too, still feeling like she owed her friend for accompanying her on this trip.

The Doppelgänger and her date were nowhere in sight when Evie and Regina finally stepped away from the bar and made their way toward their orchestra-level box seats.

No wonder they had no problem comping these tickets, *Evie thought as she settled into her seat. The seats were terrible, the box so close to the stage that Evie and Regina practically sat behind the violin section. Nevertheless, Evie reveled in the chaotic sound of the orchestra warming up. Her sharp ears picked out a cello running through scale exercises (D-minor), a trombone growling out pedal tones (A... A-flat... G...), two bassoons playing a fast passage together (the opening notes of the program's first piece). Even as one part of her brain processed every note she heard, another part continued to dwell on the Doppelgänger. Almost against her will, her eyes scoured the concert hall for another glimpse of the girl with* her *face.*

"Evie?" Regina nudged her. "Are you even listening to me?"

"No," Evie answered honestly. She glanced at Regina and could tell her friend was both worried and annoyed. "I'm sorry. I'm... distracted."

Regina snorted. "No kidding."

And then Evie found her. In a balcony box opposite.

The lights began to dim, and Evie forced herself to turn her attention to the stage. Still, her eyes wandered back to the Doppelgänger when the concertmaster appeared and the applause started. She saw the Doppelgänger turn in her seat and pull the boy in for a kiss. Evie looked away, embarrassed for having intruded on what they probably thought was a private moment concealed by the darkness—not to mention how unsettling it was to watch a girl with her *face kissing some strange adolescent boy.*

When the music started, Evie wanted to lose herself in it, but thoughts of the Doppelgänger crowded out whatever enjoyment she'd hoped to have tonight. She couldn't focus on the music or the musicians. Maybe it was just like Regina said—everyone has a doppelgänger out there somewhere. But Evie couldn't shake the odd feeling seeing her Doppelgänger gave her. It was like déjà vu on steroids. Or like being trapped in an episode of a sci-fi show. Every time Evie glanced over at the Doppelgänger, she had the distinct impression she was somehow seeing what her life could have been.

Not that Evie's life had been particularly hard or anything. Well, at least not until she'd run away from home a couple months into her senior year. But before then, she'd had it pretty good. A stable home. Good friends. Respectable grades. A decent job at the surf shop. Plenty of opportunity. Still, watching the rapture on the Doppelgänger's face as she listened to the music—and the adoration on the boy's face as he gazed at the Doppelgänger—Evie felt a strange pang of longing.

But a longing for what, she couldn't say.

Summer 2020

1

The Party

♫

It was by far the strangest Fourth of July Evie had ever celebrated in her twenty-three years of life.

No parade. No fireworks. Only masks and fear.

And for Evie's money, the masks and fear were utterly absurd. She breathed a prayer of thanks that she no longer lived in California, where she'd grown up. Even though many restrictions remained in Colorado—the state she'd called home for the last five-and-a-half years—Evie had at least been allowed to go back to work at the music store in May. From what she'd heard, Californians were still basically living under house arrest.

Fortunately for Evie, her friend and coworker Finn thought the world's response to the pandemic just as ridiculous as she did. And he was throwing a Fourth of July party to prove it.

Evie had long outgrown the partying days of her high school and college years, but after almost four months of being treated like a disease vector rather than a human person, she was more than ready to mingle. She didn't even think she'd know anyone there other than Finn. In years past, that thought might have intimidated her. Not now. While the pandemic had most people living in constant fear and suspicion, it had had the opposite effect on Evie. Being part of the minority who refused to panic made Evie feel bolder, less beholden to other people's opinions.

Even so, as she pulled up to Finn's house and parked along the curb, a familiar knot of nerves settled in her chest. Several other cars clogged Finn's short driveway, and more lined the curb on both sides of the street. Evie briefly wondered whether any of Finn's neighbors might call the cops and complain about such a large gathering.

The moment she opened her car door, the smell of hamburgers on a charcoal barbecue hit her nose, and the din of voices and classic rock floated toward her from somewhere behind the house. It made her smile. They were signs of *life*.

Red, white, and blue balloons and an arrow drawn on poster board directed guests through an open side gate. Evie walked through it and followed a line of paving stones to the backyard, where the party was already in full swing. Four men, each with a beverage in hand, played corn hole on the lawn. Several people sat at a long picnic table on the shaded patio. Other small groups of two and three stood near the barbecue or the drink coolers or the food table. A handful of small children wove between the adults, along with several dogs, all chasing each other.

Evie knew Finn rented the house with three other guys, but she had still expected something smaller and humbler. After all, Finn made less than she did at the music store, and Evie sometimes struggled to pay the rent on her crappy studio apartment in a less appealing part of Scrub Oak, the Denver suburb where they both lived and worked and had gone to music school together. It made her wonder what his roommates did for a living. This house was easily on par with the one she'd grown up in—in La Jolla.

"Evie! You made it!"

Evie turned to see a man with thick-rimmed glasses and wild blond hair waving her over. Finn. She had never figured out whether his messy hair was a stylistic choice or simple laziness. Either way, he pulled it off well.

Finn stood with a cluster of musicians they'd both known from their time at the Lockwood School of Music. She was surprised to see them —she'd assumed her former classmates would be as afraid of catching covid as the rest of the world. She was glad to be wrong.

"Whoa! Evie Vincent?" A tall, skinny man with a booming bass voice threw his arms open wide as Evie approached. She allowed herself to be enveloped by his long limbs. Because of the height difference between them, their hug was somewhat awkward, but Evie delighted in it nonetheless—when was the last time she'd hugged anyone? Months, probably.

"Hi, Tony," Evie said as she pulled away.

The other two people standing with Finn and Tony—both women—offered polite smiles but no hugs. Amelia was a flautist with curly, dark hair that had been dyed an unnatural red. The other woman was a pianist named Vanessa. The shape of her face and her limp, straight hair had always made Evie think of a horse.

"Hello, Vanessa, Amelia." Evie nodded to both of them.

"It's been ages!" Tony exclaimed. "What have you been up to?"

"She's my boss, don't ya know?" Finn answered for her. He threw an arm around her shoulders. Unlike Tony, Finn seemed to be just the right height for Evie. He was still quite a bit taller than her—everyone was—but her shoulder fit neatly and rather comfortably under his arm. "And she's the bestest boss in the whole world."

"I am not your boss," Evie protested. It was true that she'd worked at the music store longer than Finn and had recently been promoted. The promotion came with a raise and more responsibility, but it gave her no authority over Finn or the other two Bach for More employees.

"Wait, you're still working in *retail*? I would've thought you'd be playing with the New York Phil by now," Amelia said. Her voice had a snide edge to it. "Or maybe touring as a soloist. Isn't that what other prodigies do?"

Evie's cheeks burned.

"That's right," Vanessa chimed in. "We all thought that's why you left Lockwood before you even graduated—to play some cushy gig somewhere."

"Sorry to disappoint." Evie gave them a flat stare. She'd left Lockwood three semesters before she was supposed to have graduated—more than two-and-a-half years ago now—and she was angry at herself for still being so pained by the memory.

"Evie's built up a pretty solid studio at the music store. Both violin and guitar. She's in really high demand as a teacher—er, there was lots of demand before the pandemic, anyway," Finn said.

His attempt at gallantry only made Evie more uncomfortable. Not to mention the reminder of how many students—and how much income —the lockdown had stripped from her. Just before the stay-at-home order shut down the store in March, Evie commanded a studio of twelve students, almost enough for her to leave the store altogether and launch her own private studio. But only three had returned when the store reopened in late April.

"I think I'm gonna get something to eat," Evie said and walked away. She felt bad leaving Finn and Tony so abruptly—especially Tony, since she hadn't seen him in so long—but she figured there would be other opportunities over the course of the party to catch up with them.

Evie barely had time to grab a plate before she felt a light touch on her right shoulder blade—exactly in the spot where she had a tattoo of a single measure from the first movement of Tchaikovsky's *Violin Concerto*. She turned to see Finn with an apologetic look on his face.

"Sorry about that," Finn said. "I didn't think... It was such a long time ago."

Evie waved dismissively. "It's my own fault. I'm the one who was too embarrassed to ever tell anyone that I left because I failed my jury and lost my scholarship."

Finn rubbed the back of his neck but didn't say anything. It struck her that even Finn—one of only two people she'd remained friends with after leaving Lockwood—didn't know the full story of why she never finished her music degree. Evie piled food onto her plate, wondering how long he would stand there watching her.

"Can I get you something to drink?" Finn finally asked. Then he grinned and waggled his eyebrows behind his thick-rimmed glasses. "I made a special Fourth of July punch."

Evie relaxed and smiled. "Sure," she answered.

More and more people arrived as the afternoon wore on, crowding the backyard and filling the main level of the house. Evie recognized more faces from Lockwood, but she avoided them. Apparently, two-and-a-half years wasn't long enough to get over her embarrassment.

When Amelia had called her a *prodigy*, Evie was certain she'd meant it as an insult, a reminder that Amelia—and many others—thought her nothing more than a show-off. And perhaps Amelia was right. At her audition to get into Lockwood, Evie had so thoroughly impressed the string department that they offered her a full-ride scholarship—something no one else had ever accomplished as far as Evie was aware. As an incoming freshman, she'd beat out upperclassmen and grad students for chair placement in the Lockwood Symphony Orchestra, second only to the concertmaster—and the only reason she hadn't been given *that* seat was because the conductor wanted someone with more "leadership" experience filling that role. She was named concertmaster a year later, as a sophomore.

Evie never meant to let her accomplishments go to her head, and she never wanted special attention. All she ever wanted was to make her instrument sound beautiful. But maybe her accomplishments did go to her head. And maybe she had been a show-off. Maybe her peers were right to despise her.

And so she avoided them.

Instead, Evie floated from group to group, forcing herself to meet new people and enjoy the general ebullience. After a while, she realized that most of the guests were not Finn's friends, but friends of his roommates. They were teachers and marketing directors and nurses and electricians and engineers. Evie's social circle had grown so small and specific in recent years, she found it exciting—and a little overwhelming—to meet such a variety of people.

After a few hours and three cups of Finn's special punch, Evie went inside to use the restroom. When she came out of the bathroom and wove her way through the press of bodies to reach the back door again, someone grabbed her wrist.

"Evie."

Evie turned and nearly collided with a stocky man with a dark beard and close-cropped hair. She caught her breath, shocked by the sight of him.

"Liam?" she whispered.

November 11, 2017

Evie practiced her violin with her eyes closed, letting her muscle memory and her ears do the work. Between preparing for her music jury at the end of the semester and her junior recital in the spring, Evie had plenty to work on. But she wasn't worried. Having perfect pitch made it easier to memorize the music, so it was only a matter of training her fingers and bowing arm.

Repetition. That was the key. Playing it right over and over and over again until she couldn't play it wrong.

A knock on the practice room door interrupted her intense focus.

Evie opened her eyes and turned around. She liked to practice with her back to the door, which had a long, narrow window set into it, so she wouldn't be distracted by the sight of other music students passing by. But the face peering through the window now wasn't a student.

It was Liam.

He was a campus safety officer, and it was his job to clear out the music building at midnight every Thursday, Friday, Saturday, and Sunday night. A side door with a card reader lock allowed students and faculty to get into the building with a swipe of their ID between 6:00 AM and midnight every day of the week, but there was no access after midnight. Very often, Evie was the only music student still practicing when Liam made his midnight rounds—the only student he had to "kick out." And always, he left the music building with her and walked her back to her on-campus student apartment. Evie looked forward to it every time.

She smiled when she saw him, and he cracked the door open.

"Midnight?" she asked.

"Not quite," Liam answered. "It's about ten 'til."

"Then I have ten more minutes to practice," Evie said with a smirk. "Shoo."

Liam opened the door wider. "Come on. Put your violin away and grab your coat," he said. "I have something I want to show you."

He seemed relaxed. And happy. Which was good. Things had felt a little strained between them lately. If anyone had asked Evie, she would have readily admitted that she was head over heels in love with Liam. And although neither of them had ever made a move, she was sure he felt the same about her. Or that he felt something, anyway. But in recent weeks, Liam had become more subdued, distant, awkward even.

Not wanting to let his good mood go to waste, Evie obediently put her instrument away and hustled out of the practice room. They stopped by the instrument lockers, where Evie retrieved her coat and locked up her violin, and then Liam led her to the elevator.

"Do I get a hint?" Evie asked, giving him a sideways glance.

Liam grinned. "Nope."

When they reached the main level, Evie started toward the exit, but Liam pinched her coat sleeve and pulled her in the opposite direction, toward the atrium and the main concert hall.

"This way."

Evie followed him through the atrium, past a grand staircase that led to the mezzanine and balcony levels of the concert hall, and through a set of double doors. She'd practically lived in this building for three years—even before she was officially a Lockwood student, Regina had snuck her into the practice rooms almost daily—and the deeper into the building they went, the more curious she became. Down another set of stairs, they came to the door for orchestra level seating.

Liam took out an enormous ring of keys and unlocked the door.

"After you." He held the door open for her and motioned her inside.

"It's pitch black in there," Evie said, her heart beating a little faster. Did he want to get her alone in the dark? She kind of liked the idea of being alone in the dark with Liam, but it seemed unnecessary to bring her all the way to the *concert hall if that's what he wanted.*

Evie realized she could pull out her phone and use the flashlight, but she didn't want to ruin whatever surprise Liam was going for. So she waited for Liam to use his university-issued flashlight. He clicked it on and led her through the aisles up to the stage.

From the floor of the orchestra level seating, the stage was about chest-high on Evie. Liam handed Evie his flashlight, and planting his palms on the stage, heaved himself up. He turned and held out a hand for Evie.

"There are stairs, you know," Evie said, using the flashlight to point to a set of steps near the box seats.

"This way is more fun," Liam responded, grinning. He bent down, took her hand, and effortlessly hauled her up.

Liam was a thick man—thick arms, thick chest, thick legs—and judging by the way she almost flew past him when he pulled her onto the stage, Evie suspected every inch of him was muscle. With a light hand on her back, Liam guided her backstage, to a corner that she'd hardly given a second thought in her many semesters performing in this hall. Tucked into the corner was a very steep and very narrow spiral staircase she'd never noticed. When Liam stopped at the bottom of it, Evie shone the flashlight straight up. The stairs ascended beyond the reach of the light.

"Where do these go?" Evie whispered.

"Up," Liam answered.

Evie snorted.

"Are you afraid of heights?" he asked.

"No." But she was a little afraid of not knowing what was at the top of the stairs. The way they disappeared into the inky void unnerved her.

"Then shall we?" Liam held out a hand, inviting her to go first.

"Really, what's up there?" she asked, annoyed that her voice sounded a little panicky.

"One of the most magnificent views in the entire city," Liam answered softly. He pressed closer to her, and her heart stuttered.

"We're going on the roof?"

Liam smiled. "Do you want to see it? It's a long climb, but it's worth it. I promise."

Evie beamed. She couldn't help it. Finally, after all this time. It was a date... right? He was taking her to the roof for a romantic view of the city. What else could it be? Why else would he want to show her this secret, secluded, beautiful spot except to finally admit there was something more than friendship between them?

Evie turned and started up the spiral staircase, and Liam followed close behind her. He was right—it was a very long climb. Well before they reached the top, Evie's legs and lungs began to burn, and she paused to catch her breath.

"You okay?" Liam asked.

"Yeah. Great. Just embarrassingly out of shape," Evie answered. Once upon a time, when she lived in San Diego and watched the sunrise from atop her surfboard every morning, Evie had been in fantastic shape.

Liam snickered. "It's even harder coming down, you know."

"Wonderful."

Evie's legs protested, but she forced them into motion again. She didn't care how much her muscles burned—she refused to give up. Perhaps irrationally, she worried that if she failed to make it to the roof, if she proved too weak or too easily deterred, Liam would regret bringing her and wouldn't say what she suspected he wanted to say. So she pushed on.

The steps led to a square scuttle hole in the ceiling, but there was no hatch or panel—it was simply open. Evie felt a shocking drop in the temperature as her head poked over the edge of the hole. She shone Liam's flashlight around, revealing a vast, attic-like space with a vaulted ceiling and steel beams crisscrossing the floor.

"Careful where you step," Liam said from below and behind her. "Stay on the beams."

Evie climbed the rest of the way out of the scuttle hole and shuffled along a beam just far enough to give Liam space to join her. When he did, he took the flashlight from her and led her with careful steps toward a gray steel door.

"You can hold onto me if you need to," Liam said over his shoulder. "It can be kind of hard walking these beams in the dark."

Even though she hadn't surfed in ages, Evie still had remarkable balance, and she had no trouble walking along the narrow beam. But she wasn't about to pass up the offer to hold onto Liam, so she reached forward and kept a hand on his back. The material of his safety officer's coat was cold and slick beneath her palm. At the door, Liam took out his massive ring of keys again. The door swung outwards, and a blast of frigid Colorado air swept through it. Liam half-turned and grabbed Evie's hand to lead her out onto the roof.

They stood on a ledge that was maybe five feet wide. Above and behind them, the roof sloped upwards another twenty feet to the apex of the building. Below and in front of them was a sheer drop to another peaked roof perpendicular to the one behind them.

And the view... Evie could see the entire campus—the commons, the humanities building, the business building, the science and math buildings. The dorms, the campus green, the arboretum, the athletic center, the lacrosse *field. Here and there a student walking along one of the winding red brick walkways that wove through campus or a couple snuggling on a bench, so tiny from this height. Beyond campus, Evie could see the sparkling lights of the city skyline to the north and the dim outline of the snow-capped Rockies to the west.* Magnificent *was almost an understatement.*

"Nice, right?" Liam asked with a grin.

"Very."

Still holding her hand, Liam led Evie to a spot a few feet away from the door and then sat, tugging her down with him. They sat with their backs to the sloped roof, their legs stretched out in front of them. Liam let go of Evie's hand, but it was only so he could put his arm around her. She wanted to relax and enjoy the closeness, but the cold and her own excitement made her tense, almost jittery.

"Sorry it's so cold," Liam said.

"It's not that bad," Evie lied.

"It probably would have been better to bring you up here during the summer, but—" Liam took a deep breath. "I brought you here for kind of a special occasion."

Evie's gaze snapped to Liam's face. Her heart hammered in her chest. This was it, the moment she'd been longing for, dreaming of, for months.

Liam checked his watch. And waited. What was he doing?

"Liam?"

"Now," he said. He looked down at her and smiled. "Exactly one year ago, you and I met."

Evie melted. This was even more romantic than she'd imagined. Meeting her meant so much to him that he remembered the date it happened! Emboldened by the thought, Evie leaned up, closed her eyes, and pressed her lips to Liam's. His beard was softer against her chin than she expected it to be.

Liam kissed her back and squeezed her closer for several heartbeats.

But then, he broke it off. Abruptly. Unfinished.

"I'm sorry," he said, shaking his head. "I can't."

He stood, leaving Evie cold and shocked. Her mind and emotions reeled. She had precious little experience with kissing, and her first lame thought was that she'd done it wrong somehow. Her cheeks flamed, confusion and humiliation ripping through her.

"Why?" was all she could get out.

"It's just not a good idea, Evie," Liam replied. He wouldn't look at her.

Evie stood, too, her whole body shivering—whether from the cold or the intensity of her emotions, she didn't know.

"I think you're wrong," she said. "I think it's a very good idea."

"I'm on duty," Liam said with a small shrug. "I'm a campus safety officer, and you're a student." He still wouldn't look at her, which made Evie suspect he wasn't being entirely truthful.

It made her angry.

"What does that have to do with anything?" she practically shouted.

"I'm in a position of authority," Liam responded. "It would be wrong of me to take advantage of that."

"What? Liam, that makes no sense," Evie argued. "I'm the one who kissed you. And not because I felt forced or threatened if I didn't. I kissed you because I wanted to. Because I have wanted to for months. I thought... I thought you felt the same way."

Liam finally glanced at her, but only for an instant. He said nothing.

Evie felt sick. Had she been wrong all this time? Had she imagined the looks he'd given her? The sparks between them? But then... why did he bring her up here? Why mention an otherwise meaningless anniversary?

"I'm sorry I brought you up here, Evie," Liam said. "It was a mistake."

♫

Someone bumped into Evie from behind, forcing her to step even closer to Liam. She could smell his cologne, and she hated how much she liked it. She twisted her wrist out of his grasp and took a half-step back.

"What are you doing here?" Evie demanded.

"The same thing everyone is doing here, I imagine," Liam replied. He flashed half a smile, as if he didn't understand why she wasn't thrilled to see him. "Celebrating the Fourth of July."

"Oh. Of course. Did your *wife* come, too?" It was an old wound, and one she thought had mostly healed. But she couldn't keep the bite out of her voice.

Liam looked taken aback. Genuinely confused. "My wife?"

Evie narrowed her eyes. She had to hand it to him. His acting was as good now as it ever was.

"Give her my best," Evie said. She turned on her heel and escaped through the crowd.

♫

As the sun disappeared and daylight faded, someone lit a gas fireplace nestled at the edge of the covered patio, and Evie found herself in a cozy group of half-shadowed strangers near the flames. Liam hadn't followed her outside, and there were enough people at the party that they hadn't run into each other again. She was grateful. Even though she'd spent much of the afternoon avoiding former classmates, and now Liam, Evie wasn't ready to go back to her lonely apartment.

She sipped from her fourth cup of Finn's special punch.

Evie didn't drink often, and when she did, she usually didn't drink much. Being such a small person, she was a lightweight, and she hated the out-of-control feeling of being drunk. Just now, she didn't feel drunk. Four cups over several hours was just enough to give her a pleasant buzz that was made even pleasanter by the gentle heat from the fireplace.

The classic rock that had been blaring from smart speakers all afternoon suddenly died.

"Evie!" It was Finn. Evie could just make him out in the dim twilight, coming toward her. He carried something. "Someone said they saw you over here. I was worried you'd already gone home. Here."

As Finn stepped into the firelight, Evie saw that he carried a guitar. He held it out to her, and his eyes twinkled merrily. His grin was infectious.

"What do you want me to do with that?" Evie asked, playing dumb.

"Oh, you *know* what I want." Finn waggled a single eyebrow. He squished himself onto the wide patio chair next to Evie, practically hip-checking her to make enough room for the both of them.

"Hey!" Evie barked with a laugh. "If you want me to play, you gotta give me space."

"Pfft." Finn traded her—the guitar for her almost-empty cup of punch—and stood back up. But then he reached behind Evie and stole the back cushion she'd been lounging against so he could sit on it on the ground at her feet. He drank the last of her drink and gazed up at her. "Anything else, milady?"

The strangers around them watched their playful interaction with amusement. Evie fleetingly wondered if they thought she and Finn were flirting, and it made her cheeks turn a little pink. Or maybe that was the alcohol.

"I don't really do this anymore, you know," Evie said to Finn, trying to block out all the eyes watching the two of them. Almost out of habit, she started to tune the strings on the guitar.

"Come on," Finn encouraged her. "For old times' sake."

In high school and at Lockwood, she and Regina had been known to provide impromptu entertainment at parties, with Regina singing just about any song requested and Evie playing guitar and singing harmony along with her. It was a kind of party trick, in fact. Even songs she didn't initially know, Evie could listen to once and play back perfectly on the guitar. As long as Regina knew the words, they would perform.

But Evie hadn't done anything like that—heck, she'd hardly been invited to parties—since Regina graduated and landed a gig in the chorus of a touring Broadway show. Regina was the pretty one, the outgoing one, the fun one. After she left, Evie realized that most of her friends were really just Regina's friends who tolerated Evie's existence.

Except for Finn.

"I don't have anyone to harmonize with," Evie said.

"I'll sing with you," Finn replied.

"You?" Evie had never heard Finn sing.

"What, you don't believe I can?" he asked with a grin.

"I—" She stopped herself before she said something insulting. She had met many people in her life who swore they could carry a tune but actually couldn't. Her perfect pitch didn't lie. "Okay."

Before Evie could even ask Finn what he wanted to sing, a woman sitting in their cozy little circle blurted out, "Ooh, do you know that one song? Oh, what is the name of it. You know, it's got that really pretty guitar part."

"Oh, yeah, that one," Finn played along. "Come on, Evie. You know that one."

He smirked at her, and she chuckled.

"Dust in the Wind!" the woman shouted.

Evie tried not to roll her eyes. She gave Finn a look that said *don't make me play that one*. It wasn't that she couldn't. It was that someone requested that song virtually every time she played—that and *Blackbird*. And every time, the person making the request thought they were being oh-so-original.

"Umm, I don't know the words to that one, sorry," Finn said, keeping his eyes locked on Evie.

Evie mouthed the words *thank you*.

Finn smiled. "Do you know any Ray LaMontagne?" he asked with a sly look.

He knew her too well. She loved Ray LaMontagne. If Finn sang a Ray LaMontagne song and sang it well, she suspected she might swoon. On the other hand, if he butchered a Ray LaMontagne song, she would butcher him.

"*You Are the Best Thing*?" Evie suggested.

"Wow, thanks, Evie," Finn joked. "What a nice thing to say." He even put a hand on his heart, feigning to be touched.

"Hm. Maybe I should have said *Trouble* instead," Evie retorted. "Because that's what you are, Sir Gallagher."

"What about that song from that Irish movie? *Falling Slowly*?" another person from the circle interjected.

It was a good suggestion—the original was a duet for a man and a woman set to acoustic guitar. Evie looked to Finn, her eyebrows raised with the unspoken question, and he nodded. Evie closed her eyes and took a moment to bring the song to mind with all its notes and rhythms and articulations. She imagined each finger placement and picking and strumming pattern.

With a slow exhale, she played. The song began with soft, simple fingerpicking, four measures of eighth notes. On the downbeat of the fifth bar, Finn started singing the first verse. His voice was a little shaky at first—nerves, probably. But when Evie harmonized with him on the second line, he seemed to gain confidence. She was impressed— many people who weren't trained singers, even competent instrumentalists, would lose their concentration and be pulled off their own note when another voice added harmony, but Finn stayed true. By the time they reached the chorus, Finn's voice was strong and rich and intense. Evie's naturally husky voice blended with his, their intonation perfect.

They were well-matched.

Evie kept her eyes closed for the entire song. When she opened them as she played the final notes at the end, she was surprised to find that several more people had joined the group around the fire. Many of them were couples with arms around each other or leaning on one another, spellbound looks on their faces. For a long moment after the last note died away, everyone seemed to hold their breath, and the crackling fire was the only sound.

"Not too shabby for a clarinet player, huh?" Finn broke the spell.

Evie smirked.

Then all at once, voices around them started calling out song requests. The requested genres ranged widely. Evie heard one person ask for *Bridge Over Troubled Water* and another suggest *Kashmir*. Others clamored for Taylor Swift. A few begged for songs and artists she'd never heard of. Someone even threw out a Michael Jackson song, which Evie actually thought would be fun to try on acoustic. It was ultimately up to Finn, though. If he didn't know the words, it wouldn't matter whether Evie could play it. And Finn was quite selective.

Evie knew from their years of friendship that Finn had an eclectic taste in music, and almost none of what he listened to hailed from the twenty-first century. She suspected he only knew of Ray LaMontagne and *Falling Slowly* because she had a playlist of 2000s indie folk on constant repeat at Bach for More. So it came as no surprise that he said no to Taylor Swift and yes to *Bridge Over Troubled Water*.

Evie closed her eyes once more and blocked out the voices and other sounds around her, retreating into her mind's ear to focus on the chords she would need to play. Unlike *Falling Slowly*, the original recording of *Bridge Over Troubled Water* didn't have a guitar part. Rather than trying to reproduce every individual note of the original's piano part, Evie mentally pared the song down to its basic chord progression. Within a matter of seconds, she was ready.

She played. Finn sang. She harmonized.

By the end of Simon & Garfunkel's classic, even more people had crowded in around the edges of the growing circle. Evie couldn't make out most of the faces beyond the glow of firelight, and she wondered whether Liam was one of them. She hoped not. For some reason, it didn't bother her to play and sing for strangers, but she didn't want Liam to hear her. She didn't want her voice and her skill on the guitar to delight or impress him. She didn't want to give him her music because her music was her soul. She wanted to forget that he existed.

More song requests poured in, and Evie and Finn obliged for more than an hour. Evie always sang and played with her eyes closed, and every time she opened them between songs, she found Finn grinning up at her from his cushion at her feet. She wondered how many cups of punch he'd had. Whenever they sang a song with a particularly well-known or catchy chorus—*Living' On A Prayer, Sweet Caroline, Don't Stop Believin'*—others sang along.

It was fun.

Evie couldn't remember the last time she'd had fun.

Perhaps the most fun moment of the night came from an unexpected source: Amelia the flautist. With a smug look, Amelia requested a song with no vocals—a "challenge for our little guitar player."

"In school, she always bragged that she could play anything by ear after hearing it only once," Amelia announced to the whole crowd.

"Shall we test that claim?"

Some of the drunker people ooh-ed and aah-ed and clapped. Others glanced around uncomfortably. Amelia's tone was so obviously meant to provoke Evie, they probably thought a catfight was about to break out and weren't sure whether they wanted to be there when it did.

Finn regarded Amelia with a deep frown.

"You up for it, Evie?" Amelia goaded. "Any song I choose?"

Evie was confident in her ability to hear any song and identify every single note in it. She heard music the way others heard speech—the notes came to her without much thought. The question was whether her fingers would be able to keep up. But the gauntlet had been thrown. She wasn't about to leave it on the ground.

Evie nodded. "Sure, I'm game."

Amelia pulled out her phone and scrolled on her screen for a moment. The crowd waited in rapt silence. When Amelia tapped her screen, a song started to play. Spanish flamenco. With very fast fingerpicking.

Evie frowned. It was a duet. She couldn't possibly play both parts at once.

"Which part do you want me to play?" Evie asked when the song ended.

Amelia scoffed. "The whole song."

"Yes, but which of the two guitar parts do you want me to play? It's a duet," Evie responded, failing to keep the sarcasm out of her voice. As a musician who'd actually graduated from Lockwood, Amelia should have been able to hear for herself that there were two guitars playing.

Amelia hesitated, her face flushing. She'd clearly thought it was only one guitar, and her attempt to humiliate Evie was backfiring. But she recovered. Barely. "The melody, obviously."

"Okay."

And Evie closed her eyes, took a deep breath, and played it. It was slower than the recording—having perfect pitch couldn't help her fingers play unfamiliar material fast, only practice could do that—but she played the melody note for note.

When Evie came to the end and opened her eyes, Amelia was gone.

And Finn was grinning at her.

2

Without Tobias

♫

It was the saddest Fourth of July Sam had ever celebrated in her seventeen years of life. Well, maybe the first Fourth of July without her parents was sadder. But this was a close second.

Tobias had moved away. Six hundred eighty miles away. His absence made the loneliness of the pandemic even lonelier.

Sam hadn't felt this lonely since the time she and Tobias had been grounded from each other after accidentally getting drunk at Patrick's party. That was almost five years ago, and it was still the only time Sam had ever been drunk. Or even tasted alcohol, for that matter.

That was the year Sam had moved in with Tobias and his family, the Howards. Her parents had been in a car accident that hospitalized them both for months. Just when her mother seemed to be making great strides in her rehabilitation, a pulmonary embolism took her life. Shortly afterwards, Sam's father recovered enough to abandon her with a heartless note saying, "The Howards can have her."

Sam looked back on that year—her seventh grade year—with a mix of powerful feelings. The loss of her mother and the betrayal by her father left deep wounds, but the Howards had also opened her eyes and her heart to a whole new world of joy and love. Tobias's parents, Lydia and Paul, had shown her more kindness and generosity than she could ever hope to repay. After her father abandoned her, they petitioned to be her legal guardians and provided for her every need.

Tobias himself had started out disliking Sam—or at least pretending to—when she first started living with his family. He was a grade ahead of her and a year-and-a-half older, and his so-called friends teased him about Sam. For her part, Sam had already harbored a major crush on Tobias for years—ever since she was nine years old, when she and her parents had first moved to Chickenhawk, into the house right across the street from the Howards. A few months after Sam moved in with Tobias's family, he admitted he had feelings for her, too. It took a while longer to figure out how to date each other when they lived in the same house. Strict rules were put in place—no kissing, no cuddling, and no holding hands in the house—and when it became clear Sam would never be moving out, the rules became even stricter.

Sam's reminiscences brought her full circle back to the present. The *rules* were why Tobias had to leave. Sort of. In a roundabout way. As they grew older, their bodies more mature, and their hormones more powerful, the rules became harder and harder to follow. Not that they had ever crossed *The Line*—or really even come close to doing so. They were both committed to waiting until they were married. But they'd also found more clever and more creative ways to bend the rules around the house—little touches here, almost-but-not-quite kisses there, suspiciously frequent collisions with one another in the hallway, leaning into each other as they did the dishes together, footsie at the dinner table. Well, perhaps that last one wasn't so clever. Pretty cliché, actually. And the one Lydia caught most often.

The pandemic took the situation from amusing to unbearable. Before March, Sam and Tobias spent plenty of time together outside of the house—going to school and out on dates—which gave them ample opportunity to kiss and cuddle and hold hands. But then everything shut down—some places by local mandate, others by choice. School went online. They were cooped up in the house together and unable to show physical affection toward each other for days at a time—especially because Lydia and Paul were confined to the house, too, which made it harder to bend the rules even a little bit.

As Tobias's graduation neared, he proposed a solution. Or rather, he just plain proposed.

April 28, 2020

It happened on the first really warm day of spring. Eager to take advantage of the weather and the chance it afforded them to have some "together time,"

Sam and Tobias walked to a park near their neighborhood. After a long and long-overdue kiss under their favorite tree, Tobias whispered, "Marry me, Sam."

She smiled and chuffed, thinking he was just caught up in the moment.

"I'm not joking," Tobias said. "I'm asking you for real."

Sam grew serious as she looked up into Tobias's earnest face.

"I know this isn't the romantic, elaborate proposal you deserve," he continued. "I don't—I don't even have a ring. But I love you, Sam. So much. And I know—I am a thousand percent sure—that you are the one I want to spend my life with. The one I want to grow old with and have a family with. The one I want to lay my life down for. So please. Samantha Josephine Ingram, I'm asking you… begging you… will you marry me?"

"Yes!" She said it without hesitation or uncertainty.

They'd talked about marriage before in a sort of far-off future kind of way. Sam had no doubt whatsoever that she wanted to marry Tobias. But she also hadn't expected him to propose before either of them had even finished high school. She loved Tobias deeply, and she had long dreamt of spending her life with him. But the idea of marrying so young also terrified her. How would they support themselves? What if she got pregnant? Sure, he was graduating, but she still had another year of high school. And what about college?

Would Lydia and Paul even let them get married?

After the initial jubilation over his question and her answer passed, Sam made her worries known. Tobias listened and nodded, as if he'd thought about all of these things already.

When Sam brought up Lydia and Paul, Tobias said, "Well, why don't we ask them. Right now."

And they did.

And that's when everything went sideways.

Paul and Lydia kept remarkably calm. It shouldn't have been a surprise—Sam had rarely seen Lydia lose her temper, and she'd never seen Paul angry. But to Sam and Tobias's chagrin, calm did not mean supportive.

"You're way too young," Lydia said.

"I'm old enough to vote and go to war," Tobias replied. "I'm legally an adult."

"Sam is not," Lydia responded. "And until she is, we are still her legal guardians."

"I'll be eighteen in January," Sam pointed out meekly. She almost didn't. It was a discussion more than an argument, but it felt like arguing. And she hated arguing with Lydia. She loved and respected and trusted Lydia. Being at odds with her always felt wrong.

"It's not just about the number of years you've been alive," Lydia fired back. "It's about maturity. About being ready to support yourselves. Ready to support a family. Ready for children." She turned to Sam. "Are you ready to have kids?"

Sam swallowed. "No," she answered honestly.

"See?" Lydia gestured with an open hand.

"But I wasn't ready to lose my parents when I was only thirteen either," Sam continued. "It happened anyway. And God gave me everything I needed to handle it."

Lydia's face softened at the mention of Sam's parents. She'd always called Sam an old soul, even before her mother died and her father abandoned her. Those traumatic events had aged Sam's soul even more.

"I think there are some things you can never be ready for until they happen," Sam said. "Things like losing people and things like having children." She looked Lydia in the eye. "Were you ready when you had Liz? Or Catherine, for that matter?"

Liz was Tobias's older sister, the eldest of the Howard children, and Sam knew Lydia had only been twenty years old when she was born. Catherine was Tobias's little sister, just three-and-a-half years old. She had been a complete surprise, born when Lydia was forty-two and fifteen years after Tobias, the next youngest.

Lydia narrowed her eyes in a **don't give me attitude** kind of way. Sam threw up a placating hand. Oddly enough, if Sam could claim to know anything at all about children, it was only because she was already living with the Howards when Catherine was born.

"All I'm trying to say is… if I wait until I'm **ready**—" she made air quotes. "—to be a mom, I might never get married."

"Even if that's true, Sam," Lydia replied, "you still need to think about how you're going to pay for diapers and groceries and clothes and medical expenses. Not to mention rent and utilities and insurance. A car. Gas. Your cell phone. Those are all things you can and should be able to take care of **before** you get married."

"Is that it?" Tobias asked.

"You don't think that's enough?" Lydia retorted.

"What I mean is, is that the only thing standing in our way?" Tobias clarified. "Financial security? Or are there other reasons you think we should wait?"

When Lydia and Paul hesitated a beat too long, Tobias plowed on. "Because I think waiting longer than we have to is just cheating ourselves of grace. Matrimony is a Sacrament, right? Why put off receiving the grace of a

Sacrament any longer than absolutely necessary?"

Tobias's reasoning lit Sam up inside. Goosebumps raised the hair on her arms, and tears sprang to her eyes. Grateful tears. Happy tears. Loving tears. Before she'd lived with the Howards, Sam hadn't ever thought about God, let alone believed in Him. But the Howard family's steady and joyful witness of faith and love had nudged open the door of Sam's heart just enough for God to break it wide open. She came into the Catholic Church a few months after her mother died, and her faith had only grown stronger since. Tobias's had, too.

"We've already been dating for four-and-a-half years," Tobias continued, becoming more animated and passionate with each word. "How much longer do you think we need to date? One year? Two years? Four years? Because that's one, two, four more years of fighting temptation without that grace."

Lydia's mouth hung open. She had no answer. If she agreed that the grace of matrimony was real and important, she had no room to dispute Tobias's conclusion that waiting was spiritually risky. And it was unthinkable that she would disagree—the reality and power of sacramental grace was fundamental to what they believed as Catholics.

Sam wanted to cheer. She had never been so proud to be Tobias's girlfriend. No! Not just his girlfriend anymore. Whatever Lydia and Paul said, Sam had already given him her yes and had no intention of taking it back. She was his fiancée! The realization delighted her so much that she forgot about the tension in the room and grinned.

"That's a valid point, Tobias," Paul finally chimed in. He was a quiet and serious man—both traits Tobias had inherited. Sam admired the way he always took time to observe, listen, and carefully analyze a situation before formulating his own thoughts or speaking up. "I might even say it's an excellent point. And Sam, I think your insight about being ready or not ready is both wise and humble. Only pride can fool itself into thinking it's ready for every possible outcome. But that doesn't let us off the hook for making preparations for likely outcomes. And children are a likely outcome in a healthy and holy marriage. So, Tobias, what preparations have you made to support a family? And if you haven't made any, how long do you suppose you'll need to do so?"

Sam thought she saw the corner of Tobias's mouth lift. And when she glanced at Paul, she swore he had a twinkle in his eye despite his neutral expression. Had Tobias and Paul already talked about all of this? Although Paul was unfailingly practical, the voice of reason in every situation, Sam believed he was also a romantic at heart. In that moment, she felt sure he wanted to give their engagement his blessing and to help them figure out a way to marry sooner rather than later, but he wouldn't do it without winning *over his own wife first.*

"Paul?" Lydia regarded her husband with raised eyebrows.

"If Tobias has a plan, it's only fair that we hear what it is before we make any decisions one way or the other," Paul explained. He and Lydia stared at one another for a long moment, having a silent conversation only the two of them understood. Finally, Lydia relented.

"All right. Let's hear it." Her feistiness from earlier disappeared. In fact, she seemed to slump as if already defeated, and she wiped a quick hand across her eyes. Lydia cried a lot—about big things, small things, happy things, sad things, beautiful things, difficult things. For her, tears were just a standard side effect of powerful emotion. But seeing her tear up now made Sam's heart pang.

"Well," Tobias began, "you know I've been working in landscaping every summer since I was fourteen. Even though I only worked during the summer, I managed to save up a few thousand dollars from that. And you know that it's never been my plan to go to college. I'm not good at school, the jobs I'm interested in don't require a college degree, college is really expensive. So, I have already started applying for full-time positions working under an electrician or doing HVAC. Whichever one I get, I plan to work my way up through an apprenticeship. Both of those jobs make decent money."

"A few thousand dollars, you said?" Paul asked.

Tobias nodded. "That's what I have saved up already. I'll save more once I get a full-time job."

"You'll also spend a whole lot more if you're married and start having children," Paul responded. "Do you have any idea what your monthly budget would be if you and Sam were married?"

"Yes, sir," Tobias answered. "I've done a lot of research on budgeting and cash flows and all that. I made some..." His ears turned pink. "Some spreadsheets."

Sam gazed at Tobias in surprise. She'd had no idea that he'd had their future on his mind long enough to make spreadsheets. *But Paul didn't seem surprised at all.*

"So you know how much you need to make to be able to pay expenses and *put some money into savings each month?"*

"Yes, sir."

"And these jobs you're applying for... they pay that much?"

Tobias hesitated. "We won't be able to afford this—" Tobias motioned at the beautiful suburban house around them. "—kind of lifestyle until I'm a journeyman probably. Maybe not even then. But we will be able to afford the necessities. Plus some."

Paul nodded for a time, thinking over Tobias's answers. "Since you know your monthly budget, you should be able to calculate how much six months of expenses would be."

Tobias's brow furrowed. "Yes, sir."

"Is that how much you have saved?"

Tobias hesitated again. And deflated a little. "No, sir."

"And what about Sam's engagement ring? Did you forget to give it to her when you proposed this afternoon? Or can you not afford one?"

Tobias looked at Sam, but she couldn't read his expression. Apologetic? Hopeful? "I have a design picked out, but I don't know your ring size," he said to her. "I thought we would go together to get your finger sized after... after you said yes."

Again, he surprised her. And she loved him for it. When had Tobias had time to go ring shopping? And make spreadsheets? And plan their whole future? Just how long had he been planning to propose? He had to have started before the pandemic—jewelry stores were certainly not among the essential businesses *that had been allowed to stay open.*

"That sounds wonderful," Sam said softly.

Tobias smiled at her, and for a moment, lost in each other's gaze as they were, Sam forgot Lydia and Paul still hadn't given them permission to marry.

"Tobias," Paul gently recalled their attention. "I would like to offer a compromise."

"Okay," Tobias said uncertainly.

"Like your mother, I believe you are both very young to be getting married, especially considering your current financial situation." Sam noticed he hadn't said too young, *only* very young. *"You have some money saved, but not enough, and you have no current employment, though you do have some prospects. On the other hand, I believe your intentions are sincere and that they won't change no matter how much time passes. Your desire to marry one another is not rooted in fickle infatuation or mere physical attraction, but in true, authentic, deep love. Love that's already been tested in many ways. I believe that."*

Paul paused. It made Sam worry about what he would say next.

"This diocese requires a minimum of six months of marriage prep." It was not what Sam had expected Paul to say. She hadn't realized that marriage prep classes at their parish would need to figure into their timeline. Even if Paul and Lydia gave immediate consent, they'd still have to wait at least six months. "My offer is this. You may ask Father Bernard to begin marriage prep after the following conditions have been met: first, that you have a full-time job; second, that after you have bought and paid for Sam's engagement ring in

full—no debt—you then have enough money in savings to cover six months of expenses—expenses according to how much it will cost to live as a married couple, not as a single young man; and third..." Paul took a deep breath.

Sam almost couldn't bear the suspense.

"You have to move out."

♫

Paul never said Tobias had to move *six hundred eighty miles* away, just that he had to move out.

But after looking at all the options and making a lot of calculations with his spreadsheets, Tobias realized the quickest way to save six months of expenses would be to move to Scrub Oak, Colorado and apprentice under one of Sam's uncles, Steve, who owned an HVAC company. He could live with Steve and his wife, Kristy, and save on rent.

Sam sat at the piano in the family room and fiddled with the sparkling ring on her left ring finger. Even after a couple of months, the weight of it still felt strange when she played piano.

Tobias spent an enormous chunk of what he'd saved over the previous four summers to pay for the ring in cash. Sam protested that she didn't need anything quite so fancy—that she didn't even need real diamonds—but her attempt to help Tobias save money only hurt his feelings. Apparently, he had put a great deal of time and thought into choosing her ring, and he misinterpreted her frugality as disapproval of the design choices he'd so carefully and lovingly made. Sam quickly realized her mistake and tried to backtrack, profusely praising the design and style of the ring. But the hurt didn't leave Tobias's eyes until Sam apologized outright and told him she was only worried about the money because it meant waiting longer to be married—and she didn't want to wait longer.

"I hope you've been practicing the national anthem on that thing," said a friendly voice behind her. "You messed it up pretty bad last year."

Sam spun around on the piano bench and found Bear, Tobias's older brother, standing in the doorway and grinning at her. She hadn't even heard him come into the house.

He wore the cassock of a seminarian, having just come from serving at Mass. Every summer, the seminarians of the diocese were assigned to serve in various parishes and learn from the pastors who hosted them. Miraculously, Bear had been assigned to their very own parish that summer. He stayed at the rectory with Father Bernard, but he spent many of his days off at his parents' home.

"That wasn't last year," Sam replied, mirroring his grin. "That was four years ago. And I was sight-reading. From a phone."

"Four years?!" Bear exclaimed. "You've lived here for four years? And you still put up with these goofballs?"

"I heard that!" Lydia called from the kitchen.

"Almost five," Sam said. "And I wouldn't trade these goofballs for the world."

"Keeping that halo shiny, huh?" Bear said with a wink.

Sam's smile slipped. "Not shiny enough."

She knew and understood why Paul had made Tobias's moving out a condition of their deal. Tobias needed to prove he could stand on his own two feet before taking on the responsibility of providing for a family. But each day of Tobias's absence made Sam just a little more bitter about it. She missed him, and it was hard not to blame Paul and Lydia for the ache she felt. As a result, she'd found herself snapping and arguing more often, even saying deliberately hurtful things.

Bear settled on the piano bench next to her. It creaked beneath his generous weight.

"What's up, Sam?" he asked in a low voice, one that Lydia wouldn't be able to hear in the kitchen.

Sam leaned her head against his giant shoulder and sighed. From the moment the Howards had taken her in all those years ago, Bear had treated her like one of the family. He'd been a big brother to her from the start.

"Lydia and I had a fight this morning," Sam said. Tears welled in her eyes, both from shame at the hurt she'd caused and from the hurt she still felt. "I asked if I could go visit Tobias in Colorado, and she said no, and I blew up." Sam sniffed. "She doesn't trust us not to… whatever."

Bear took a deep breath, allowing several moments to pass before responding. "Wow. I really didn't see that coming."

"What?"

"Your first mother-in-law fight. And you're not even married yet. Geez."

Sam snorted a laugh and wiped her tears with her fingertips. "Is that what this is? Because it sucks. I don't want to spend the rest of my life fighting with Lyds just because she's my mother-in-law. I love her too much." That's why it hurt so much that Lydia didn't trust her.

"It's just a weird situation, Sam, and she's doing her best to do what she thinks is right. She feels responsible for both of you. For your souls. Most parents just have their own kid's soul to worry about, which is plenty, but she's in the weird position of worrying about her son *and* her son's girlfriend. She's doing for you what she would do for her own daughter. I think."

"I just thought, after all this time... we've been together for four-and-a-half years, and we've never once even come close to stepping over the line. And we won't. But she acts like we're feral animals ready to rip each other's clothes off all the time. It's... it's insulting," Sam vented.

"Is that really why she won't let you go? Is that what she said?" Bear asked.

Sam hesitated. "No. She didn't say that."

"What did she say?"

"She didn't give me a reason," Sam said. A beat. Then, "Er, I guess, I didn't give her a chance to give me a reason. I just... went off on her."

"Hm." Bear crossed his large arms and stroked the close-trimmed beard on his chin.

Sam sat up and looked at him. "You think I should apologize."

Bear shrugged. "Or you could let it fester and become a much bigger deal than it needs to be. Up to you."

♫

Sam found Lydia in the kitchen. She sat at the breakfast table with Catherine, drawing mermaids for the little girl to color in. Lydia looked up when Sam entered.

"Where's Bear?" she asked.

"He went up to change," Sam answered. She took a seat at the table, stroking the top of Catherine's head as she did so. She loved Tobias's little sister as much as she loved all the Howards. It took her a few moments to work up her courage. When she did, she took a deep breath and said, "Lydia, I'm sorry about the things I said this morning. I have no right to be anything but grateful to you and Paul. You've never owed me anything, but you've always given me everything. I acted like a spoiled brat this morning, and I'm very sorry." She didn't quite make it all the way through her little speech before the tears returned.

Catherine looked at her askance. "Why are you crying, Sam?"

"Because my heart hurts," Sam answered.

Lydia reached across the table with an open palm. Sam placed her own hand in it, and Lydia squeezed.

"I'm sorry, too," Lydia said. "I know how hard this is for you. You and Tobias have never been apart this long, and I know you miss him. I miss him, too." She paused. "I do trust you, Sam. I want you to know that. You and Tobias have been model kids, always. Well, except for that time you got drunk."

Sam quirked a smile. The drunk episode had long since become a joke between all of them because it had been so out of character for both her and Tobias.

"I just don't want you traveling across state lines while things are so crazy," Lydia explained. "Between the pandemic and the riots, I just don't think it's a good idea to send you off on an airplane by yourself. Travel restrictions are all over the place and changing every day, it seems like, and I don't want to risk you getting stuck in Colorado. And I don't want you driving that far by yourself. Paul can't take time off to go with you, so that leaves me. But where I go, Catherine goes, and I don't want to be traveling with a three-year-old with everything that's going on."

Sam nodded. She should have known Lydia had a perfectly practical reason for not letting her visit Tobias. Her emotions had gotten the best of her, though, and she'd jumped to all the wrong conclusions.

"If or when things settle down, you can absolutely go visit Tobias," Lydia said. "On one condition."

Sam raised her eyebrows in a silent question.

"That you give him a great big hug from me when you see him," Lydia said with a gentle smile. "Deal?"

Sam shot out of her chair and came around the table to throw her arms around Lydia's neck. Lydia stood to return the hug properly. The top of Sam's head barely reached Lydia's chin, and Lydia planted a kiss on her hair.

"Do you forgive me?" Lydia asked.

"Yes," Sam said, her face buried in Lydia's shoulder. "Do you forgive me?"

"Of course I do."

"My soul magnifies the Lord,
and my spirit rejoices in God my Savior,
for he has regarded the low estate of his handmaiden.
For behold, henceforth all generations will call me blessed;
for he who is mighty has done great things for me,
and holy is his name.
And his mercy is on those who fear him from generation to generation.
He has shown strength with his arm,
he has scattered the proud in the imagination of their hearts,
he has put down the mighty from their thrones,
and exalted those of low degree;
he has filled the hungry with good things,
and the rich he has sent empty away.
He has helped his servant Israel,
in remembrance of his mercy,
as he spoke to our fathers,
to Abraham and to his posterity for ever."

Luke 1:46–55

3

A Strange Encounter

♫

"Bless me, Father, for I have sinned. It's been a month since my last confession."

Evie waited a beat. It was silly. In all the times she'd ever gone to confession, no priest had ever responded at this point. Whichever priest she confessed to, he only spoke after she actually started naming her sins. But for some unknown reason, Evie always waited for him to say *something* at this part. When—as always—the priest didn't say anything at all, she continued.

"I have been extremely judgmental of the way people react to the pandemic. I think terrible thoughts about them. That they're stupid. Or cowards. I have failed to exercise compassion. I know it's real and that people are really getting sick and dying, but… I just get so angry about the whole thing. I get especially frustrated with two of my coworkers, and I snap at them when they don't deserve it."

Evie paused. She'd confessed that very thing last time, too. A firm purpose of amendment—the sincere intention to avoid sins in the future—was part of a valid confession. But her anger about the pandemic was something she didn't know how to avoid. The best she could do was try to avoid lashing out at people for their fear.

"I went to a party yesterday, and I saw someone there who… who used to be a friend—er, more than a friend. I'm not sure, actually. Anyway, things didn't end well between us, and I thought I had forgiven him, but I still felt angry when I saw him. He tried to talk to me, but I… didn't give him a chance. I guess I'm still holding a grudge.

"And then, I also was angry at some people I used to go to school with. I think I humiliated one of them, and what's worse is that I enjoyed humiliating her. I gave in to pride and vanity. I acted like a show-off.

"And then, I was embarrassed and ashamed of being a show-off, and I left the party without saying anything to my friend who was hosting the party. I made him worry, and I probably hurt his feelings. At the very least, I'm guilty of being ungrateful and inconsiderate."

Evie paused. Finn's party loomed too large in her mind to remember any of the other sins she was sure she'd committed in the last month.

"For these and for any sins I have forgotten, I am truly sorry."

Evie heard the rustle of clothing as her confessor shifted in his seat behind the screen.

"Thank you for a good and honest confession." It was Father Michael's voice. He was a young-ish priest, recently ordained. "What does Jesus say? He says, 'Take my yoke upon you, and learn from me, for I am *meek and humble of heart.*' Humility. Humility doesn't mean putting yourself down or allowing yourself to be abused by others. It means seeing yourself as you truly are—as God sees you. How does God see you?"

"I don't know," Evie whispered. She thought the question might have been rhetorical, but she answered anyway.

"Hm. Perhaps you should ask him," Father Michael said, and Evie could hear the gentle smile in his voice. "For your penance, pray the Magnificat—do you know it?"

"Um… no."

"It's in the Gospel of Luke, chapter one, verses forty-six through fifty-five. Reflect especially—"

"I'm sorry, Father," Evie interrupted. "Can you write that down? I… I'm not good at remembering numbers."

"Oh." A beat. "I don't have anything to write on. Or to write with." Another beat. "Do you have your phone?"

"Yes…"

"Here. Take a picture."

Evie heard the sound of pages being turned—thin pages, a Bible. The confessional was designed so that penitents had the option of sitting face-to-face with the priest or kneeling behind the screen. Evie preferred kneeling, but she saw Father Michael's hand appear around the edge of the screen holding his open Bible.

"It's there on the left side, first column. Luke one, forty-six to fifty-five."

Evie pulled out her phone and snapped a picture of the verses.

"Got it," she said.

The Bible disappeared around the corner.

"Good. Now, pray with those verses. They're Mary's words. And as you're praying, reflect especially on the part that speaks about how God scatters the proud and lifts up the lowly. Do you think you can do that?"

"Yes, Father." Evie stared at the picture on her phone. *My soul magnifies the Lord, and my spirit rejoices in God my Savior, for he has regarded the low estate of his handmaiden…*

"Okay. Please say your act of contrition."

Evie closed her eyes. This was why she preferred kneeling behind the screen. She always messed up her act of contrition when she confessed face-to-face, but behind the screen, she could pray it flawlessly.

"O my God, I am heartily sorry for having offended you, and I detest all my sins because of your just punishments, but most of all because they offend you, my God, who are all-good and deserving of all my love. I firmly resolve, with the help of your grace, to sin no more and to avoid the near occasions of sin. Amen."

"God, the Father of mercies, through the death and resurrection of his Son has reconciled the world to himself and poured out the Holy Spirit for the forgiveness of sins; through the ministry of the Church may God grant you pardon and peace, and I absolve you from your sins in the name of the Father, and of the Son, and of the Holy Spirit."

Evie made the sign of the cross as Father Michael invoked the Holy Trinity. At the end, she said, "Amen."

"Go in peace," Father Michael said.

"Thank you, Father."

♫

Evie dreaded seeing Finn at work on Monday morning. Even after going to confession and receiving absolution, she still felt awful about the way she'd left Finn's party. And about the way she'd humiliated Amelia at the party.

But it was more than that. Singing with Finn had made Evie see him in a new way, a way that confused her.

Making music—not merely singing or playing, but *making music*—with another human being was intimate business. It required vulnerability and trust, attentiveness and awareness of the other. Being in tune and in balance with one another demanded listening, responding, adjusting, fitting inside each other's sound. When perfect intonation and balance were reached and individual voices subsumed into a single sound, the feeling was like nothing else in the world.

Obviously, Evie had made music with dozens of other human beings before—playing in the orchestra and string quartets and other ensembles—and it never got weird. But duets were different. It had never been weird with Regina either, but then again, Regina was her best friend.

Finn was a good friend. And Evie wanted it to stay that way. Until they'd sung together, she never even considered that Finn could be something other than a good friend. Well, that wasn't entirely true. She had considered it once or twice in the five years they'd known each other, but she'd always known that no man would pick her while she was standing next to Regina, so she'd always dismissed such considerations immediately.

But she was no longer standing next to Regina. And the memory of her and Finn's voices blending together so well that it was difficult to tell who sang the melody and who sang harmony—and the image of Finn grinning up at her from the cushion at her feet—made her wonder if things were about to get weird between them.

Along with her recent promotion, Evie had been given a key to Bach for More. Terry, the store's owner, hoped to dial back his involvement in the business's day-to-day operations—a first step toward his eventual retirement—and he'd handed off many of his daily tasks to Evie. Opening the store was one of them.

When she arrived Monday morning, two men waited outside the door. One looked to be in his thirties, the other college-aged. The older one had a three-day growth of beard and dirty fingernails. The younger one was tall and lean with a handsome, clean-cut face and dark, fashionably cut hair. Something about him seemed vaguely familiar.

Evie's eyes flicked to the only other vehicle in the parking lot, a utility van with a decal that read *Emory's HVAC Services*. She'd almost forgotten—the air conditioning had quit working Friday afternoon. Evie regarded the two men at the door again. The older one fit the bill all right, but the younger one looked more like a jock than an HVAC technician.

"Sorry," Evie said as she approached with the key. "I didn't realize you guys would be here so early."

They both turned, and the younger one's big brown eyes bulged and his mouth opened when he saw her. He didn't say anything, though.

"Party a little too hard this weekend, did ya?" the older one said.

Evie smiled politely but didn't answer. She unlocked the door and held it open so they could enter, but the younger man reached around and grabbed the door behind her, motioning her inside first.

"Thanks," Evie said.

"Sure," he answered. The young man continued to stare at her in a way that made her uncomfortable. He didn't leer or anything. It was more like… like he was frightened by her.

"I'm Joe, that's Tobias," the older man said when they were all inside. "I'm teaching him the ropes, ya know." He stopped in his tracks and cussed. "Sorry, did you want us to wear masks while we're inside?"

Evie groaned inwardly.

♫

When Finn arrived, Evie breathed a sigh of relief.

Sure, she'd dreaded seeing him. But that was before she met the HVAC men. She didn't like being alone with them, especially because every time she glanced over at them, she caught the young one—Tobias—staring at her. It was even more unsettling after he and Joe put their cloth masks on—despite Evie's insistence that she didn't care one way or the other—and all she could see were his staring eyes. He quickly averted his gaze every time she caught him, but after the fourth time in ten minutes, Evie almost texted Finn to tell him to come to work early.

"Good morrow, Lady Vincent!" Finn greeted when he came in. "How art thou?"

Normally, Finn's goofy antics would make Evie smile or laugh. Or quirk an eyebrow at the very least. He must have been able to tell she wasn't in the mood this morning, though, because he toned it down right away. His entrance drew the attention of the HVAC men. Tobias looked from Finn to Evie as if trying to judge their relationship. But again, he dropped his eyes as soon as Evie looked his way.

"Glad to see you're alive," Finn quipped as he joined her behind the counter.

"I know. I'm sorry," Evie said. "You had no reason to be worried, though."

"Says you," he responded. "I didn't know ninety percent of the people at that party. Any one of them could have been a serial killer or a talent scout for an evil movie executive—"

"What?"

"—or a human trafficker."

Evie flinched at that last one, but Finn didn't seem to notice.

"You're what—five feet tall and less than a hundred pounds, I bet," he continued. "It wouldn't take much for a guy who's had one or five too many drinks to overpower you and carry you off to who knows where. And knowing my roommates, I can tell you there were plenty of guys at that party who would do exactly that kind of thing. And do you know how horrible I would feel if something like that happened to you at a party I invited you to?"

Evie was half-touched and half-insulted by Finn's concern. Sure, she was little. But she could take care of herself. She'd had to since she was seventeen. Then again, hadn't she just been hoping Finn would rescue her from being alone with the HVAC men?

"Okay, Sir Gallagher," Evie said in a low voice. "I get it. I'm sorry I didn't tell you when I left the party." She paused. "And thank you for looking out for me. You're a good friend."

Finn smiled. "You know Regina would have my hide if I let anything happen to you. She made me promise to keep an eye out for scoundrels and ruffians when she left."

Evie punched him in the shoulder. "*Scoundrels and ruffians*? She did not say that."

"No, she used far more colorful language, for sure," Finn agreed, chuckling and rubbing his shoulder.

Evie rolled her eyes. "All right. Well, ready thyself, good sir, because scoundrels and ruffians are afoot, and I require your knightly presence."

"Every night? Holy crickets, Evie, I had no idea you felt that way."

Evie's cheeks and ears burned, and she punched his shoulder again. "Knightly, like a knight in shining armor." Somehow, that made it worse. She *knew* things would get weird. Her words came out in a rush. "I don't mean a romantic knight in shining armor. I mean like a guard or something. Like a protector. I need protection."

"Protection?" Finn's expression turned serious. "From what? Did something happen, Evie? Are you okay?"

"Yes. I mean no." Evie huffed. "Yes, I'm okay. No, nothing happened. But—" she jerked her head in the direction of the HVAC men. "—see those guys working on the A/C?"

Finn's blue eyes darted to the men behind her and then back to her face. "Yes."

"The tall one with dark hair… he keeps staring at me, and it's giving me the creeps."

"You want me to tell him to leave?"

"No!" Evie sighed. "We need the A/C fixed. Just… don't leave me alone with them. Okay?"

"You got it, boss," Finn answered. His words were light, but his tone and his face were not.

"Thanks. And I'm not your boss."

The morning passed slowly with only a handful of customers to take care of. When a mother and her adolescent son came in looking to buy a guitar, Evie tried to sell them on lessons as well. The boy seemed more interested in his smartphone than guitar lessons, though, and the mother seemed horrified by the suggestion of in-person instruction. No surprise considering the woman had entered with not one but two masks smothering her face and strictly maintained a distance of six feet from Evie and Finn at all times. Evie wondered how the woman could stand having two masks on in a building with no air conditioning in the middle of a hot summer—and whether she'd treated retail workers as if they were disgusting bugs instead of humans even before the pandemic stole her sanity.

As the woman and her son left, Evie turned to the guitar display with a sigh and set about putting guitars back on their stands and hooks. They hadn't even bought a guitar in the end.

"You play guitar?"

Evie jumped at the sound of Tobias's voice so close to her. He stood at her shoulder admiring the guitars. He'd taken his mask off, revealing his boyishly handsome face.

"Yes," Evie answered. Where was Finn?

"What about piano?" Tobias asked.

"Um… no," Evie said. "Are you wanting to take piano lessons? We have a piano instructor. He teaches here on Thursday evenings."

"Oh. No, I don't want to take lessons," Tobias replied. "I *know* someone who plays piano." The way he said it made it seem like he was speaking in code, and she was supposed to interpret it. He turned and looked intently at her. "She's amazing at it. Her name is *Sam*." Again, as if there was some hidden meaning in his words.

Evie couldn't decipher any hidden meaning, though, so all she said was, "Oh."

"You guys finished with the A/C?" It was Finn, and Evie had never been so happy to hear his voice. He stepped between her and Tobias. Tobias was a good bit taller than Finn, so Evie could still see his face clearly over Finn's shoulder.

"Yeah. It might take a while to cool the whole room down, but you should notice a difference soon," Tobias answered. He offered a half-smile.

"Where's your partner?" Finn asked.

"Just getting the paperwork from the van," Tobias said. "I..." His eyes returned to Evie. "Do you know Steve Emory, the owner of Emory's HVAC?"

Evie frowned at the non sequitur. What was the matter with this kid? Did he have some kind of developmental disability?

"No, I don't," Evie said.

Tobias opened his mouth as if he were about to ask another bizarre question but thought better of it. "Well, I should probably get going." He turned to leave but paused. "I might come back to look at some of your piano music, though. For Sam. Not today, but..." He looked at Evie again. "Do you work here every day?"

"Hey, buddy." Finn took a step closer to Tobias. "She's not interested."

Tobias looked surprised. Mortified, even. The tips of his ears turned bright red. "Oh. No. That's not... I'm sorry, I didn't mean to... I'm engaged. To Sam. Sam is my fiancée. The girl who plays piano. I'm not... I don't want..." He stopped himself. Finally. He took several breaths. "I'm sorry."

He turned and hurried out of the store without looking back.

After a long moment of silence, Finn turned to Evie. "I understand why that kid creeped you out."

"Beware then of useless murmuring, and keep your tongue from slander; because no secret word is without result, and a lying mouth destroys the soul."

Wisdom of Solomon 1:11

4

He's Hiding Something

♫

Tobias called Sam for a video chat every night at exactly 8:00 PM Central, 7:00 PM Mountain.

Tonight, his call came early, interrupting the post-dinner family rosary. When her phone rang in the middle of a *Hail Mary* and she saw Tobias's name on the screen, Sam's heart skidded. Surely, something was wrong.

"It's Tobias."

She excused herself from the table and answered the call as she left the dining room.

"Hey, is everything okay?"

Tobias wrinkled his fine brow. "Yeah, why?"

Sam stopped on the bottom step of the staircase that led to the upper floor, where her bedroom was. "Do you know what time it is?"

Tobias looked somewhere off screen. "It's five-thirty."

"Yeah."

"So?"

"We're in the middle of the rosary."

"Oh, shoot." Tobias slapped his forehead. "I totally forgot, I'm sorry. I'll call later."

"Okay…"

Tobias smiled weakly. "Love you."

"Love you, too."

And he disappeared from Sam's screen. She frowned as she put her phone in her back pocket and slowly returned to the dining room. Paul and Lydia gave her questioning looks as she retook her seat.

"Well?" Lydia said. "Is everything okay?"

"I'm not sure," Sam answered. "He said there was nothing wrong, but…" She couldn't put a finger on it. He'd spent his entire life praying a family rosary after dinner. He knew that's what they would be doing, what they did every night at the same time. How could he have forgotten? What would make him forget? "I don't know. He said he'd call later."

Lydia shrugged and restarted the *Hail Mary*.

♫

Sam sat back against the plush pillows on her bed, watching seconds tick away on the clock across the room. Waiting.

She'd tried not to think about Tobias calling again while they finished the family rosary, but an anxious pit had formed in her gut. There was nothing definitely unusual about her conversation with Tobias—he'd said nothing out of the ordinary—but something about it nagged at her. Without understanding how, she just *knew* something was wrong.

Her phone rang for only half a second before she answered it. Tobias's handsome face filled her screen. Even after four-and-a-half years, the sight of him made her heart beat a little faster.

"Hey," she said.

"Hi," Tobias greeted in turn. "Sorry again about calling too early. I just… I didn't even think about it before I hit call."

"It's okay," Sam replied. "You kind of scared us, though. We all thought something must be wrong if you were calling during the rosary."

Tobias turned down the corners of his mouth and shook his head. "Nope. Nothing's wrong. Just wasn't thinking."

"You sure?"

"Positive."

"Okay." A beat. "How was your day?"

Tobias nodded for a while and looked away as if he were considering how to answer. "Fine."

Now Sam was sure something was wrong. *Fine* was the kind of curt answer he would've given her before they started dating, back when he was trying to convince everyone, including himself, that he didn't like her. On a normal nightly call, he readily shared even the mundane details of his day—how much he was learning from her uncle and how much Joe annoyed him and how odd some of his customers were and how hot and beautiful Colorado was in the summer. *Fine* meant everything was *not fine.*

"You wanna expand on that, buddy?" she prompted. "What was *fine* about it?"

Tobias's brows went up, and he shrugged. "I don't know. Joe and I worked on a bunch of A/C units today."

"That's it? No crazy customer stories or gross jokes that Joe made?"

Tobias half-smiled. Joe's gross jokes really got on his nerves, and Sam had spent many of these calls listening to him gripe about it.

"No. No gross jokes. But…" Tobias hesitated. "I guess there was one sort of interesting thing. Our first call today was at a music store. It made me think of you. There was a girl who worked there—" His inflection made it seem like the sentence would keep going, but Tobias didn't continue.

"A girl?" Sam repeated. The anxious pit in her stomach tightened. *A girl* was the interesting thing about his day?

"Yeah. She was… short."

Sam had the distinct impression that he had been about to say another word besides *short* but changed his mind. She did her best to keep her expression neutral.

"Anyway, how was your day?" Tobias asked.

"My day was super awesome," Sam said blandly. "I watched Catherine's favorite princess movie with her for the seven-hundredth time." Tobias huffed a laugh. "Helped Lyds demolish the weeds in the backyard. Practiced *Rhapsody in Blue*—got another few measures mastered. Daydreamed about how I would be spending the day if you were here."

"Hm." Tobias rubbed his chin. "Did it involve the park? And a certain tree?"

The anxious knot loosened, and Sam grinned. "Maybe."

"What else did we do in your daydream?" Tobias asked, his eyes alight with mischief.

"We played basketball in the driveway, and I beat you," Sam said, feigning seriousness.

Tobias snorted. He had been a star player on the varsity basketball team in high school, and Sam didn't have an athletic bone in her body. Sam cracked a smile, too.

"Not really. That wasn't actually in my daydream. No, in my daydream," Sam said, closing her eyes as she recalled her imaginings, "we took a canoe out on the river. I fell into the water, and you rescued me. And we went on a hike. I twisted my ankle, and you had to carry me all the way back to the trailhead."

Tobias laughed. "Why do all your daydreams involve you getting hurt or needing to be rescued? Those are awful daydreams."

Sam opened her eyes and grinned again. "Oh no, they're wonderful. In every one of them, I end up in your arms. There's nowhere I'd rather be."

Tobias groaned. "Gosh, I miss you."

"Same."

They settled into a comfortable silence, and Sam's mind drifted back to the mysterious girl at the music store. The anxious knot tightened again, and she wasn't sure why. Of course Tobias would be meeting girls in Colorado. Members of the female sex made up half the population—it was unavoidable. And it was something that had never even crossed Sam's mind as something to worry about. She didn't feel jealous exactly. No, it was more a sense that Tobias was hiding something. Sam didn't like the feeling at all.

"So… this short girl at the music store," Sam said, trying to sound nonchalant and probably failing. "Tell me more about her."

Tobias seemed to hold his breath, though it was hard to tell over video chat. "There's not really anything else to tell," he said.

"The most interesting thing about your day was that you met a short girl at a music store? But there was nothing else interesting about her except that she was short?" Sam pressed.

Tobias nodded. "Yeah, I think she might even be shorter than you."

Sam frowned. It was true—she hadn't grown much after junior high, topping out around five-foot-two. Tobias, on the other hand, had continued to sprout through high school and was well over six feet tall. That's not what bothered her, though.

"Did this short girl have a name?" Sam asked, irritation slipping into her voice.

"Um… Evie, I think."

Sam cursed herself for asking such a stupid question. Of course the girl had a name. And now she was annoyed that Tobias actually knew what it was. Then again, she was a customer. Of course Tobias would know her name. Why were her emotions being so ridiculous?

"Was she pretty?" Sam didn't mean for that question to slip out, but it was too late to take it back. She hated that she was acting jealous. She wasn't jealous. Was she?

Tobias took too long to answer, and the anxious knot in Sam's gut spread to her heart. Finally, he said, "That's not a fair question, Sam. If I tell you the truth, you'll be mad that I said she was pretty. If I lie and say she wasn't, you'll know anyway and be mad that I lied to you."

So she *was* pretty. This mysterious short girl at the music store named Evie was pretty.

"But that's not what made her interesting," Tobias said.

Great. She was interesting, too.

Sam closed her eyes, struggling to control her thoughts. She needed to stop interpreting his words in the worst possible way, but some evil little voice jumped inside her brain and twisted her thoughts around.

"Okay, so, what made her so interesting?"

"What are you doing, Sam?" Tobias asked.

Sam opened her eyes and saw that Tobias's face had darkened. Her irritation was becoming his.

"Yes, Evie was pretty. And she was short. And she was a musician. She reminded me a lot of you, in fact, and I didn't want to tell you that because I didn't want you to take it the wrong way. And I was right. You are taking it the wrong way."

"I can't help it, Tobias," Sam returned, her voice heated. "You scared me when you called earlier. I thought surely something was wrong. And now I find out that the thing that distracted you so much that you forgot what time it was, was a pretty and interesting girl?"

"Who made me think of *you* and made me want to call *you* as soon as possible because I miss *you* and wish *you* were here with me," Tobias shot back.

Sam opened her mouth to respond but couldn't think of anything to say. His explanation was actually quite satisfactory, but Sam's emotions were still all over the place. She took a moment to collect herself, and Tobias didn't rush her.

"I'm sorry," she said, her chin trembling. She put a hand on her forehead. "I don't know what's wrong with me, Tobias. I feel like I'm just fighting with everyone all the time, and I don't know why." She paused. "I just miss you, I guess. I hate not having you next to me at the dinner table and not seeing you come down the stairs in the morning. I hate that I have to say goodnight to you over a screen. I feel like I'm going crazy or something."

Tobias sighed. His expression had softened into one of sorrow and compassion. "You're not crazy, Sam. I feel it, too. It's stressful, this whole situation. It's like... like we're being tested or something." He paused. "We just gotta promise each other that we won't fail the test."

Sam nodded. A moment passed in which neither of them said anything. After a while, Sam broke the silence. "Tobias, I promise that I will not take things the wrong way as long as you promise not to hide things from me. Even if something happens that you think I won't like, I want to hear about it. Okay?"

Tobias smiled. "You sound like my mom."

Sam smiled, too. It did sound like something Lydia would say. In fact, Lydia had said something very similar to Sam when she'd first moved in with the Howards.

"She's a wise woman. She knows the value of honesty," Sam said.

Tobias nodded in agreement.

They talked for a while longer before wishing each other goodnight and sweet dreams. It wasn't until the call ended that Sam realized Tobias never actually made the promise she asked of him. And that left her with only one conclusion.

He was still hiding something.

5

An Unexpected Pupil

♫

By the end of the week, Evie forgot all about the creepy kid from the HVAC company.

She couldn't forget about singing with Finn at the party, though. He treated her no differently than he had before the party, and she hoped the same could be said about the way she treated him. She didn't want their friendship to change.

But one thing definitely changed.

Finn had gained a new confidence in his singing, and now he sang constantly around Bach for More. Whatever played on the store's sound system, he sang along with. Evie found it odd that, in all their years of friendship, she had never heard him sing before the party. Clearly, he'd been hiding his true talent.

After listening to Finn sing all week, as he was crooning along with some 1940s big band song from one of his own playlists, Evie asked him about it.

"Why did you never sing before? You obviously enjoy it. And you're good at it," she said.

"Oh, I've always sung," Finn answered. "Just not around you."

"What? Why?"

Finn gave her a look like she had asked a stupid question. "Why, indeed. Do you have any idea how intimidating it is to sing in front of someone with perfect pitch?"

Evie's brow wrinkled in consternation. "You thought I would judge you?"

"I knew you would," Finn said. "You can't help it. You hear what you hear, right? But the flip side is that it's fantastically affirming to be told by someone with perfect pitch that you're a good singer." He grinned and waggled his eyebrows.

"Well, you are," Evie said. "And I'm glad you've finally come out of your shell so I can tell you so."

"Actually," Finn started, growing more serious, "there's something I've been meaning to tell *you*. And I guess now is as good a time as any."

Evie's heart jammed into her throat. She *knew* it would get weird. Her mind raced to think of the right words to respond.

"I'm starting a master's program in the fall," Finn said.

Evie barely registered the words, they were so wildly different than what she'd expected.

"I'm sorry, what?" she said.

"I'm going back to school in the fall," he repeated. "To get my master's degree."

"In music?" Her heart slowly returned to its proper place in her chest.

"Sort of," Finn answered with a shrug. "It's a master's program in sacred music."

"Sacred music?" Evie knew Finn was Catholic, just like her. But they never talked about it. Why was that? Evie bookmarked the thought to ponder later. "I didn't even know such a thing was offered."

"There aren't many programs out there, it's true," Finn said. "Being a music director at a parish isn't exactly a lucrative career."

"Is that what you want to do?" Evie asked.

Finn half-nodded, half-shrugged. "Maybe." He looked at her as if gauging whether to tell her more. "This is going to sound like the nerdiest thing ever, but... when things first shut down in March, I got real bored, and I started reading a lot. Like, everything I could get my hands on. And one of the things I read was a Church document on sacred music. It just got me thinking... it's kind of a lost art, you know? And I don't want it to be lost anymore."

Evie studied Finn's face. The earnestness in his blue eyes. And a horrible thought hit her.

"Where?" she demanded. "Will you have to move?"

"Yes, I will have to move," Finn said. Then, he grinned. "But not far. Just to my parents' house. It's a remote program, at least for now. But I can't afford to pay for both school and rent, so my parents have generously offered to let me move back in until I finish my master's."

"Oh, good grief, Finn," Evie breathed, punching him in the shoulder. "Don't scare me like that."

"Scare you? Are you telling me you'd be sad if I left?" Finn gave her a mischievous look. "That you'd miss me?"

Ugh. She *knew* it would get weird. Why had she said that? No, it wasn't weird. There was a perfectly reasonable explanation for why she didn't want Finn to leave.

"Of course I'd miss you," Evie said. "You're my friend. And maybe you haven't noticed, but I don't have many friends. None besides you and Regina, actually. And Regina's off living her dreams, so yeah… it would suck if you left."

Finn's face softened. He opened his mouth to say something, but the bell over the door announcing a customer interrupted him. They both turned toward the newcomer, and Evie froze.

It was Liam. He had a girl, seven or eight years old, with him.

His daughter.

November 25, 2017

The shock of the news rocked Evie. She couldn't breathe.

Liam had been shot.

They'd hardly spoken since the night on the roof almost two weeks ago, and Evie still felt hurt and confused by his rejection. But her heart remained unchanged. She was still in love with him. And the knowledge that he'd been shot caused her physical pain.

The university had broadcast a school-wide emergency text message during the active shooter situation. Campus security had responded to a late-night altercation on the campus green, and one of the students involved had pulled out a gun and started shooting when they arrived. One person had been shot before the student was apprehended.

Some hours later, just before dawn, the university released the name of the campus security officer who'd been shot: Liam Davis. He'd been taken to a hospital near campus in serious condition.

Evie didn't trust herself to drive to the hospital, so she begged Regina to take her. Regina agreed—reluctantly. Although she'd never met Liam herself, she'd heard every detail of Evie and Liam's relationship. With the fierceness only a best friend can muster, Regina hated his guts for breaking Evie's heart.

They found Liam's room at the hospital easily. Several campus security officers as well as city police officers clogged the waiting room on his floor. One of them pointed Evie and Regina toward the right room and said Liam was in pain but awake and alert.

"I'll wait here," Regina said, making herself comfortable on a sofa next to a good-looking policeman.

Evie made her way down the hall to Liam's hospital room. The door was mostly closed, but she could hear voices inside when she got close. She paused just outside the door, not wanting to interrupt another visitor or perhaps the medical staff.

"It was a clean through-and-through." Liam's voice. "Nothing vital hit. Just straight through my shoulder. I'll be out in a few hours."

"A few hours?" A woman's voice. Young. Or at least, not old. "So what, they'll just send you home with a bunch of pain meds? That's crazy."

"What's that, Dada?" A little girl's voice.

"That's called an IV, baby." Liam's voice again. "It puts the medicine straight into my veins. Don't worry, it doesn't hurt."

Evie's mouth hung open, and she clutched the front of her shirt as the reality sank in. For the second time that morning, she couldn't breathe. He had a daughter? And that woman… his wife. Evie turned around and fled.

She never wanted to see Liam again.

♫

Finn could have had no way of knowing who Liam was.

"Good morning," he greeted cheerily as he approached Liam and his daughter. "Can I help you find something?"

Liam smiled pleasantly at Finn. "Yes. My daughter, Bridget, wants to start playing the violin."

Evie clenched her jaw.

"Oh, well, you are in luck, young lady," Finn gushed, turning his attention to the girl. "Because my friend and colleague over there, the illustrious Lady Vincent, is the very best violinist I have ever met. I bet she'll help you pick out the *perfect* violin. And she might even agree to give you some lessons."

The girl smiled shyly and looked up at Liam.

"I think that sounds pretty good," Liam said to his daughter. "What do you think?"

The girl nodded.

Evie cursed Finn under her breath. She had to remind herself that he

58

didn't know. He couldn't know.

Finn led Liam and his daughter to where Evie stood near the counter.

"Evie, this young lady—Bridget?" Finn glanced at the girl, who nodded. "Bridget would like to look at violins and maybe sign up for some lessons." Finn gave Evie a look of triumph, surely thinking he was doing her a huge favor. He must have seen something else in Evie's face, though, because his expression quickly changed to one of confusion.

Evie forced herself to smile at Bridget, telling herself that it wasn't the girl's fault her father was a philandering, duplicitous liar.

"How old are you, Bridget?" Evie asked.

She looked to Liam. "Go on. You can tell her," he encouraged.

"Seven," Bridget mumbled.

"Wow," Evie said. She couldn't help but think—that would have made her four years old when Evie heard her voice in that hospital room. "Do you know how to read music?"

Bridget shook her head as if she didn't quite understand the question.

"That's okay," Evie said. "I didn't know how to read music when I started playing violin either." She smiled at Bridget, and Bridget smiled back.

Evie had to steel herself before shifting her gaze to Liam. His daughter was precious and innocent, but he was not. Somehow he had tracked her down here and trapped her, using his own daughter as a pretext to talk to her. She pinned him with an icy glare.

Liam met her gaze calmly. "I owe you an explanation."

Evie scoffed. "After almost three years, I don't think I want to hear it."

Bridget looked between the two of them with wide eyes.

So did Finn. "You know each other?" he asked.

Liam turned to Finn. Liam was a tad shorter but much brawnier than Finn. He carried himself with confidence, and his almost-black hair and eyes and beard added to his rugged bearing. If Evie had been a man, she might have found Liam intimidating. But much to her aggravation, she was a woman and only found him stupidly attractive.

"Would you mind taking my daughter to look at the violins while I speak with Evie for a few minutes?" Liam said to Finn.

Finn's face darkened, and he made eye contact with Evie. "Are you okay?"

She wasn't, but she nodded anyway. Whatever tongue-lashing Liam deserved, his daughter didn't need to hear it. Liam had never given her reason to fear him. She only feared he would somehow worm his way back into her fragile heart.

"Go with this man and look at the violins, baby," Liam said to Bridget. "When you find the perfect one, you come and show it to me, okay?"

"Okay," Bridget murmured.

"This way." Finn led the little girl away, casting glances back at Evie as he moved toward the string section of the store.

Liam watched them for a moment before facing Evie again. He opened his mouth to speak, but Evie cut him off.

"Does your wife know you're here?" she said.

Liam shook his head. "Why do you think I'm married, Evie?"

"Really?" Evie held out a hand toward Bridget. "I thought it was kind of obvious."

"I'm not and never have been married to Bridget's mother," Liam said. "And you implied that I was married at the party... *before* you met Bridget. Why?"

"You're demanding an explanation? Funny, I could have sworn you said *you* owed *me* an explanation," Evie shot back. Her voice rose in volume with each word. "So explain, Liam. Explain to me why you led me on. Why you lied to me. Why you broke my heart."

Liam flinched.

Finn poked his head over a set of shelves in the string section, but she ignored him.

"Evie," Liam said quietly, "I have spent the last three years regretting what happened—and what didn't happen—between us. I never meant to lead you on or break your heart, and I'm sorry that I did. I mean it, Evie. I am so sorry." He paused. "If it makes any difference, I broke my own heart, too."

Evie didn't want to believe him, but he delivered his apology with such sincerity and sadness in his eyes that she had to.

"That's not an explanation," she said hoarsely.

Finn and Bridget returned before Liam could say more.

"Look at this fine instrument we found," Finn announced. "What you do think, Evie? You're the expert here. I'm just a woodwind player." He looked down at Bridget with a wink. "With a stunningly suave singing voice, I might add." His levity sounded forced, but Evie appreciated his attempt to protect the little girl from the tension in the room.

Finn handed the tiny violin to Evie for her inspection. It was a one-eighth violin, sized for small children to learn on.

Evie cleared her throat. "I think this one might be a size too small. Let me see you hold it."

She handed the violin to Bridget. "Bring it up and put it under your chin. Like this." Evie gently moved Bridget's left hand along the neck of the violin and helped her tuck the instrument under her chin in a proper hold.

"Yeah, definitely too small. I think you're ready for a quarter violin. A big-girl violin," Evie told her.

Bridget beamed.

"Quarter violin. Right," Finn said. He clearly did not want to leave her alone with Liam again, but Evie tried to communicate with a look that she was fine. Turning to Bridget, he said, "Come, milady. We shall find ye a quarter violin."

As soon as Finn and Bridget were out of earshot, Liam jumped right in. "Have coffee with me."

"No."

"Please, Evie," he begged. "I'll never get to say everything that needs to be said here. Just one coffee. Please."

Evie wanted to kick him and kiss him at the same time. How long had she waited for him to ask her out to coffee? Or drinks? Or dinner? Or anything? She would have settled for anything back then. Would she now? He wasn't married as she'd thought. He did have a daughter, and he had lied about it. Or at least, he had omitted it, which was basically the same thing considering how close they'd become during those months at Lockwood. But perhaps, if he really wasn't married, he hadn't been as dastardly as she'd assumed. Perhaps there was more to the story. Perhaps he deserved a chance… to explain himself, anyway.

"Fine," she said.

"What time do you get off work?" Liam pressed.

"Five-thirty."

"The coffee shop across the street okay?"

"Sure."

Liam took a deep breath and exhaled loudly. Then he smiled. "Thank you."

"Does your daughter actually want violin lessons? Or was that just an excuse so you could corner me at work?" Evie asked. The ice hadn't melted completely. Not even close.

Liam's smile remained. "She really does. And my daughter deserves the best. Don't forget, Evie, I've heard with my own ears how good you are. You have no idea how many nights I just sat outside your practice room and listened to you play for a while before I had to interrupt you and make you leave. When I saw you at that party, I realized someone there must know how to get in touch with you. I asked around until I found that someone. She told me where you work."

Evie didn't know how to respond.

"You will teach her, won't you?" Liam said. "Whatever happens between us."

Whatever happens between us. What did that mean? What did he expect to happen when they went to coffee? Evie felt torn. A warning voice in the back of her mind screamed that she shouldn't go down this path with Liam again. If he'd broken her heart once, there was no reason to believe he wouldn't do it again. But when she glanced over at Bridget cradling a quarter violin in her arms and the delight on her face as Finn showed her the bow, Evie shoved that warning voice aside. She still didn't trust Liam. But she couldn't say no to teaching his daughter.

"Of course I will."

"Pardon one another so that later on you will not remember the injury. The recollection of an injury is itself wrong. It adds to our anger, nurtures our sin and hates what is good. It is a rusty arrow and poison for the soul. It puts all virtue to flight."

St. Francis of Paola

6

Coffee with Liam

♫

Evie's stomach twisted and squirmed with nerves as she closed up Bach for More for the night.

Finn had already gone home. After Liam and Bridget left, she could tell Finn wanted to ask her how she knew them, but he never did. Evie wasn't sure why she didn't just come out and tell him anyway, without making him ask. Perhaps after meeting Liam for coffee, after hearing his explanation, she would fill Finn in. Not because Finn was anything more than a friend. Because she knew how awkward the entire interaction must have seemed to him, and he deserved to know what he'd found himself in the middle of.

Bach for More and the coffee shop, Jack the Dripper, occupied adjacent street corners, and the street between them was a side street with little traffic. Evie crossed it without even looking for cars. She saw far fewer pedestrians than there should've been on a Friday evening in this part of town, and many of the ones she did see wore those stupid face diapers. When would things go back to normal? Ever?

Liam waited at a table on the outdoor patio in front of the coffee shop. The heat of the summer day hadn't yet begun to wane, but umbrellas at the tables provided shade to make the heat more bearable. Liam's face lit up when he saw Evie, and annoyingly, her heart did a little flip. He stood as she neared his table.

"One coffee," Evie said. "You better make it count."

Liam's smile slipped just a tad. "Thank you for coming."

They went inside to order drinks, but Evie turned around at the door when the barista told her she needed to have a mask on. "Order me a chai latte," she told Liam, who had obediently covered his face. It was ridiculous. With his beard, a mask was worse than useless.

Evie settled herself at the table on the patio and took several deep breaths to try to calm her nerves as she waited. What could Liam possibly say? How would she react? How *should* she react? Why had she even agreed to this meeting? Was there any possible explanation that would make her change her mind about him? Why did it matter to him anyway? Hadn't they both moved on? The questions zipping through her mind made her more anxious, and she considered bailing. But the moment she resolved to do so, Liam appeared with the drinks.

"All right," Evie said once he sat. "Explain away."

Liam took a deep breath and held it a moment before exhaling. "Where to begin…"

"How about the part where you made me believe you had feelings for me and then rejected me. Or maybe the part where you had a daughter that you never told me about. Or who that woman in your hospital room was."

"My hospital room—" Liam's brow furrowed in confusion. He studied Evie's face, which she worked to keep expressionless. Then, it finally dawned on him. "When I was shot. You came to the hospital when I was shot?"

Evie didn't answer.

"You already knew about Bridget," Liam continued, evidently piecing it together for himself. He nodded to himself. "No wonder you hate me."

Evie didn't deny it.

"Her mother," Liam said. "That would've been Bridget's mother in my hospital room. We weren't together anymore, but she brought Bridget to see me." He shrugged. "I mean, she wanted to see me, too. She's not heartless. She still cares even if things didn't work out between us."

"What's her name?" Evie couldn't think of anything else to ask. Actually, she had a million questions she wanted to ask, but she was afraid of the answers.

"Jessica," Liam answered. He stared down at the table. "We started dating when she was in college and I was at the police academy. She got pregnant just a couple months after I graduated. I was twenty-one… barely twenty-two when Bridget was born. And by then, things were not good between me and Jessica. We tried to make it work for a while, but…" Liam sighed. "Anyway, I quit the police force and started working private security when we split up. I thought it would be better for the times Bridget was with me. Better schedule. Less dangerous—" he gave a short, mirthless laugh. "And then, eventually, I found the campus security job. It paid more than the job I had at the time, and working weekend nights seemed like a good fit with the custody arrangement."

Liam looked up and into Evie's eyes.

"And then I met you." He half-smiled. "And the timing couldn't have been worse."

Evie frowned.

"Jessica and I were talking about getting back together around the same time," Liam explained. "I thought it would be the best thing for Bridget, to have both her parents in the same home. And I wanted to make it work for her sake." He sighed. "Which meant I couldn't—or at least wouldn't—do anything about the fantastic, beautiful, talented girl I met on my rounds at the music school."

"That's not how it felt," Evie said. "You didn't have to walk me home every night. You didn't have to listen to my sob stories about my childhood, about running away, about my father. If you were really trying to keep your distance…" Now it was Evie's turn to shake her head. "You did a terrible job."

Liam nodded in agreement. "I know. And I'm sorry. I have no other excuse except to say that I enjoyed spending time with you. Having someone to talk to."

"Except I'm the only one who ever talked," Evie retorted. "I told you everything, but you told me next to nothing about yourself. I didn't notice at the time. Or maybe I just didn't want to. It should have been a red flag. But I was blind."

"I should have been upfront with you," Liam admitted. "I purposely hid my private life from you. I knew if I let you in, I would be entering dangerous territory. I knew I wouldn't be able to keep any distance at all."

Evie scoffed. "If I knew you had a daughter and that you were trying to make things work with her mother, I would never have acted around you the way I did. I would have treated you like you were off limits—because you were. I would never have let myself fall for you if I knew."

"I know that now," Liam responded. "I probably should have

known it then, but I don't know what to say, Evie—I was confused."

"You were selfish," Evie corrected. "You were only concerned about protecting your own heart. You didn't even think about mine."

Liam looked away. Evie saw him swallow hard.

"You're right," he said huskily. "You're right. I'm sorry."

A long silence stretched between them. Evie's nerves had disappeared, but curiosity still niggled at her.

"The night on the roof," she said. "Was it because you were still with Jessica?"

Liam barked a sarcastic laugh and shook his head. "Add cowardice to my faults. No, I wasn't with Jessica. That's why I took you up there. I wanted to tell you how I felt. How I'd always felt since the moment I met you. And I was finally free to do something about it. But when we kissed, it hit me—how much you would hate me when you found out that, for a whole year, I hid the fact that I have a kid. And I didn't have the courage to tell you. I didn't know *how* to tell you."

Evie didn't respond. She felt relieved and validated and disgusted and angry and sorry and sympathetic all at once.

"And then I stopped seeing you at the music school," Liam continued. "And I suspect you blocked my number because my calls always went straight to voicemail. And then I got shot and left that job. So I never had a chance to come clean with you. Until now."

Evie shrugged. "Even if you'd stayed, you wouldn't have seen me anymore. I left Lockwood at the end of that semester."

"Why?" Liam asked. "Please tell me it wasn't because of what happened between us."

"In a way, it was," Evie answered honestly. "But it wasn't *just* that. There were other things going on. I was not in a good place mentally or emotionally. For a lot of reasons."

"Your father?" Liam guessed.

Evie nodded. "All of it, happening all at the same time… I couldn't handle it. And I failed my music jury."

"Your what?"

"Juries—they're like final exams for performance majors," Evie explained. "You have to perform for the department faculty, and it's pass/fail."

"And you failed?" Liam was incredulous. "How is that even possible? I've heard you play. You're… you're… magical."

Evie cracked a smile. Her musical skills had been called many things, but *magical* was a first. But her smile disappeared as she recalled that horrifying day at Lockwood.

December 12, 2017

Evie wanted to vomit. She paced in the green room of the recital hall, cradling her violin and trying to call her jury pieces to mind. Performing had never given her this kind of anxiety before, but she blamed the many sleepless nights she'd had since... actually, she couldn't remember the last time she'd slept well.

First, Liam had broken her heart.

Then, that meeting with her father...

And then Liam got shot, and she found out he was married and had a daughter.

And now it was finals week, and she still had two more final papers to write before the end of the week.

Plus, she'd been putting in extra hours at Bach for More so she could afford a new car—her old beater was on its last leg—or tire?—and she didn't even feel safe driving it anymore.

Evie was a wreck, and she knew it.

The door between the green room and backstage opened, and Henry, a grad student violinist, came through it. He smirked at Evie as he held the door open for her.

"Break a leg," he said, a nasty edge in his voice. Evie had stolen his position as concertmaster last year, and he loathed her for it.

Evie brushed past him into the cool darkness of the backstage area. She shoved aside the heavy curtain to step onto the lit stage. The lights were so bright, she squinted. With a hand on her forehead to shade her eyes, she spotted the string faculty sitting together in floor level box seats.

"Hello, Evie," said Professor Chin, the department chair and her own studio professor. Professor Chin taught very few violin students personally anymore, and Evie had always felt the enormous privilege of studying with such a legendary woman. "What are you playing for us today?"

Evie blanked. She couldn't remember.

String students were not allowed to play from sheet music for their juries. They were expected to memorize their music, as professional soloists did. Playing from memory had never been difficult for Evie—her perfect pitch made memorizing music incredibly easy.

But just now, her mind was nothing but a void. She couldn't think of a single note.

"Evie?" Professor Chin prompted. "Are you playing the Sibelius? That's what you've been working on this semester."

"Um, yes," Evie stuttered. The Sibelius. Right.

How did that one go?

Panic gripped Evie. What was happening to her? Why couldn't she remember how Sibelius's violin concerto went? She'd listened to it a million times. Played it a million more. She couldn't even think of what key it was in or what note it started on.

Evie lifted her violin, hoping the music would come to her if she went through the motions. She rested the bow on the strings and closed her eyes.

Nothing happened. Nothing came to her.

The string faculty waited in silence.

After a long, painful battle to remember anything, a single note even, Evie lowered her violin.

"I'm sorry," she managed to say, though she wasn't sure her voice carried past the edge of the stage.

Numb, she turned and walked out.

♫

"They had no choice but to fail me," Evie said. "And I lost my scholarship. I couldn't afford to stay, so I didn't."

Liam regarded her with a slack jaw. "I am so sorry, Evie."

Evie pursed her lips. "Probably served me right, actually. I needed the lesson in humility. I had started to think that having perfect pitch meant I was a perfect player, that I was unbeatable and unstoppable. Flawless. But I'm not. Never have been."

Evie inwardly chastised herself. What was she doing? Why was she revealing her innermost heart to Liam again? Hadn't she learned anything at all?

"I should get going," she said abruptly. She hadn't even touched her chai latte.

"Of course," Liam said. "I'm sure you have things to do. So do I."

They both stood.

"Thank you for meeting me," Liam said. "I knew I'd never get it all out with your coworker buzzing around."

"Finn? He can be a little overprotective sometimes." It was kind of sweet, actually, but Evie didn't think Liam needed to know that.

"Anyway," Liam continued, "Thank you for letting me explain. I know they're all poor excuses, but at least now you know… my feelings for you were real, and I didn't back off that night on the roof because of anything you did. You never did anything wrong, Evie."

Evie sighed. "Maybe not, but I can at least admit how foolish and immature I was. I allowed myself to fall for someone I didn't know, someone who never shared anything about himself, never even asked me on a date. I got so wrapped up in a fantasy—a relationship that, by any meaningful definition, didn't actually exist—that I failed my jury, lost my music scholarship, and sabotaged my future. For that, I have only myself to blame."

Despite her lingering anger toward Liam, Evie had long recognized her own part in the way things played out between them, but she had never quite been able to articulate it before. Saying it now, she felt an enormous sense of relief, as if a stone she'd been hauling around on her back was finally gone.

"Can I walk you to your car?" Liam asked. "Where are you parked?"

"In Bach for More's lot." Evie jerked her head in that direction.

They left the coffee shop's patio and crossed the little side street.

"I hope you're not worried about Bridget taking lessons with me after what I told you about my jury," Evie said, a slight smile on her face. "It was a temporary lapse, I assure you."

Liam grinned. "Oh, I'm not worried. I heard you at the party. I know you weren't playing your violin, but I figure you must be one of those people who can play any instrument you touch."

Evie laughed. "No, I can't. I'm garbage at wind instruments, especially brass. I can't do the lip buzzing thing. And I'm only so-so at piano. Though I suppose if I spent time practicing it, I could be pretty good at piano, too."

"What were you saying again about humility?" Liam teased.

Evie rolled her eyes playfully.

They reached her car. Evie turned and held out her hand, intending a handshake as a sign of peace between them. But Liam held open his arms, an invitation for a hug.

"Oh," Evie muttered.

She started to move her arms to hug him, but he pulled his arms in and held out his hand for a shake. They laughed at the awkwardness.

Evie held out her hand again, and Liam took it.

"I know it's a long shot after the way I treated you," he said softly, "but my feelings for you haven't changed, Evie. I just need you to know that."

Evie tried to withdraw her hand from his, but he held on and drew her a step closer.

"Liam..." Evie said, shaking her head. Her heart fluttered, and she didn't quite know whether panic or attraction caused it. "I appreciate the explanation and the apology. But it's been three years, Liam. My feelings *have* changed."

Liam clenched his jaw. He still didn't release her hand from his grasp.

"You're seeing someone?" he asked.

Evie recoiled, startled by the question. "No, I'm not."

"But you have feelings for someone else," he said, his brow creasing into a frown.

Evie opened her mouth to deny it but stopped herself. Liam had no claim over her heart anymore. Why should she tell him what feelings did or did not exist there—for him or anyone else? She tugged her hand away, and he finally let her go.

"I'll see you Wednesday for Bridget's lesson," Evie said, half-hoping her rejection would make him want to cancel his daughter's violin lessons.

"Absolutely."

7

Faith

♫

Evie had been raised Catholic and received all her Sacraments, but Sunday Mass had always been optional when she was growing up, and religion rarely came up in conversation. When Evie ran away, her faith—though not terribly well-formed—was one thing she took with her.

Lonely, angry, frightened, and deeply wounded when she arrived in Colorado, Evie sought out the comfort of something familiar and stable: the Mass. Years later, she would look back on that time and recognize God's guiding and protecting hand. She could easily have chosen wild rebellion and self-destruction—most people in her situation probably would have—but something, or rather Someone, had drawn her to go to church instead. In some way, in fact, going to Mass every Sunday and making God an important part of her life felt more defiant than anything else she could have done.

Eventually, the grace of receiving the Eucharist every week began to transform Evie from the inside out. Her heart softened, and her grudges faded. She became curious about scripture and Church teaching. Going to church became a matter of love for the Lord more than a desire for comfort.

An avalanche of trials halfway through her junior year at Lockwood —including Liam's rejection and her failed jury—nearly undid Evie, and her faith was, once again, all she had left. The months that followed were some of the darkest of her life, but the Lord provided a tiny light for her to cling to and follow: a random Bach for More customer raving about a physically demanding and spiritually transformative pilgrimage in Spain called El Camino de Santiago, The Way of Saint James.

For almost nine months, Evie planned and saved and thought of nothing but the Camino. It gave her direction and purpose at a time when her life otherwise felt utterly rudderless. Terry generously granted her extended vacation time of five weeks so that she could walk the entire French Route of the Camino—almost five hundred miles.

Her Camino was the best and hardest thing Evie had ever done. Every step, so physically and mentally draining, brought emotional and spiritual healing. She carried four stones with her, each one representing what she felt were her greatest wounds, to the Cruz de Ferro—a cross of wood and iron some two-thirds of the way along the French Route. She left them there, and with them, her bitterness and anger. Leaving the stones behind at the foot of the Cross lightened her backpack and her soul.

September 18, 2018

Day 21. San Martín del Camino to Astorga, 22.92 kilometers.

In the first few days of the Camino, the sun had been blazing hot. From Los Arcos to Logroño, Evie slogged through an entire day of rain. But mostly, the weather had been quite comfortable.

Not today.

Evie had felt the cold blowing in the night before when she retrieved her shirt, shorts, and undergarments from the clothesline in the front yard of the municipal albergue. The albergue had no heat, and she'd shivered in her thin sleeping bag all night long. Unable to sleep and hoping that walking would help her warm up, Evie left the albergue well before sunrise.

Walking didn't help. Not with the cold wind blowing in her face. It seemed that autumn had arrived in Spain overnight.

Few things made Evie quite so grumpy as being cold.

Still, she was in better spirits than she had been some days ago, before she met Patty and Deana, step-sisters in their fifties. The flat, straight nothingness of the Meseta had turned a physically strenuous pilgrimage into a mental battle. Evie lost count of the times she thought about quitting the Camino in that stretch. But after running into Patty and Deana a few days in a row and eating dinner with them twice, Evie began to appreciate the simplicity of the Camino.

As Deana had put it, "This is real luxury, having nothing else in the world to worry about except walking from point A to point B."

Her simple statement changed Evie's entire perspective. Now, every pilgrim she met, every albergue she stayed in, every meal she ate felt like a gift. She had everything she needed — clothes, food, shelter at night — and no responsibilities, no demands on her time, no work or relationship problems to deal with or stress about. Deana was right. Life on the Camino was luxury.

But just now, the cold wind did not feel like luxury.

Evie stopped for a café con leche *and* tostadas con mantequilla *at Hospital de Órbigo. Relishing the warmth of the cafe, she took her time and watched the glow of the rising sun bathe an impressive thirteenth-century Roman bridge in hues of pink and orange. The coffee, the toast, the warm cafe, the sunrise... gifts, each one.*

When she finished her small breakfast, Evie reluctantly hoisted her backpack and hiking poles and set out into the cold, vicious wind once more. She wore as many layers as she had with her — a short-sleeved shirt under a long-sleeved shirt and a fleece over both — but the wind cut through the fabric easily. Soon, her teeth were chattering, and the demons of despair that had threatened her resolve in the Meseta returned.

Within a few kilometers, Evie entered another small village, Villares de Órbigo. She followed the yellow arrows, the famous waymarkers of the Camino, along a winding village street. As she rounded a corner, she spotted a sign for sellos — stamps.

Pilgrims on the Camino collected stamps in their pilgrim's passport from every albergue they stopped at. Churches, monasteries, cafes, and other places along the Way offered stamps as well. Upon reaching the end of the Camino in Santiago de Compostela, pilgrims had to show a passport full of sellos *to prove they'd actually walked the route. Without it, they could not receive the Compostela, the official Church-issued accreditation recognizing the completion of the holy pilgrimage.*

Eager for both a stamp and shelter from the cold wind, Evie followed the sign and ducked into a small garage-like space. An old, weathered man welcomed her with a wide smile and, in Spanish, offered her a cup of hot, black coffee. She gratefully accepted. The man gestured for her to sit on a cozy little couch and enjoy some little biscuits with her coffee. The coffee was not very good, but it was hot, and that was enough for Evie.

The walls of the room were covered in maps and hundreds of pictures of pilgrims who had passed through over the years. The man spoke very little

English, and Evie spoke very little Spanish, but they managed to have a rudimentary conversation in which he asked where she was from and she claimed Colorado as her home. Delighted, he pointed out pictures of other pilgrims who had been from Colorado.

There were a great many hospitable souls along the Camino—people who spent their days offering refreshments to weary pilgrims. Many of them had once been pilgrims themselves, and the experience inspired them to dedicate their lives to providing succor and encouragement to those on the Way. Some offered sellos *as well, and most had a bucket or basket for donations—whatever a pilgrim could or wanted to give to provide for the next day's refreshments for the next day's pilgrims.*

But this man was the first Evie had met who refused even donations. All he requested in return for the coffee and biscuits and stamp was a little bit of time for conversation. It was clear that helping pilgrims gave him immense joy, and his kindness and warmth gave Evie the strength she needed to keep going.

With another stamp in her pilgrim's passport and more caffeine in her veins, Evie wished the man well and walked on. The wind continued to bite, and the route took an uphill slant. Evie saw few other pilgrims on the path, which seemed unusual. Perhaps it was because she'd left so early in the morning.

Some ten kilometers later, as the terrain leveled out, Evie happened upon another oasis of hospitality, this one in the middle of nowhere. The nearest village was five kilometers in either direction, but some kind soul had erected a pilgrim's haven here. Under a makeshift canopy, there was a huge round table with fruits and nuts and even an orange juice maker. A smaller booth offered beverages—tea and coffee and water. Nearby, log seats surrounded a fire pit, where Evie found two other pilgrims warming themselves. There was even a hammock strung between two trees where a truly tired pilgrim could find some rest. The man who supplied it all conversed with the couple by the fire, and Evie heard him say something she'd heard many others say along the Way.

Today, she felt the truth of it.

"The Camino provides."

♫

El Camino. The Way. Jesus told His apostles that He was the Way.

Above all, Evie's Camino taught her a radical reliance on God. In her darkest moments, on the most desperate days, He'd given her what she needed to keep going: Patty and Deana, an old man with bad coffee and cheerful conversation, an oasis in the middle of nowhere, a community dinner in Hontanas, a young Romanian man who encouraged her to go to Mass in Frómista even though her feet were covered with blisters and she didn't think she could walk another step, a monastery with Eucharistic adoration in Carrión de los Condes, a man from Chicago who inspired her to offer her tired body and sore feet as penance for herself and others.

The Camino, the Way, Jesus provided.

Because of the Camino, Evie began to cling to and live by a verse in John's Gospel—a verse in which Jesus tells His apostles, *Apart from me you can do nothing.*

And so, after meeting Liam, Evie placed herself at the foot of the cross in the Blessed Sacrament chapel at one of the parishes she frequented.

Liam was back in her life. What did it mean? What did she want it to mean? Evie searched her heart, asking God to shed His light on the dark corners and hidden feelings there. She'd told Liam that her feelings had changed, but she couldn't deny that he still commanded a strange attraction for her. Had her feelings truly changed? Or had they just been obscured by time and space, waiting to reemerge when the opportunity arose?

How deep had her feelings ever been to begin with?

Evie wondered. Philosophically, she'd always assumed that depth of attachment and depth of wound were directly correlated—a deep wound could only be inflicted if there was a deep attachment. And Liam had indeed wounded her very deeply. But perhaps she'd mistaken intensity for depth. Three years ago, her feelings for Liam were intense, certainly, but did they ever truly run deep?

She'd barely known him. How deep could they have been?

Liam… Bridget… did Evie have the fortitude to teach his daughter? To build a relationship with her? To see Liam every week? *Apart from me you can do nothing.* Right. With God's grace, she could do it. She had to. She'd promised she would.

Besides, Finn would be at the store on Wednesdays. He would have her back if she needed someone to run interference with Liam.

Poor Finn. He'd seemed so confused and worried about her when she was talking to Liam, and she hadn't even bothered to explain anything to him afterwards. Finn really was a sweetheart, always so gallant and protective. And when he sang… or when they sang together…

Evie's heart lurched. She came here to pray for guidance in her situation with Liam. How had her thoughts turned to Finn?

Evie glanced up at the tabernacle guiltily. But another thought popped into her mind, and strangely, it didn't feel like the thought came from her. Hadn't she started her prayer asking God to shed light on the hidden feelings in her heart? Did that mean…?

Evie shook her head. No. Finn was a friend. Nothing more.

And Liam… well, Liam wasn't even that much. Perhaps she and Liam could be friends eventually. And after that, maybe something more. *If* he could prove himself trustworthy.

And it would take a lot more than a chai latte and an apology to regain Evie's trust.

Saint Joseph,
Illustrious offspring of David,
Light of Patriarchs,
Spouse of the Mother of God,
Chaste guardian of the Virgin,
Foster father of the Son of God,
Diligent protector of Christ,
Head of the Holy Family,
Joseph most just,
Joseph most chaste,
Joseph most prudent,
Joseph most brave,
Joseph most obedient,
Joseph most faithful,
Mirror of patience,
Lover of poverty,
Model of workers,
Glory of the domestic life,
Guardian of virgins,
Pillar of families,
Solace of the afflicted,
Hope of the sick,
Patron of the dying,
Terror of demons,
Protector of Holy Church,
pray for us.

Litany of St. Joseph

8

Trust

♫

"Bless me, Father, for I have sinned. It's been a week since my last confession."

The Sacrament of Reconciliation was one of Sam's favorite parts about becoming Catholic. The awareness of her need for forgiveness and mercy, and a recognition that confession offered what she needed, had been a driving force in her conversion. Since coming into the Church, she'd made confession a regular part of her routine, going at least once a month. At the beginning of the pandemic, when Masses stopped but confessions continued, she and the Howards started going more frequently—partly because they needed to and partly because it was the only sacramental grace available to them for a time. When Tobias moved away, Sam found herself in the confessional once a week or more—she couldn't seem to go more than a couple of days without fighting with someone or entertaining impure thoughts.

"I had another fight with Lydia," Sam started. Father Bernard had heard so many of her confessions by now and had known the Howards for so long, she had no need to explain who Lydia was to her. "I said some awful things to her and interrupted her and was just… mean."

"Have you apologized since fighting with her?" Father Bernard asked.

"Yes," Sam answered. "And she forgave me."

"Good. Do you have more to confess?"

"Yes." Tears pricked her eyes. She often cried in confession, but she felt like everything made her cry lately. "I had a fight with Tobias, too."

"Mm-hm."

"I mean, it wasn't exactly a fight," Sam clarified. "But... he was telling me about this girl he met in Colorado, and I acted all jealous and suspicious. I know it hurt his feelings, but..."

"But what?"

"I still feel suspicious, Father," Sam admitted. "I think there's something he's not telling me, and it makes things strained when we talk."

"Sam, are you and Tobias engaged?" Father Bernard asked.

The question caught Sam off guard. She and Tobias had agreed not to ask Father Bernard to start marriage prep with them until Tobias had saved up enough money, and neither of them had mentioned their engagement to him. He must have noticed her ring.

"Yes," she answered. "But it's still sort of unofficial, I guess. Lydia and Paul want us to wait until Tobias can support a family. And I'm still a minor, so..." Sam shrugged even though Father Bernard couldn't see her through the screen.

"Hm." Sam imagined Father Bernard nodding on the other side of the screen. "Trust is the bedrock of a good marriage. Think what it means to marry, to give your very *self* to another person. Can you give your entire self—body, soul, heart, future—to someone you don't trust?"

Sam swallowed.

"Or will you always be holding back something of yourself?"

Sam didn't answer, but his words made her heart hurt. Did he mean that she lacked trust? Or that Tobias did? Either way, what did it mean for their future together?

"Is that it?"

"No, there's more," Sam murmured. She hesitated. For some reason, the fighting was always easier to confess than the impure thoughts. Especially since Father Bernard knew both her and Tobias. "I had... certain thoughts... about Tobias."

"Certain thoughts? About hurting him?"

"No," Sam said, feeling her cheeks burn. When Father Bernard said nothing, she knew he was waiting for her to come out and say it. He'd taught her long ago that one of the requirements of making a good confession was actually confessing—naming the sin, not just hinting at it. "I entertained impure thoughts about Tobias," she said as quickly as possible. "And that's everything."

"Sexual desire is not a sin, Sam," Father Bernard said. "And in marriage, the sexual embrace is a beautiful and holy expression of the gift of self that spouses make to one another. But indulging in fantasies turns that desire inward, turns it into self-love. It becomes a desire to take rather than a desire to freely receive—a desire to use rather than to love. Do you understand?"

"Yes, Father," Sam responded, and this time, the tears spilled over— partly from sorrow for her sins, but partly from pure embarrassment.

"Thank you for a good and sincere confession," Father Bernard said. "Our Heavenly Father never withholds His mercy from those who ask for it. In fact, like the father in the parable of the prodigal son, God is overjoyed every time we return to Him, whether we've strayed just a little or very far. He delights to call you His beloved daughter, Sam. Never forget that."

"Thank you, Father."

"For your penance, pray the Litany of St. Joseph," Father Bernard said. "And now, your act of contrition."

"My God, I am sorry for my sins with all my heart. In choosing to do wrong and failing to do good, I have sinned against you whom I should love above all things. I firmly intend, with your help, to do penance, to sin no more, and to avoid whatever leads me to sin. Our Savior Jesus Christ suffered and died for us. In his name, my God, have mercy."

"Deus, Pater misericordiárum, qui per mortem et resurrectiónem Fílii sui mundum sibi reconciliávit et Spíritum Sanctum effúdit in remissiónem peccatórum, per ministérium Ecclésiæ indulgéntiam tibi tríbuat et pacem. Et ego te absólvo a peccátis tuis in nómine Patris et Fílii et Spíritus Sancti."

"Amen."

♫

When Sam arrived home after confession, she found Lydia watering the flowers in the front yard while Catherine splashed around in a kiddie pool in the driveway. Sam parked her car—a car that was Tobias's before it was hers and Bear's before that—along the curb.

"Sam! Watch this!" Catherine called when Sam got out of the car. The little girl threw a water toy in the air, spraying water everywhere. She squealed in delight, thinking it the most magnificent trick, and

Sam laughed.

"Whoa!" Sam indulged her. "That looks like fun. Can I try?"

"No," Catherine said. "You're too old."

"Oh, ouch," Sam chuckled. She saw Lydia crack a smile from across the driveway. Sam headed toward her, barely dodging a splash from a giggling Catherine on her way.

"What's up, buttercup?" Lydia asked as Sam neared.

Sam shoved her hands in her pockets, not sure how to begin. "Um… I'm worried about Tobias."

Lydia glanced over at her, alarmed. "Why?"

"Because I think he's hiding something from me."

"Oh." Lydia's look of alarm settled into a thoughtful frown. "What makes you think that?"

Sam chewed her lip. "I don't know. He started to tell me about this girl he met at a music store earlier this week, but he was being super weird about it. And it's just been kind of awkward ever since." Sam paused. "I trust Tobias… but it's hard when it feels like there's something he's not telling me."

"Maybe you should tell him that," Lydia said.

"But how?" Sam asked. "I mean, has Paul ever hidden things from you?"

Lydia chuckled. "In a quarter century of marriage? What do you think?"

Sam felt like it was a trick question. "Yes…?"

"Tobias is a lot like Paul, you know," Lydia said. "Sometimes it takes a little extra work and patience to get them to open up and tell you what's going on in their heads."

"I know that, but… it feels different this time," Sam said. "Not like he's just being quiet or reserved or not saying things because he doesn't think they're important. It's more like he's purposely keeping something from me because he doesn't want me to know."

"Hm." Lydia frowned again, but it only lasted a moment. "I'll tell you something my mother told me when Paul and I were engaged. It's probably some of the best advice I've ever been given. It's saved our marriage more than once."

Sam raised her eyebrows. She'd always thought of Paul and Lydia's marriage as perfect, and it seemed strange to her to think it had ever needed saving.

"*Always assume your spouse's best intentions,*" Lydia said. "Or, in your case, your fiancé's best intentions. See, no husband, no wife, no boyfriend or girlfriend is perfect. We all do dumb things. We all make mistakes. We all hurt each other from time to time. But most of the time—not all of the time, but most of the time—we don't actually mean to hurt each other. It's hard enough to forgive when the man you love hurts your feelings unintentionally. It's even harder when you assume he did it on purpose. But if you always assume that he has the best of intentions, give him the benefit of the doubt, it makes forgiveness a whole lot easier. And knowing Tobias, you'll probably be right if you assume his good intentions."

Sam thought about it. "You think he's protecting me from something?"

"Maybe," Lydia said. "Maybe it's something he thinks you wouldn't want to know if given the choice. Or maybe it's a burden he doesn't want you to have to bear. That's usually when Paul would keep things from me—trying to be the stalwart hero and bear some burden all by himself. I broke him of that habit years ago, though. He knows better now." Lydia grinned to herself. "And so do I. Every burden is more easily borne by two than one."

♫

That evening, when Tobias called for their 8:00 PM video chat, Sam knew what she needed to say.

"Tobias, I owe you an apology," Sam said almost the instant his face appeared on her screen.

His eyes widened. "You do?"

"Yes," she said. "I was upset when you told me about the girl at the music store, and I've been hanging onto it all week. I'm sorry for being so petty and jealous and suspicious."

"Suspicious?" Tobias looked hurt. "Like, you suspected that I was doing something wrong?"

When he said it like that, it made Sam understand exactly what Lydia meant. Without meaning to, she'd assumed the worst rather than giving Tobias the benefit of the doubt, and her suspicion both wounded Tobias and made her own hurt worse.

"I didn't mean to," Sam said. "I *know* you would never do anything… like that. But I let my emotions get the better of me. It seems to be happening a lot lately."

Tobias didn't respond right away. Sam didn't know whether his silence was angry or merely thoughtful.

"I went to confession today," Sam said, unable to bear the silence any longer. "And Father Bernard said that *trust is the bedrock of a good marriage.*"

"Did you tell him we're getting married?" Tobias asked. He didn't sound angry. He sounded surprised.

"I kinda had to," Sam said. "He must've seen my ring at Mass or something because he asked me if we were engaged, and you know, I think lying in confession might make the whole thing invalid, so I told him the truth."

Tobias smiled but said nothing.

"Anyway," Sam continued, encouraged by his smile, "*trust is the bedrock of a good marriage.* And I failed to trust you, Tobias. I'm sorry, and I promise to trust you completely from now on. No matter what."

Tobias scrubbed a hand through his hair. Sam recognized it as a nervous gesture, but she refused to let it make her suspicious again.

"I really don't think you have anything to apologize for, Sam," Tobias said. "I know I was acting weird. You had every right to be suspicious."

Sam's heart dropped into her stomach. Was he admitting something? *No!* She reined in her thoughts and told herself to let him finish.

But he didn't continue.

Sam took a deep breath and exhaled slowly, silently praying for fortitude. "Here's the thing, Tobias. Trust has to go both ways. I get the feeling that there's something going on, or that something happened, that you don't want to tell me about. For whatever reason. I'm not saying it's a bad reason. It's probably a good reason. Like you're trying to protect me from something or you don't want to burden me with something. But I can't be the only one doing all the trusting here. Please, trust me. Let me help you carry this burden, whatever it is."

Tobias looked away from the screen and rubbed his face. It seemed to Sam that he was debating with himself. Finally, he nodded and looked back into the camera.

"You're right," he said, and Sam's heart squeezed painfully. "There is something—something about the girl at the music store—that I didn't want to tell you. But now it seems... I don't know... like I imagined it maybe. At first, I didn't tell you because I didn't want to get your hopes up. But now, I just think it sounds stupid. Crazy."

He paused.

"Just tell me already!" Sam said, exasperated. She couldn't even begin to imagine what he was about to tell her. Get her hopes up? Stupid? Crazy?

"This girl—Evie," Tobias started again. "I told you she reminded me of you, but it was more than that. She looked *exactly* like you. Well, not *exactly*. Not like twins. But the resemblance was crazy, Sam. Even her expressions. Like, the way she looked at me like I was a weirdo, it was the same look you give me when you're not sure whether I'm joking or not." He paused. "It's the same look you're giving me right now, actually."

He stopped and looked at her expectantly.

"Okay…" Sam said, unsure what he expected.

Tobias sighed. "It freaked me out, Sam. How similar she was to you. And it was crazy, but I just kept having this thought… what if this is Sam's sister?"

Sam caught her breath.

Late January, 2016

Sam lost track of the days after her mother died, but on one of them—a day when Tobias and Bear were at school and Paul was at work and Lydia was meeting with the funeral director or her mother's case manager or someone else—she walked across the street and unlocked the door of her parents' house.

It was dark and cold and quiet.

No one had been inside this house since they'd moved the piano in early November. Sam shut the door silently behind her and tiptoed toward the hallway. It felt wrong to disturb the stillness here, as if she might awaken some ghost or monster if she made too much noise.

Her destination was her mother's hobby room.

Since the accident, it had often crossed Sam's mind to come here and find out, once and for all, what that file cabinet in her mother's hobby room contained. But every time, she convinced herself it would be an invasion of her mother's privacy. Now that her mother was gone, Sam needed *to know what was in that cabinet. Whatever secret the cabinet held was a piece of her mother's life that Sam had never been allowed to see, and she was desperate to find and hold onto anything her mother had considered so precious.*

When she opened the door to the hobby room, the smell overwhelmed her. The smell of her mother.

Sam choked back tears, not ready to let them have their way with her again. Closing her eyes, she inhaled deeply and breathed it in, that smell, and let it soak into her being.

She crossed the room to the file cabinet.

It was locked, and she had no idea where to even look for the key. Knowing it would be locked, though, she'd had the forethought to find a crowbar among Paul's tools in the garage and didn't think he'd mind if she borrowed it. She reasoned that she had every right to break into this file cabinet. Whatever was inside had belonged to her mother. Maybe it belonged to her father now—she didn't know how those things worked—but why shouldn't she have as much right to it as he did? It wasn't like he was in any shape to care anyway.

The cabinet had two deep drawers, one on top of the other. Sam wasn't quite tall enough to get the right leverage on the top drawer, so she jammed the crowbar into the seam at the top of the bottom drawer. Prying it open was harder than she thought it would be. But finally, with a loud metallic bang!*, the lock snapped and the drawer slid out.*

Sam set the crowbar aside.

There were several file folders neatly organized inside, each containing a ream of paper. Sam pulled the first folder out and opened it. The top sheet looked like some kind of title page for a novel: A Summer of Passion *by R.R.* Ingram. *Sam flipped to a page somewhere in the middle, and sure enough, it was a manuscript. And what Sam read made her eyes go wide and her cheeks blush. She slammed the folder shut and set it down, more than a little uncomfortable thinking of her own mother writing such things.*

Sam pulled out a second file folder and opened to the title page. Another manuscript, this one titled Forbidden Fruit *by R.R. Ingram. Sam didn't bother to look further, suspecting whatever she found would only make her more uncomfortable.*

Her mother's secret hobby had been writing steamy romance novels? It was not at all what Sam had expected or hoped to find. She had hoped to find something that would make her feel close to her mom again, but now she just felt awkward.

Maybe the top drawer would have something else.

Sam tugged on it—it had come loose when she broke the lock on the bottom drawer—but it jammed partway out. She pulled harder and only managed to tip the entire cabinet forward. Thinking perhaps the tracks were dented or crooked, she bent down to look at the underside of the drawer. But it wasn't damaged tracks that caused the drawer to stick—there was something taped to the underside of the drawer.

A small, wooden trinket box.

Sam ripped it loose from the tape. She ran her fingertips over the intricate carving on the lid, a carving of mountains and pine trees. This is what she had hoped for, but now that she had it, she was scared to open it. What if she found out something else about her mother that she didn't want to know? Steeling herself, Sam snapped open the clasp and lifted the lid.

Her breath caught.

A blue crystal rosary. The crucifix and medal and chain links looked old and tarnished, but the crystal beads were still sharp and shiny.

Tucked under the rosary was a folded piece of paper. With shaking fingers, Sam gently pushed the rosary aside and pulled the paper free.

She unfolded it, and everything changed.

> *For Samantha, if I should die before I'm brave enough to tell you*
>
> *My dear Daughter,*
>
> *I have so much to tell you, I don't quite know where to begin. We've hidden many things from you, and part of me still understands why. But the other part of me hopes that I have the courage to tell you these things face-to-face and that you'll never have to read about them here. If you are reading these words, it is because my cowardice won out, and for that, I am deeply sorry.*
>
> *Before I tell you any of the things we've kept from you, let me first tell you something I hope I never kept from you—I love you. If I have made mistakes and been a poor mother, it is because I am a flawed person. It was never because I didn't love you. If, when you read this, there are things I did for which I didn't have a chance to beg forgiveness, I beg it now. You are my heart, dear Daughter, and I regret all the ways my actions may have hurt you in the past and the ways they may continue to hurt you for years to come.*
>
> *I grew up in a big family. You never knew that. As far as I know, my parents and my three siblings are still alive. The last time I saw them, my parents were still living in the house I grew up in, in a small farming community in Eastern Colorado. My siblings and their spouses and children lived near them. My maiden name is Emory, if you ever care to look them up. The rosary in this box belonged to my mother, and her mother before her. I'm not even certain why I kept it, but it seems right to pass it on to you.*
>
> *I met your father when I was a freshman in college. As you know, he is several years older than I. We met at a bar I used to go to with my girlfriends. He was a businessman—at least, that's all I thought he was at the time. We fell in love quickly, and before I knew it, we were*

married and moving to another state.

We had moved three times and been married four years before I found out the truth. By then, blind and naive as I was, I had allowed your father to isolate me from everyone and everything I had known before, and I was too ashamed (and still am) to reconnect with my family. They tried to warn me, you see, but I was headstrong and so madly in love. I left your grandparents on very bad terms.

I was also, by the time I learned what your father was really up to, pregnant with our first child. Yes, my Daughter, this is indeed a very difficult truth to reveal. **You have an older sister out there somewhere.** *I don't even know her name. We were in such an impossible situation at the time, we gave her up for adoption (your father didn't even want me to carry the child to term, but in that, at least, I stood up to him).*

You must be wondering what was so terrible that I had to leave my family behind and give up my first-born daughter. I'm still hopelessly in love with your father, Samantha, but he is not a good man. He is and always has been involved with drug trafficking and other smuggling activities. Even if I knew all the details of his work, I think I would spare you having to read them. Suffice it to say, it is dangerous to linger too long in any one location and to make too many friends, which is why we've lived the way we have your whole life. It hasn't been fair to you, I know, and I am so very sorry.

If I've kept you at arm's length, my dear Daughter, it's been to protect you. I am weak and fragile. Hiding the truth always seemed the best way to keep you safe, and I knew if I allowed myself to get too close to you, I risked bringing you too close to danger. This I regret most of all, as I think we could be great friends if we ever have the chance.

Do not judge me too harshly, sweet Daughter. My mistakes are many and grave, but they were made honestly. Remember that your poor mother loved you and wanted only to protect you.

With all the love in my heart,

Your Mother

♫

"Sam? Are you going to say anything?"

She didn't.

"I mean, it's crazy, right?" Tobias said. "Like, what would be the odds? I kept going back and forth about whether to tell you or not because it seems so… so *bizarre*. I even tried to ask her questions to find out more about her—er, at least I was going to, but I think I must've come off wrong because her boyfriend got in my face and kinda told me to back off. Anyway, I had this plan to find out as much as I could before I told you anything. But now that it's been a few days… it's like I'm not even sure that I saw what I saw, you know?"

Sam's mind buzzed—part of it telling her it was impossible and part of it wishing more than anything that it was true. In the first year after her mother's death, she'd brainstormed ways to search for her older sister, but she came up empty. She had no name, no place or date of birth, no information at all except a vague notion based on the timeline in her mother's letter that her sister must be five or six years older than her.

"Sam? Are you okay?" Tobias asked, sounding worried.

Sam blinked. "Yes. I'm okay."

"You don't look okay."

"I'm just… processing," she said.

Tobias waited patiently.

"How old is—" Sam almost said *she*, but realized halfway through the question that she'd avoided using the girl's name and didn't want to anymore. "—Evie?"

"I didn't get a chance to ask her," Tobias answered, "but I would guess early twenties."

Sam's skin crawled with goosebumps, and she drew a shaky breath. Sam knew the likelihood that Tobias had just happened to run into her long-lost sister was practically zero—a coincidence that would beggar belief—but her heart hammered with hope anyway.

"Are you still mad at me for not telling you right away?" Tobias asked sheepishly.

"What?" The question took a moment to register. "Oh. No. I'm not mad. I'm… bewildered. Do you really think she could be my sister?"

Tobias sighed. "I don't know what I think, Sam. I mean, maybe I was just delirious and saw things I wanted to see instead of seeing things as they really are."

Sam fidgeted and chewed her bottom lip. She knew what she was about to ask was ridiculous. "Do you think you could go back to the music store and talk to her again? Maybe… take a picture that you could send me?"

Tobias coughed. "Definitely not. I'm pretty sure she would think I was stalking her or something."

"What? Why?"

The tips of Tobias's ears turned pink. "You have to understand, Sam. I was so freaked out about how much she looked like you."

"And?"

"I acted like a complete weirdo," Tobias confessed. "I think she thought I was being awkward because I was trying to hit on her."

Sam raised her eyebrows. Tobias rethought his words.

"I wasn't trying to hit on her," he scrambled. "But I was definitely being awkward. Because I was freaked out, not because I was trying to hit on her. She misinterpreted the reason for my awkwardness."

"Hm." Sam fell into a thoughtful silence. How else could they find out more about Evie?

"Sam?"

"I'm thinking."

"About?"

"Maybe if I tell Lydia…" Sam muttered, more to herself than to Tobias.

"Um… what?"

"Maybe she'll actually let me come out there if I tell her," Sam continued. "And then *I* could go to the music store."

"You don't think that would be weird?" Tobias asked. He pitched his voice an octave higher. "'Hi, Evie, my name's Sam. I heard that you looked like me so I flew all the way out here from South Dakota to find out if we're sisters. Totes normal, am I right?'"

"Number one, I do not sound like that," Sam said, a smile creeping onto her face. "Number two, I would probably drive, not fly. And number three, don't ever say *totes* again."

Tobias chuckled.

"But you're right," Sam admitted. "It would be weird. I have no idea what I would say to her." She sighed and fell into silence again. When she imagined telling Lydia about Evie, Sam began to appreciate why Tobias had tried to keep it to himself in the first place—she could already see the look of incredulity Lydia would give her.

"I don't want you to get your hopes up for nothing, but…" Tobias said after a while. "If it really means that much to you, Sam, I'll go back. I'll talk to her again."

"Really?" Sam heard the hope in her own voice.

"Really," Tobias said.

Sam kissed the camera lens on her phone. "You are the best fiancé ever."

Tobias grinned.

"He will provide the way and the means, such as you could never have imagined. Leave it all to Him, let go of yourself, lose yourself on the Cross, and you will find yourself entirely."

St. Catherine of Siena

9

He's Back

♫

On Saturdays, Evie worked at Bach for More with the store's two part-time employees, Lety and Trent. Lety had played French horn in high school but was currently studying something to do with IT at a community college, and Trent was a retired high school band director. Both had fallen prey to the pandemic panic and wore masks everywhere.

Although Finn didn't work the front of the store on Saturdays, he used one of the studio rooms in the back to teach clarinet lessons, just as Evie taught violin and guitar lessons on Wednesdays. With only two students, Finn typically spent no more than a couple hours at the store on lesson days.

During Finn's second lesson, while Evie sorted and stocked a shipment of inventory in the stockroom, they both received a group text message from Regina:

> *Hope you fools don't have any plans sept 26 cuz I already got you comp tix* 😹 *Sorry E prolly have to wear a mask* 😁

She included a link to the touring schedule for the show she was in. They would be in Colorado for two weekends.

Evie screeched with delight and jumped into the air with a fist pump. She missed her best friend dearly and couldn't wait to see her. Since Regina's graduation two years before, her rehearsal and touring schedule had kept her busy enough that she had never made it back to

Colorado. All her off time was spent visiting her family, who still lived in California, where Evie and Regina had grown up together.

Evie almost ran to Finn's studio room to celebrate with him, but she decided against it—she didn't want to interrupt his lesson. He probably hadn't even checked his phone yet. Instead, she sent a GIF of dancing characters from *The Office*—a favorite show of hers and Regina's that they had spent an absurd amount of time bingeing when they were both students—to the group text. It was then that she noticed Tony was part of the group message, too, and her excitement rose. It would be like old times, the four of them—her and Regina and Finn and Tony! She didn't even mind that she would probably have to wear a mask to the performance. Or even if she did mind, she felt it would be worth the sacrifice.

Trent appeared in the doorway of the stockroom.

"Everything okay in here?" he asked.

"Yeah. Why?" Evie responded.

"Oh. I thought I heard you scream," Trent said. "Thought maybe you fell or dropped something heavy on yourself."

Evie laughed. "No, sorry to alarm you. I just got some really good news and got a little excited, I guess."

Trent's eyes crinkled with a smile Evie couldn't see under his mask. "Oh. That's good. Glad you're okay."

He left Evie to finish sorting and stocking. Almost at the same time she returned to the counter out front, Finn's lesson wrapped up. His student, a greasy, gangly boy in middle school, passed Evie and Trent and Lety without a word or even lifting his head to look at any of them. He ducked out the front door and climbed in a waiting SUV as if hoping no one would catch him coming out of the music store. Evie shook her head—why were middle school boys so awkward?

A moment later, Finn appeared with his clarinet case in hand. Evie knew she wore her excitement about Regina on her face, but she knew Finn would be just as excited. Maybe even more—for a time during her freshman year, Evie positively believed Finn fancied her tall, gorgeous, fun-loving friend. Although no hard evidence of such an attachment had ever emerged, the impression had lingered in Evie's mind. She took it for granted that all men preferred Regina over her.

As Finn approached Evie at the counter, he must have noticed her excitement because a slow grin spread across his face.

"You look positively mischievous, Lady Vincent," he said.

"Have you looked at your messages?" she asked.

"Why?" Finn asked. "Did I miss my own birthday or something?"

Evie laughed. "No. Just look."

Finn set his clarinet case on the counter and dug his phone out of his pocket. Evie enjoyed the play of emotions that caused his eyebrows to crease together and then go up and then relax. The corners of his mouth twitched, but he put his phone calmly back in his pocket and looked up at her with a controlled expression.

"Aren't you excited?" she asked.

"I don't know what you're talking about," Finn answered. "I just have a bunch of messages from silly girls—one who doesn't know how to spell and one who has terrible taste in television."

Evie punched him in the shoulder.

"Ouch!" Finn said with a laugh. "I take it back. You don't have terrible taste in television."

She punched him again.

"Hey! That's about enough of that, Lady Vincent."

With a faux look of fierceness, Finn poked her in the abdomen—not hard, just enough to tickle. She yelped and laughed in surprise. She swatted his hand, and they both chuckled.

"Oh, man, it's been so long," Finn breathed. "It'll be like old times, you and me and Regina and Tony."

Evie laughed again. She couldn't help it. Hadn't she thought the same thing only minutes ago?

"Dance party," Finn said suddenly. "Right now. We gotta celebrate. Trent—" Finn whirled toward Trent, who seemed oblivious to their shenanigans as he organized sheet music. "What's your vibe, my man? Are you a soul kinda guy? Disco? EDM?"

"Pardon?" Trent asked.

Evie made eye contact with Lety, who raised a single eyebrow and shook her head ever so slightly. What did that mean?

"All right, the king of dance parties it is. Good choice," Finn said, though no one had made any suggestions. He grabbed his phone again and scrolled through his music as he made his way to the sound system receiver. He plugged his phone in, spun the volume dial, and Michael Jackson's *Off the Wall* blared through the store's speakers.

Lety rolled her eyes, and Trent scowled.

But Evie didn't care. She felt too good to care. As Finn boogied his way back toward her, she let the song's funky rhythm work its way through her body and started dancing. The two of them shimmied and grooved through the store, completely ignoring the looks Trent and

Lety gave them. Finn, of course, sang along.

But after one particular twirl, which ended with Evie facing the door, her joyful exuberance turned abruptly to startled embarrassment.

Tobias, the creepy kid from the HVAC company, stood there wide-eyed. How long had he been watching her dance?

Evie ran to turn the music down to an appropriately subdued level.

"Hey!" she heard Finn call from behind a drum display. "The song wasn't over yet."

When he came around the corner and looked at Evie, she subtly nodded toward Tobias. Finn saw him, and his expression turned sour.

Tobias ran a hand through his hair as he approached Evie. Finn reached her side at the same time.

"Hi," Tobias said with an uncomfortable smile. "Um... I'm the... I was here fixing the A/C earlier this week."

"We remember," Finn said with a hint of menace. Evie elbowed him. They should at least wait to hear what the creepy kid had to say before being rude to him.

Tobias looked back and forth between Evie and Finn. The tips of his ears turned pink.

"I know I acted kind of like a weirdo the last time I was here," Tobias said, his words hesitant and his breathing heavy. "I'm sorry about that. And I wanted to explain."

The fact that he recognized the strangeness of his own behavior made Evie want to hear him out. But his obvious nervousness also made her wary.

Tobias licked his lips and cleared his throat. "So, this is going to sound crazy. And it probably is crazy. But hopefully, it'll make sense why I was so weird."

Evie felt Finn tense next to her. She was grateful he hadn't left the store yet. What would she have done if Tobias caught her alone? Well... Trent and Lety were there, but having Finn there made her feel safer somehow.

"Okay, here goes," Tobias said, apparently pumping himself up for whatever he had to say. He gestured toward Evie. "You look *exactly* like my girlfriend—er, my fiancée—Sam."

"Buddy, that pickup line went out of style before it was ever in style," Finn said.

"No, it's not a pickup line," Tobias said, shaking his head. He fished his phone out of his pocket. "Look, I'll show you." He turned the screen toward them, and Evie caught her breath.

The brightly smiling teenage girl in the wallpaper picture did, indeed, bear an uncanny resemblance to Evie. It's strange enough to see your Doppelgänger once… but Evie had seen this girl before. She would swear it. And when she looked back up at Tobias's face, she realized she'd seen him before, too.

Evie felt herself grow lightheaded and clutched at Finn's arm to steady herself. He gave her a worried look.

"You okay?" he whispered.

"What did you say her name is?" Evie asked.

"Sam," Tobias answered. "Samantha Ingram."

Evie couldn't breathe. Her head spun. She squeezed Finn's arm harder.

"You think it's weird, too, right?" Tobias said. "How much you two look alike?"

"Yeah," Evie breathed, barely keeping herself together. "Super weird."

Tobias sighed and put his phone back in his pocket. "Can I ask you a… well, kind of a personal question?"

"I don't think so—" Finn started.

"Yes," Evie interrupted him.

"Okay. Please don't take this the wrong way if you weren't, but… were you adopted?" Tobias asked.

Evie's heart stopped.

"Okay, it's time for you to leave." Finn gently pried Evie's hand from his arm and stepped toward Tobias to escort him out of the store. Tobias put his hands up in a gesture of surrender.

"Why would you ask that?" Evie managed to blurt out.

"Because Sam knows that she has a sister somewhere that her parents gave up for adoption before she was even born—before Sam was born, I mean," Tobias spat out quickly. He likely knew Finn wouldn't let him talk much longer. "I know it's probably impossible, but when I saw you the other day, I just kept thinking… how much you both look alike, and you're both musicians, and you're the same height—well, she's a little taller, maybe, but not much—but you even have kinda similar voices. I just had to ask. I'm sorry if I… I didn't mean to cause trouble at all."

Evie raised a shaky hand and covered her mouth with the tips of calloused fingers.

Tobias studied her face. He must have seen something in her expression because his eyes widened. "Am I right? Are you her sister?"

Evie shook her head, but she couldn't get any words out. What she wanted to say was, *I can't believe it, but yes, I think I am.* But nothing would come out. And because she was shaking her head instead of nodding, Tobias's face fell.

"All right, time's up," Finn said. This time he physically turned Tobias around and pushed him toward the door. Tobias didn't resist. He left with shoulders slumped. Finn watched out the door to make sure he got in his car and drove away before he returned to Evie.

"What's wrong with that guy?" Finn muttered. "I mean, who asks a complete stranger if they were adopted? Sure, that girl kinda looked like you, but so what? There are almost eight billion people in the world. There are bound to be a few who look alike. That guy had some real cojones coming back here just to ask you that—"

"Finn," Evie interrupted him. She looked up into his blue eyes with an apologetic look. "There are some things I need to tell you."

His eyebrows pinched in concern.

10

A Difficult Call

♫

Tobias felt like a fool. And he did not look forward to calling Sam.

Even though he'd teased her about her idea to come out to Colorado and talk to Evie herself, Tobias wished now that he'd encouraged her to do just that. Sam was so much better at talking to people. Especially people older than them. Adults loved Sam. And judging by Evie's reaction to Sam's picture, maybe the sight of Sam in the flesh would have made her more receptive to the possibility that they were sisters.

Of course, when he'd asked her outright, Evie had denied that they could be sisters. But on the other hand, she had never actually answered his question about whether she was adopted. Her boyfriend had intervened before she'd had a chance to.

Even though Tobias dreaded disappointing Sam, he knew he couldn't wait until their normal evening call to tell her how his second meeting with Evie went. He hadn't met anyone his own age since moving to Colorado, in large part because the pandemic kept many activities and places closed. And while he didn't mind living with Sam's Uncle Steve and Aunt Kristy, they weren't exactly the type of people he wanted to spend his Saturday afternoon hanging out with. With nothing to do and no one to distract him, Tobias knew he would drive himself crazy if he waited until 7:00 PM to call his beloved.

Steve and Kristy had offered their entire basement for Tobias to live in. He had his own entrance through a sliding glass door and a small kitchen where he could make himself simple meals. They offered to let him live there for free, but he insisted on paying rent. He would give his dad no reason to claim he couldn't handle the responsibilities of adulthood. What he paid Steve and Kristy was less than half the average rent for a one-bedroom apartment in Sioux Falls, so he was still saving money, but he was also proving—to his dad and to himself—that he was capable of managing a budget and paying expenses.

He initiated a video call to Sam the moment he walked through the sliding glass door.

"Hey," she said when the call connected. Tobias could see the headrest of his old car behind her.

"Are you driving?" he asked, incredulous.

"No, of course not," Sam said. "I'm in a parking lot. I got bored at home, so I just got in the car and started driving around. I ended up at the frozen yogurt place."

"Oh," Tobias said. His stomach growled at the mention of frozen yogurt, and his heart ached to share a cup with Sam.

"You look sad," Sam said. "And you looked that way before I mentioned the frozen yogurt, so I know it's not because you wish you were here."

"I do wish I was there, Sam," Tobias replied. "Or that you were here."

Sam leaned her head back against the headrest and sighed. "I promised Lyds I wouldn't ask again. Not until things calm down or whatever. She won't let me travel alone with the pandemic and the riots still going on."

"Maybe if we gave her a better reason, she'd let you come."

Sam's head snapped forward, and her eyes bored into her screen.

"A better reason? Like a sister? Tobias, did you go back there already? Did you talk to her? Is Evie my sister?" She spit out questions faster than a machine gun.

Tobias didn't know which one to answer first. "Yes, I went to the music store. I just got back. And I did talk to Evie."

"Well? What happened? What did she say? What did *you* say?" Sam's eyes were wide and hopeful.

Tobias looked down, trying to think of a way to explain what had happened. When he looked back up, he saw that his hesitation had already done the damage he'd been hoping to avoid. The look of disappointment on Sam's face crushed him.

"It's okay, Tobias," she said. "We both knew it was a long shot."

"I'm sorry, Sam," Tobias said. "I didn't get to talk to her for very long before her boyfriend kicked me out of the store—"

"You got yourself kicked out of the store?" Sam interrupted. The corners of her mouth lifted a bit. "For me?"

Tobias cracked a smile. He hadn't given Sam enough credit for her resilience. He knew how much she longed to find her sister, how much she had dared to hope when he told her about Evie, and how much it must have pained her to have that hope dashed. But he also should have known that—just as she had when she lost her parents—Sam would bear this cross with grace.

"You won't tell my parents, will you?" Tobias said.

Sam raised her eyebrows. "The last time you asked me not to tell your parents something was when you pummeled Jason the Meathead for bullying me. And your mom flipped when she found out."

Tobias grinned at the memory. Not the memory of bloodying Jason's face with his fist—that part still filled him with shame, even after all these years. But the memory of the events that bloodying Jason's face had set in motion. After his violent reaction to Jason's bullying, Tobias panicked and admitted to Sam that he liked her. And then she admitted the same thing back to him. But then Tobias had bungled things by telling her they couldn't be together. After that, it took both of them a few weeks to get their hearts and their heads all straightened out and on the same page, but they ended up together, and that's all Tobias cared about.

"Okay, I guess you can tell them," Tobias said with a sigh. He could already imagine the text messages he would get from his mom when she found out he'd been kicked out of a store.

"I think I need to hear the rest of the story first," Sam said. "Exactly what did you do to get yourself kicked out?"

"I asked Evie if she was adopted," Tobias replied. He actually wasn't sure the exact moment Evie's boyfriend decided to push him out the door, but the moment he'd asked that particular question seemed like a good guess.

"And she said no?" Sam asked.

Tobias considered his answer carefully. Evie hadn't given him a definite yes or no to *that* question. She'd only shaken her head when he asked whether she could be Sam's sister. But she had said *something* when he asked about adoption. What was it? Her boyfriend had been talking at the same time, and everything after that happened so quickly.

"I didn't get an answer before her boyfriend kicked me out," Tobias finally said.

"So there's still a possibility?" The hope returned to Sam's eyes.

Tobias wouldn't lie to her. "I don't think so, Sam. I showed her your picture, and I think I told her I thought you might be sisters—I don't remember exactly what I said, I was kind of babbling by then—but she seemed pretty sure you weren't. She just kind of… shook her head… when I asked if she was your sister. And that's when her boyfriend shoved me out the door."

Sam listened attentively, her eyebrows knitting in thought, but the hope didn't leave her face.

"So there's still a possibility?" she asked again.

"Sam, I just told you—"

"You just told me she never really answered you. And a shake of the head could mean anything," Sam insisted. "Think about it, Tobias. How would you respond if someone stalked you at work just to ask if a random dude was your long-lost br—" She stopped herself.

Tobias did have a long-lost brother. Not as long-lost as Sam's sister —Jake had been a troubled teen who ran away when Tobias was eleven—but Sam must have realized her hypothetical wasn't as hypothetical as she thought it was when she started her speech.

"Anyway, you would have done more than shake your head, right?" Sam went on.

"It doesn't matter, Sam," Tobias said, desperate to protect her from more broken dreams. "If I go back again, I'm pretty sure she's going to call the cops on me. Or her boyfriend is going to fight me. We need to let this go. There's nothing more we can do."

"There's nothing more *you* can do," Sam said.

Her words hurt his pride, and Tobias tried not to let it show. That single sentence made him feel like he'd failed her, which made him angry. Not at her, but at himself.

"You've already gone above and beyond, my love," Sam added gently. "And I am so, so grateful that you went and talked to her again. I know it was risky and difficult and probably awkward, but you did it anyway because I asked you to. So, now…" Sam paused and took a breath. "Maybe it's my turn to make a fool of myself."

Tobias didn't like the sound of that. Not one bit.

11

Secrets

♫

Evie and Finn left the care of the store in Trent and Lety's hands while they shut themselves in one of the studio rooms and sat down for a conversation Evie never imagined having.

"I probably should have told you a long time ago because we're friends and friends know this kind of stuff about each other, but… I *was* adopted. As an infant," Evie confessed.

Finn couldn't quite control his look of shock, but Evie gave him credit for trying.

"My adopted parents, Pete and Cassidy, had been trying to conceive for years and couldn't, so they decided to adopt. All the arrangements were made before I was even born, but it was a closed adoption, so they never met or knew who my biological parents were."

"Evie, I had no idea…"

Evie gave a sad laugh. "Neither did I until I was seventeen."

Finn's eyes grew wider, and his eyebrows rose higher. "Are you serious?"

Evie nodded. "Pete and Cassidy never planned to tell me at all. But Gemma and Gentry—they're twins, Pete and Cassidy's real kids; they finally got pregnant six months after they adopted me, go figure— anyway, Gemma and Gentry overheard a conversation between Cassidy and her mother…" Evie had to pause. It still hurt even though she had forgiven all of them long ago. "Cassidy's mom—supposed to be my grandma, right?—told Cassidy that the reason I was so much trouble was because I was adopted."

"Whoa. That's awful," Finn said.

"Yeah," Evie said. "And I really wasn't even that much trouble. I was just a girl who didn't understand why her parents loved her less than they loved her siblings."

Finn leaned forward, resting his elbows on his knees and clasping his hands. His blue eyes, intent on Evie's face, were full of compassion.

"I didn't believe Gemma and Gentry at first," Evie continued. "Or didn't *want* to believe them. I told Cassidy about it, thinking I would get them in trouble for spreading rumors and just generally being jerks to me, but that's not what happened. Cassidy told me the truth, and it devastated me."

"I can't even imagine," Finn whispered.

"I mean… my whole life… my whole identity…" Evie said. "It was all a lie. I felt like, suddenly, I had no idea who I even was." She paused. "I'm still not sure I know," she mumbled, more to herself than to Finn.

He waited for her to continue, saying nothing but somehow managing to offer support. She liked that about Finn—his solidness, his concreteness, his there-ness.

"That's how I ended up here, in Colorado," Evie said. "I was so hurt and angry that I ran away. Regina was already here, going to school. I didn't know where else to go, and she offered me a place to stay until I could figure something out."

"I can't believe I never knew any of this," Finn said. But his tone wasn't reproachful, just amazed.

"Hardly anyone knows," Evie replied. "I don't like to talk about it."

"Regina must know, though, right?"

"Of course. We grew up together. She felt almost as betrayed—lied to—as I did," Evie said. "And Professor Chin knew. I kinda had to tell her when I auditioned. I had to explain why I didn't have high school transcripts or my parents' signature on anything."

"Wait. You never finished high school?" Finn looked impressed.

Evie shrugged. "I was only a few weeks into my senior year when I ran away. I got my GED a couple months after I got to Colorado, though."

Finn studied her. Evie could practically see his brain working through all she'd told him and drawing further conclusions. He had more questions, she could tell. She waited patiently for them, ready to offer answers to anything he asked. To her great surprise, it felt good to tell Finn her long-held secret. It felt right.

"Holy crickets, you got a full ride to Lockwood, didn't you?" Finn said suddenly, sitting back and digging his hands into his wild blond hair. "There's no other way you could've done it."

Evie smiled a little and nodded.

"Evie… *no one* gets a full ride to Lockwood," Finn said.

Evie shrugged. "Maybe Professor Chin took pity on me."

Finn grinned. "I don't believe that. I think you're just that good."

Evie smiled, but then her face fell. "Whatever the reason, it didn't matter in the end. I failed her when I failed my jury. She might have bent the rules for me when I auditioned, but she couldn't save me from *that*. I failed so spectacularly, they had no choice but to yank my scholarship."

Finn leaned forward again. "You're still the most talented musician I know, Evie. So what if you didn't finish your music degree? The point of going to music school is to train you so you can get a job as a musician. I'd bet my life savings that you could audition for any orchestra in the country and get a job right now. You don't need a piece of paper with your name on it to play the way you do."

Evie looked into Finn's eyes and saw sincerity there. "Your life savings, huh? What's that, like three dollars?" she teased.

Finn chuckled. "Less. I think I'm in negative territory now that I'm going back to school."

They were both quiet for a while, but Evie suspected Finn would eventually remember the reason she was telling him all this in the first place—Tobias. And Sam. Sure enough, after a few moments, Finn's brow creased, and he titled his head.

"So… do you think that kid—Tobias—was onto something?" Finn asked. "That you might be related to his girlfriend?"

Evie took several breaths to keep her emotions in check before finally answering.

"I'm sure of it."

November 19, 2017

The moment felt surreal.

Evie sat at a small table in a room full of federal penitentiary inmates meeting with their loved ones or their lawyers. The way some of the inmates looked at her made her skin crawl, and her stomach was tight with nerves.

But she promised herself she would not leave until she met him. Robert Rice. Her biological father.

Months earlier, Liam had helped her identify him. It had seemed like a long shot, but she had begged him to use his contacts in the police department to find out whether her DNA was a familial match with anyone in their database. He refused the first several times she asked him, insisting that it was a completely inappropriate use of law enforcement resources, but he eventually relented. She didn't know any details about who at PD helped him. He just took a mouth swab from her one week and came back the next with a file folder containing the criminal record of Robert Rice.

Drug smuggling. Human trafficking. Bribery. Extortion. RICO. Money laundering. The list of convictions was startling, and the sentences for all of them added up to more than a couple life sentences.

Evie had tried writing Robert Rice letters, but she never received a response. Unsure whether he didn't want to respond or whether the penitentiary's mail system was to blame, Evie resolved to pay him a visit. After all, the federal prison where he was serving his many sentences was, unbelievably, only a two-hour drive from where she lived.

She knew him the moment he entered the room escorted by two guards. His mugshot had been in the file folder Liam had given her, of course, but she would have known him anyway. She owed many of her own features, including her gray eyes, to his genetic contribution. Unlike Evie, though, Robert Rice's face bore several jagged and patchy scars, as if he had been in some terrible accident.

Robert Rice sat down across from her with a stony expression. His gray eyes seemed almost lifeless, soulless. Like a shark.

"Hi," Evie said, not sure how else to begin.

"You grew up fast," he said.

"You know who I am?" Evie asked, surprised.

He snorted. "Did you think I wouldn't? Did you think the accident would turn me into a slobbering idiot like your mom?"

Evie looked at him in confusion. But the callous mention of her mother as a slobbering idiot *pierced her heart. So far, she'd been unable to uncover any information at all about her biological mother. "I'm sorry, I don't know what you're talking about."*

Robert Rice studied her more closely and uttered a foul curse. "You're the other one, aren't you?"

"The other one?" Evie's confusion deepened.

"The one she told me she got rid of," Robert Rice said. "Let's see, when was that? When we were living in California?"

"I'm your daughter," Evie said forcefully, wanting to bring crystal clarity to their conversation. "My name is Evelyn Rose Vincent. You and my mother arranged for me to be adopted before I was even born."

"Her decision, not mine," Robert Rice said. "I told her to get an abortion."

Evie reeled. This man had no heart. He was a monster. How could she be his offspring?

"I'm glad she didn't listen," Evie said, defiance lacing her words. "Where is she now? My mother."

"Dead," Robert Rice answered without a hint of emotion.

"How? When?" Evie asked. Although she'd never known the woman who gave birth to her, the news still sent a shock of pain through her. Now she would never know her.

Robert Rice shrugged. "Time has no meaning in this hellhole. A year? Two? A stroke or some such thing. Whatever it was put the stupid woman out of her misery. We were both in a car accident, and she was nothing but a drooling mess after that."

Evie stared at him in disbelief. How could someone be so heartless? It was clear Robert Rice and her mother had carried on a relationship for years after Evie's birth. How could he speak about her with such contempt and disgust? As much anger as she still felt toward Pete and Cassidy, she could never imagine them speaking about one another the way this man spoke about her mother.

"What was her name?" Evie asked.

"Renee."

"Where is she buried?" Evie made an inward vow that she would visit her mother's grave, wherever it was. Obviously, Robert Rice, the man with whom Renee had spent much of her life, would never visit it. Everyone deserved to have someone *visit their grave.*

Robert Rice shrugged again. "Somewhere in South Dakota, I imagine."

South Dakota? A memory sparked in Evie's mind. A memory of an audition, and a symphony concert, and a face that looked too much like hers to be mere coincidence. And that's when something Robert Rice had said earlier finally sank in. That Evie was the other one.

"Did you and Renee have any other children besides me?"

"Another girl," Robert Rice said with a nod. "Probably sixteen by now."

"Probably? You don't know? Did you give her up for adoption, too?" Evie peppered him with questions.

"No, we kept her. Until Renee died anyway. Cursed woman ratted me out before she died. I didn't have much choice but to disappear. Left Sam with some neighbors. Not that it mattered. I got nabbed a few months later, and

here we are." He spread his arms as a gesture to the prison around them.

"I have a sister named Sam?"

"Samantha, yeah. Annoying, mousy little thing."

Evie couldn't stand to hear him insult anyone else. She didn't know Renee or Samantha, but based on what little she now knew of Robert Rice, she was inclined to believe they were saints for having put up with him for more than five minutes.

"Thank you for meeting with me. I won't take up any more of your precious time," Evie said as she pushed away from the table. The nearby guards reacted to her sudden movement, drawing closer and putting their hands on Robert Rice's shoulders.

He smirked.

"Don't bother sending any more letters, Evelyn," he said. "I won't answer them."

Evie left with a heart full of grief.

♫

"Wow. Robert Rice sounds like a real peach," Finn said.

Evie snorted a laugh despite the seriousness of her revelations.

"I don't want to throw a wrench in the works," Finn said with more gravitas, "but didn't Tobias say his girlfriend's name was Samantha Ingram? If she were your sister, Robert Rice's daughter, wouldn't her name be Samantha Rice?"

"That's exactly the mistake I made when I tried to look her up," Evie responded. "Sometime after I met Robert Rice, I decided to search the internet for a Samantha Rice in South Dakota who would be a few years younger than me. The only Samantha Rices I found were way too old or way too young."

"So…"

"Robert Rice is his real name. But when he was arrested, he was operating under an alias. And he operated under other aliases before that," Evie explained. "One of them, one he used for many, many years, was John Ingram."

♫

Evie and Finn talked a while longer after she told him about Robert Rice, a.k.a. John Ingram.

She told him how she'd reconnected with Pete and Cassidy and

Gemma and Gentry a year after running away, but that her relationship with all of them was still rocky. She told him how she'd gone to Sioux Falls, South Dakota for an orchestra audition and seen who she now believed had been Sam and Tobias at a symphony concert. How the sight of her Doppelgänger had inspired her to start searching for her biological family, and how the search had been mostly fruitless until—

"Who's Liam?" Finn asked. "You keep saying his name like I should know who he is, but I don't. Was he a student at Lockwood and I just don't remember him?"

The question surprised Evie, and her mind raced through the previous day's events and conversations—Liam bringing Bridget to Back for More and asking Evie to coffee. Finn had never heard her say Liam's name. He had no idea.

Evie's stomach clenched with guilt. Her family history wasn't the only secret she'd kept from Finn. For some reason, she'd never thought of them as secrets before. And for some reason, she found this one much harder to tell Finn.

"Um… you remember the guy who came into the store with his daughter yesterday?"

Finn's eyebrows rose.

"That was Liam."

Evie knew she owed Finn more of an explanation than that, but she felt awkward about revealing her romantic wounds and didn't quite know how much or what to say.

Finn waited. Evie said nothing.

Finn scoffed softly. "Okay, Evie. You don't have to tell me who he is or how you know him or whatever, but as your friend, I have to point out that you just spent the last hour telling me how much it hurt you when people you loved didn't tell you the truth."

His words hit her like a gut punch, and Evie gasped. Her anger flared hot and fast. "It's completely different, Finn! First of all, I had a *right* to know I was adopted. They kept something from me that I had a right to know. You have *no right* to know about my history with Liam. It has nothing to do with you. Secondly… I can't think of a secondly, but the point is that the situations are completely different."

"You're right," Finn acknowledged. "They are different. But I literally just threw a guy out of the store for you—unjustly—because of things I didn't know. Things you never told me. And seeing *Liam* yesterday obviously upset you, so at least give me enough information to know what to do if he ever comes in again. Is he a threat? A nuisance?"

"Neither. His daughter is starting lessons with me on Wednesday, so just treat him like a normal customer."

"Fine. I will."

"Fine."

Evie crossed her arms even though it felt childish to do so. How had things gone from a heartfelt conversation between friends to uncomfortable so quickly?

"Don't be mad, Evie," Finn said.

"I'm not mad."

"Yes, you are." Finn chuckled to himself, then sighed and rubbed his face. "Way to go, Gallagher."

Evie uncrossed her arms and relaxed a little. "Okay, look. It's just awkward. I used to have a huge crush on Liam, and he rejected me, and I was still a little salty about it when I saw him yesterday. That's all."

Finn studied her. It was clearly *not all*, and she knew that he knew it. But he didn't press her further.

Instead, he stood and held out his hand. "Milady."

She took the offered hand, and he pulled her to her feet and drew her into a warm hug. A friendly hug. A comforting hug. They stayed that way for a while. Probably longer than they should have. But it felt good to be held, and Evie couldn't make herself pull away.

"Thank you," Finn murmured quietly into her hair. "For telling me your whole life story."

Evie chuckled into his shirt. "Sorry."

"No, I'm serious," Finn said. "It means a lot to me that you told me." He paused. "And I'm sorry if I did the wrong thing kicking Tobias out."

Evie didn't respond. She didn't know how to. The shock of Tobias's visit had worn off, but her heart and mind felt too muddled to see the next step.

"You said something yesterday," Finn said after a moment. "About me and Regina being your only friends. And I got to thinking… wondering… I sometimes do stuff with the young adult group at my parish, and I thought maybe you could come with me sometime. Meet new people. Nicer people than the ones we knew at Lockwood."

Evie sighed. "I don't know, Finn. Maybe it wasn't the people at Lockwood. Maybe it was me."

Finn leaned away so he could look down at her face. "False. Repeat after me."

"What?" Evie laughed uncertainly.

"Repeat after me," Finn said again. "I, Evelyn Vincent…"

"Finn—"

"That's not what I said. I said, 'I, Evelyn Vincent…'"

Evie rolled her eyes but smiled despite herself. "I, Evelyn Vincent…"

"… am a wonderful person…"

"I'm not saying that."

"Okay, fine. Then I'll just tell you, and you'll have to believe that it's true," Finn said. "You, Evelyn Vincent, are a wonderful person. You are a beloved daughter of a Royal King, which makes you a royal princess, and you deserve to be treated as such. Anyone who knows you—really knows you—also knows how immeasurably enriched their life is with you in it. Anyone who doesn't know that needs to have their head examined."

Evie swallowed and felt her cheeks blush. Her mouth suddenly felt dry.

A knock on the door of the studio room made them both jump, and they separated hurriedly. Lety's masked face peered through the window. Evie motioned her inside.

"A customer has a coupon I don't know how to key in," Lety said, eyeing the two of them with a knowing look.

"Right," Evie breathed. She moved for the door.

"Evie," Finn called when she reached the hallway. "Mass tomorrow at ten-thirty. Hike afterwards. I'll text you the details."

"Sounds good," Evie answered with a smile.

♫

After she closed Bach for More at the end of the day, with her heart and head full of Tobias and Sam and Finn and Regina and Liam, Evie once again found herself on her knees in the Blessed Sacrament chapel. Her mind buzzed with a million thoughts and jumped from one to the next before she could grab onto any of them.

Sam… she had no doubt that Samantha Ingram was her sister. Robert Rice's second daughter. The daughter he kept but apparently disliked. And now Finn knew she had a sister, too.

Finn… where to even begin with Finn? A friend, a close friend, so endearing and so confusing at the same time. Her friendship with Finn had seemed so simple for so long, but now it seemed… not simple. It all started when they sang together. She *knew* it would get weird.

Regina… her best friend was coming to town. Did Regina like Finn? Did Finn like Regina? Did it matter? What would Regina tell her to do about Sam?

Sam… Tobias… if she trusted in God's Providence, could she trust that God had arranged this, too? Now that she knew who and where her sister was, what was the next step? *Apart from me you can do nothing.* But what? What was she supposed to do? Or what was she supposed to let the Lord do for her? Maybe she should talk to Finn about it again.

Finn… why had it taken her so long to tell Finn about her past? Why couldn't she tell him about Liam?

Liam… what would he think if—

Her phone buzzed, jarring her from her scattered thought-prayers. She blushed with embarrassment even though she was the only person in the chapel—she usually turned her phone on silent when she came to the chapel. Before she could retrieve the phone from her back pocket, it buzzed again.

Two messages from Finn:

> *10:30 mass at St. Thomas Aquinas. Bring a change of clothes, meeting at the trailhead immediately afterwards. Hike's 3 miles, nothing strenuous. Lunch will be provided.*

And:

> *Wanna ride together? I can pick you up at 10.*

Evie looked from her phone to the Blessed Sacrament and whispered, "What are you trying to tell me?"

Apart from me you can do nothing.

Evie sent her response:

> *Sure. See you at 10.*

12

Damage Control

♫

When Sam asked, Tobias refused to give up the name of the music store where Evie worked. Sam had it in her mind that she would call the store and talk to Evie herself, but the idea made Tobias want to hurl. He could just imagine how such a scenario would play out.

Evie, rightly concluding that Tobias was the only possible person who could have told Sam her location and rightfully feeling targeted, would either lodge a complaint with Emory HVAC or press charges against Tobias. In the best case, he would lose his job. In the worst, he would be arrested for harassment or stalking.

Sam relented when he laid it all out that way. Although she was disappointed, she assured him before the call ended that she understood and that she wouldn't do anything that might get Tobias in trouble—with her Uncle Steve or the law.

Despite disappointing his beloved, Tobias felt relieved. Evie's face had haunted him all week, but he sincerely believed he had done all he reasonably could to find out whether she was related to Sam. The way he saw it, he'd pushed his luck returning to the store and asking her such personal questions. The fact she hadn't already pressed charges made him feel like he'd dodged a bullet, and he was glad to put the whole mess behind him.

So when Steve shouted down into the basement that someone from Bach for More had called the Emory HVAC on-call number asking for Tobias, his heart jammed into his throat.

Tobias met Steve at the top of the stairs and took the smartphone from him with shaky fingers. Steve didn't seem angry or concerned, so Tobias forced a smile.

"It's on mute," Steve said as he handed the phone over. "You can come get me if they have questions you don't know how to answer." He clearly assumed the call was about the A/C repair Tobias and Joe had done.

Tobias nodded. "Will do."

Steve left him with the phone and disappeared.

Tobias waited until he reached the bottom of the stairs before he cleared his throat, took the phone off mute, and raised it to his ear.

"This is Tobias speaking," he said. He didn't have much experience speaking to customers on the phone. He hoped he sounded professional.

"Tobias, this is Finn," a male voice said. "From Bach for More Music Store."

Tobias froze. He had expected Evie to be on the other end of the line. Was Finn her boyfriend? Or maybe Evie had complained to a supervisor he hadn't met?

"Hello? Are you there?"

"Yes, sir." Tobias didn't know what else to say.

Finn chuckled. "Come on, dude. There's no way you thought I was intimidating enough to call me *sir*. Or old enough."

"Um..." How to answer that? "I was trying to be polite. I know I upset your girlfriend today, and I don't want to cause any more trouble."

"My *girlfriend*?" Finn laughed. "Please don't let Evie hear you call her that. She will murder me if she thinks I've been telling people she's my girlfriend."

"Oh. You just work there, then? I thought... You just seemed really protective," Tobias said. "As you should be. I was way out of line. I never should have asked her those questions. Never even should have come back to the store. You will never see me again, I promise." Tobias felt a little cowardly for babbling on like that, but then again, the idea of going to jail for stalking did scare him.

"Calm down, my man," Finn said. "I called to apologize. For throwing you out of the store. I thought I was doing Evie a favor, but it turns out... well, it turns out that you were right. Evie *was* adopted, and she's pretty darn sure that she and your lady are, in fact, sisters."

Tobias almost dropped the phone. His brain screeched to a halt, paralyzed with shock.

"Tobias? You there, my man?"

Tobias coughed. "Is this a joke?"

"No," Finn said. "Evie told me after you left. I think you surprised her so much she didn't know how to react, and then I threw you out before she *could* react, so… now I'm trying to repair the damage."

Tobias still didn't believe him. It could be a setup, a trap to get him back to the store so he would incriminate himself further as a stalker. Or maybe just a prank to cause him trouble the way he'd caused them trouble. He should test Finn.

"What makes Evie so sure Sam is her sister?" Tobias asked.

"Is Sam's father a man named John Ingram?" Finn returned with his own question.

Tobias's skin prickled with goosebumps. Still…

"I told you Sam's last name. And John is a very common name. What else?"

Finn huffed. "A few hours ago, you were desperate to convince us Evie and Sam were sisters. Now you doubt it? What changed?" he asked.

"I'm not getting Sam's hopes up again unless I'm absolutely certain," Tobias replied. "If Evie is so sure, why did she say no when I asked if they were sisters?"

Silence. Tobias waited for an answer.

"I don't know," Finn finally said. "Maybe she was just caught off guard."

"I need more than John Ingram's name," Tobias said.

He heard Finn sigh. "Look, according to Evie, John Ingram isn't even his real name. It's an alias. His real name is Robert Rice, and he's a convicted felon sitting in the federal penitentiary right here in Florence, Colorado. Evie knows for a fact that Robert Rice is her father because she found him through some kind of familial DNA search. She went to visit him, and he told her he had another daughter with Evie's mother, whose name was Renee, and their second daughter's name was Samantha. Oh, and he mentioned South Dakota. Apparently, Renee passed away while they were living in South Dakota, and Robert Rice left their daughter with neighbors and went on the lam. Is that enough?"

Tobias didn't know what to think. *Renee. South Dakota. Left their daughter with neighbors.* All details that matched Sam's life story precisely. The only detail that didn't fit was Robert Rice. If John Ingram had truly been nothing more than an alias used by Sam's father, Tobias was sure Sam had never been aware of it. Could Robert Rice really be the same man? When Sam's father abandoned her, he had indeed been wanted by the police, but wouldn't they have contacted Sam if they'd caught him? How could he have been arrested, convicted, and sentenced to time in a federal prison without Sam knowing?

"Tobias?"

"Okay, say it's true. Say they're sisters," Tobias said. "I can pretty much guarantee Sam will want to meet Evie, but does Evie want to meet Sam?"

"I don't see why she wouldn't want to," Finn answered.

"She didn't say?" Tobias asked.

"No."

"I'm not telling Sam until we know for sure," Tobias declared. "I don't want her to get pumped about meeting her sister only to find out Evie wants nothing to do with her."

"Seems reasonable," Finn said. A pause. "I'll tell you what. I'm hanging out with Evie tomorrow. I'll ask her and let you know."

"Really?"

"Really."

"Tomorrow?"

"Tomorrow."

Tobias thought about it a moment longer. Finally, he said, "Okay."

They exchanged numbers—Tobias didn't want Finn using the Emory HVAC on-call line to get in touch with him—and left it at that.

Tobias wrestled with his conscience the rest of the day and well into the night. He'd promised Sam never to keep things from her again, even to protect her. But Sam's life had already been filled with so much rejection and abandonment—why add to that unnecessarily if Evie didn't want to meet her?

Finn would text him Evie's answer tomorrow. Just one day. Hopefully, she would be eager to meet Sam, and Tobias would only need to keep this secret for one day.

Hopefully.

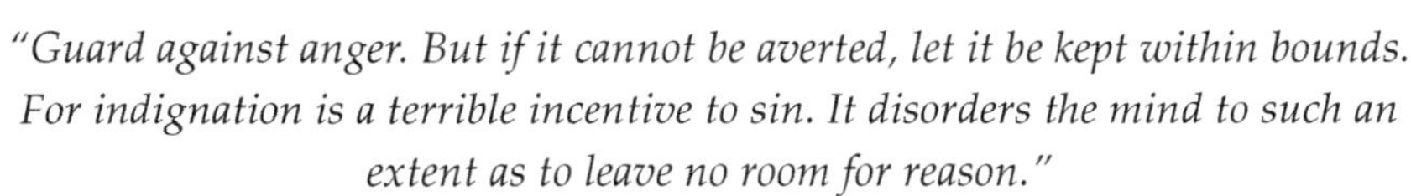

"Guard against anger. But if it cannot be averted, let it be kept within bounds. For indignation is a terrible incentive to sin. It disorders the mind to such an extent as to leave no room for reason."

St. Ambrose

13

Broken

♫

Evie paced her little studio apartment in a summer dress she had forgotten she owned. The yellow dress had wide straps that concealed most of the Tchaikovsky tattoo on her right shoulder blade—only the clef and key signature showed. She wondered fleetingly whether she should grab a cardigan in case the air conditioning in the church was too cold. As she paced, Evie unconsciously practiced fingering exercises on her right wrist. She glanced at the huge treble-clef-shaped clock on her wall.

It was 9:59 AM.

Evie had tried calling Regina after her visit to the Blessed Sacrament chapel the night before. She hoped her best friend would give her some perspective on the events of the past week, but as usual, Regina didn't answer. Although Evie was genuinely happy that Regina had found success pursuing her dream career, her friend's busyness often kept them from speaking for weeks, sometimes months at a time. She found Regina's unavailability especially frustrating now, when she so badly needed someone to help her sort through her tangled thoughts. How could her friend possibly be so busy when half the world was still shut down for that stupid virus?

Evie's phone buzzed, interrupting her musing. Finn.

> *I'm out front*

Surprisingly, Evie felt relieved. What had she even been anxious about? That Finn wouldn't show up? No. That he would come up to her apartment to get her. Perhaps because it was a studio—there was no delineation between living space and bedroom—letting Finn see the inside of her apartment would have felt… intimate.

Evie shook the disconcerting thought from her mind as she grabbed the small backpack she'd stuffed with hiking clothes and headed out the door. When she reached the bottom of the stairs and looked through the cloudy glass door, Evie saw Finn's sky-blue Subaru Outback parked in front of her building and Finn leaning against the passenger door, waiting.

His blond hair was as messy as ever, but he wore a pink button-up shirt and a navy tie. It struck Evie that the only time she'd ever seen Finn dressed up was for performances during college, when they had been required to wear concert black. At work, he always wore jeans and a graphic tee.

Finn straightened and smiled when Evie came out of the building. He opened the passenger door for her and held out his hand as if he were a footman helping her into a carriage.

"Lady Vincent," he said.

"Sir Gallagher," Evie returned with a nod, but she didn't take his hand.

When Finn took his place in the driver's seat, he picked up his phone from the cupholder and scrolled through it.

"What's your vibe this morning?" he asked.

"I don't think you have my vibe on your phone," Evie answered.

"False. I have all the vibes," Finn returned with a grin. "If you don't pick, I will."

"Surprise me." Evie enjoyed the disparate genres included in Finn's tastes. His knowledge of songs and artists was encyclopedic, and whenever she let him choose the music playing at Bach for More, he managed to broaden her own mental repertoire.

"Brave girl," Finn muttered as he made his selection. "I have to warn you, this song makes me dance."

"Even while you're driving?"

Finn pulled away from the curb as the first notes played—a quick series of perfect fourths and fifths from a piano followed by the rest of the rhythm section and saxophones. And then a funky trumpet playing the melody.

"Even while I'm driving." Finn wiggled his shoulders and got into the groove.

Evie laughed. She had to admit, the song made her want to dance, too, and she bobbed her head in time with the beat. Whatever remained of the tension she'd felt waiting for Finn to pick her up melted away.

"What is this?" she asked.

"Al Hirt. *Java*." Finn glanced over at her and waggled his eyebrows. "You like it, yes?"

"I like it, yes."

♫

The only time Evie had ever truly struggled with her faith was the day bishops all over the world began announcing that public Masses were suspended due to the pandemic. She had come to believe—because it had been her lived experience time and again—that the grace received in the Eucharist gave her the strength to face any trial, any challenge, any loss, any cross. The one cross she was not prepared to carry, then, was losing the Eucharist itself. So when public Masses resumed in her diocese, Evie felt profound gratitude and relief.

Still, the sight of pews taped off to mark the requisite six-foot social distancing, the signs reminding parishioners to don their masks, and the empty holy water fonts made her clench her jaw in frustration. Every intervention they'd been forced to endure "out of an abundance of caution" seemed designed to chip away at their humanity. Masks to hide their human faces. Distance to deny their human connections. Isolation to break their human spirits.

Technically, the way Evie understood the "rules," she and Finn should have sat six feet apart from each other. Only families or those who lived in the same household were supposed to sit together, and she and Finn weren't family and certainly didn't share a house. But when they entered the church, Finn followed her to a pew toward the front and sat right next to her. She glanced at his masked face as she lowered the kneeler and almost got the giggles—his glasses were completely fogged up from his hot breath leaking through the gap at the top of his mask.

Evie found it difficult to concentrate during Mass. The same thoughts that had zipped through her mind all through adoration the night before plagued her now.

Finn… sitting right next to her. Close enough that their knees might touch if they weren't careful. Foggy glasses aside, he really looked quite dapper in his shirt and tie. *Stop it.*

Sam… Evie had a sister named Sam. And she now knew how to get in contact with her. Was she ready for that? What if Sam was a monster like their father, Robert Rice? What if Evie didn't like her? Worse, what if Sam didn't like Evie? What if Evie was too moody, too broken, too difficult to love? Could her heart handle being rejected by her little sister? Gemma and Gentry had never been overly fond of Evie, but somehow the thought of being unlikeable to her *real* sister made Evie's chest tighten with anxiety.

Tobias seemed nice enough… when he wasn't being weird and creepy. What kind of girl would he date? What kind of girl would date him? No, he'd called her his *fiancée*. What kind of girl would marry him? What kind of girl would he want to marry?

Wait… how old was Sam? Robert Rice had said *probably sixteen*. That had been almost three years ago. That meant she could only be eighteen or nineteen now if Robert Rice's guess was right. The fact that it was a guess—he was her father, for goodness' sake—disgusted Evie. She thought back to the symphony concert where she'd first seen Sam —she was now convinced it had been her. When was that? Freshman year? January? More than four years ago. If Robert Rice was correct, Sam would have been fourteen or fifteen then. But that didn't seem right. From what Evie remembered, her Doppelgänger had seemed younger than that. Twelve or thirteen maybe.

Either way, what kind of girl got herself engaged when she was still just a teenager? Tobias had a boyishness about him, too. He had to be near Sam's age, and by his looks, Evie would guess he was also under twenty. So young, both of them, to be getting married. Perhaps he'd gotten Sam pregnant. Did Evie already have a niece or nephew on the way?

What kind of childhood had Sam experienced, being raised by Robert Rice and Renee… was it Rice or Ingram? Had she married him when he was Robert Rice and used Ingram as an alias as he had? Or had she even known the man she married? Had they been married at all? Evie hated that she still knew so little about her mother, and she felt a stab of jealousy that Sam had at least had the opportunity to know their parents. She was sure Robert Rice had been a terrible father, which dulled the stab a bit, but what kind of mother had Renee been? Did she and Sam have as turbulent a relationship as Evie and Cassidy? Or did they bond over the shared misery of being shackled to Robert Rice?

Tobias had said she was a musician. A piano player. Which parent had they both inherited their love and talent for music from? No one in Evie's adopted family was musically inclined, and she'd always felt like the odd duck among them. There was something comforting in the thought that she and her *real* sister had music in common.

"You ready?" Finn whispered in Evie's ear.

Her mind had wandered through the entire Mass. Her body had gone through all the motions, but she couldn't recall a single word from the readings or the homily. *I'm sorry, Lord.*

"We can change in the bathrooms here. We'll meet up with the others at the trailhead," Finn whispered.

Evie nodded and followed him out of the pew.

♫

When they arrived at the trailhead—one of many around Chatfield State Park—Finn introduced Evie to five other people: a software engineer named Bryan, a labor and delivery nurse named Jackie, a law student named Winnie, an elementary school teacher named Meg, and a veterinarian named Daisy. They all greeted her with cheerful smiles and handshakes.

Growing up in San Diego, Evie had been an avid surfer, but she learned to enjoy hiking almost as much as surfing when she moved to Colorado. As much as her feet and hips hurt when she finished all five hundred miles of the Camino, the pilgrimage had only increased her love of hiking. The fresh air and beautiful vistas, the wonder and awe of God's creation, made hiking a rejuvenating and profoundly spiritual experience.

But within the first half-mile of Evie's hike with Finn and his church friends, she wanted to strangle whoever had suggested a midday hike in the middle of July. The sun was murderously hot. Evie started the hike with her bobbed hair loose, but before long, she pulled a workout headband from her backpack and put it on to keep her hair from sticking to her sweaty face.

"You look hot," Finn said.

"Excuse me?" She was used to Finn kidding around, but the comment seemed unusually bold.

Finn laughed and blushed—Evie didn't often see him blush. "Sweaty hot, not… I mean, you are… never mind. I'm gonna get myself in trouble if I keep going. Forget I said anything."

Daisy, the veterinarian, fell back to match pace with them, and Evie found herself walking between Daisy and Finn. Bryan, Jackie, and Meg chatted amiably in front of them.

"So, Evie, Finn tells us you work together at a music store. He says you're a fabulous musician," Daisy said.

Evie gave Finn a look, and he smirked.

"I play the violin and the guitar," Evie replied.

"And she has an amazing voice," Finn added.

"I do not." Evie glanced at Finn but quickly returned her attention to Daisy. "I can carry a tune, but I don't really like the quality of my voice," she explained.

"Are you kidding me?" Finn exclaimed. "Don't believe her, Daisy. Her voice is beautiful."

"No, it's not," Evie said. "I grew up singing with Regina. I know what a beautiful voice sounds like, and mine is not it."

"Well, yeah, but she's an operatic soprano," Finn argued. "That's a very specific kind of singing. You're more like… like a Julie London."

"Who?" Evie asked. She felt keenly aware of Daisy watching her and Finn banter.

"Here. Listen." Finn pulled out his phone, ever ready to share his vast knowledge of songs and artists. He hit play on a song and turned the volume all the way up so Evie and Daisy could hear it as they walked.

Julie London sang in a lower register than most female vocalists—as Evie did—and her voice had a breathy, seductive quality. It reminded Evie of being wrapped in a soft, warm blanket.

Daisy's eyebrows went up.

Evie looked at Finn. "Is that really how I sound?"

Finn tilted his head in an *I'm just sayin'* kind of way. Evie felt heat in her cheeks as the song continued.

"And she has perfect pitch, so she never sings a wrong note," Finn said to Daisy.

"Julie London? Or Evie?" Daisy asked with a quirk of a smile.

"Evie," Finn answered, returning the smile.

"Okay, you can stop now," Evie said, Finn's praise making her uncomfortable. She turned to Daisy again. "Tell me more about your work. Do you own your own practice?"

Finn hit stop on the song and put his phone away.

"No, I'm just starting out really. I work at an animal hospital with several other vets," Daisy said. "Do you have any pets?"

Evie shook her head. "We had dogs when I was growing up, but it seems unfair to have a dog or a cat in a tiny apartment like mine. Leaving it alone all day long most days. It would be lonely."

"You live alone?" Daisy asked.

"Yes."

"Don't *you* ever get lonely?"

Evie frowned.

"I'm sorry," Daisy said. "That was kind of a rude question. I just… I have a lot of siblings, and I've always had roommates ever since I left home. I can't imagine living alone. I need community too much."

"No, it's fine," Evie assured her. "To be honest, it never really bothered me until the pandemic. It's nice to go home to a quiet apartment, but it's less nice when you can't leave."

"Hm, yeah." Daisy nodded. "Do you have any siblings?"

For the first time in her life, Evie didn't know how to answer that question. Before she could make up her mind what to say, Finn spoke.

"You should tell her about Sam," he said.

Evie halted in her tracks and stared at Finn in disbelief. Finn and Daisy stopped a step later and looked back at her in concern. Daisy glanced between the two of them, obviously sensing that she'd inadvertently kicked up a hornet's nest.

Evie turned around and started back toward the trailhead. She heard Finn tell Daisy to keep going, that they would catch up, and then she heard his footsteps hurrying to catch her. She didn't look at him when he fell in beside her.

"Sorry, I thought—"

"Shut up." Evie couldn't even fully understand why she was so upset, let alone tell Finn what he'd done wrong. But she *was* upset. Very upset. "Leave me alone."

"Evie, what… I said I'm sorry. I didn't mean to put you on the spot like that," Finn tried again.

"That's not it," Evie replied. She increased her walking speed, hoping to leave Finn behind, but her short legs couldn't outpace his longer ones. Soon, they were both huffing.

"Then what? Why are you so mad?" Finn asked between breaths.

Evie didn't answer him. Her mind scrambled to sort out the tumultuous emotions rolling through her. She was mad, as Finn said, but it was more than that.

They were only a few dozen yards from the trailhead when Finn finally pulled her to a stop and turned her to face him.

"Evie, I need you to talk to me. What's going on?"

"Everything I told you yesterday, I told you in confidence," Evie spat. "I didn't expect you to go blabbing it to your friends, people I barely even know."

Finn recoiled in confusion.

"Why would I want to tell a complete stranger about a sister I've never met?" Evie continued. "What would I even say? I know nothing about her. Nothing at all. Maybe she's a horrible person. Or maybe she would think I'm a horrible person. Maybe it's good we've never met. Anyway, am I supposed to tell Daisy my whole life story? I told you everything, so now all of a sudden I'm supposed to tell everyone I meet about all the horrible things I've been through? That's not how it works, Finn."

"Okay, okay. I understand, and I'm sorry. I shouldn't have said anything about Sam in front of Daisy," Finn said with his hands up in surrender.

"Maybe you haven't realized, Finn, but I have some pretty major trust issues, and this—" Evie waved at their surroundings. "—is not helping. I told you what I told you yesterday because I thought I could trust you."

"You can trust me," Finn insisted.

Evie sighed and shook her head, trying to rein in her anger. "Just forget it. Take me home."

"I don't want to forget it, Evie," Finn said, stopping her from turning back toward the trailhead. "How can I make it up to you?"

"Never mention Sam again," Evie answered, dead serious. "In fact, never mention anything I told you yesterday ever again."

Finn looked taken aback.

"Whoa, hold on. You've been looking for your sister for a couple of years, and now you know who and where she is… but you want to pretend like she doesn't exist?" Finn said, incredulous. "That makes no sense, Evie."

"Why do you care?" Evie snapped.

"Because if I were in your shoes, I would jump at the chance to meet my sibling," Finn said. "Especially since—" He cut himself off and glanced away uncomfortably.

"Especially since what?"

"I just think you should meet her, that's all. Tobias said she was a lot like you, so she must be pretty great."

"That's not what he said," Evie retorted, ignoring the compliment.

"He said we look and sound alike, and we're both musicians. He said nothing about her personality. What were you going to say, Finn? Especially since what?"

Finn licked his lips. "You just seem like you could use a sister."

Evie scoffed. "What's that supposed to mean?"

"Just what I said," Finn responded. "You don't have a great relationship with your adopted family. You said yourself you don't have any other friends besides me and Regina, and Regina is harder to get ahold of than quicksand—"

"Is that why Daisy asked me if I was lonely? Did you tell her I have no friends?" His assessment was spot on, but it only made Evie angrier that he was right.

"What? No!"

"I know I must seem pathetic to you, but I don't need you to fix me, Finn," Evie said.

"That's not what I'm… I don't think you're pathetic, Evie. I think you're fantast—" Again, he cut himself off and looked away. He rubbed the back of his neck. "I'm sure you and Sam would be two peas in a pod if you just gave her a chance."

"I'm. Not. Meeting. Her." Evie wasn't sure when she'd made the decision, but saying the words out loud cemented it in her mind.

They both stood in awkward silence for a moment.

"Anyway, after yesterday, it doesn't matter. Tobias left the store thinking he was wrong about me. It's too late now," Evie said after a while. She felt the falsity of her own statement. It wasn't too late. She knew where Tobias worked. She could reach out any time she chose.

"Actually, it's not," Finn said.

Evie rolled her eyes, knowing he was about to call her out on her lame excuse. But that's not what happened.

"I already called Tobias and talked to him about—"

"You did *what*?" Evie was stunned. And furious.

"He said Sam—"

Evie came uncorked. She shoved Finn, and he stumbled back a step, bewildered.

"How dare you, Finn Gallagher?" She shoved him again. "How *dare* you?" And again. Harder.

Finn tripped on a root behind him and crashed to the ground. His glasses flew off as he went down, and he landed on them with a crunch.

Evie covered her mouth with both hands, horrified that she'd lost control. But she was also furious with Finn. She couldn't move. She just watched him pick himself up, dust himself off, and look mournfully at his shattered glasses. He refused to look at her as he turned and trudged toward the trailhead.

He'd only gone a few feet before he stopped and said over his shoulder in a voice full of humiliation, "You're gonna have to drive. I can't see without my glasses."

♫

They drove in silence to Finn's house, Evie stewing in rage and Finn wallowing in mortification. Evie only spoke once she turned onto his street.

"Where am I supposed to park?"

"Anywhere in the driveway," Finn answered hoarsely.

Evie pulled the Outback into the driveway and put the car in park. She reached into the backseat and grabbed her backpack.

"Evie," Finn said as she opened her door.

She ignored him and got out, slamming the door behind her. She started for the sidewalk, intending to walk to the convenience store a couple blocks away. Better to wait there than here with a presumptuous traitor.

Finn scrambled out of the passenger seat and caught up with her.

"Evie, wait. Where are you going? You're not gonna walk home," Finn said.

"Nope. I'm not."

"Just wait. I have an old pair of glasses upstairs. Let me drive you home," Finn pleaded.

"I think you've done enough already, Finn," Evie retorted.

"How are you going to get home?"

"Not your concern."

"It is my concern." Finn dragged her to a halt. The blue of his eyes seemed especially intense without his glasses, but his gaze was unfocused. She probably looked blurry to him. "*You* are my concern, Evie. I know you're pissed at me right now, but I need to know you're going to be okay."

"Fine, you wanna know how I'm gonna get home?" Evie said. "I'm gonna text Liam to come pick me up." Actually, she planned to order a rideshare, but she was feeling vindictive and sensed that mentioning Liam would draw blood.

Finn frowned. "The guy who broke your heart? The one you were yelling at in the store two days ago? That Liam?"

Evie narrowed her eyes, but she wasn't sure Finn could see it.

"Wow. So all a guy has to do is wait two days to get back in your good graces? Two days from now, you'll be asking for my help again?"

Evie slapped him. She'd never slapped anyone in her life, and it happened before she even really knew what she was doing. It shocked her almost as much as it shocked him.

"Finn, I—" She didn't know what to say. She didn't want to apologize. Not when she was so furious with him. But she didn't like that she was turning into a violent termagant either.

Finn lifted a shaky hand to his stinging cheek. "Way to go, Gallagher," he whispered.

"Finn—"

"You don't have to say it, Evie," he interrupted her. His unfocused gaze dropped to the ground in front of him. "I won't bother you anymore."

He walked toward his house, his hand still on his cheek, his face miserable.

Evie refused to feel sorry for him. He was the one who'd wronged her. He'd gone behind her back, betrayed her trust, presumed to act on her behalf in a deeply personal matter without consulting her. She had every right to be angry.

Didn't she?

By the time Evie reached the convenience store and ordered a rideshare, panic started to creep around the edges of her anger. How could she possibly face Finn at work in the morning? How much had he told Tobias? Would Tobias come looking for her again? Would he bring Sam the next time? She felt vulnerable, exposed. No longer in control of her own life.

The panic fed her rage, and her rage fueled her panic.

When she walked into her apartment, one thought clanged and echoed around her brain like church bells gone haywire: *I have to get away. I have to get away. I have to get away.*

"And I saw that truly nothing happens by accident or luck, but everything by God's wise providence… for matters that have been in God's foreseeing wisdom, since before time began, befall us suddenly, all unawares; and so in our blindness and ignorance we say that this is accident or luck, but to our Lord God it is not so."

St. Juliana of Norwich

14

To Colorado

♫

Sam flew down the stairs as soon as she got off the phone with Tobias, her mind exploding. She hurried into the family room, where Lydia and Paul were watching TV. Her breathless entrance caught their attention immediately.

"Sam? Is everything okay?" Lydia asked.

Sam threw herself on the couch next to Lydia and clutched her hands.

"You have to let me go to Colorado," Sam said.

"Sam, we already talked about this—"

"I know, but just hear me out. Please," she begged.

Lydia raised her eyebrows. It was probably an expression of impatience, but Sam took it as encouragement to make her case.

"Tobias found my sister," Sam blurted. "Her name is Evie, and she works at a music store less than ten miles away from Uncle Steve's house, and she looks just like me, and she knows we're sisters because she met my dad, he's in prison, and John Ingram isn't even his real name, but he told her all about me—"

"Sam, Sam, slow down," Lydia managed to say.

Paul said nothing, but he scooted forward to the edge of his seat.

"Sorry." Sam took a deep breath to calm herself down.

She took out her phone and pulled up the picture Tobias had sent her not five minutes ago. A picture Finn had sent Tobias. A picture of Evie. Her sister. Her big sister. Her very own big sister! Sam's heart

137

had burst with joy and excitement and love the moment she saw the picture. She handed her phone to Lydia so she could see the picture—that wonderful, beautiful picture of Sam's big sister!

Lydia's eyes bulged, and Sam grinned at her reaction.

"Tobias found her. He found my sister," Sam gushed.

"I'll admit, the resemblance is… remarkable," Lydia said, studying the picture.

Evie wasn't the only one in it. It was a selfie of her and Finn from her twenty-first birthday—or so Sam had been told. Finn had told Tobias the picture was a couple of years old now—Evie had turned twenty-three on June 18—but Tobias assured Sam that Evie hadn't changed much.

"You mentioned your father, Sam," Paul reminded her.

"Yes, that's how Evie knows we're sisters," Sam said, nodding. "Or maybe *know* is the wrong word. I guess we can't *know* without a DNA test or something… but the coincidences are too crazy to be just coincidences."

"How did Tobias find her?" Lydia asked.

"He fixed her air conditioning," Sam answered with a grin. "Isn't God great? Only He could have planned it that way."

Lydia smiled at Sam's enthusiasm.

Sam launched into the whole story, everything Tobias had told her about Evie and his visits to the music store and his conversations with Finn. Lydia and Paul listened patiently, their expressions oscillating between wonder and what Sam interpreted as worry.

"Evie told Finn, who told Tobias, who told you, that she doesn't want to meet you?" Lydia said when Sam finished.

"Yes, and I totally get it," Sam replied. It had stung a little when Tobias told her that, but Sam's optimism couldn't be quashed. "She's just scared, that's all."

"How do you know that?" Lydia asked.

"Just a feeling," Sam answered with a shrug. "The only member of our family she's met is our father. I can't blame her for being nervous about meeting me." Sam wrinkled her brow. "I suppose it could be resentment, too. After all, I'm the one our parents kept. Being the one they gave away can't be easy to come to terms with."

Lydia offered a sympathetic look. "Sam, if she doesn't want to meet you, what exactly were you planning to do if we let you go to Colorado? Ambush the poor girl?"

Sam sighed and sat back against the cushions. "That's not the word I would use."

Lydia tilted her head.

"She's my *sister*, Lydia," Sam said, leaning forward again, her eyes misty. The initial rush of excitement from Tobias's phone call was waning, and deeper emotions were beginning to catch up with her. "Why would God put all these pieces in place if He didn't want us to be in each other's lives? I need to meet her. And I think she needs to meet me, too. She just doesn't realize it yet."

Lydia stroked Sam's cheek. She turned to Paul, and they exchanged a long look.

"It's a ten-hour drive. She could do it in a day," Paul said. "And Tobias won't let anything happen to her."

Sam's heart soared. She knew Paul would come through for her!

"Plus all my mom's family," Sam added. "They've always said, anything I need… Oh! I don't think Evie knows about them! She has no idea she's been living so close to her own uncle! And our grandparents, too!" The excitement she'd felt earlier returned. She couldn't wait to tell her sister about the rest of their family—family she'd learned about herself only after her mother's death.

Lydia drew Sam into a hug. "My sweet girl. Remember to give Tobias a hug for me."

Sam squeezed Lydia tight. "Thank you."

♫

Sam packed enough clothes for a week, but Lydia and Paul gave her permission to stay in Colorado longer if things went well with Evie. Half-afraid Tobias would try to dissuade her from coming—not because he didn't want to see her, but because he might think her plan a fool's errand—Sam texted rather than called him to deliver the news. Of course, her phone rang seconds after she sent the message.

She didn't even say *hello* when she answered. Instead, she led with, "You're not gonna talk me out of it."

"I wasn't gonna try," Tobias said, a little startled, but still grinning from ear to ear. "I just wanted to make sure you weren't kidding."

"Not even a little bit," Sam said. "I'm in the middle of packing right now. I'll leave here in the morning and be knocking on your door by dinnertime."

Tobias somehow managed to smile even wider.

"Can't wait."

♫

The shortest route from Chickenhawk to the southern suburbs of Denver took Sam south into Nebraska, zigzagging along two-lane state highways until she hit I-80 and headed east toward Colorado. She preferred to think of the drive as peaceful rather than boring. There wasn't a great deal to see until the Front Range came into view in the last couple hours of the trip.

Each of her last four summers, Sam had visited Colorado. Her maternal grandparents, Jack and Celeste Emory, lived in a small town in the eastern part of the state, along with two of her mother's siblings and their families. All told, she had ten cousins from her Aunt Sharon's and Uncle Bill's families. Sam's Uncle Steve was her mother's older brother and the only living Emory sibling to have moved away from the town where they all grew up. Kristy was Steve's third wife—his first had divorced him after two years, and his second had passed away from cancer. Kristy had two grown children from another marriage, but Steve had no children of his own.

Sam hadn't known any of them before her mother died and left her that letter. That first summer after her mother's death, Lydia had accompanied Sam to Colorado to visit her newfound relatives.

June 18, 2016

Sam awoke to the sound of retching, and it made her own stomach turn uncomfortably. Faint gray light seeped in through the cracks in the shutters, telling her the sun wasn't up quite yet. A moment later, she heard the toilet flush, and Lydia came out of the bathroom and returned to the bunk bed below Sam.

The bunk bed was the only accommodation Grandma and Grandpa Emory could offer. Other rooms that had once been bedrooms had long ago been turned into office and storage space, but they'd kept the bunk bed for babysitting grandchildren overnight.

"Lydia? Are you okay?" Sam whispered.

She heard Lydia sigh. "I think so."

"Is it food poisoning?" Sam pressed. She mentally reviewed all the things she and Lydia had eaten in the last twenty-four hours. They'd eaten all the same things. Would she get sick, too?

"No, honey," Lydia answered. Sam heard the rustle of sheets as Lydia shifted in the small bed. She sighed again. "I was going to wait a little longer before I told you and Tobias and Bear, but it seems silly to hide it now."

Sam's heart lurched. Was Lydia seriously ill? She didn't know if she could handle another loss so soon.

"I'm pregnant, Sam," Lydia said.

"Ha!" Sam slapped her hand over her mouth. She hadn't meant to laugh, but she was so thoroughly surprised. And delighted.

"Yeah, that's about how I feel, too," Lydia said, and Sam could hear the smile in her voice.

"I didn't know… I mean, Tobias is almost fifteen," Sam said, trying to be delicate. Truthfully, she'd thought Lydia was too old to have more children.

"Yes."

"And Liz just got married." A thought crossed Sam's mind, and she gasped. "What if she's already pregnant, too? What if you guys have kids at the same time? Won't that be weird? You'll be a grandma."

Silence. And then, "Yes."

"And then Liz's kid will have an aunt or uncle that's the same age as them," Sam continued in wonder. "Wait, did you mean yes, she's pregnant? Or yes, that would be weird?"

She heard Lydia sigh again. "She hasn't told anyone yet."

"Ha!" Sam burst again, but this time she got the giggles and couldn't stop. It wasn't that she thought it was funny — well, maybe a little funny — but more that the thought of new Howards coming into the world made her so happy.

"Thanks a lot," Lydia said, but she was giggling, too.

"I'm sorry," Sam said. "I'm just happy, that's all. I think it's wonderful."

"It is wonderful," Lydia agreed. "Unexpected. But wonderful." Her voice turned sober. "Sam, honey, I don't want you to get too excited yet. Most miscarriages happen in the first trimester, and since I'm older, that risk is higher."

"I understand," Sam said. After a few moments, she asked, "How far along are you?"

"About eight weeks."

Sam did the math in her head. Liz's wedding had been about eight weeks ago. The thought made her want to laugh again.

"How far along is Liz?"

"Only about four weeks."

"Maybe your baby and I will share a birthday," Sam said, guessing the due date. "Wouldn't that be fun?"

"You might not think it's fun when you have to spend the entire day in the hospital while I'm in labor," Lydia responded.

Sam fell silent. The mention of the hospital made her think of her last birthday. They'd celebrated at the inpatient rehabilitation center where her mom was relearning things like dressing herself and writing with a pen. It was the last time Sam saw her mother alive. A pulmonary embolism killed her the next day.

Sam hated hospitals.

"You don't have to stay at the hospital the entire time, of course," Lydia amended. Perhaps she'd sensed the change in Sam's mood. "Paul will let you all know when the baby's close, and Bear can bring you and Tobias over then. Or... you don't have to be there at all. You can wait until we bring the baby home if you want."

"Lydia," Sam said.

"Yes?"

"I love you." Sam wasn't sure why she needed to say it right then, but it was true—she felt closer to Lydia and Paul than she'd ever felt to her own parents.

"I love you, too, Sam."

♫

Sam smiled at the memory. She'd once told Tobias how romantic she thought Paul and Lydia's marriage was. After looking like he wanted to puke, Tobias admitted that he admired them. He refused to use the word *romantic* to describe his own parents, though.

Because of the pandemic, Sam's grandparents had suggested canceling her annual trip to Colorado. She didn't mind that much—she loved her mother's family because they were family, but her visits felt more obligatory than enjoyable. She had little in common with most of them, and her grandparents and Aunt Sharon often spoke disparagingly of her mother. They'd never forgiven her for running off with John Ingram and cutting them out of her life. Sam's relationship with her mother had left much to be desired, to be sure, but the constant jibes and judgments at her mother's expense wore on her. She began to understand why her mother had been so eager to escape.

The sight of the Rocky Mountains reminded Sam why she liked Colorado so much, though. At least one day of her visit every summer was spent in the mountains—she'd been to Estes Park and Vail and Grand Lake so far—and the (literally) breathtaking peaks never failed to impress her.

The ten-hour drive gave Sam plenty of time to rehearse what she would say to Evie when she met her. Based on what Tobias had told her—which was based on what Finn had told him—Evie would probably be upset at first. She'd said she didn't want to meet Sam, but Sam reasoned that the vast majority of people had no choice about whether they met their siblings or not. Why should Evie get a pass? In any case, Sam was sure they'd be the best of friends after they got to know one another. The mere fact that they both loved music gave Sam great hope that they could spend hours discussing their favorite composers and swooning over sweeping symphonies.

As Sam neared her Uncle Steve's house, her stomach began to flutter with excitement. Tobias had been in Colorado for almost seven weeks. It was the longest they'd been apart since… well, ever. Even before she moved in with the Howards, their families had been neighbors and, if nothing else, she and Tobias would see each other playing out in the yard and wave hello almost every day (she did most of the waving in those days, while Tobias generally did nothing more than blush). When she turned onto her Uncle Steve's street, she broke into a wide grin.

Tobias stood in the driveway waiting for her.

She pulled up to the curb and almost forgot to put the car in park before unbuckling and opening her door. The car beeped at her, and she cursed it for delaying her for even a second. With the car in park and the engine off, Sam jumped out and ran at Tobias. He caught her up into his arms and lifted her off the ground, burying his face in her neck and hair. She wrapped her arms around his neck and clung to him as if she would never let him go again.

Tobias did not let her down when he pulled his head back to look into her face. There was more than a foot difference in their heights, and she enjoyed being eye-to-eye with him.

"Hi, you," she said.

"Sam," he whispered.

He kissed her, and the rest of the world disappeared.

15

To Iowa

♫

The middle of a pandemic was a horrible time to relocate and look for a new job, but the prospect of doing so scared Evie far less than staying in Colorado and facing Finn and Liam and probably Tobias and maybe Sam. She was done being cornered and ambushed.

Evie decided on Iowa. Her decision was based almost exclusively on covid restrictions, or rather, the lack thereof. Iowa was one of only a few states that had never issued a stay-at-home order, and she'd heard their governor promise there would never be a mask mandate either. As much as Evie had come to love the rugged beauty of Colorado, her attachments to living there had been stripped away one by one.

Finn was the last.

It had only taken her a couple of hours to pack everything she owned into her Toyota RAV4. Everything but her bed, that is. She'd knocked on doors in her apartment building asking if anyone wanted it, and an old guy with missing teeth and disheveled hair took her up on the offer. He and his sister—who had just as many missing teeth and even less hair—hauled it away as soon as she had removed the sheets and pillows. Evie owned no other large furniture, hardly any artwork or knickknacks, and only enough kitchen items to make simple meals. Her violin and parlor guitar, clothes, and toiletries were all she had ever required to live comfortably.

Evie made three phone calls as the Denver skyline shrank in her rearview mirror. The first was to Regina, who—of course—didn't answer. Evie left a voicemail saying she wouldn't be able to make it to her friend's September show after all. She provided no other details.—

The second call was to her landlord to tell him she had vacated her apartment. With the government-ordered moratorium on rent collections, he was more than happy to accept her offer to pay for August and call it good even though her lease ran through October.

The third call was to Terry. Leaving Bach for More's owner in the lurch was Evie's one regret about moving away so quickly. He had been kinder and more patient with her than she ever deserved over the years that she'd worked for him, and he had made a rather big deal out of promoting her. She kept her reasons for leaving vague but said just enough about her destination to make him believe it all had to do with the pandemic. Everyone knew a statewide mask mandate was coming down the pike in Colorado, and perhaps Evie would have left when that happened anyway. Although Terry was disappointed, especially with the hastiness of her departure, he told her he understood and offered to write her a letter of recommendation if she needed one. His magnanimity tugged at her heart and almost made her turn around.

Almost.

The drive to Des Moines was about six hundred eighty miles, close to ten hours. Since she left so late in the afternoon, Evie stopped in Kearney, Nebraska for the night, figuring that would put her in Des Moines by early afternoon the next day. After settling into her hotel room, Evie texted Liam to let him know she could no longer offer his daughter violin lessons—she felt she owed him that much, at least. A minute later, he replied with a million questions. When she didn't respond to his flurry of text messages, he tried calling her. She didn't answer.

Instead, Evie used her time in the hotel in Kearney to research job openings and apartments to lease in Des Moines. An apartment was easier to find than a job posting, and by the time she went to bed, she'd booked viewings at three different apartment complexes.

Her job search began with music stores and widened to organizations that offered private music lessons or classes. Even without a degree—or a high school diploma, for that matter—Evie felt confident in her credentials as a private violin and guitar instructor. The only postings she found, though, were for part-time positions. She could work to build up her own studio as an independent private instructor, of course, but that would take time—months, probably—

and she didn't know whether her savings would stretch that far.

Almost on a whim, she searched professional symphonies in the area and found that, miraculously, the Des Moines Symphony was holding auditions for the principal second violinist later that very week. Evie hadn't performed on violin since failing her junior year jury —she'd only practiced on her own and played with her violin students. Although performance anxiety had never been an issue for her before that catastrophic jury, she half-worried that the memory of her onstage meltdown would become a mental barrier for future performances. But as she stared at a webpage listing audition repertoire, a thrill raced through her veins.

What she wouldn't give to play with an orchestra again! No other experience quite captured the sublimity of making music with so many other humans—of being engulfed by perfect harmony and resonance and at the same time contributing to it, of all the instruments' voices and timbres blending into a single glorious sound, of dozens of minds and souls working as a single organism to produce something incomprehensibly beautiful.

With a spot in the orchestra, a part-time position at a music store, and a few private students, Evie could make it work. She didn't have the sheet music for most of the pieces listed in the audition repertoire, but it didn't matter. She'd played many of them before with the orchestra at Lockwood, and the ones she hadn't played, she'd heard enough times to know by heart. For Evie, hearing a piece was as good as reading the sheet music for it.

She submitted her resumé.

16

Where's Evie?

♫

Tobias had told Steve and Kristy nothing of Evie or of Sam's reason for visiting before she came. The four of them ate dinner together when Sam arrived, and she revealed the truth about her visit as they ate. Steve seemed only mildly interested in finding out more about his newly discovered niece, which struck Sam as odd, but Kristy responded with more enthusiasm. She convinced Steve to give Tobias a day off so he could go with Sam to Bach for More.

Despite Sam's protestations that she was perfectly happy sleeping on the couch in Tobias's basement abode, Tobias insisted that he take the couch and she take his bed. Secretly, and somewhat guiltily, Sam relished the thought of sleeping in Tobias's bed—even if he couldn't sleep there with her yet. The pillows smelled like him.

Even with the comfort of pillows that smelled like Tobias, though, Sam hardly slept. She was too excited about meeting her sister, and her mind raced with the possibilities. When morning came, she learned that Tobias had slept poorly as well—only in his case, it was because of the lumpy couch. Distracted as she was by thoughts of Evie, Sam felt more like herself than she had in weeks.

Watching Tobias eat his cereal, his hair still askew from sleeping, she realized why. The Howard house was where she lived, but Tobias was her *home*. He caught her staring.

"I missed eating breakfast with you," Sam said, smiling.

The tips of his ears turned pink—a boyish attribute that

embarrassed Tobias but which Sam had found ridiculously adorable ever since she'd known him—but he smiled in return.

Bach for More opened at 9:00 AM. As hard as it was to wait, Sam determined that they should give Evie the courtesy of getting her day started before interrupting her. In fact, Sam debated waiting until closing time. If the meeting went well, she and Evie would surely want to have a very long conversation to catch up on the seventeen years of sisterhood they'd been deprived of—a conversation that would be impossible while Evie was still on the clock.

But by midmorning, Sam got antsy and announced that she was ready.

♫

Sam and Tobias walked hand-in-hand from the parking lot toward the front of the building.

"You okay?" Tobias asked, looking down at her and giving her hand a little shake.

"Yeah. Great." Sam could barely breathe. The reality of what was about to happen had walloped her brain halfway to the music store, and she'd almost vomited from nerves.

"We don't have to do this. We can still turn around," Tobias said, slowing their pace.

Sam whipped her gaze to his face. "Are you crazy? I'm meeting my sister, and no one can stop me."

Tobias's eyebrows lifted a bit, but he wisely said nothing.

A sign on Bach for More's door prompted them to put masks on. Sam groaned. She'd forgotten hers in the car.

"It's okay, come on," Tobias said and opened the door for Sam. He leaned close and spoke in a low voice. "Both times I've been here, Evie wasn't wearing a mask. I don't think she's much of a rule follower."

Sam took a deep breath, bracing herself, and walked inside. Tobias followed close behind, their hands still intertwined.

Her eyes scoured the store. Violins, violas, cellos, and double basses lined one wall. A huge selection of guitars occupied the adjacent one. Brass and woodwind instruments were displayed on the wall opposite the strings, with aisles of sheet music and instrument accessories taking up the floor space between. A long checkout counter ran along the back wall, and beyond it, Sam could see a hallway leading further into the building—perhaps toward rooms for instrument repair or lessons. A Frank Sinatra song played over the speakers—a sad one about heartbreak and loneliness.

The only other person in the store was an older man behind the counter. He wore a mask, so Sam couldn't make out much about his features, but his eyes widened when he saw her.

"Who's that guy?" Sam whispered to Tobias.

"I have no idea. I've never seen him before."

They approached the counter slowly. As they got closer, the man's brow furrowed—whether in confusion or disappointment, Sam couldn't tell.

"Um, hi," Sam said as she reached the counter.

"Hello. Can I help you find something?" The man's voice was muffled by the mask.

"Yes, actually," Sam replied. "Er, not some*thing*, but some*one*. I mean, I'm here to see someone specific." Egads, what was she saying? *Just spit it out already.* "My sister. Evie. Is she here?"

The man's eyes widened again. "You're Evie's sister? That explains the resemblance."

"Yes, sir," Sam answered. Tobias squeezed her hand reassuringly.

"But... didn't she tell you?"

Sam's heart dropped. "Tell me what?"

"She's gone," the man said. "Doesn't work here anymore. She called me Sunday night to give notice and tell me she was moving to another state."

Sam reeled. She'd missed her.

"Finn!" Tobias suddenly said.

A twenty-something man with messy blond hair and thick-rimmed glasses had appeared from the hallway behind the counter. Sam recognized him from the selfie he'd sent Tobias. But in the selfie, he'd looked happy—smitten, in fact, if Sam had judged correctly. Now, he looked miserable.

Finn's gaze landed first on Tobias, then on Sam. The corner of his mouth lifted in a half-smile. It didn't take the sadness from his eyes, though.

"You're her," he said.

"Yes," Sam responded.

Finn came to stand beside the older man and slapped him on the shoulder like they were buddies. "Terry, this is Sam Ingram, the sister Evie's always had but never met."

Terry tugged his mask down to reveal his mouth. He glanced

between Finn and Sam. "I'm sorry, I don't understand."

"My parents gave Evie up for adoption before I was born," Sam explained. "We only recently found out about each other. I came… I came all the way from South Dakota…" *Ugh.* Of course, she would start crying now. Sam tried to hold it in, but as soon as Tobias let go of her hand and put his arm around her, she buried her face in his shirt and sobbed.

"Oh my," Terry said, sympathy in his voice. "I'm so sorry you missed her. She… didn't she know you were coming?"

The question pierced Sam, and she cried harder. Evie hadn't *known* she was coming, but she'd likely guessed it and fled to avoid meeting her. It was probably Sam's fault she was gone.

"It's my fault, Sam," Finn said gruffly, as if he'd read her guilt-ridden thoughts. "I made a mess of everything. If I'd let Evie take her time and do things her own way instead of…" He paused. "I betrayed her trust. It's me she's mad at. Me she's running away from."

Sam snapped her attention to Finn and wiped her eyes. Terry handed her a tissue.

Running away.

Memories cascaded through Sam's mind—memories of moving every year or two for much of her childhood, never settling in one place for too long. Her parents stayed in the Sioux Falls area longer than they'd stayed anywhere, but then… her father had eventually run away from there, too. Even before Sam was born, both her parents had had a habit of *running away*. Was it in Evie's DNA to run? Was Sam's sister doomed to repeat their parents' mistakes?

No. Sam wouldn't let her.

"Have you talked to her?" Sam asked Finn.

Finn shook his head. "I tried texting and calling. She won't answer. I stopped after the first couple tries. I don't think she's blocked my number, and I don't want to give her a reason to."

"Would you give *me* Evie's number?" Sam pressed. "Maybe she'll talk to me."

Finn sighed, reluctant. "I don't know, Sam. She was so angry when she found out I talked to Tobias without her permission. If I give out her number without her consent… And to you, of all people…"

"Why doesn't she want to meet me?" Sam demanded, her disappointment slowly hardening into frustration.

Finn shrugged. "Your guess is as good as mine."

Tobias rubbed a soothing circle on Sam's back. "Maybe it's because of me."

Sam looked up at him. "You? Why? What did you tell her about me?"

"No, I don't think it's because of anything I told her… just that I acted like such a dork," Tobias said. "I didn't make a good impression. Maybe I ruined it for you."

"Evie's not that shallow," Finn said, a little heat in his voice.

"I'm not saying she is," Tobias returned, matching Finn's tone.

"She's been hurt a lot," Finn said. "It clouds her judgment about people sometimes."

"If she even gives them a chance to begin with," Tobias retorted.

"Tobias…" Sam admonished quietly. She didn't want him to make the situation worse by picking a fight with Finn.

Terry and Finn suddenly looked toward the door behind Sam and Tobias as a customer entered. Finn's expression darkened, which prompted Sam to glance over her shoulder at the newcomer.

He was a burly bearded man with an intimidating scowl on his face. His facial hair made it difficult for Sam to judge his age, but she guessed thirty-ish. He headed straight for their group, his glare focused on Finn.

"Where is she?" he barked when he reached them. "Where's Evie?"

"I beg your pardon, sir," Terry bristled. "But—"

The man pointed an accusing finger at Finn. "It's you, isn't it? You're the reason she turned me down. The reason she's avoiding me again. Is she here?" He looked past Finn and Terry toward the back hallway. "Evie!"

"Sir, I don't know who you are," Terry tried again, more forcefully this time, "but the young lady you're looking for is not here."

The man finally seemed to notice Sam and Tobias, and he did a double-take when he saw Sam's face. She felt Tobias pinch the back of her shirt and tug her closer to him and farther from the stranger. The bearded man had arms as thick as tree trunks, and his manners were deplorable. She couldn't blame Tobias for feeling protective.

"Who—"

"None of your business," Finn interrupted the man. "It's none of your business where Evie is, and it's none of your business who this customer is. In fact, I don't believe you have business here at all."

The man turned his scowl back to Finn, who met it with a fierce look of his own. Finn nodded toward the door, a clear invitation for the man to leave.

The store's phone rang, making all five of them jump. Terry picked it up.

"Bach for More, this is Terry," he greeted. He stepped several feet away to speak to the caller, and despite the mounting tension between Finn and the stranger, Sam remained peripherally aware of his side of the phone conversation.

"It is my business," the man growled at Finn. "She promised to teach my daughter violin lessons."

His statement surprised Sam. She would have pegged him as a spurned lover, not a disappointed customer. Her sister must have been a heck of a teacher.

"Well, I guess she changed her mind—" Finn started. Sam cut him off with a motion.

"Yes, she taught violin lessons here," Sam heard Terry say. Following Sam's gaze, the three others turned toward Terry on the phone. "Extraordinarily talented." A pause as he listened. "I believe it had something to do with tuition. She wasn't able to afford her last few semesters. That's when she started working full-time here at the store and teaching violin and guitar lessons." Another pause. "Yes… Yes, she would be an invaluable addition to your organization." Another pause. Terry nodded as he listened. "I have no doubt you'll be impressed. Her skill and work ethic are unmatched." Another pause. "No. None… Thank you. Bye."

Terry hung up the phone and turned to see all four people watching him intently. For a moment, no one said anything. And then, the stranger spoke.

"You were talking about Evie, weren't you?" the bearded man asked. "Who was that? Is she applying for another job? That was it, right? She listed you as a reference? Where? Where is she applying?"

Terry hesitated. Had Evie confided anything to him? Was he like a father figure for her? Judging by the phone conversation, he thought quite highly of her.

"I'm sorry, sir," he finally said. "I'm not at liberty to say."

The man ground his teeth.

"If she wanted you to know, she would've told you herself," Finn said. "Maybe you should take the hint and leave her alone."

To be fair, Evie hadn't told any of them where she was going—or even *that* she was going. Still, Sam appreciated Finn and Terry's instincts to protect her sister from this bearded man. He reminded her of Jason the Meathead, the brute who'd bullied her in junior high.

The bearded man cast one last, mean glance at all of them, huffed furiously, and left.

Sam waited until he was well out of sight to turn back to Finn.

"Who was that guy?" she asked.

Finn's jaw clenched. "His name is Liam. He and Evie… have a history."

Sam's eyebrows rose. She had more questions—questions about why Liam thought Finn was the reason Evie turned him down, for instance—but there was a more urgent matter at hand. She turned to Terry.

"That phone call. You know where she is, don't you?" Sam asked gently.

Terry met her gaze, and his face softened. "The Des Moines Symphony," he said. "She's auditioning there on Thursday."

They fell into silence as they digested the news. Another customer entered, and Terry excused himself to tend to their needs, leaving Sam and Tobias and Finn to themselves.

Sam's brain kicked into high gear. She knew exactly what Evie would be doing on Thursday. It wouldn't be hard to find out where and what time the auditions were being held. And Des Moines couldn't be that far of a drive—certainly comparable to her drive from Chickenhawk. Would Evie despise her for tracking her down? Was it a risk Sam was willing to take?

Definitely.

"I'm going to Des Moines," Sam announced. She looked first at Finn, then at Tobias. "Anyone who wants to join me is welcome to come along."

Tobias held her gaze a moment before shaking his head. "Sam, I can't miss more work. Not if… not if I'm going to save up what we need…"

She reached up and caressed his cheek. "My love. You worry too much." He raised his eyebrows, and she smiled softly. "God will provide what we need, when we need it. Like right now, I need you. And look—He gave you to me!"

Tobias cracked a smile. He placed his own hand over hers and turned his head to kiss her palm. "I'll ask Steve for the rest of the week."

"Ask Kristy," Sam said with a grin. She turned to Finn. "You comin'?"

Finn swallowed. He shook his head slowly. "I don't know. She's already plenty mad at me. I don't want to push her even further away."

Something about Finn's bespectacled face and messy hair had made Sam like him right away, and her heart went out to him.

"Do you love her?" Sam wasn't quite sure what possessed her to ask such a bold question, but she was sure she already knew the answer.

Finn blushed but didn't reply.

"We'll leave in the morning," Sam said. "You have until then to make up your mind."

O Jesus, meek and humble of heart, hear me.
From the desire of being esteemed,
From the desire of being loved,
From the desire of being extolled,
From the desire of being honored,
From the desire of being praised,
From the desire of being preferred to others,
From the desire of being consulted,
From the desire of being approved,
From the fear of being humiliated,
From the fear of being despised,
From the fear of suffering rebukes,
From the fear of being calumniated,
From the fear of being forgotten,
From the fear of being ridiculed,
From the fear of being wronged,
From the fear of being suspected,
deliver me, O Jesus.

Litany of Humility

17

Love and Fear

♬

"Bless me, Father, for I have sinned. It's been nine days since my last confession."

Evie took a deep breath. She'd made some difficult confessions in her life—like the time she finally confessed running away from home—but this one seemed especially hard to spit out.

"I slapped a friend… one of my best friends… out of anger a couple days ago. And right before that, I pushed him to the ground and broke his glasses."

"Have you attempted to repair the relationship?" the priest asked from the other side of the screen.

Evie's eyes filled with tears, but she swallowed them back. "No."

"Was this friend violent toward you also?"

"No."

"Then attempting to repair the relationship would not compromise your safety?"

"No."

"Then you must at least attempt it. You do not have to be successful—your friend may not be open to reconciliation—but you must do what you can to make reparation."

Which is exactly why Evie had dreaded making this confession. She knew the priest would say something like that, but she didn't know if she was ready to call Finn. Not because she wasn't sorry for hitting him, but because he'd broken her trust. She could apologize. She wasn't sure she could forgive.

"Do you often respond with violence when you are angry?" the priest asked.

"No, never. It's the first time I've ever hit anyone," Evie said. "I mean, when I was a kid, I got into fights with my siblings, but… you know… that's different."

"What are you afraid of?"

Evie wasn't sure she'd heard the priest correctly. It seemed like a non sequitur, and she didn't know how to respond.

"Anger—wrath—is often provoked by fear. Fear of loss. Fear of rejection. Fear of what we don't know or don't understand. What are you afraid of?"

"I don't know," Evie whispered.

"Hm. Ask the Lord to reveal it to you. And once He brings your fear to light, ask Him to heal it. Saint John tells us, *There is no fear in love, but perfect love casts out fear.* Ask the Lord to remove your fear and replace it with love."

The priest's words struck a deep chord in Evie's soul. She *was* afraid. Of betrayal. Of being lied to. Of being disillusioned. Of being made a fool of. Of not being in control.

"For your penance, please pray the Litany of Humility. You'll find it on the back of the prayer cards in the kneeler."

Evie leaned back and saw a stack of prayer cards tucked into the kneeler's built-in shelf. She took one off the top. The image on the front showed three hearts, all burning with flames of love. The first was the Sacred Heart of Jesus, wounded on one side and crowned with thorns. The second was the Immaculate Heart of Mary, pierced by a sword of sorrow and surrounded with roses. The third, adorned with lilies, Evie had never seen, but she assumed it represented the Heart of Joseph. She flipped the card over and saw the prayer on the back. As she skimmed some of the lines, her own heart quailed.

From the desire of being praised, deliver me, O Jesus… From the desire of being consulted, deliver me, O Jesus… From the fear of being humiliated, deliver me, O Jesus… From the fear of being wronged, deliver me, O Jesus…

"Your act of contrition?"

Evie prayed it and meant it.

The priest gave her absolution, which usually brought a sense of peace and relief. Not this time. Evie left the confessional with a feeling of heaviness in her heart. *Apart from me you can do nothing.* Evie knelt in a pew to carry out her penance. She prayed the Litany of Humility—

every petition was just as difficult to ask for as the ones she'd skimmed in the confessional—and prayed, too, for the courage to call Finn.

Ask the Lord to remove your fear and replace it with love.

In a moment of startling clarity, Evie realized why she was afraid to call Finn. It wasn't because she didn't love him.

It was because she did.

♫

"Tell me about my sister," Sam said, pushing away a plate of mostly eaten food. Tobias dragged it in front of him and began gobbling up the leftovers.

A grin spread over Finn's mouth. There was still a sadness in his eyes, but Sam enjoyed watching his face light up at the mere mention of Evie.

Sam and Tobias had arranged to meet Finn for dinner when he got off work. She still held out hope that he would join them on their road trip to Des Moines in the morning.

"What do you want to know?" Finn asked.

"Everything," Sam replied. "I know she looks like me. I know she's twenty-three years old. I know she plays the violin and the guitar." Sam gave Tobias a sidelong look. "I know she's *short*."

Tobias gave her a sheepish smile, his cheeks stuffed with her leftovers.

Finn laughed. "That she is. I'm average height, but Evie makes me feel tall."

"What else? I want to know everything," Sam said, leaning forward.

Finn rubbed his chin. "I don't know. She's… Evie. Evelyn Rose Vincent."

"Vincent is her adopted name?"

Finn nodded.

"Is she close with her adopted family?"

Finn hesitated a moment. "Not very. She still goes back to San Diego for Christmas and sometimes Thanksgiving, but I don't think she talks to them much more than that."

"San Diego? That's where she grew up?"

"Yes."

"When did you meet her?"

"We started at the Lockwood School of Music the same year. She was majoring in violin performance, and she kicked everyone's butt even as a freshman," Finn said with a proud grin. He leaned forward conspiratorially. "In fact, she's the only person I know of in the history of Lockwood who earned a full-ride scholarship to attend."

"Wow," Sam breathed. She was delighted to hear that her sister was so talented. Tobias had already told her that Evie was a musician, of course, but it struck her afresh that music tied them together—it had been the one thing she'd had in common with her parents, too. "She must be incredible."

"She is," Finn replied. "And equally talented on guitar, though she probably wouldn't say so. She's one of those people who can hear a song once and play it back perfectly. She has perfect pitch."

"Oh, what I wouldn't give to have perfect pitch," Sam said. "I play piano, but I also like to compose music. Perfect pitch would make composing so much easier."

"You compose?" Finn sounded excited.

Sam nodded.

"I'm starting my master's in the fall, studying sacred music," Finn said. "I only did a little bit of composition in college, but I want to learn more when I go back to school. Maybe I can pick your brain sometime."

"Sacred music? Like *Catholic* sacred music?" Sam asked.

"Yes."

"That's amazing!" Sam almost came out of her chair.

Finn chuckled. "Is it?"

"You don't understand. My parents didn't believe in anything when I was growing up," Sam explained. "And they never taught me to believe in anything. But then, when I moved in with Tobias's family—" she smiled at Tobias and squeezed his knee. "—I learned about God and church and everything. But I didn't really *get it* until I made the connection between Mass and music—sacred music. The beauty of sacred music helped me believe in something—Some*one*— transcendent." She returned her gaze to Finn. "Sacred music is a huge part of the reason I became Catholic."

He stared at her, his eyebrows raised, his mouth slightly open. "Evie's Catholic, too, you know."

"I didn't know!" Sam's excitement grew. The more she heard about her sister, the more she loved her and couldn't wait to meet her. Sam sighed. "I hope I'm not building her up too much in my mind, but I just think we're gonna be such good friends, me and Evie. She sounds so perfect."

"She is," Finn said softly, and his expression became sad once more. He stared at the table.

Tobias squeezed Sam's hand under the table, and they exchanged a brief look. "What do you think she'll say when we show up in Iowa?" Tobias asked.

Finn rubbed his left cheek. "No idea."

"What would *you* say to Evie?" Sam asked. "If you were going with us."

Finn met her eyes. "I'm sorry."

"Have you ever told her how you feel about her?" He'd never answered Sam when she asked if he loved Evie, but she'd taken his silence as affirmation that her suspicions were correct.

Finn blushed, just as he had when she'd asked him before. "I never knew how. And now I'll probably never have a chance."

"If you come with us, you'll have a chance," Sam replied. "She deserves the truth, doesn't she?"

Finn sighed. "To what end? If I ever had a shot with Evie—which I'm not at all sure I ever did—I blew it when I started meddling in things I had no business meddling in. If I tell her now, she'll just hate me even more."

"How much do you love her?" Tobias asked. "Would you lay down your life for her?"

"In a heartbeat," Finn answered.

"What about your pride?" Tobias said. "Are you willing to lay that down?"

Finn opened his mouth to reply but stopped and thought about Tobias's words. After a moment, he said, "I hadn't thought about it like that."

Sam grinned. "So you'll come?"

Finn looked at her. "It's one thing for me to risk my own pride. But what about you? What if me being there ruins *your* chance to talk to Evie?"

"We just have to plan it right," Tobias jumped in. "We know when and where she's auditioning. That's our opportunity. But if you and I stay out of sight until Sam has had a chance to talk to her..." He trailed off, leaving the rest to their imaginations.

Finn looked back and forth between Sam and Tobias. Finally, he sighed and nodded. And despite his protests, the grin that appeared on his face told Sam that he'd wanted to join them all along.

"For what it's worth, I think Evie would be lucky to have you," Sam said earnestly.

"I think she's already lucky to have you," Tobias added. "Every girl deserves a guy who's willing to stand up for her. Like you did when you threw me out of Bach for More."

Finn snorted.

"Yeah, and the way you told that guy—Liam—to get lost today," Sam put in. She nodded sagely. "Took guts."

Finn chuckled. "Or stupidity. Did you see that guy's arms?"

"I would've backed you up," Tobias said.

"You said he had a history with Evie," Sam said. "What did you mean?"

Finn clenched his jaw. "I don't really know that much. Just that Evie used to like him, but he broke her heart. And then he showed up at the store last week asking for violin lessons for his daughter."

Sam frowned. Had her sister been involved with a married man? "I wonder what she saw in him," she mused, almost to herself. Then, she looked up at Finn. "What does she value in a person?"

Finn's face fell. "Trust." He sighed. "She values a person she can trust."

*"Put aside your hatred and animosity. Take pains to refrain from sharp words.
If they escape your lips, do not be ashamed to let your lips produce the remedy,
since they have caused the wounds."*

St. Francis of Paola

18

Inklings

♫

None of the apartment complexes where Evie viewed apartments would accept her lease application because she was unemployed. It was Evie's first inkling that she'd made a mistake leaving Colorado so impulsively. When she'd run away from San Diego, Regina had provided a safety net—a place to stay and time for Evie to get her feet under her. No such security existed in Des Moines, Iowa.

Unwilling to spend her savings on another hotel room, Evie found a public parking garage and slept in her car for a night. It wasn't comfortable, but she convinced herself that it was no worse than some of the albergues she'd stayed in along the Camino. She couldn't practice her violin in her car, though, and she knew she needed to find a place to stay if she expected to prepare for the symphony audition.

Desperate, Evie responded to a listing for a detached mother-in-law suite that advertised suspiciously low rent. The woman renting the space sounded nice enough on the phone, and when Evie went to look at the property, nothing about it made her think it was a scam—just a rundown little house in a rundown little neighborhood. The woman renting it lived in the main house. She seemed as desperate to find a renter as Evie was to find a place to stay. They signed the lease on the spot, and Evie moved her meager belongings in just after dinnertime.

After a small fast food dinner, Evie planned to spend the entire evening practicing for the audition. In addition to several orchestra excerpts, she would be asked to play the first movement exposition of a violin concerto of her choice. She knew exactly which one she wanted to play—Tchaikovsky's, the same one that had earned her a full-ride scholarship to Lockwood, the same one tattooed on her shoulder.

As Evie began to practice, the niggling thought that she should really call Finn as the priest in the confessional had advised distracted her. She lowered her violin and growled in frustration. She feared that if she didn't resolve things with Finn, she might choke in the audition the way she had at her final Lockwood jury.

But the realization she'd had during her prayer made her more terrified than ever to call him. What would she say to him? *I'm sorry for slapping you, and also, I think I might be in love with you, you big goof?* What if he rejected her apology? How would she possibly focus for an audition after that? No, it was better to wait.

Evie's phone rang, and her heart jumped into her throat. What if it was Finn? Had he heard her thoughts across two state lines? She pulled out her phone, and to her great relief, saw Regina's name on the screen.

"Regina!" Evie practically squealed when she answered.

"Hey, girl, what's this nonsense that you're not coming to my show?" Her friend sounded worried, not angry.

"I know, I'm sorry," Evie apologized. "I was so excited to go, but… my circumstances kinda took a turn, and I'm not actually living in Colorado anymore."

"Come again?"

"Um, yeah." Evie chuffed. "Do you have time for a long story?"

"Must be a good one if it means you're turning down a free ticket to see your girl in the hit show of the season," Regina responded.

Evie pressed her back against the wall and slid to the floor of her new abode—she had no furniture yet. She cradled her violin in her lap and settled in for a long-overdue conversation with her best friend.

"Do you remember when I met my biological father, and he told me that I have a sister?" Evie said, not sure where else to start.

Regina audibly gasped. "You found her! Was she in South Dakota like you thought? Is that where you are? Did you move there to be close to her?"

The firehose of questions put Evie on her mental backfoot, and she stuttered trying to answer. "Uh, no. I… Well, yes, I found her… sort of. Not in South Dakota. Well, maybe there. But… I'm in Iowa."

"Okay, back up. Start at the beginning. How did you find her? And why are you in Iowa?"

Evie almost laughed. "Those questions have very different answers. Which one do you want first?"

"The one about your sister, obviously. I mean, this is huge, Evie. You found your sister!"

The way Regina said it was Evie's second inkling that she'd made a huge mistake leaving Colorado without even giving Tobias a chance to introduce her to Sam. She took a moment to collect her thoughts and then launched into the entire story of the last week-and-a-half, starting with Tobias fixing the air conditioning at Bach for More and finishing with her slapping Finn and driving to Iowa. It took her the better part of two hours, and Regina listened as only a best friend could.

"Did you for real slap Finn?" Regina asked at the end.

"For real."

"Girrrrrl." Regina paused. "Okay, sorry, back to your sister. Just… help me understand… you don't want to meet her? Ever?"

The priest's words came back to Evie: *What are you afraid of?*

"I'm scared to meet her," Evie admitted. "What if we don't like each other?"

"Then you'll be normal siblings," Regina said without missing a beat. Then, "I kid, I kid. Siblings can be tolerable on occasion." Regina had two siblings, an older brother and a younger sister, whom Evie happened to know she adored. "But, for real. Evie. I'm not pretending I know what it's like to have the opportunity to meet a previously unknown sister, but I do know that sometimes you have to take the risk and put your heart out there. If you're always stuck at *what if,* you are going to end up very lonely."

"I have you and—" Evie almost said *Finn,* but that wasn't true anymore. "I don't need a lot of friends as long as I have my *best* friend."

"Well, that's sweet, E, but…" Regina trailed off and switched tacks. "Okay, well, what about Finn? Are you just gonna leave things like they are? Slap 'n' go?"

Evie snorted. Leave it to Regina to turn a serious situation into a punchline. She'd told Regina the entire story… except the part where she'd realized she had feelings for their charming, messy-haired friend. "I will apologize… when I find my courage."

"And?"

"And what?"

"Come on, Evie," Regina said. "Don't act like you don't know."

"Know what?" Evie's heart rate picked up a notch.

"That Finn's been crazy in love with you since you guys were freshmen. Don't tell me that's changed."

"What?" Evie was stunned. "You're joking. I always thought he had a thing for you."

Regina actually laughed. "Oh, girl, I am not his type at all. I never was, but especially after Tony and I hooked up."

"Wait, you hooked up with Tony?" Evie's mind spun. How had she been so oblivious about her friends' lives? Perhaps she really was as self-absorbed as her Lockwood peers had implied. "When?"

"Oh, a long time ago," Regina answered. "It was only a couple of times before we realized we were all wrong for each other. But, you know, they were roommates, and… well, Finn caught us once."

"What?"

"Yeah. Super awkward," Regina said. "Anyway, obviously, he never would have gone for a girl like me before that, but after that… whew. No way."

"Okay," Evie said, "but that doesn't mean he has a thing for me. Or ever did."

Regina laughed again. "You're cute, E. You seriously didn't know?"

"Stop laughing, it's not funny," Evie said, but soon she was laughing, too.

"I mean, I'm kinda shocked you guys have never… you know," Regina said. "Take away that boy's goofy glasses and comb his hair, and he'd be downright delectable."

"Regina!" Evie screeched, her cheeks blushing furiously.

"Well, you know what I mean. I know you guys *wouldn't*… you're both such goodie-goodies. I just mean I'm surprised things have never progressed beyond friendship. Honestly, the two of you are perfect for each other."

Evie's laughter died.

June 18, 2018

Evie didn't like to have expectations. Expectations were always ripe for disappointment. But even she *had expected more pomp and festivity to surround her twenty-first birthday than reality granted her.*

Only six months out from discovering that Liam was married and had a kid and from failing her jury and dropping out of music school, Evie's heart was still raw. She'd purposely lost touch with all her fellow music students, unable to face the shame of her mighty fall. All except Regina and Finn, of course. But then Regina graduated at the end of the school year and almost immediately won a part in the chorus of a touring musical.

So, by the time Evie's birthday rolled around, it was just Finn.

He offered to throw her a whopping big party, but she declined. Instead, she told him he could take her to a bar for her first legal drink.

He did not take her to a bar.

He took her swing dancing.

Evie had taken ballet and tap lessons as a little girl, but that experiment had only lasted a few months. Her feet were not nearly as talented as her ears. Finn swore he would teach her the steps and that all she really had to do was follow his lead anyway.

The first song they danced to, Evie spent the entire time watching her feet. During the second song, she risked a glance up at Finn now and then and always caught him grinning at her. By the third song, she felt confident enough to keep her head up and grin back at Finn. Swing dancing was far more fun than she'd anticipated.

After the third song, they took a break at the bar, and Finn bought Evie a drink. It wasn't her first alcoholic beverage—she'd had a couple beers at parties in high school, and a few harder drinks in college. But for the most part, she'd spent more time singing and playing guitar at those parties than drinking. Alcohol had never held the attraction for her that it seemed to for others. Still, her first legal *drink seemed worth celebrating, and she was glad Finn was the one to buy it for her. It was a gin and tonic, which she'd never tried before. She found it surprisingly refreshing. Finn drank a local craft beer.*

"Happy birthday, Lady Vincent," Finn said grandly, holding out his glass for a toast. He practically shouted to be heard over the music and general din. "And many happy returns."

Evie clinked her glass against his and took a sip. "Thank you, kind sir."

Finn took out his phone and swiped to the camera. He flipped the lens to selfie mode and scooted closer to Evie.

"For Regina," he said, leaning close so he didn't have to shout so loud. "She made me promise since she couldn't be here."

Finn slipped an arm around Evie's waist and pulled her close so they both fit in the frame. Evie lifted her gin and tonic, and they both smiled at the camera until Finn snapped a picture.

"So what do you think? Is it as awful as you'd thought it would be?" Finn asked.

"No, it's actually quite delicious," Evie answered.

Finn laughed. "Not the drink. The dancing. I saw that look on your face when we got here. You thought you'd hate dancing, didn't you?"

"No, honestly!" Evie protested. But then, "Okay, maybe I was skeptical. But really, I'm having a lot of fun. I didn't know you were such a good dancer."

Finn waggled his eyebrows, and Evie laughed.

"You're a good partner," he said.

Evie raised her eyebrows doubtfully. She'd stepped on his toes every couple of measures.

"Especially when I start teaching you fancy moves. You're so tiny," he said and pinched her arm. She smacked his hand away. He chuckled. "You'll be easy to throw around."

"You are not *throwing me around," she said, laughing.*

"Lifts?" he said hopefully.

"No."

"Turns, then," he pleaded. "I promise, it'll be easy. I'll do all the work, and all you have to do is follow my lead."

"Fine."

They returned to the dance floor after finishing their drinks. Finn started with some basic moves and turns, guiding Evie with surety and strength. Then he got a little fancier, instructing her to slide her hand along his waist or cradling her in his arms for a few beats. Her cheeks flushed a little, but she chalked it up to the gin and tonic.

The next song sped up, and Evie allowed Finn to whip her around in spins and turns and hand changes. Her mind could barely keep up. Finn spun her outward and back at what felt like lightning speed. Their hands missed each other, and wham!*, Evie's face slammed right into Finn's chest. Blood poured out of her nose, and she held a hand over her face to keep it from spilling all over the dance floor.*

"Oh my gosh, Evie! I'm so sorry! Are you okay?" Finn sounded panicky, but Evie was having a hard time not giggling.

Finn guided her toward the restrooms and nearly followed her into the ladies' room.

"I can handle it from here," she said, still laughing through her hand and the blood dripping from her nose.

Evie had difficulty stopping the bleeding and finally settled for twisting a corner of a paper towel and stuffing it up her nose, leaving part of it hanging out. She looked at herself in the mirror and touched the top of her nose. It was tender, but she laughed to herself again. It was just her luck to have a bloody nose on her twenty-first birthday. And now she'd have to go out there and weave through the crowd with a paper towel hanging out of her nose.

Finn didn't control his reaction well when she emerged from the restroom. He clapped both hands over his mouth and then ran them through his hair.

"It won't stop?"

Evie shook her head and laughed. "I think you should probably take me home now."

"Oh, Evie, I'm so sorry," Finn said.

They headed for the exit and Finn's sky-blue Subaru. It took halfway to Evie's apartment to get Finn to laugh about it with her—he felt so awful about giving her a bloody nose. He insisted on walking her up to her apartment—something about the loss of blood and not wanting her to pass out on the stairs.

At her door, she turned to him. He stood close, and she could smell his cologne. It was pleasant. It's the gin and tonic.

"Thank you for celebrating my birthday with me, Sir Gallagher," Evie said. "For buying me my first drink." She looked down and gingerly pulled the paper towel out of her nose. She sniffed a few times and wiped her nose with her fingertips to make sure the bleeding had truly stopped. She looked back up, and Finn seemed even closer. Her heart stuttered.

"Lady Vincent, 'twas a pleasure." Finn's gaze dropped to her mouth for just the briefest moment, and Evie held her breath. But then he found her hand and brought her knuckles to his lips instead. "Sleep well, fair lady."

"Good night, fair... knight," Evie responded lamely. She cringed, and Finn snorted a laugh.

He left, and Evie watched him go, uncertain how to feel about whatever had just happened. Had Finn wanted to kiss her? Would she have let him? Now that she was thinking about it, Evie thought Finn might be a pretty good kisser, being a wind instrument player who practiced tonguing all the time.

She shook herself.

It's the gin and tonic.

♫

"Do you really think Finn has feelings for me?" Evie asked. "Or did, at some point?" If he'd ever had feelings for her, slapping him probably diminished them beyond repair.

"I haven't talked to him in a while, but I know for certain that he carried a torch for you all through college," Regina replied.

"How do you know *for certain*?" Evie challenged.

"He told me."

"What? When?"

"After you left Lockwood," Regina answered. "He was worried about you. Scared you'd stop talking to him like you stopped talking to everyone else. He didn't want you to completely cut yourself off from everything and everyone."

Regina's words were like knives. Evie had never considered that her leaving Lockwood had hurt anyone but herself. That anyone had even cared.

"E…?" Regina prodded.

"Hm?"

"How do *you* feel about Finn?"

Evie leaned her head back against the wall and sighed. "I feel like an idiot."

"That's not exactly what I was asking."

"I don't know what to do, Regina," Evie said. "I've ruined everything. It doesn't matter how I feel about him because what I did to him is unforgivable."

"Do you love him?"

Evie couldn't lie to Regina. "Like crazy."

"Then don't give up."

♫

By the time Evie got off the phone with Regina, she had missed two other phone calls. The first was from Liam. She had paused her conversation with Regina to look at the caller ID when it beeped in, but she'd chosen to ignore the call, annoyed that he hadn't given up yet and thinking it might be time to block his number again. When a second call beeped in a few minutes later, she didn't even bother looking, figuring it was just Liam trying a second time. It wasn't.

It was Finn.

She didn't see that it was him until her call with Regina ended, and by then, it was late at night—too late to call Finn back, but not too late to practice. She practiced until well after midnight and, having left her bed with the toothless neighbors in Colorado, slept on the floor. After spending the previous night in her car, she slept soundly despite the hardness of her makeshift bed.

When she rose the next morning, she made herself coffee and ate a small breakfast before resuming her practice. Repetition. Repetition was key. Her ears were perfect, but her fingers were not. Repetition was the only way to make them perfect. After her conversation with Regina, Evie felt more focused, less distracted. Even though she still owed Finn a phone call, one that would not be easy to make, she was able to shove thoughts of him to a corner of her mind where they wouldn't interrupt her while she practiced.

Shortly after noon, Evie took a break for lunch and allowed thoughts of Finn to come out of their compartment and occupy the forefront of her mind. She needed to call him and apologize. She *wanted* to tell him she missed him. Cared for him. Loved him. She mentally rehearsed a dozen different ways to say what she wanted to say, but in her imagination, Finn never reacted the way she wanted him to. The conversations she conjured in her mind made her more nervous than ever, but she refused to let her fears defeat her.

She pulled up Finn's number and called.

It went straight to voicemail.

She hung up.

She hadn't rehearsed a message to leave on voicemail. Without Finn responding or interrupting her, she could say *anything*. She could say *everything*.

No. She didn't want to reveal the depths of her feelings over voicemail. That would have to wait until she could talk to him face-to-face. He deserved that much. Just the apology, then.

Evie called again. It went to voicemail again.

"Finn. Hi. This is Evie. I know I haven't been answering your calls, and I'm sorry about that. I just… I needed some time. I, uh, I also want to apologize for… for what happened before I left…" *Shoot*. She was getting emotional already. She took a breath before continuing. "I am so, so sorry for slapping you. And for pushing you. For breaking your glasses. For yelling at you. Basically, for being a horrible, horrible person and treating you horribly. You mean so much to me, Finn… you have no idea how much…" *Shoot*. She wasn't supposed to say that yet. Her mind went blank. "Um. I'm in Iowa. Des Moines. I'm auditioning for the symphony here. I don't know what will come of it, but… I just really hope that whatever happens, we can still be… I hope I didn't permanently damage our… *friendship*. Please, call me back."

Evie hung up and facepalmed. "Real eloquent, Evelyn."

She set a timer on her phone. Five minutes. She would give herself five minutes to wallow. After that, practice. Focus. Repetition.

Instead of wallowing, though, it was more like reminiscing. She thought of the way Finn always called her *Lady Vincent*. The hundreds of times Finn had been there for her when no one else was. The way they'd danced on her twenty-first birthday and how he'd looked like he wanted to kiss her. How he'd held her and told her she deserved to be treated like a princess. How it felt to sing with him, to hear their voices intertwine.

And then she started daydreaming. About what it would be like to hold Finn's hand. To kiss him. To wake up next to him. To sing lullabies to their children together. *Evelyn Rose Gallagher. Evie Gallagher. Lady Gallagher.* She liked the sound of it.

Her timer went off, startling her. She knew she was being ridiculous. Even if Finn called her back, and even if he accepted her apology, and even if he still had feelings for her, there were still more *ifs* between the present moment and a future with Finn—like what if she won the audition with the symphony? What if they started a romantic relationship and it didn't work out? What if—

Evie remembered Regina's words from the night before. *If you're always stuck at 'what if', you are going to end up very lonely.* Regina was right. There would always be more *what ifs*. Evie couldn't consider them all, know them all, plan for them all. At some point, she just had to decide that it was worth the risk.

"Finn," Evie said out loud. "Finn Gallagher, you are worth the risk."

Evie stood and resumed her practice. For hours, she practiced. Every so often, she stopped to check her phone—to see whether Finn had returned her call—but by the time she stopped to eat dinner, she began to lose hope.

It was Wednesday. Finn worked open to close at Bach for More on Wednesdays. She had called just after noon, but of course, she was an hour ahead of him now. It would have still been morning for him. She checked the time on her phone. 6:24 PM. Bach for More closed at 5:00 PM. Why hadn't Finn called her back yet?

After Evie finished her dinner, sleepiness set in. She wondered if she should have spent part of her day shopping for a bed instead of practicing—a good night's sleep would do as much or more than a little extra practice to keep her mind sharp during the audition. She shrugged to herself. Too late now.

Evie curled up on her pile of blankets and pillows on the floor and fell asleep.

19

Road Trip

♫

They met in the parking lot at Bach for More and left Scrub Oak in Finn's sky-blue Subaru Outback at 8:00 AM.

Sam and Tobias fought over who would ride shotgun—only instead of trying to claim it for themselves, each one advocated for the other. Sam wanted Tobias to sit up front since he was so tall, but Tobias wanted to be a gentleman and let her take the front since she was a girl. She suspected it was more about the pressure of carrying on a conversation with the driver, Finn, than anything else. Tobias, she knew, would rather sit in silence for ten hours than drum up topics of discussion with someone he barely knew. So in the end, Sam agreed to take the front passenger seat and pulled it all the way forward so Tobias, with his long legs, could sit as comfortably as possible behind her. Finn said nothing the entire time, but Sam thought she saw him smirk at her and Tobias bickering.

Finn plugged in his phone and dialed up some tunes before hitting the road. Sam's breath caught in her throat when the first song began, for it held a very specific and painful memory for her. Finn had likely chosen it because of their conversation about sacred music the night before and couldn't know how difficult it was for Sam to hear it.

"Mozart's *Requiem*," she whispered.

"Sublime, as Salieri might say," Finn said.

"Do you mind if we skip it?" Sam asked.

"Um… sure," Finn said and tapped the forward button on his

steering wheel. A song from a completely different genre came on, a song Sam didn't recognize. "Not a fan of Mozart?"

"Huge fan, actually," Sam said. "I just… I went to a concert where they played Mozart's *Requiem* the same night my mom died. I haven't been able to listen to it since without thinking of that night."

"Holy crickets," Finn said. "I'm so sorry."

"You didn't know," Sam said with a sad smile. Wanting to change the subject, she asked, "Who's this?"

"Ray LaMontagne," Finn answered. "Evie's favorite."

Sam closed her eyes and listened to the aching lyrics and the slow, soulful melody. It was a song about friendship, but the longing with which the singer sang the words made Sam think it was about a still deeper desire. Without opening her eyes, she said, "You can tell a lot about a person by the music they listen to, you know."

"Oh? What does this song tell you about Evie?" Finn asked.

"I need more than a single song or even a single artist," Sam answered, opening her eyes and looking over at Finn. "What else does she listen to?"

"Well, she has *this* guy on constant repeat, and other songs like it, any time she has control of the sound system at Bach for More," Finn said. "But she loves orchestral music, too, of course."

"*Orchestral music* is too broad," Sam said. "Someone who loves Bach is very different from someone who loves Bartók. Who's Evie's favorite composer?"

"Tchaikovsky, hands down," Finn replied. "She loves him so much she has a tattoo of his music on her shoulder. Right here." Finn tapped his own right shoulder blade with his left hand.

Sam gasped dramatically. "See? I knew Evie and I would be best friends. I'm a sucker for the Late Romantics."

Finn chuckled. "Okay, but what do Ray LaMontagne and Tchaikovsky tell you about her?"

Sam closed her eyes and listened to a few more bars of the Ray LaMontagne song.

"She feels emotion *very* intensely," Sam said, again without opening her eyes. "Maybe so intensely that her emotions overwhelm her reason when she makes decisions. It's probably why she's so impulsive. Why she runs away when people disappoint her. I would be willing to bet she feels positive emotions just as deeply and intensely, though. The intensity of her passion makes her both fragile and resilient—easy to hurt, but never defeated."

Sam opened her eyes and glanced at Finn. He kept his eyes on the road, but he was slack-jawed. Sam twisted in her seat to find that Tobias listened intently to their conversation.

"Am I wrong?" she asked Finn.

"There's something I didn't tell you about Evie," Finn said. "Something I didn't even know about her until recently. This isn't the first time she's run away." He glanced at Sam. "She ran away from home—from her adopted parents—when she was in high school."

Sam frowned, feeling her stomach sink. "Why?"

Finn sighed. "It's her story to tell, not mine," he said. "That's why I didn't tell you when you asked about her adopted family last night. But when you said…" He chuffed and shook his head. "You said she runs away when people disappoint her. There's no way you could have known just how true that is."

"Oh." Sam's mind darted from one possibility to the next. Had Evie run away from her adopted family because she was like Tobias's brother, Jake? Caught up with the wrong crowd, a slave to substance abuse? The idea didn't seem to line up with Finn's descriptions of Evie, but it was possible she'd turned her life around during college.

Sam glanced back at Tobias and saw a frown on his face, too. She knew he must be thinking of Jake as well.

Of course, it might not have been Evie's fault at all. Perhaps she had run away because her adopted parents were abusive. That thought made Sam's blood boil. Although she'd never witnessed it, the letter her mother left her had led her to believe her father might have been abusive. He'd struck Sam exactly one time. She'd laid low enough to avoid him—and his wrath—the vast majority of the time. For the most part, he seemed content to forget she even existed. As long as she didn't remind him of her existence, he had no reason to hit her. But that one memory—the memory of her father's backhand splitting the top of her right ear and knocking her to the ground—was enough to make her sick thinking that Evie had possibly grown up with abusive parents.

The Ray LaMontagne song ended, and an instrumental pops piece started. With an orchestra backing a jazzy piano solo, Sam pegged it as something from the 1960s. The song brightened Finn's face, and he grinned.

"Okay, what about me? What does my music selection tell you about me?" he said to Sam.

"Well, so far, all I've heard is a song you picked for my benefit, a song by *Evie's* favorite artist—I noticed you didn't say he was *your* favorite artist," Sam said, "which in and of itself tells me you pay attention and like to make other people feel comfortable—"

Finn smiled self-deprecatingly.

"—and… whatever this is." Sam waved toward the radio controls.

Finn feigned shock. "Whatever this is!" He turned the volume up. "This, my dear girl, is Peter Nero, one of the greatest pianists of the twentieth century, playing a delightful Rodgers and Hart gem called *Mountain Greenery*."

Sam laughed. "I apologize. Clearly, I need to brush up on my Great American Songbook."

Finn sniffed.

"Okay, so what else do you listen to when you're left to your own devices?" Sam asked.

"A little bit of everything. I get bored if I stick to one genre for more than a few songs," Finn said.

"Who's your favorite artist?"

"Evelyn Vincent," Finn answered without hesitation.

Sam chuckled. Even though she didn't know Evie yet, it gave her heart joy to know that her sister was adored by a nice guy.

"No joke, she's got a great voice," Finn said. "But that answer probably just tells you something you already knew." He gave her a meaningful look. "So I'll say Benny Goodman."

Sam raised her eyebrows in pleasant surprise.

"I'm a clarinet player," Finn explained. "BG is my boy. Although Artie Shaw, Woody Herman, Glenn Miller, Tommy Dorsey, Xavier Cugat, Julie London, Ella Fitzgerald, Doris Day, Tom Jones, Michael Jackson, Lou Rawls, and Judy Garland are all at the top of my list, too. And Frank and Dean and Nat and Bing, of course. Perry Como. Otis Redding. Etta James. Ray Charles. Carpenters. Cass Elliot. You want me to keep going?"

"No, that's plenty," Sam said with a laugh. Of all the artists he'd listed, she was familiar with maybe half of them. But from that half, she decided he had good taste. "What's one genre you absolutely will *not* listen to?"

"Modern country," Finn said. Sam laughed at the expression of disgust on his face. "Although I do like the classic stuff. Patsy Cline. Johnny Cash. Loretta Lynn. Hank Williams."

"Okay, one more question," Sam said. "If you had to choose… Bach, Mozart, Beethoven, Brahms, or Stravinsky?"

"Geez louise. What a choice," Finn said. He thought about it briefly and sighed. "Mozart. Final answer."

"Okay, here goes," Sam said. "You enjoy adventure and surprises. You're playful and have a good sense of humor. Even though you like to make other people comfortable, you have definite opinions and don't really care whether other people agree or not. You're countercultural, an old-fashioned gentleman with old-fashioned values, which is why you're drawn to music from generations past."

Finn laughed. "What are you, a psychology major?"

Sam burst out with a laugh of her own. "No. I haven't even graduated high school yet."

"No kidding?"

"I start my senior year in thirty-five days."

Finn glanced back at Tobias. "What about you? You're not still in high school, too, are you? Please tell me I didn't just help two high schoolers run off to elope or something."

"I graduated this past May," Tobias said, a slow grin spreading across his face. "You don't have to worry. My parents know where we are. We're not planning to elope."

"Your parents… what about—" Finn cut himself off and shot a glance at Sam. "Who… I mean, since your mom passed away and your dad is in prison…"

"Tobias's parents are my legal guardians," Sam said, rescuing him from trying to formulate such a delicate question.

Finn's eyes flicked to the engagement ring on her left hand.

"Isn't that kind of awkward?" he asked. "Doesn't that make you two like… brother and sister or something?"

Tobias choked, and Sam laughed. "Definitely not," she said. "I told Lydia—that's Tobias's mom—a long time ago that I didn't want to be adopted by them for that very reason. I knew…" She looked back at Tobias. "I didn't want to be her daughter. I wanted to be her daughter-in-law."

Tobias smiled, and the desire in his eyes made her cheeks flush. She turned back around in her seat, hoping Finn didn't notice.

"So you two have been a couple for quite a while," Finn said.

Sam nodded. "Four-and-a-half years."

"Holy crickets," Finn said. "And you're going to be a senior in high school? So what, you've been together since you were…"

"I was in seventh grade," Sam filled in the blank. "Tobias was in eighth."

"I don't want to sound skeptical," Finn said, glancing at her. "But… have you ever even dated anyone else? Either of you?" His eyes flicked to Tobias in the rearview mirror.

Sam had, in fact, been on exactly one date with one other person. But even that date had ended with her kissing Tobias.

"I met the girl of my dreams when I was eleven," Tobias said. "And she told me she loved me when I was fourteen. Why would I bother dating someone else?"

Finn chuckled. "Fair enough."

♫

They stopped in Kearney, Nebraska for gas and lunch. When Finn pulled up to the pump, Sam jumped out before the boys could even unbuckle.

"I got it," she said.

Tobias hurried out next and stopped her hand before she could swipe her debit card.

"What are you doing?" he asked in a low voice.

Finn exited the car and came around the hood.

"I'm getting gas. What does it look like?" Sam said to Tobias.

Finn gazed past them, and his expression darkened, but he shook himself out of it almost as quickly.

"What is it?" Sam asked.

"Just had a weird déjà vu moment," he said with a shrug. "I swear I keep seeing the same white SUV a few cars behind us, and a white SUV just pulled into the gas station across the street. Must be a popular make and model."

Sam and Tobias followed his gaze across the street, but the white SUV pulled up to the pumps on the far side of the rival gas station, where it was hidden from view.

"Like I said, just weird déjà vu. Anyway, I'm going to use the facilities," Finn said. He turned and headed toward the building.

Sam shrugged and turned back to the pump.

"Sam, of the three people in the car, you're the only one who doesn't have a job," Tobias said, stopping her hand again. "Me or Finn should pay for it."

"Finn or I," Sam corrected.

Tobias gave her a hard look.

"Look, I'm the reason the three of us are here," Sam replied. "Well, I mean… Evie's the reason we're all here, but neither of you would have come if I hadn't said I was coming first. So I should pay for it."

"With what money?"

Sam felt her cheeks redden, and she bit her lip. She hadn't known how or when to tell Tobias… it seemed now was as good a time as any.

"The money my mother left me."

Tobias tilted his head in confusion.

"After the accident, but before she died, my mom put everything she had in a trust in my name and listed me as her only beneficiary in her will," Sam explained. "Your mom and dad are the trustees. I wasn't supposed to have access to those funds until I turn eighteen, but your dad said I would need travel money, so they transferred some of it to my bank account before I left South Dakota."

"How much?" Tobias asked.

"How much did they transfer? A couple thousand dollars. They said they would transfer more if something important comes up," Sam answered. She watched Tobias's face. She knew he was wondering how much was in the trust, but he was too gentlemanly to ask. She looked around surreptitiously and motioned him closer. He leaned down, and she cupped her hands around her mouth as she whispered in his ear. "There's another nine hundred ten thousand, two hundred sixteen dollars and thirty-three cents in the trust."

Sam had never seen Tobias's eyes get so big. The blood drained from his face, and he swayed. She grabbed the front of his shirt to keep him steady.

"Don't tell anyone," she said, grinning.

"Sam, that's almost—" He stopped and lowered his voice to a whisper. "That's almost a million dollars."

She nodded.

"Did you know she left you that much? Before now, I mean?"

Sam bit her lip. "I didn't really pay attention to the amount when she died. I knew she left her money in a trust for me, but I had no idea she had anything more than a small allowance from my father. She never had a job during my lifetime. The only thing I can think of is that my father must have been trying to hide how much he was making from whatever criminal activities he was engaged in and put a lot of it in an account in my mother's name. I don't think he expected her to change her will and name me her sole beneficiary before she died. The house was in her name, too. *Only* her name. Which means I inherited all the money from the sale of the house, too."

Tobias stared at her, speechless.

"But, my love," she said carefully. "Your dad made it absolutely clear that this doesn't change the deal. He still wants you to save up before we talk to Father Bernard about starting marriage prep. I think it has less to do with the amount of money and more to do with making us work for it. To show that we're willing to sacrifice for each other."

Tobias nodded in understanding.

"Besides, I don't know how much of the money I want to keep," Sam continued, which caused Tobias to react. "I mean, if it really is money my father made from whatever awful crimes he committed, it's dirty. I think we should give it away to a drug rehab center or some organization that helps victims of human trafficking or something. It may not help the people he hurt directly, but it'll help people who've been hurt by people like him."

Tobias smiled and drew her into a hug. "I'm marrying a saint."

"I'm not a saint. I'm not dead yet," Sam said and felt Tobias's chest rumble with a chuckle. He kissed the top of her head.

"I love you, Samantha Ingram."

"I love you, Tobias Howard."

They stood that way for a while, simply resting in each other's embrace. Eventually, Tobias gently pushed Sam back and looked down into her face.

"Actually," he said with a mischievous grin, "I know exactly who should get that money."

♫

When Sam, Tobias, and Finn finally reached Des Moines, they were all tired, hungry, and grumpy. They checked into a reasonably priced hotel in the downtown area, and Finn went his own way for a late dinner. Although Tobias and Sam each had their own room, Finn had to put their rooms under his name because the hotel didn't allow guests under twenty-one to book a room. Sam offered to pay for all three rooms, but neither of the boys allowed her to do so.

Sam and Tobias ordered delivery and ate dinner together in Tobias's room. With so many things to think about and feels to feel, Sam had a hard time eating.

She was both excited and nervous to meet Evie, even more than she had been when Tobias took her to Bach for More. Her conversations with Finn at dinner the night before and during the drive had given her greater insight into her sister, but she almost regretted knowing so much. How much would Finn's words color her own impression of Evie?

She was also both excited and nervous to be traveling with Tobias without any real chaperones. The clerk had actually scoffed when they asked for separate rooms, which made Sam's cheeks burn and Tobias's ears turn pink. Finn didn't judge one way or the other, but he also seemed too preoccupied with his own upcoming reunion with Evie to pay much attention to Sam and Tobias's behavior. When Tobias invited Sam to his room for dinner, she felt a curious flutter in her stomach.

Now that she was here in his room, sitting cross-legged on his king-size bed with a bowl of Japanese noodles, the flutter wouldn't let her eat. Tobias sat at the desk, shoveling food into his mouth. The situation didn't seem to faze him at all.

"Tobias," Sam said.

"Hm?"

"Do you… do you struggle… at all… with… No. How do I ask this?" Sam tried to take a deep breath, but her lungs wouldn't seem to expand that far.

Tobias looked up from his meal, his expression a mix of concern and confusion.

Sam started over. "I think I'm finally starting to understand the reason for the rules."

"What rules?"

"I mean, I've always understood *intellectually* why your parents didn't want us kissing or cuddling at the house," Sam said. "But I'm starting to understand *experientially*."

Tobias frowned. "What are you talking about?"

"Temptation, Tobias," Sam said, exasperated that she didn't know how to say what was on her mind. "Your mom once told me the rules wouldn't have been as strict if we didn't live together. She said it's one thing to stop at a kiss goodnight when you drop a girl off at her door. It's a whole lot harder to stop when you live in the same house."

"Okay…" Tobias said. "We kissed each other goodnight at Steve and Kristy's."

"This feels different," Sam responded.

"Because we're in a hotel? We've been in hotels together, too. I mean, not in the same room, obviously, but… we have separate rooms this time, too. It's no different than going on vacation with my parents."

"Except your parents aren't here."

A goofy look came over Tobias's face, and the tips of his ears turned pink. "What are you saying, Sam? That you're *worried* because they aren't here? Or… *glad* because they aren't here?"

Sam felt her own cheeks flush. She hadn't thought about it that way, but now she wondered if he was *glad* they were unsupervised.

"I'm worried."

"Don't be. I would never go that far," Tobias said. Then, as almost an afterthought, "I guess I shouldn't say *never*. When we're married, I'll definitely go that far."

Sam set down her bowl of noodles and buried her face in her hands, starting to feel self-conscious. She peeked at him between her fingers. "That's not helpful."

Tobias chuckled. "I'm sorry. I get what you're saying. And I agree, this feels different. But I think it's good for us. If we can only say *no* when someone else is around to say *no* first, our *yes* won't mean much on our wedding night."

His words worked their way through her brain. They made sense. Sam took her hands from her face and put them in her lap. "I like that."

"What was that word you used? You said you understood the rules intellectually before, but now…"

"I understand *experientially*," Sam said. "Through experience."

"I'm still not sure I know what you mean," Tobias said with a tilt of his head.

It felt embarrassing to admit, but she supposed that if she were going to give her entire *self* to Tobias in marriage, she might as well get used to telling him even the things that embarrassed her. "When we first started dating, I was so young… sex never even really crossed my mind. Ever. I liked holding your hand, and kissing was fun, but I don't know… I just never thought about anything more intimate. Physically, I mean. But I'm not thirteen anymore. Now… I *do* think about it. So now… I know from experience why those rules were necessary."

Tobias nodded along as she spoke, which made her feel less awkward. "I get it now. I can't say I *never* thought about it when we first started dating, but it's definitely… *more* now," Tobias admitted.

Sam felt heat in her cheeks again.

"I think it's a good sign," Tobias continued. "Husbands and wives are supposed to want each other that way. I mean, it would be kind of weird if you still never thought about it… right?"

"I guess so," Sam said.

"If it would make you feel better, we can set our own rules," Tobias said. "For when we don't have anyone else around to hold us accountable."

"Like what?"

"Like… we are only allowed to kiss if both of us have both feet flat on the ground," Tobias said.

Sam giggled. But she thought about it, and it actually seemed like a pretty good rule. It would indeed be difficult to go too far with both feet flat on the ground.

"We already broke that rule," Sam said, thinking of when she'd arrived at Steve and Kristy's and Tobias had picked her up to kiss her.

"It wasn't a rule yet."

"Also, you're really tall," Sam said. "Am I not supposed to stand on my tiptoes even?"

"Okay, you can stand on your tiptoes," Tobias conceded. "Rule amended."

Sam laughed again. "Okay, what else?"

But before Tobias could reply, there was a knock on the door. They exchanged a look before Tobias got up and went to answer it. Sam stayed put and listened—she couldn't see the door from where she sat on the bed.

"Hey, what's up?" Tobias said. "Is everything okay?"

"No." Finn's voice. He sounded on the verge of tears. "I have to go home."

"What? Why?" Tobias asked.

"My dad fell," Finn said. "He was up on the roof. He's in really bad shape. My mom just called. She needs me to come home and watch the kids—my siblings—so she can be at the hospital with my dad."

Sam jumped off the bed and hurried to join Tobias at the door.

"Finn, that's awful," she said. She knew how it felt to get that kind of news.

"Oh. Sam." Finn glanced between the two of them. "I'm sorry, I didn't know you were here, too. But I'm glad you are. It means I only have to do this once."

Sam reached out and touched his arm in sympathy. "Do we need to pack up and leave tonight?" she asked. She hoped he didn't notice her disappointment. Her heart felt like it was ripping down the middle. How many times would her plans to meet Evie be thwarted?

Finn looked at her in surprise. "No, you don't need to leave. Just me."

"But we came in *your* car," Tobias said.

"I know." Finn pulled his car keys out of his pocket and handed them to Tobias. "And I'm trusting you to bring her back safely."

"Your car? Or Evie?" Tobias asked gently.

Despite his worry for his father, Finn smiled. "Both, if you can manage it." He paused. "She called me while we were on the road. I set my phone to *Do Not Disturb* while I'm driving, though, so I didn't know until I got to my room. She apologized…" He paused again. "I called her back, but she didn't answer. I left her a message, though, and I told her everything. I told her I was sorry and that I'm crazy about her and… I even told her that we're here in Des Moines."

"You told her we were here?" Sam repeated, feeling a little panicked. "You don't think she'll run again?"

Finn's smile faded. "She might."

Sam slumped against the doorjamb.

"I'm sorry, Sam," Finn said. "I had to be honest with her."

"I know," Sam said. She gave him a small smile.

Finn returned the smile, but only for a moment. "Anyway, my mom called after that. I managed to get a red-eye flight that leaves in a couple of hours." He looked at Tobias. "Do you think you could take me to the airport?"

"Absolutely," Tobias said. "You're sure about leaving your car?"

"I trust you, brother," Finn said with a nod.

Sam glanced between Finn and Tobias. She was fascinated by men— how, in a matter of days, they'd gone from Finn throwing Tobias out of Bach for More to Finn trusting Tobias with his car.

Finn turned to Sam. "I'm sorry I won't be there when you meet Evie tomorrow."

"Do you have any last-minute advice?" Sam asked.

Finn thought about it a moment. "Just be you and let the Lord do the rest."

20

Twitterpated

♫

Evie awoke to the sound of cats fighting in the alley outside her bedroom window. It was a horrid sound, and it took her heart several minutes to return to a normal pace.

She looked at the time on her phone. It was 1:08 AM.

And she'd missed a call.

From Finn.

He'd left a voicemail.

Wide awake now, Evie sat up and accessed her voicemail. She put the phone to her ear and listened.

"Holy crickets, Evie, I can't believe I missed your call. I... I don't even know where to start, I have so much I need to tell you. I didn't leave a message before because I thought... well, I thought maybe you blocked my number. I didn't want to keep bothering you. But then I got your message, and you said *call me back*, so here I am calling you back. And I'm rambling. I'm so sorry. I just... I'm so glad you called. And, okay, first things first. Apology accepted. I forgive you. I was a little... bewildered... when you slapped me, but really, truly, it's forgotten. I promise I will never do anything again to make you want to slap me because... yeah, not fun. But also, I owe you an apology. I am sorry that I talked to Tobias without talking to you first. It was just... dumb. I was dumb. I thought I was helping. I thought you were disappointed that I threw him out of the store before you had a chance to tell him the truth, and I thought I could make it right by telling him the truth, but obviously, that was a terrible idea because it was based on an assumption I had no right to make. Ass. U. Me. Right? Well, I certainly feel like an ass. And I am really sorry, Evie. I never, ever want to hurt you. I… the truth is… I should have told you a long time ago that I am just absolutely nuts about you. Like, stupid in love with you. I don't mean it's stupid that I'm in love with you. I think it actually makes me pretty smart. No, that's not… Wow, I am messing this up so badly. It's just… it makes perfect sense that I would be in love with you because you're perfect, and anyone with one eye and half a heart would be madly in love with you. Like I am. Holy crickets, I sound like an idiot. Anyway, what I mean to say is that hurting you is absolutely the last thing in the world I want to do. Um… so… in the spirit of trying to be forthcoming and honest and trustworthy, I need to tell you —"

The message cut off.

Evie couldn't believe it. She stared at her phone, cursing it for having a time limit on voicemail messages. But at the same time, her heart danced with joy. She started the message over and listened to it again.

And then she listened to it a third time.

After the fourth time, she felt a little ridiculous again.

Evie couldn't call him back at this hour. But she also didn't want to wait until morning to respond. So she typed up a text message.

> *I only got part of your message. Stupid voicemail cut you off. But I liked the part I heard. Very much. I hope we can catch each other tomorrow. I miss you* ♥

She debated the heart emoji for a long time. Was it too much too soon? But she'd heard it four times. He was in love with her. *Nuts* about her. It gave her an idea. She erased the heart emoji.

> *I only got part of your message. Stupid voicemail cut you off. But I liked the part I heard. Very much. I hope we can catch each other tomorrow. I miss you* 🥜

If Finn remembered what he'd said, he would understand what she was getting at. If he didn't remember… Evie laughed. He'd think *she* was nuts.

And she was.

Nuts about Finn.

♫

Evie woke with the sun and found that Finn had sent her a text while she slept. It had come in a little after three in the morning.

> *Lady Vincent. I miss you too. I'm dreadfully sorry I can't be there to cheer you on at your audition (I'll explain later), but I know you will rock their faces off. You are the most amazing musician I know and (if you'll pardon a humble knight for being so bold) the fairest lady in the land.* 🌹

It was a lovely way to wake up. She didn't quite understand why he would need to explain about not being there for her audition, though. Did he think she expected him to come to Iowa just to support her? On such short notice? It was a nice thought—she wouldn't mind seeing his goofy grin and waggling eyebrows before and after her audition—but she had no expectation that he would drop everything and fly to Iowa just to sit in a lobby and wait for her. Had she even told him when the audition was? She couldn't remember.

Evie wanted to call him, to hear his voice. But she didn't want to wake him. It was an hour earlier in Colorado, after all, and judging by the time he'd sent the text, he must have been up quite late. So she settled for another text.

> *Sir Gallagher. You are too sweet. I'll call you after the audition.* 

This time, she didn't think twice about the heart emoji.

♫

The audition wasn't until 10:00 AM, and Evie thought she might go crazy if she sat in her unfurnished mother-in-law suite until then. Nerves stole her appetite, so breakfast was out of the question.

Mass. She could go to daily Mass. The rhythm and familiarity of the liturgy would help her stay calm and focused. Most parishes had a morning Mass. Surely, she could find one nearby that would still give her plenty of time to get to the Des Moines Civic Center, where the audition was being held. Evie did a quick search on her phone's map app and found a Catholic church in the downtown area, just a few blocks from the Civic Center, with Mass at 8:30 AM. Perfect.

Evie showered and dressed comfortably. The audition was blind— the judges wouldn't be able to see her—so dressing to impress was pointless. With her violin tucked into the backseat of her RAV4, she headed downtown.

Annoyingly, even though masks were not required by government mandate, the parish required them. Evie donned her cloth mask begrudgingly, but with Finn's lovely message still on her mind, not even the pandemic could ruin her morning. Every time she thought of his words, she smiled to herself. Perhaps wearing a mask just now wasn't so bad—without it, the other people at Mass might wonder why she was grinning like a silly goose. But between thoughts of Finn and thoughts of the audition, Evie hardly even noticed the other Mass-goers anyway.

"I sought the LORD, and he answered me, and delivered me from all my fears."

Psalms 34:4

21

That's Her

♫

Sam felt Tobias nudge her as she knelt with her head bowed in prayer. She looked up at him, and he nodded his head toward a woman walking past them up the aisle toward a pew close to the front. She frowned, uncertain why he was drawing her attention to the woman. He leaned in close to her ear and whispered through his mask.

"That's her."

It took Sam half a second longer than it should have to know who he meant by *her*, but the moment it clicked, she stopped breathing.

Her hair was styled differently than it had been in Finn's selfie, and she wore a mask now. In fact, Sam wondered how Tobias had recognized her so quickly. Or at all. How could he be certain?

"What do you want to do?" Tobias whispered.

"You're sure it's her?" Sam whispered back, tears clouding her vision.

Tobias nodded. "Do you want to try to talk to her after Mass?"

Even though Finn had left, Sam and Tobias agreed to follow the same general plan they had discussed before leaving Colorado. They would go to the Des Moines Civic Center during the violin auditions, but Tobias would wait in the plaza across the street until Sam had a chance to introduce herself to Evie. If all went well, she would text Tobias to join them.

Painfully, Sam shook her head. "I don't want to distract her before her audition. We'll stick to the original plan—er, the modified original

195

plan." It was a risk. Evie was right there in front of her, and there was no guarantee that their plan to catch her after the audition would succeed. But Sam wouldn't start her relationship with her sister by sabotaging Evie's chance to play with a professional orchestra.

Tobias rubbed Sam's back comfortingly. "Whatever you want."

The priest entered, and everyone stood. Sam's heart pounded, and she felt like her knees might buckle, so she leaned into Tobias. He put his arm around her and pulled her close, supporting her with his strength.

Sam did her best to concentrate on the Mass, but her gaze constantly wandered to Evie's back. She had straight, light brown hair that was cut short—not quite chin-length. The tank top she wore hid part of a tattoo on her right shoulder blade—Sam thought she could make out a treble clef and remembered Finn saying it was part of a Tchaikovsky piece. At one point, during the Gospel, Evie clasped her hands loosely behind her, and Sam noticed tattoos on her wrists as well—a quarter rest on her right one and an eighth rest on her left. The fingers of her left hand moved constantly, as if she simply couldn't stop practicing. Sam had found herself doing the same thing now and then, the muscle memory of whatever piece she happened to be learning at the moment working itself out on an imaginary piano. The similarity made her smile beneath her mask.

As she walked up the aisle during Communion, Sam kept her head bowed, letting her long hair hide her face. She was terrified that when she pulled down her mask to receive the Eucharist, Evie would look up just at that moment and see her. But no such thing happened. When Sam risked a glance at her, Evie had her own head bowed, her eyes closed and her forehead resting on her clenched hands, as if she were deep in prayer.

When Mass ended, Sam used her hair to hide her face again as Evie passed. She didn't know if Evie would recognize her, but she knew if she didn't hide her face, *she* wouldn't be able to keep from staring, which might draw Evie's attention. Tobias seemed to have the same idea—he scratched the side of his head, obscuring his face until Evie was gone.

Sam released a breath she didn't realize she was holding.

"You okay?" Tobias asked in a low voice.

"Ask me again this afternoon."

22

True Colors

♫

Evie still had an hour before the audition, but she wanted to get to the Des Moines Civic Center early to warm up anyway. She could have walked there from the church, but she didn't want to leave her car in the church's lot, so she drove to a public parking garage a couple blocks closer to the Civic Center.

As she approached the main doors of the building, she caught sight of a familiar figure sitting on a bench out front. Evie stopped dead in her tracks, shocked. Her brain struggled to make sense of what—or rather, whom—she was seeing.

"Evie!" Liam called as he stood and half-jogged toward her.

"What are you doing here?" she asked, bewildered. She almost wondered if she was hallucinating. Liam's presence made no sense.

"I wanted to wish you luck before your audition," he said with a disarming smile.

But Evie was not disarmed, only more confused. And more than a little annoyed. Finn and Regina were the only people she'd told about her audition. And frankly, the only people she would have been happy to see at that moment.

"And I wanted to make sure you're okay," Liam continued before she could speak. He stepped closer. "When you told me you couldn't teach Bridget, I knew something was wrong. I knew you wouldn't let my daughter down without a very good reason."

Evie felt a stab of guilt remembering Bridget's beaming face as she cradled her brand new violin. She regretted leaving all her Bach for More students, of course, but her studio had been so decimated by the pandemic anyway, she'd only given them a cursory thought. Liam had been the only parent she reached out to personally. Now she wished she hadn't.

"But why are you here?" Evie said. "You could have just called." As soon as the words were out of her mouth, she remembered all the calls she'd ignored and cringed inwardly.

"I tried," Liam replied, a hard edge slipping into his voice. "Many, many, many times." His voice softened to a tone of concern. "You didn't answer, which made me worry even more. I didn't know if you still had my number blocked or if something terrible happened to you."

"By why are you *here*, Liam?" Evie asked again, exasperated. "You followed me all the way to Iowa because I can't teach your daughter violin lessons? That's crazy."

He smiled sheepishly. "I was kind of hoping you'd think it was romantic."

"Romantic?" Evie scoffed and took a half-step back. "I'm sorry if I didn't make it clear before, but whatever feelings I ever had for you are long gone. And frankly, it's not romantic that you're here. At all. It's creepy."

Liam's face darkened. "Is that what you're gonna tell that joker you work with? What's his name? Finn?"

Evie felt like she'd been slapped. "Excuse me?"

"Yeah, I can't wait to hear you tell him what a little creep he is," Liam went on, his words now laced with venom. "He should be here shortly."

Evie reeled. "What are you talking about?" she breathed. She looked around wildly, half-terrified and half-hopeful that Finn would suddenly appear.

Liam stepped in close and brought his face near to Evie's. "Is it because I have a daughter, Evie? Because I've made mistakes?"

Evie froze. The frenetic intensity in his eyes and voice frightened her. She'd never seen him like this.

"I know I'm not good enough for you, Evie," Liam murmured. "Not by half."

He brought his hand up and touched her face. Once she had craved such tenderness from him, but this felt all wrong. Evie pushed herself away from him, but Liam caught her wrist and dragged her close again. She thought she might cry.

"It's time to stop running, Evie," he whispered.

"You're hurting me," Evie whimpered, trying to twist her wrist free.

Liam pressed his mouth to hers roughly, but she turned her head to break the contact. His grip on her wrist tightened painfully. He tried to kiss her again, more forcefully this time. Panicking, Evie reached up with her free hand and scratched his face. It surprised him enough that he released her. Evie turned and ran for the building. She yanked open a door and dashed inside, nearly colliding with someone coming the other way.

"Sorry," she mumbled.

She spotted the sign for the restrooms and hurried toward the ladies' room. Once inside, she locked herself in a stall and collapsed to the tiled floor, trying desperately to control her breathing. It didn't work. She hyperventilated and passed out.

♫

Evie opened her eyes, and the base of a public restroom toilet slowly came into focus.

How long had she been out?

She pushed herself to a sitting position and checked her phone. It was still only 9:21 AM. She must have lost consciousness for only a minute or two. Her left wrist throbbed. Gritting her teeth, Evie tested it, flexing her wrist and moving her fingers the way she would if she were playing her violin. It hurt.

The reality of what had just happened crashed into her, and Evie choked on a sob. She had been on her own since she was seventeen, but this was the first time she'd ever felt truly afraid for her safety. When she'd run into the building, she'd been too panicked to pay attention to whether Liam had followed her inside. He might still be lurking out there, waiting for her to emerge so he could... Evie shuddered.

Her phone buzzed. A text message. From Liam.

Evie didn't even bother to read it. She deleted the message and blocked his number again, furious with herself for ever unblocking it.

"Hello? Are you okay in there?" a woman's voice called from somewhere in the restroom.

Evie hiccupped. "Yes." And then, "No."

"Do you need me to call someone?" the voice asked.

Evie worked to get her crying under control, to catch her breath enough to respond. "Can you just... can you tell me if there's a man outside? Dark hair, beard?"

"Um... sure," the voice responded.

Evie heard heels click on the tile and leave the restroom. As she waited, she tried to corral her jumbled thoughts. How in the world could she play an audition now?

How had Liam found her? When she'd texted him to cancel Bridget's violin lessons, she'd offered no explanation. She certainly hadn't told him she was leaving Colorado. It was possible, she supposed, that he'd called the store, and Terry had told him she was moving to Iowa. But how had he known she'd be at the Des Moines Civic Center for an audition that morning? He had a law enforcement background. Maybe she hadn't given his investigative skills enough credit.

But then something Liam said pricked at her memory. *I can't wait to hear you tell him what a little creep he is. He should be here shortly.*

What did he mean? Finn had given her no indication that he was in Iowa—or had he? Evie suddenly remembered that, just before his voicemail message got cut off, he had been about to tell her something *in the spirit of trying to be forthcoming and honest and trustworthy.* And his text that morning apologizing for not being at her audition—not as if she'd expected him to be there, she realized, but as if *he'd* expected to be there. But then... Liam had seemed sure he *would* be there. What was the truth? Was Finn in Iowa or not?

And none of Evie's thoughts could make any sense of *why* Liam knew anything about where Finn would be and when. They barely knew each other—in fact, Evie was a little surprised that Liam even remembered Finn's name. And yet... Liam had acted jealous of Finn, as if he not only knew him but knew how he felt about Evie... and how Evie felt about Finn. Had the two of them talked to each other? About her? Had Finn told Liam where she was?

Evie pulled up Finn's text message from that morning, hoping to find a clue.

> *Lady Vincent. I miss you too. I'm dreadfully sorry I can't be there to cheer you on at your audition (I'll explain later), but I know you will rock their faces off. You are the most amazing musician I know and (if you'll pardon a humble knight for being so bold) the fairest lady in the land.* 🌹

Instead of revealing answers, reading his message again just made Evie's heart ache. She wished Finn had been the one waiting for her in front of the Civic Center. She would have happily accepted a kiss for luck from him. The memory of Liam forcing her to kiss him enraged her.

The click of heels on tile signaled the mysterious woman's return.

"There's no one in the lobby except a bald man. No one in front of the building either," she said.

"Thank you for checking," Evie said.

"Did this man—the one with dark hair and a beard—did he hurt you?" the woman asked.

"Yes… er, at least, he tried. I think."

Evie stood and slung her violin case over her shoulder. She opened the stall door and found a middle-aged woman in a business suit standing near the sinks. The woman's eyes widened at the sight of her, and Evie wondered just how puffy and red her face was from crying.

"You're auditioning today?" the woman asked.

Evie swallowed. "I was supposed to, but… I'm not sure I'm in the right frame of mind anymore." She rubbed her tender wrist. Her frame of mind wasn't the only thing Liam damaged.

The woman noticed, and she uttered a soft curse at Liam's expense —though, of course, she didn't know his name. "Would you like to reschedule your audition?" she asked.

Evie was taken aback. "Are you one of the judges?"

The woman smiled kindly and extended a hand. "I'm the concertmaster. Linda Pogoda."

Evie shook her hand, stunned. "Evelyn Vincent." She felt doubly self-conscious about how awful she must look.

"Ah, yes, I remember your resumé," Linda said. "Your violin professor and your employer at the music store both had very nice things to say about you. It was funny, actually, they both used the same word to describe your playing—*unmatched,* they said. It made me eager to hear for myself."

Evie swallowed, humbled by the praise of two people she admired —two people she knew she'd disappointed.

"I certainly understand if you don't feel able to play today," Linda said. She rummaged through her purse. "Grace Chin is an old friend of mine. Her word carries a lot of weight in my book. If she says you're the cat's meow, you must be out of this world. I don't want to miss the opportunity to play with talent like that." She pulled out a business card and handed it to Evie. "Give me a call when you're ready to audition."

Evie accepted the card, speechless.

"Are you sure there's no one I can call for you? Someone to come pick you up?" Linda asked.

"Thank you, I'll be okay," Evie said, though she still felt far from it.

"Okay, then." Linda headed toward a stall. "It was nice to meet you, Evelyn. I hope I see you again soon."

"Thank you," Evie responded.

She left the restroom and stopped in the lobby, wondering what she should do.

Apart from me you can do nothing.

Evie looked at the time. 9:32 AM. Closing her eyes, she said a silent prayer, begging for guidance. For strength. For help.

She rotated her wrist in slow circles, stretching the muscles. She worked her fingers along her right forearm, carefully at first and then faster and faster. She brought to mind every note of the audition repertoire. It was all there, crystal clear, ready to transform from thought into sound. She could do it. She *would* do it.

The pain in her wrist remained, but she let it fuel her resolve. She had allowed distress over Liam to destroy her college career. She wouldn't let it happen again.

Evie read Finn's text one last time. *I know you will rock their faces off. You are the most amazing musician I know.* It gave her courage. Confidence. A desire to succeed.

Whatever the truth was about Finn and Liam, it would have to wait. Evie had an audition to win.

23

Hug-O-Gram

♫

After Mass, Sam and Tobias walked back to their hotel for breakfast before walking to the Des Moines Civic Center. Sam didn't eat much, her stomach and heart tied in too many knots. Tobias always had an appetite, no matter the circumstances, but he continually glanced at her with a look of worry as he ate. She was glad he was there with her.

When Tobias finished eating his and Sam's breakfasts, they headed through the lobby. Tobias's phone vibrated as they reached the doors leading outside.

"It's from Finn," he said when he looked at it. "He says his dad is stable, but the house is chaos." Tobias grinned and chuffed. "He's the oldest of eleven."

Sam's eyes bulged. "That's even bigger than your dad's family."

Tobias nodded. "He says to tell you to give Evie a hug for him."

Sam smiled to herself as they left the building and started down the sidewalk. "I'm turning into the world's most in-demand hug messenger. Maybe I'll start my own business—hug-o-grams."

"What are you talking about?" Tobias said with a laugh.

"When I left South Dakota, your parents told me, *Give Tobias a hug for me*," Sam said, pretending like the whole thing was a terrible chore. "Now Finn is demanding I deliver his hug to Evie? Seriously, I'm going to start charging."

Tobias snorted. "Why bother? You're practically a millionaire."

Sam elbowed him. "Hush. You can't say things like that out loud.

You never know who's listening."

"Pfft." Tobias nudged her back, knocking her slightly off balance. She scowled at him, but he grinned.

They reached the street corner.

"Besides," Tobias said, pressing the pedestrian button, "if you were charging, your customers should demand a refund."

"What?"

"I don't recall ever receiving my hug-o-gram. You failed to deliver," Tobias said.

The stoplights changed, and they started across the crosswalk.

"I've given you plenty of hugs," Sam replied.

"Yes, but those were all *your* hugs. I never received my parents' hugs."

Sam dragged Tobias to a halt in the middle of the crosswalk and threw her arms around his torso, squeezing as tightly as she could. He tried to laugh but it came out as more of a cough because she'd squeezed the breath right out of him. Then she released him.

"Thank—"

She interrupted him with another squeeze. "There. That's both of them." She let him go and started toward the sidewalk without waiting for Tobias.

He caught up with her and claimed her hand, weaving his fingers through hers. "Thank you," he said. After a few steps, he added, "I don't think that's how you should hug Evie, though. Breaking her ribs might not make the best first impression."

Sam snorted and smiled, but it faded quickly.

"I'm glad you're here, Tobias," she said seriously. "I don't think I could do this without you."

"Do you want to change the plan? Do you want me to wait with you at the Civic Center?" he asked.

Sam considered the offer, but, "No. I'll be okay as long as I know you're close."

He kissed the back of her hand, and she looked up at him. "Always."

24

Audition

♫

The audition was held on the stage of the concert hall itself. A partition had been erected that split the stage in half. Evie knew the judges sat on the other side of it, but she couldn't see them, and they couldn't see her. The man who'd checked her in and escorted her to the stage had warned her not to say a word or even cough or clear her throat. The point of the blind audition was to ensure impartiality—that musicians would be judged on playing alone and not on sex, race, age, appearance, or anything else.

A music stand was the only item on Evie's side of the partition. Others who had auditioned had probably used it for the orchestra excerpts. Evie couldn't have used it if she wanted to—she didn't have a single sheet of music with her.

"Applicant number six," her escort announced. He left without another word.

"You may begin with your selected concerto, the first movement exposition, whenever you're ready," a voice instructed from the other side of the partition. Evie smiled. She recognized it as Linda's voice. Somehow, it put her at ease.

She lifted her violin and set her chin on the rest. After a couple of deep, calming breaths, she raised her bow and began the first movement exposition of Tchaikovsky's *Violin Concerto*. She could never articulate what it was about this piece that captivated her, but she'd played it so many times, it practically pumped through her veins. It was a bar from the exposition's secondary theme that graced her shoulder.

Legend had it that Tchaikovsky dedicated the piece to a specific violinist, but when he presented the sheet music to the violinist—supposedly a virtuoso in his time—he declared the piece so difficult as to be unplayable. The legend had some truth, some exaggeration, and there were other works that most violinists considered to be more difficult. But Evie had always found secret joy in playing the famously unplayable piece.

Evie poured herself—her anger and insecurities, love and joy, regrets and failures, triumphs and hope—into her violin. She held nothing back. The sweeping themes and the demanding variations rang out, filling the world—or at least the concert hall—with Beauty. It was Evie's gift, and she gave it away freely, happily, with abandon.

November 26, 2005

Eight-year-old Evie listened, enraptured.

Ballet dancers swirled across the stage, but she hardly paid any attention to them. It was the music. *It did something to her soul. Her ears were in ecstasy, the sounds coming from the pit below the stage filtering into her brain in a perfect kind of logic. It made sense to her as nothing else ever had.*

Her parents owned a piano, but it was more decorative than anything. Evie had tried playing it a few times, but the noise annoyed her mom. Truthfully, it annoyed Evie, too, but for different reasons. Without understanding why, she simply felt that the piano was not playing the notes correctly.

As she listened to this glorious sound of ballet music—Tchaikovsky's The Nutcracker—*Evie pictured the matching piano keys that would produce the same notes. She catalogued the melodies in her mind, eager to go home and reproduce the songs on the piano—at least as closely as she could with a piano that didn't play quite right.*

At intermission, Evie turned to her best friend, Regina, with a look of wonder.

"That's the most beautiful thing I've ever heard," she said earnestly. Her own parents never listened to music like this. A whole new world was opening up for her.

"You're supposed to say it's the most beautiful thing you've ever seen," *Regina replied with a giggle. "It's a ballet, silly."*

"Oh, yeah," Evie said, embarrassed. "The dancing was pretty, too."

Regina's mom leaned forward to speak around Regina. "Would you ladies like to look into the pit? See some of the instruments?"

"Yes, please!" Evie answered with enthusiasm.

Regina's mom herded them toward the front of the seating section to the edge of the stage. Regina, being a year older and a few inches taller, looked over the ledge and gasped excitedly. Evie was too short to see over the ledge, so Regina's mom lifted her and set her on the lip of the stage so she could gaze down into the pit where the orchestra played. Many musicians had already abandoned their seats to take a break during the intermission, but a handful had stayed to continue fiddling around on their instruments. Evie was especially drawn to the instrument being played by a fellow in the front row on the left side of the orchestra. She recognized the sound as the one that had dominated many of the ballet's melodies.

"What do you call that one?" she asked, pointing.

"That's a violin," Regina's mom answered.

"A violin," Evie whispered to herself. She would remember that. It would be the first thing she asked her parents when she got home—if she could learn to play the violin. She couldn't wait.

December 25, 2005

Evie had been morose for weeks, ever since going to the ballet with Regina. Her parents had told her no when she asked if she could learn the violin. Her mom said she wouldn't be able to stand the noise because it would take too long for Evie to learn to play it well. Her dad seemed more sympathetic, but in the end, he always agreed with her mom. They also said if they got Evie a violin, they'd have to get instruments for Gemma and Gentry, too, to be fair— but instruments were expensive.

Evie settled for playing the melodies she'd heard at the ballet on the piano. She got them right on her first try, but the notes felt just slightly off—none of the keys on the piano would play the notes exactly as she'd heard them. When she tried to explain that to her parents, they told her she was probably just doing it wrong. But then her dad actually heard her pound out a melody with a single finger, and something in his face told her she'd been right. He hired a piano tuner that very week, and suddenly, the keys played the notes the way they were supposed to. Evie was delighted.

But her young heart still longed for a violin. The piano was lovely, but it didn't compare to the sweet resonance of the violin.

What Evie's parents denied her, Santa Claus did not.

On Christmas morning, she found a child-sized violin with her name on it under the Christmas tree. Her heart nearly burst with joy.

Until she tried to play it. She drew the bow across the strings just as she'd seen the fellow in the pit orchestra do, but it didn't make a sound at all. Thinking she'd somehow already broken the beautiful instrument and terrified that her parents would take it away to punish her, she felt tears pool in her eyes.

"What's the matter?" her mom asked. "Don't you like it? Isn't it what you wanted?"

"Oh, I almost forgot," her dad said.

He gently took the bow from Evie's fingers and turned a knob at one end. The fibers stretching the length of the bow tightened.

"Santa showed me how to do this," he said with a wink. "When you put it away, you have to turn the knob in the other direction to loosen it again."

"Why?" Evie asked.

"See these fibers?" He pointed. "They're made out of horsehair. From a horse's tail. The strands of hair will wear out over time, but if you remember to loosen them every time you put your violin away, they'll last longer."

Evie beamed and eagerly reached for the bow.

"Hold on. Santa also told me you have to use this first," her dad said, holding a block of something out to her. "It's called rosin. You have to rub it on the bow. That's what makes it make a sound on the strings. But be careful not to touch the horsehair with your fingers. Horsehair is very delicate, and the oils from our skin can damage it."

He showed her how to apply the rosin—Santa had shown him, he said—and then Evie tried again. This time, the violin rang out with a squeal. Evie giggled, overjoyed that it had made a sound. Carefully, she drew the bow across the thinnest string and knew exactly which key on the piano it matched. She drew the bow across the next string and the next and the next. Without knowing how, she instinctively understood the relationship between each of the strings. But...

"It's not in tune," Evie said.

Her dad looked at her in surprise. "It's not? How can you tell?"

In tune *was a term she'd heard the piano tuner use. She knew what it meant now.*

"Can't you hear it?" Evie said. She drew her bow across the thinnest string again. "It's too low."

"It sounds plenty high to me," her mom quipped with a look of annoyed resignation.

But her dad regarded her with a look of awe. "Evie, sweetheart... come here."

He led her to the piano and made her sit on the bench. He took the violin and bow from her and set them aside.

"If I sing a note, can you play that note on the piano?" he asked her.

Evie nodded her head. What a silly thing to ask. It was like asking if she could pick out the color red on her mom's hideous Christmas sweater. A toddler could do it.

He sang a note, and Evie cringed. "That's between the keys, Dad."

"What do you mean?"

"It's not this note—" she played the key just below his pitch. "—or this one." She played the next key up, which was higher than what he'd sung. "There's nothing in between. You didn't sing a note that's on the piano."

His look of amazement intensified.

"What?" she asked.

"Can you play anything *you hear?" her dad asked.*

Evie shrugged. "I know which keys match, but I'm not very good at playing them."

"Will you play a Christmas song for me?"

"Which one?"

"Jingle Bells," he said.

Evie obliged. She didn't play the rhythm precisely right, pounding each note out with one finger, but the notes were all there.

"O Come All Ye Faithful," her dad requested.

Again, she obliged, playing it note for note but not quite in rhythm.

Her dad chuffed in wonder. "That's incredible." He turned to her mom. "Honey, are you hearing this?"

Evie didn't think it was incredible. It was natural. Pitches were like words —she understood them the same way she understood her dad speaking to her. She didn't have to stop and parse each individual word.

Music was the same way. It just made sense.

♫

When Evie came to the end of the exposition, she finished with a flourish, allowing the final note to resonate and fade into the cushioned seats of the performance hall. She breathed heavily, exhilarated.

"Thank you." Linda's voice again, and Evie thought she could hear a smile in her voice. "Let's move on to the orchestra excerpts. We'll go with Mendelssohn first. The *Scherzo* from *A Midsummer Night's Dream.*"

Evie closed her eyes and brought the music to mind. As soon as she heard the notes in her head, she began to play. The challenge of playing music by ear rather than from sheet music was not the notes, but all the other things—things like articulation and dynamic markings. Even the notes were not always easy to hear on a recording of a full orchestra—other instruments might cover the violin parts, obscuring the full complexity of the written music. Fortunately, Evie had played this excerpt for a chair audition at Lockwood and knew every note, articulation, and dynamic. As she finished the excerpt, she breathed a silent prayer that the next one they asked for would be as easily accessible from her mental repertoire.

"Fabulous, thank you." A man's voice this time. "*Die Zauberflöte*, the second violin part, please."

A curveball.

Evie had played *Die Zauberflöte* before, but she had been the concertmaster then—she'd played the first violin part. Still, with her perfect pitch, she'd memorized the second part just as easily from hearing ten of her fellow violinists play it over and over and over again in rehearsals. She closed her eyes and heard the notes in her mind's ear and played, emphasizing the dynamic changes from *piano* to *forte* and back again.

Partway through the excerpt, she remembered that she'd heard this very piece performed the night she first saw Sam and Tobias. Rather than distract her, the memory fortified her focus. In her imagination, she was performing on that stage in Sioux Falls, playing Mozart for her little sister.

When Evie concluded the excerpt, she heard three voices conferring quietly with one another behind the partition. She waited.

"Thank you, that'll be all," Linda said.

The abrupt dismissal startled Evie. She'd prepared four times the number of excerpts she'd been asked to play. Was it a good sign that the judges didn't feel the need to hear more? Or a bad one?

Evie resisted the urge to say *thank you*, remembering just in time that they weren't supposed to hear anything that could identify her. She exited the stage and found her way to the green room where she'd left her violin case.

Once her violin was safely stowed, Evie checked her phone. She half-expected to see another message from Finn, but there was nothing. As much as she wanted to call him right then, she decided it would be better to wait until she was back at her mother-in-law suite. Then she could focus on nothing but *him*. On *them*.

Evie smiled to herself. *Them*. She liked that thought. She liked it very much.

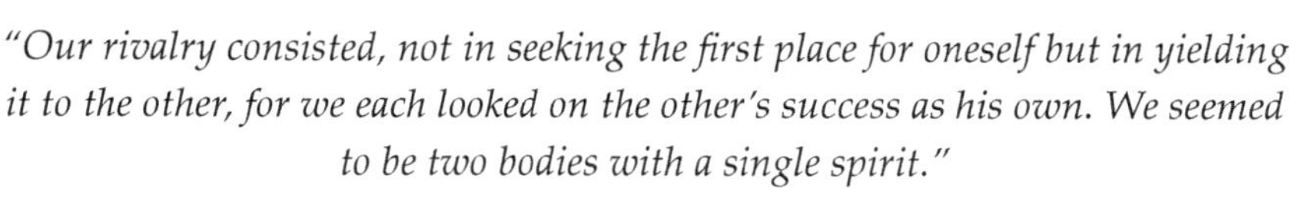

"Our rivalry consisted, not in seeking the first place for oneself but in yielding it to the other, for we each looked on the other's success as his own. We seemed to be two bodies with a single spirit."

St. Gregory of Nazianzen, on his friendship with St. Basil the Great

25

Sisters

♫

With her violin case slung over her shoulder, Evie walked through the lobby, feeling a bizarre combination of elation and trepidation. She approached the glass doors cautiously, worried that Liam might still be out there somewhere. She gazed through the glass.

Evie's heart jumped into her throat.

It wasn't Liam she saw.

It was a teenage girl with long, wavy brown hair. She sat on a bench, swinging her feet back and forth. She wore brightly colored crew socks with sandals, which Evie found… endearing. Evie's reaction to seeing her in the flesh—and so close—was unexpected. She felt a surge of love and longing that stole her breath.

Evie pressed the push bar on the glass door and opened it slowly. The girl did not notice. Evie could hear her humming to herself. Tchaikovsky, in fact. And right on pitch. It wasn't the *Violin Concerto*, but the second movement of his *Serenade in C Major*. Evie felt goosebumps raise the little hairs on her arms despite the humid heat of a Des Moines summer day.

"Sam."

♫

Sam turned at the sound of her name and caught her breath.

Her sister.

Her sister had said her name.

Sam stood slowly and raised a shy hand in an awkward wave. For a moment, the two women just stared at each other.

"Hi," Sam said. Her legs felt like jelly.

"Hi," Evie said back.

She took a few tentative steps forward, and Sam forced her own legs to move. They met each other halfway. Evie was a little shorter than her—Sam wasn't used to anyone being shorter than her—and when her mouth curved into a smile, Sam noticed dimples just below the corners. They were adorable.

Sam took a breath, but she didn't know what to say. She'd rehearsed a thousand times, but nothing came to her now that the moment was here. Not knowing what else to do, she drew Evie into a fierce hug.

♫

Sam's boldness surprised Evie, and she stiffened when Sam first hugged her. But then she exhaled and wrapped her own arms around the girl—her little sister. She felt Sam shudder with a sob, and Evie stroked the back of her head to comfort her, to reassure her.

They stood hugging each other and saying nothing for a very long time.

Finally, they pulled away, both with tear-streaked faces—Evie hadn't even realized she'd started crying, too—each marveling at the woman in front of her. Evie dug into the zippered pocket of her violin case and pulled out a package of tissues. She offered one to Sam, who laughed and accepted, and grabbed one for herself, too.

"We just met, and you're already taking care of me like a big sister," Sam remarked with a hiccupping laugh.

Evie shook her head. "We haven't even properly met yet." She stuck out a hand. "I'm Evie."

Sam took her hand and shook it. "I'm Sam."

They both laughed through more tears.

Evie steered Sam back to the bench so they could sit and have a proper chat. She set her violin case at her feet and turned toward her sister.

"I don't understand. How did you... what're you doing in Iowa?" Evie asked.

"You're not angry, are you?" Sam asked, a worried look on her sweet young face.

"I'm not angry." Evie felt that, somewhere in her brain, all the pieces were there, but she was too overwhelmed to put them all together. Liam and Sam… and Finn.

"Tobias told me he found you—found my sister—on one of his HVAC jobs," Sam explained, "so I drove to Colorado to meet you for myself, but you were already gone by the time I got there. Tobias and I just happened to be at the store when the symphony called your boss. He told us where you were, that you were auditioning. The details of the audition weren't too hard to find on the symphony's website. So we came."

Evie looked around. "*We*? Who else came with you?" *Please say Finn.*

"Didn't Finn tell you?" Sam asked.

Some of the pieces clicked into place. Finn's voicemail… *in the spirit of trying to be forthcoming and honest and trustworthy, I need to tell you…* Just how much had he told her that she never heard when her phone cut him off?

"I think he tried," Evie replied, chuckling at the absurdity of it all. "His voicemail got cut off. He said he had something to tell me, and then it just… ended."

Sam's eyes went wide. "Oh my."

"Why? What else am I supposed to know?" Evie asked, a little worried now.

Sam heaved a sigh. "Everything, I suppose. What *do* you know?"

"I'm not even sure what I *do* know is accurate, so why don't you just tell me the whole story, from the beginning," Evie suggested.

"Okay," Sam agreed. She took a moment to think about it. "Tobias called me on Sunday night and told me that you knew we were sisters but didn't want to meet me." Evie felt a stab of guilt, and Sam must have seen it in her face. "I don't blame you at all. It's… I was getting so nervous sitting here, I almost decided to call the whole thing off. So I get it. No hard feelings."

Evie chuffed in wonder. She liked Sam. A lot.

"Anyway, I decided most people don't get a choice of whether they meet their siblings or not—they're just born into the same family and grow up together—so I wasn't gonna let you have a choice," Sam said with a half-smile. "That probably wasn't very charitable of me, but I just had to meet you, Evie. I just had to. You're my *sister*. I've never had a sister."

Evie nodded in understanding and returned the smile.

"So I drove from Sioux Falls—that's where I'm from—"

"I know," Evie interrupted.

"You do?"

"I saw you there once," Evie admitted. "A long time ago. At a symphony concert. You were with Tobias. I was there with my friend Regina, and she saw you first. She said you were my doppelgänger."

Sam's face turned very serious. "I was there with Tobias?"

Evie nodded.

"They played Mozart's *Requiem*," Sam said.

"Yes," Evie said, "and overtures from some of his operas."

"January 16, 2016," Sam said.

"Yeah, that sounds right. Why? You didn't see me, too, did you?" Evie asked with a laugh. Wouldn't that be strange?

But Sam didn't laugh. Her face paled, and she looked away from Evie. "That's the day my… *our* mother died."

Oh.

Evie reached out and took Sam's hand. "Were you two close?"

"Not very." Sam shrugged. "I think she wanted to be a good mother, but she didn't know how to be with… There were a lot of secrets." Sam looked at Evie. "You've met our father."

Evie nodded.

"I think Mom wanted to protect me from him… from his crimes," Sam said. "But it ended up just creating a lot of distance between us. Until the end. We… the last few weeks of her life, we were *closer*. But still not all that close." Sam paused. "It used to make me feel guilty to admit it, but the truth is that I've always felt much closer to Tobias's mom, Lydia. She and Tobias's dad, Paul—they're my legal guardians. I've lived with them for almost five years now."

Evie had so many questions. But first…

"So you drove from Sioux Falls…" she prompted.

Sam's smile reappeared. "A little town outside of Sioux Falls actually. Called Chickenhawk. It's kind of a silly name for a town, isn't it?"

"Almost as silly as Scrub Oak."

Sam's grin widened. "So, I drove to Scrub Oak from Chickenhawk on Monday. Stayed with Tobias and my uncle—oh, he's your uncle, too! Steve Emory. He owns the HVAC company Tobias works for. He's our mother's older brother. All of her family lives in Colorado, actually, but most of them are in Eastern Colorado."

Evie was dumbfounded. Her blood relatives had been living close by all along? Sam chuckled at what must have looked like shock on her face.

"Anyway, we went to your music store on Tuesday," Sam continued. "But you weren't there. Your boss and Finn were there, though. Finn looked so sad, like his world had ended. Did you hear that part of his message, at least?"

"Which part?"

"The part where he admitted that he loves you."

Evie felt herself grinning, though she tried to control it. "We can talk about that later. Keep going with your story."

Sam's eyes lit up, and she gasped dramatically. "Do you love him, too?"

Evie declined to answer, which only made Sam giggle. She was a teenager, after all.

"Okay, sorry," Sam said, regaining control of herself. "So, long story short, all three of us—Finn, Tobias, and I—overheard your boss's conversation with the symphony…" Sam glanced at Evie as if she didn't know how to say the next part. "Actually…"

"What?" Evie asked.

"Tell me about Liam," Sam said. "What's his deal?"

Evie sucked in a breath. More pieces clicked into place.

"*Liam* came with *you*?" she said, stunned. Then, panicking, she looked around wildly again. "He's not here, is he?"

"Wait, what?" Sam asked. "No. Liam didn't come with us. Finn told him off, and he left the store with his knickers all in a knot because your boss wouldn't tell him where you were."

Evie frowned, unconsciously touching her sore wrist. That could only mean—

"You don't like him anymore, do you?" Sam asked.

"What?"

"Liam," Sam said. "Finn said you had a history with him. That you used to like him, and he broke your heart."

Evie rubbed her forehead, her head spinning. All her worlds had collided in a matter of days, and somehow, it had all happened without her.

"No, I don't like him anymore," she finally said.

"Good," Sam said. "I don't know what it is, but something about him rubs me the wrong way. I'm glad you don't like him." She paused, then added cheekily, "And that you love Finn."

Evie backhanded Sam's shoulder. It was an expression of sisterly affection that seemed to come naturally, even though they'd only just met. Sam laughed, and Evie smiled. Part of her was still preoccupied with worry that Liam might be lurking nearby, though.

"Finn *did* come with us—with me and Tobias," Sam said. She waited for Evie's reaction.

But Evie felt a mix of emotions finally having it confirmed. She wanted so badly to see him, but according to Sam, he had already known where she was *before* she told him. And if he came with Sam and Tobias, it meant he had left Colorado before she'd even called him. Yes, she wanted to see Finn *now*. But he couldn't have known that when he left Colorado. He'd hunted her down in Iowa, just like Liam had. It was disappointing.

"It took a while to convince him, though," Sam continued when Evie didn't respond.

Evie perked up.

"He said you were already mad at him for meddling—because he told Tobias who you were—and that you'd only hate him more if he came to Iowa without talking to you first. But Tobias and I basically told him to get over himself."

Evie snorted, feeling her heart lighten a bit.

"He was afraid he'd lost his chance to tell you how he really feels about you," Sam continued. "I told him you deserved to hear it in person." Sam smiled. "I guess he sort of jumped the gun when he called you."

Evie smiled, too. Finn wasn't like Liam. Not at all. Liam came expecting Evie to love him for it. Finn came knowing she'd be angry. He came after she'd slapped him and broken his glasses and before she'd apologized for it. He came offering his heart and expecting nothing in return.

"But..." Sam's face fell. "It turned out he couldn't be here to tell you in person anyway. He had to fly home last night. He had a family emergency."

"What happened?" Evie asked, disappointment and concern deflating her.

"His dad fell off the roof. He's in the hospital," Sam said.

Evie covered her mouth. "Is he okay?"

"Finn told Tobias this morning that he was stable," Sam said. "Oh, that reminds me—" She drew Evie into another hug, a tight one. When she released her, Sam said with a grin, "That's from Finn."

Evie smiled. "Thanks."

They fell into silence and once again simply stared at one another.

"Evie," Sam said after a while.

"Sam."

"I like you."

♫

They hadn't even talked about music yet, but Sam already loved her sister dearly, and she wanted her to know it. She watched Evie's chin tremble and tears fill her eyes.

"I like you, too, Sam."

They hugged again—not for Finn or anyone else this time, just because they were sisters who liked each other. Evie pulled more tissues out of her violin case. Sam was a sympathetic crier, so she gladly accepted another tissue from Evie.

"This is so bizarre," Evie said with a sigh after she blew her nose. "You're my sister, and I know nothing about you. I don't even know how old you are."

"Seventeen," Sam said. "I'll be eighteen on January 15."

She watched Evie absorb the information and make the connection.

"January 15. The concert… She died the day after your… thirteenth birthday?" Evie asked.

Sam nodded. The car accident that sent her parents to the hospital had been on Tobias's birthday the August before. Birthday celebrations had never quite felt the same after that year.

"I'm so sorry, Sam," Evie said. "I can't even imagine. I wish I had known her. I wish I had known *you* then."

"Tell me about your adopted family," Sam requested. "How did you grow up?" Her heart tensed in anticipation, hoping she wouldn't hear Evie confirm her fears.

Evie seemed to slump. "Pete and Cassidy Vincent are my adopted parents. They live in San Diego. They have two natural children, twins named Gemma and Gentry, who are fifteen months younger than me." She rattled off the facts dispassionately, as if she were listing baseball statistics or something.

"You don't get along with them?" Sam asked. Even if Finn hadn't already told her that Evie ran away from her adopted family, she could have guessed by Evie's demeanor that she didn't particularly like them.

"They don't feel much like family," Evie said. "Growing up, I always struggled with the feeling that my parents loved Gemma and

Gentry more than me, and I didn't know why. When I was seventeen—your age—they finally told me the truth. That I was adopted. And then it made sense."

"Wow."

Evie nodded. "I ran away from home after that. I was furious. Shattered, really. I felt like I'd been living a lie all my life, and leaving that life behind was the only way to find out who I really was."

"They didn't... abuse you or anything, though, did they?" Sam asked with trepidation.

"No, never," Evie answered. She sighed. "Pete and Cassidy are fundamentally good people, I think. They just didn't know how to love me the way they love their *real* children."

Sam thought, if it were a contest, it might be a tossup which one of them had it worse growing up. Even though she'd lost both her parents when she was thirteen—and before that, they had been emotionally distant at best, downright neglectful at worst—at least she'd felt supremely loved by the Howards. From the outside, Evie's life might have looked like the perfect one. But in reality, she had had no one.

"About a year after I ran away," Evie continued, "I called them up and told them where I was, but I still don't talk to them very often. We don't really have much in common. Never did."

Sam grabbed Evie's hand and held it in her lap. Evie looked over at her. "I think God knew we needed each other," Sam said. "He knew I needed a big sister, and He knew you needed a little one." She paused and grinned. "Even though you're actually shorter than me."

Evie scoffed but laughed. "Yes, just what I needed. A little sister to make fun of my height."

"I can't help it," Sam said. "I have to savor this. *No one* is shorter than me. You should see Tobias's family. They're like giants."

"Where is your fella, anyway?" Evie asked. "I think I probably owe him an apology."

Sam jerked her head toward the plaza across the street. "Waiting over there for me to text him and tell him it's okay for him to join us."

Evie looked down at their clasped hands. No, Sam realized. Not at their hands. At Sam's ring.

"Can I ask you a personal question?" Evie asked.

"Of course," Sam said. "We're sisters. I have nothing to hide from you." She meant it. She was ready to reveal her deepest heart to Evie.

"Are you... pregnant?"

Sam laughed out loud. "No, definitely not."

"Then why… I mean, you and Tobias are so young…" Evie stumbled over her words. Her cheeks flushed.

"I know it's weird," Sam admitted, sparing her sister further embarrassment. "We are young. But we've been dating for four-and-a-half years. And we've lived together for five." Sam caught herself. "Not like *that*, though. We've lived together for five years because his parents took me in. Tobias and I have never… we're not… we don't believe in sex before marriage, which is why I couldn't possibly be pregnant." Why was she getting so flustered?

Evie merely raised her eyebrows.

"Anyway," Sam continued, "since we've lived in the same house for so long, there's not much we don't know about each other at this point. He was there during the most awful parts of my life. He's seen me at my worst. And my best. We could keep waiting, I guess, but for how long? Do we need to date for six years before we get engaged? Seven? Eight? That seems silly to me when I *know* he's the man who's going to help me and—God willing—our children get to heaven."

"Are you really only seventeen?" Evie asked, incredulous.

Sam smiled. "Tobias's mom calls me an old soul." She shrugged. "Maybe it's true." And then a thought struck her and she almost squealed with excitement. "Evie!"

"What?" Evie looked startled.

"Will you be my maid of honor?" Sam held her breath, hoping against hope.

Evie chuckled. "You barely know me."

"That's not true," Sam said, shaking her head. "I mean, yes, we just met a few minutes ago, but I already feel like I've known you forever. You're my sister, and we haven't even talked about music yet, but I know anyone who loves Tchaikovsky enough to have his music tattooed on their shoulder must be a kindred spirit."

Evie glanced at her shoulder. "How did—"

"Finn told me," Sam said. "I know I probably should have waited, but I just couldn't help it. I asked him all about you. And we did spend ten hours in the car together yesterday."

Evie frowned. "That's right. You and Tobias and Finn." She paused. "How did Liam get here?"

Sam felt a shock go through her. "Liam is here?"

"You didn't know?"

Sam shook her head vehemently. "No. The last time I saw him—the only time I've ever seen him—was at the music store. He left before your boss told us where you were. He—" Sam caught her breath. The white SUV Finn had seen on the road, at the gas station. "He must have followed us."

Evie pulled her hand away from Sam and covered her face. Sam felt sick. They'd led Liam right to her sister. She reached out with a gentle hand and rubbed Evie's shoulder.

"Are you okay?" she asked.

Evie let her hands drop, took a deep breath, and sat up straight. "Finn was right. Liam did break my heart, but it was as much my fault as his. I was young and naive, and I thought I was in love with him. But I know now it was just infatuation. I hardly knew him. He rejected me, and I didn't know why. And then I found out some things about him—like, that he had a daughter, and for a while, I thought he was actually married—and suddenly it made sense why he didn't want to get involved with me. And then last week, he just... he reappeared. I went to coffee with him to hear him out, maybe get some closure. I agreed to teach his daughter violin lessons. But then... well, I never got to teach her any lessons before I left Colorado. And then today, before my audition, Liam was already here waiting for me."

Sam slumped. "I'm sorry. If I'd known he was following us... If *any* of us had known..." Evie was clearly not happy that Liam had found her. Guilt ate at Sam even though they hadn't led him to Iowa on purpose.

"It's not your fault," Evie said. "He used to be a cop, and he was determined to find me. So he did." She paused and swallowed. "When I told him I wasn't interested, that I didn't have feelings for him anymore, that I thought he was being a creep, he grabbed me..." Evie rubbed her left wrist. "And he tried to... he forced me to kiss him. I scratched his face and got away from him."

"No!" Sam's blood burned with rage. How *dare* he do that to her sister? "I *knew* there was something off about him. I'm so sorry, Evie." And then, "You should tell Tobias. He'll beat him up if he ever tries to touch you again."

Evie gave her a skeptical look. "I'm sure Tobias is a strong guy, but... have you seen Liam?"

"Believe me, when Tobias is properly motivated, he can handle even a brute like Liam," Sam assured her, picturing Jason the Meathead's bloodied face after it met Tobias's fist. He'd been a beefy bully, too, but he was no match for Tobias's protective instincts.

"Well, thank you," Evie said. "In any case, it makes me feel better knowing I'm not alone. I was honestly scared to come out of the building after my audition." Evie nodded her head toward the glass doors of the Civic Center. Then, she looked at Sam and smiled. "Until I saw you sitting out here."

"Liam better be ready to have his eyes gouged out if he ever crosses my path again," Sam said with complete seriousness, still stewing over what he'd done to her sister. "Any man who does that to any woman deserves to be castrated."

Evie chuckled. "Agreed."

"Also, any man who would up and leave his daughter to go chasing a woman who's not even interested in him..." Sam shuddered. "What a slime. I've been that daughter. Not that Dad ever went chasing after women. Or maybe he did. I don't know. But I've been the daughter whose dad abandoned her for his own selfish pursuits—" Sam stopped and caught her breath, the realization dawning on her. "That's what it was. Why I didn't like him. He reminded me of Dad."

Evie's eyebrows rose.

"Sorry," Sam said with a sigh. "That's a wound that's still... healing."

"You don't have to apologize," Evie said. "Not to me. The man wanted me dead, so... I'm not a huge fan either."

Sam's heart squeezed painfully. Her mother's letter had said as much, but she had no idea Evie knew. Remembering the letter reminded Sam of something else.

"I have something for you," she said. She reached into her pocket and pulled out her mother's rosary. She handed it to Evie. "It was Mom's. She never... I never saw her pray with it, but she left it in a box I found after she died. She left a letter, too. That's how I learned I had a sister." Sam smiled, and Evie smiled back. "In the letter, she said it seemed right to pass the rosary on to me, but... you're her eldest daughter. I think you should have it."

♫

Evie closed her fingers around the blue crystal beads of the rosary, overwhelmed by the gesture.

Apart from me you can do nothing. He had been guiding her all along. Just like He had on the Camino. He provided exactly what she needed when she needed it. Even when she tried to run away, He sent His love running after her—in the form of her little sister.

"Thank you, Sam," she whispered.

Evie kissed the rosary and tucked it gently into her pocket. She heaved a deep sigh. Sam was right—it already felt like they'd known each other forever. Like two halves of the same soul.

"There's more," Sam said.

Evie raised her eyebrows. "More what?"

"I inherited all of Mom's money," Sam said, "but I believe with all my heart that if she had known how to find you, she would have left half of it to you."

Evie shook her head. "Sam, I can't take your inheritance."

"But that's what I'm saying, Evie. It's not mine. It's ours."

Evie swallowed, again overwhelmed by Sam's ready generosity.

"I think I'm going to give most of my share away anyway," Sam continued. "It's… I have a feeling most of it is money Dad made from drugs or whatever, and I want to make up for all the evil things he's done. But you can do whatever you want with your half."

Evie chuffed. "How much is it?"

"Total… a little over nine hundred thousand dollars," Sam answered with a straight face.

Evie thought her eyes might pop out of her head. Sam wanted to just *give* her almost half a million dollars?

"Sam, I can't accept that kind of money," she said.

"You can, and you will," Sam insisted stubbornly. "If you won't take it for my sake or Mom's sake, take it for the sake of poetic justice. Think how much it'll irk Dad to know that *both* the daughters he never wanted have all the money he tried to hide away."

Evie chuckled, amused by her rationale. "I guess I can get behind that."

Sam grinned. "Good. It'll make a nice little nest egg for you and Finn."

Evie almost choked. "What?"

"Isn't that the right word? *Nest egg*?" Sam said, her cheeks turning pink.

"Just what did Finn tell you about me that makes you think we need to have a *nest egg* together?" Evie asked, chuckling despite herself. Shocked as she was by Sam's candid suggestion of what to do with the money, she recalled thinking to herself how nice *Evie Gallagher* sounded. A *nest egg* seemed much more concrete and less fanciful than imagining the sound of taking Finn's name, though.

"Well, nothing, really," Sam admitted. "Other than how he feels about you, of course. But… I don't know… I just like him and think he would make an excellent brother-in-law."

Evie laughed, both embarrassed and giddy in that ridiculous, twitterpated kind of way.

"Only if he can learn some boundaries," Evie said, only half-joking.

"You're still mad at him for talking to Tobias behind your back," Sam said. It was a statement, not a question.

Evie shook her head. "I forgave him for that. But I didn't know when he apologized that he was already on his way to Iowa. I left Colorado to get some distance from him, and he didn't respect that."

Even if coming to Iowa hadn't been Finn's idea—if he only came because Sam and Tobias convinced him to—his ultimate choice to do so when he still believed his presence would be unwanted felt invasive somehow. Presumptuous.

"Are you mad at me for being here? For following you to Iowa?" Sam challenged. She'd asked earlier, and Evie had denied being angry. And she wasn't, truly. Not at Sam anyway. "Because I would have come anyway, with or without Finn. I would have come alone if I had to. And if I didn't find you here, I would have kept looking, whether you wanted me to or not. Finn didn't want to go behind your back again. I asked him for your phone number so I could call you, and he wouldn't give it to me. And he wanted to—tried to—tell you we were coming so you wouldn't be surprised. So don't be mad at Finn. If you're gonna be mad, be mad at me. I'm the one who convinced him to come. Plus, I'm your sister. I can take it."

Evie felt chastised by Sam's outburst.

"Do you love Finn?" Sam asked for a second time. "Because if you do…" She paused. "Lydia—Tobias's mom—says when you love someone, you should always assume their best intentions. They will still hurt you sometimes because no one's perfect and everyone makes mistakes, but it's easier to forgive someone when you assume they at least did it for a noble reason. Whatever Finn has done, I think he's a noble guy who does things for noble reasons. Don't fault him for that."

Evie was surprised at how deeply she felt Sam's reprimand. She'd let her little sister down somehow.

"Yes," Evie said.

"Yes what?"

"I love him." Evie swallowed. She felt her cheeks burning, but she wanted to share her heart with Sam. "I only recently realized… We've been friends for so long, and I think I've been scared to admit how much he means to me because I don't want to mess it up. But, if I'm honest, I can picture a future with Finn." No. More than that. "I *want* a future with Finn."

"Does he know that?" Sam asked, placing a gentle hand on Evie's arm.

Evie sighed. "My last few text messages kinda hinted at how I feel, but I haven't said explicitly, *Finn, I'm in love with you.*"

"Well, you should tell him," Sam said. "I like him. I approve of this match."

Evie laughed. "Good to know." She paused. "But... how do I tell him?"

Sam grinned at her. "Are you asking for my sisterly advice?"

"Well, you are an engaged woman," Evie said. "You must know something about matters of the heart."

Sam nodded in a self-satisfied kind of way. "Indeed." She assumed a thoughtful look, and Evie wasn't sure if it was for show or genuine. Suddenly, Sam's thoughtful expression turned to one of mischief.

"I have an idea."

"I am the vine, you are the branches. He who abides in me, and I in him, he it is that bears much fruit, for apart from me you can do nothing."

John 15:5

26

I Could Write a Book

♫

"You're sure about this?" Evie asked.

Actually, she thought Sam's idea was brilliant and was a little annoyed with herself for not having come up with it first.

"Definitely," Sam said. "I haven't known Finn long, but… ten hours in the car together, remember? He's gonna love it."

Sam had texted Tobias, and the three of them had headed back to Evie's mother-in-law suite. Her lack of furnishings embarrassed her, but Sam and Tobias made no comment. Evie and Tobias apologized to one another for whatever misunderstandings had happened between them. Now that she saw Sam and Tobias together—and how ridiculously adorable they were—she ached to tell Finn how she felt. She wanted what they had, and she knew in the deepest part of her heart that she could have it if she could just be honest with Finn.

"Which one did you pick?" Sam asked.

"You'll see," Evie answered with a mischievous grin. She was nervous—almost as nervous as she had been before her audition—but she reminded herself that Finn had heard her play guitar and sing plenty of times.

Evie sat cross-legged on her floor, her guitar tuned and ready. She'd popped her earbuds in and listened to her chosen song three times to make sure she had all the lyrics right. The pain in her wrist had receded to a dull ache, barely noticeable.

Sam knelt a few feet in front of her, her face alight with excitement.

231

She had Evie's phone, ready to dial Finn's number when Evie gave her the word. Tobias hovered near the door. As soon as Evie finished her song, Sam would hand the phone over and politely slip away with Tobias so Evie and Finn could have some privacy.

"Are you ready?" Sam asked.

Evie closed her eyes and heard the song in her mind's ear. "Yes."

Sam initiated the video call with the camera on her own face. They decided it would be a clever way to relay to Finn just how well the sisters' meeting went—again, Sam's idea.

"Ev—" Finn stopped before he finished her name and laughed. Evie loved the sound of it. "You're not Evie."

"Nope," Sam said with a grin. "I'm just the camera operator. Hold on."

She flipped the camera around and cued Evie to begin.

She felt a little awkward playing to the lens of the phone—Sam kept the screen facing her so she could keep Evie in frame—but Evie did her best to imagine Finn sitting in front of her. She smiled and started strumming chords.

And then she sang. A Rodgers and Hart tune called *I Could Write A Book*.

It was probably a little on the nose, but Sam had assured her that this was no time for subtlety. *Leave no doubt in his mind where you stand,* she had said. Tobias had nodded in agreement.

Evie tried to look into the lens as she sang so Finn would know she was not just singing *for* him but *to* him. Sam's grin behind the phone threatened to steal her concentration, but Evie was determined to maintain her focus to the last chord.

At the end of the song, Sam flipped the camera back to her own face and whispered loud enough for everyone to hear, "In case you didn't get it, that was Evie confessing that she's madly in love with you. Don't mess it up."

Evie's cheeks flamed, and she was speechless when Sam handed her the phone and snuck out the door with Tobias.

For a moment, she just stared at Finn's face on the screen. He was grinning from ear to ear.

Suddenly, before Evie could make her tongue operate properly, a blur swiped across Finn's screen, and the camera bounced around wildly. When it stopped, all Evie could see was the ceiling of Finn's parents' house.

"Finn?"

She heard multiple voices, several of them belonging to children, all talking over each other. Above the din, she heard Finn shout, "Can I just have five minutes, please? The girl of my dreams just told me she loves me, and I'd kind of like to enjoy it. Go! Out of here! All of you!" The clamor died down, and a door clicked shut somewhere out of frame. The view on the screen whirled until Finn's face reappeared.

"Sorry about that," he muttered. "Little fiends." His glasses were a little lopsided, and his hair was even messier than usual. Evie imagined brushing it aside with her fingers.

"How's your dad?" she asked. It was foolish, but she suddenly felt desperate to talk about anything other than the feelings she'd just professed.

"He took quite a tumble," Finn answered. "Broke a few ribs. One of them punctured his lung. Got a pretty big bump on his noggin, too. He's stable, though. My mom said he should be able to come home tonight, but she wants me to stick around and keep these hooligans out of her hair so she can concentrate on helping my dad."

"It's good you can be there to help out," Evie said, hoping it sounded supportive and not sulky.

"I'd rather be there in Iowa," Finn replied. "Looks like you made a new friend."

Evie grinned. "Go on. You can say it."

"Say what?"

"That you told me so," Evie said. She glanced out the front window of her little abode and saw Sam and Tobias sitting on a garden bench under a leafy tree on the other side of the overgrown lawn. Sam rested her head on Tobias's shoulder and hugged his arm. Tobias said something, and she laughed. "I've only known her for a few hours, and I already adore her."

"She's a good kid," Finn said. "Tobias, too."

Evie shook her head. "No, she's not a kid. She's way more mature than I am."

"You noticed that, too?" Finn said, then immediately added, "That came out wrong."

Evie laughed. "I knew what you meant."

They fell into silence, both smiling, each taking a turn breaking into a happy, awkward giggle.

Finally, Finn cleared his throat. "So, Lady Vincent. What happens next?"

"What do you mean?"

"You… you *moved* to Iowa," Finn said. "But I'm… here."

Evie didn't have an answer for him, and she knew it showed on her face. She bit her lip. If the symphony called and offered her the position, would she give it up for Finn?

Finn's gaze was suddenly pulled somewhere off screen. He spoke to someone out of frame. "Can it wait? I'm on the phone. Just… ask Penny… What? Holy crickets." He turned his attention back to Evie. "Evie, I'm sorry, I have to go… there's a… situation."

"Of course."

"I'll call you back when I can," Finn promised.

"Okay."

"Bye."

"Bye."

Evie slumped against the wall. It had started so well, but the way the call ended left an uncomfortable knot in her stomach. Her gaze drifted beyond the window to Sam and Tobias again, so happy, so comfortable in each other's arms. She felt a pang of jealousy. They made it look so easy. But because of her own impulsiveness, her own insecurities and fears, she'd already ruined any chance of her and Finn having it easy. She'd made it hopelessly complicated by running away to another state and auditioning for the symphony—a job she desperately wanted.

Could they make a long-distance relationship work?

Would Finn be willing to move to Iowa if she got the position with the symphony?

Could she even afford to move again if she didn't get the position?

Evie put her head in her hands. "Way to go, Vincent."

27

Victory

♫

Sam treated Tobias and Evie to dinner that night. After her call with Finn, Evie seemed less elated than Sam had expected, but she said it was because their conversation had been cut short by Finn's siblings. Sam suspected there was more to it, but she'd pressed her sister for enough personal details for one day.

"How long will the two of you stay before heading back to Colorado?" Evie asked with a mouth half-full of chicken parmigiana.

Sam and Tobias exchanged a look.

"We'll probably leave tomorrow," Tobias said. "I have to get back to work. And return Finn's car to him." Tobias glanced at Evie. "Are you... staying?"

Evie set her fork down slowly and sighed. "I don't know. Until I hear back from the symphony, I don't really know what comes next for me."

Ah. So that was it. Finn had probably asked her to move back to Colorado, and she wasn't ready to.

Sam remembered when Tobias told her he liked her but wasn't ready to date her yet. Those few weeks had been torture for both of them, and in hindsight, totally unnecessary. Sam didn't want to see Evie and Finn make the same mistake. Although things worked out for Sam and Tobias in the end, they might not have—Sam had been especially cruel and petty, going on a date with another guy just to make Tobias jealous, and she knew a lesser man might not have forgiven her. Of course, they had both been in junior high at the time. Finn and Evie were, hopefully, more mature than that.

Still…

"What will you do if you get the job?" Sam asked. "About Finn, I mean."

Evie met her eyes and shrugged sadly.

"Will you move back if you don't get the job?" Sam pressed.

Evie shrugged again. "I don't know." She looked down at her plate. "You two seem to make the long-distance thing work okay."

Tobias snorted, and Sam shook her head. "Only because we know it's temporary. I couldn't do it if there was no end in sight," Sam said.

"What would you do if it wasn't temporary?" Evie asked, evidently surprised by Sam's admission.

Sam took a moment to ponder the possibilities. She loved Lydia and Paul and never wanted to disappoint them. But she wouldn't give up Tobias for anything or anyone.

"I'd make it temporary," Sam said. "Join Tobias in Colorado as soon as possible, with or without Lydia and Paul's blessing," Sam said. She glanced at Tobias, and his worried look made her doubt that he agreed. "No? You'd rather call it quits?"

"Never," Tobias said. Under the table, he squeezed her hand, the one with his ring on her finger. "You're stuck with me for life."

Sam quirked a smile but made an effort to return to neutral when she looked at Evie.

"Jobs will come and go, Evie," she said. "There's only one Finn."

♫

It was like Sam could see straight into her soul. It was unnerving.

Evie suddenly felt vulnerable and self-conscious, as if all her flaws and interior ugliness were on display. She fought the urge to flee the dinner table and the restaurant and Iowa. She couldn't keep running. Her wounds and weaknesses would always follow.

"You think I should go back to Colorado?" Evie asked. "Even if I get the symphony gig?"

"Or tell Finn to move his butt out here," Sam replied with a shrug.

"Whoa," Tobias said. "Hold on. Have you even talked to Finn about any of this?"

Evie sighed. "We were about to get into it when his siblings interrupted."

"Well, he's the one you should be talking to, not us," Tobias said. Sam looked like she was about to argue with him, but he continued before she could. "If you and Finn want to be together, you should figure out the how *together*. Don't make up your mind without his input. And definitely don't try to make up *his* mind."

It was a good point, and Evie was glad to have a male perspective at the table.

"Have you prayed about it?" Sam suddenly asked.

They'd only brushed up against topics surrounding faith and religion so far. Evie had picked up hints that Sam had a vibrant faith, and their mother's rosary made her think she was probably raised Catholic. But neither of them had said anything explicit about their beliefs.

Apart from me you can do nothing.

Evie closed her eyes and said a mental prayer right then and there. *Lord, I want to be with Finn. I also want this symphony job. But more than either, I want to do what You want me to do. Show me what You want, and I will do it.*

She opened her eyes. "Yes, I have."

Her phone rang at that exact moment, causing her to jump. Evie picked it up. She didn't recognize the phone number, but it was from Des Moines.

"Hello, this is Evie Vincent," she answered.

"Evelyn Vincent?" A woman's voice. Linda's voice.

"Yes, this is Evelyn," Evie said. Her heart hammered, and she closed her eyes to block out Sam and Tobias's inquiring gazes.

"Evelyn, this is Linda Pogoda, from the Des Moines Symphony. We spoke earlier today."

"Yes, I remember. Thank you again for your kindness. It helped more than you know."

"Oh, I think I have a pretty good idea, actually. We heard a lot of fantastic violin players today, but the decision was unanimous: Applicant number six blew the competition away. I was delighted to find out that applicant number six was Grace Chin's star student."

Evie covered her mouth. "Thank you," she breathed.

"We would like to offer you the principal second violinist position with the Des Moines Symphony."

Apart from me you can do nothing. Was this the answer to Evie's prayer?

"You can take some time to consider, of course. I imagine if you aren't already, you will be in high demand—if you keep playing the way you did today, anyway—and we can't offer the kind of pay full-time orchestras do. The spot is yours if you want it, though."

Evie swallowed, hoping Linda couldn't hear the emotion in her voice. "Can I take the weekend to think about it and let you know on Monday? I have some… things… I need to get in order first." She wanted to accept without another thought, but her impulsiveness had made things complicated enough already. Tobias was right. She needed to talk to Finn.

"Of course. I look forward to hearing from you on Monday."

Sam was grinning when Evie lowered her phone and opened her eyes. "You got it, didn't you?"

Evie nodded. A laugh of surprise and excitement burst from her.

The satisfaction she felt was from something more than simply winning a professional gig, a highly competitive spot. She'd conquered *herself*—her own fears and anxieties, her distractions and worries. She'd proven to herself that she could still perform under pressure, that her failed jury so long ago hadn't obliterated her confidence altogether. She felt victorious. And free.

"Congratulations," Tobias said.

"I'm gonna buy season tickets," Sam announced, bubbling over with excitement. "Des Moines can't be that far of a drive from Chickenhawk. We could make a weekend of it every time you have a concert. A sisters' weekend!"

Evie snorted, and—to her horror—a bubble of snot came out of her nose.

Sam laughed so hard Evie thought she might fall out of her chair. Tobias chuckled, too, but the tips of his ears turned pink—he must have been embarrassed *for* her. Evie wiped her nose with her napkin and allowed herself to chortle at her own expense.

When the trio's laughter finally settled down to a wheeze, Evie picked up her fork and twirled the last bits of spaghetti on her plate.

"You said you two are driving back tomorrow?" she asked, trying to sound nonchalant.

"I could stay and spend more time with you," Sam replied. "If it's okay with you, I mean. It doesn't seem fair to find my long-lost sister—who, by the way, is quickly becoming one of my favorite people on the planet—only to leave a day later. Tobias needs to get back for work, but I have nowhere to be. I can fly back to Colorado any old time."

Evie did her best to keep a straight face. Gemma and Gentry had never taken kindly to a little good-natured teasing, but she had a feeling Sam was different. "I'm sorry, Sam. As lovely as that sounds, I'm afraid I have to say no."

Sam's face fell, and Evie saw her swallow.

"Because I was sort of hoping to catch a ride back to Colorado with you and Tobias," Evie said. She watched Sam's face light up again, and she grinned.

"Really?" Sam practically squealed.

Evie nodded. "I need to see Finn. Talk to him. Linda gave me until Monday to make a decision about the position with the symphony. I think I want Finn to have a say in that decision." She looked at Tobias, and he smiled.

"Are you gonna tell Finn you're coming?" Sam asked, mischief in her expression. "Or are you gonna surprise him?"

Evie liked the way her little sister's brain worked.

28

Sir Gallagher

♫

Bach for More was already closed for the day by the time Tobias pulled Finn's Subaru Outback into an empty parking spot. Tobias's little Honda Civic sat where they'd left it a couple days earlier.

All three of them had kept their eyes peeled for a white SUV following them during the drive, but they'd seen nothing suspicious. Evie still felt anxious knowing Liam was out there somewhere, possibly waiting to ambush her again. She promised herself she wouldn't let him within feet of her if she ever saw him again—she would run the other way, wherever she was. While part of her believed he would never actually hurt her, another part of her knew that abusive relationships often started with seemingly small violations. She praised God that He'd maneuvered her life away from Liam when she had been most tempted by him.

Tobias and Sam gathered their things from the trunk of Finn's car and loaded them into the Civic. Tobias handed Evie the keys to the Subaru.

"Thank you, Tobias," she said. She glanced at Sam. "If it weren't for you, I never would have met my little sister."

The tips of his ears turned pink, and he smiled.

Sam threw her arms around Evie, almost knocking her over. Evie laughed and returned the tight squeeze.

"I love you, Evie," Sam said. "I've loved you ever since I knew I had a sister. But now that I know you…" She couldn't finish her sentence before tears choked her.

Evie's eyes grew moist, too, but she didn't let them spill over.

"I love you, too, Sam," Evie said hoarsely. "Thank you for not giving up on me."

They held onto each other for a while longer.

When they finally let go, Sam said, "Promise you'll come stay with us if Finn's family doesn't have room."

"I promise."

"And promise you'll call me and tell me everything if you don't stay with us."

"I promise."

"And promise you'll give Finn a hug for me."

"A hug-o-gram," Tobias added, and Sam grinned at him.

Evie laughed.

"I promise."

November 26, 2015

Evie pulled up to a two-story suburban house on a tiny lot and double-checked, triple-checked the house number. Didn't Finn say he was the oldest of nine? How in the world did a family of eleven fit in this house? How in the world would she fit in there with them?

She almost regretted accepting Finn's invitation to spend Thanksgiving with his family. But he'd been so sweet about it when he found out she had nowhere to go for the holiday, she couldn't decline.

She hadn't told him the truth about why she had nowhere to go, instead letting him believe she simply couldn't afford to fly back to San Diego. It wasn't a complete lie—although her relationship with Pete and Cassidy would never be the same after the way they'd lied to her and the way she'd run away from home, she had agreed to at least consider going back for Christmas this year. Going back for both Christmas and Thanksgiving was out of the question —mostly because she didn't want to spend that much time with her adopted family, but her finances would have made it difficult in any case. So what Finn believed was sort of true.

Maybe someday she would tell him the whole awful story. But not now. It had barely been a year since she'd found out she was adopted, since she'd found out her entire life, her entire identity was a lie. Who was Evelyn Rose Vincent? Evie no longer knew, and the intervening year hadn't helped her figure it out—much. Maybe when she did figure it out, she'd be ready to talk about it.

Would she and Finn still be friends when that day came? Who knew?

They'd only known each other a couple of months, both freshmen at the Lockwood School of Music. Evie initially thought he was cute in a nerdy kind of way, with his thick-rimmed glasses, intensely blue eyes, close-cropped blond hair, and easy-going smile. She and Finn were in the same group during freshman orientation week, had music history and music theory classes together, and both played in the orchestra, all of which helped them bond quickly. But, of course, as soon as Finn met Regina, who was a gorgeous and witty sophomore, Evie quashed any attraction she might have felt. Regina and Finn just seemed to click. Granted, Regina seemed to click with everyone.

Evie was greeted at the door by Finn's mother and two young children who followed her like little puppies. The clamor of voices beyond set Evie on edge. She didn't like chaos, and she had a feeling this house was nothing but.

Finn's mother led Evie into the eye of the storm. The house was split-level, with the kitchen overlooking the living room. A long table stretched across much of the living room space. It had benches on either side, and there was little room to walk around it. Two teenagers were busy setting the table, and in the kitchen, three more Gallaghers were on the verge of a food fight. A sliding glass door led to the backyard, where Evie could see Finn and his dad monitoring a smoker. Finn held a toddler who kept trying to pull his glasses off his face.

Finn's mother opened the glass door and yelled, "Finn, your friend is here!"

Finn hustled over and let his toddler sibling down once they stepped inside. His cheeks and nose were rosy from the crisp fall air, and he broke into a bright smile when he saw Evie.

"Happy Thanksgiving! Welcome to Gallagher Castle," he said, holding his arms out wide.

One of his teenage brothers snorted. "Bro, your nerd is showing."

"Is that bird almost done, Finn?" his mom asked. "We're just about ready in here."

"Yeah, Dad's just about to take it out," Finn answered. He turned to Evie. "Come. Sit. Can I get you something to drink?"

He steered her toward a seat at the table.

"Water would be great, thanks," Evie said. "But, um... before I sit... where's your restroom?" She didn't actually need to use the restroom. She just needed a retreat from the overwhelming noise.

"Oh! Right this way." Finn led her back toward the front door and showed her a bathroom near the entryway. "I definitely recommend locking the door.

Some of the littles don't quite understand about privacy yet. But it's kinda tricky." He showed her an old-fashioned skeleton key that rested in the lock on the inside of the door. "It's old. Turn the key, but leave it in the lock. If you take it out, you can see through the keyhole."

Fantastic. Why did I come here? *Evie wanted to flee this bedlam, but she didn't want to be rude. Finn was a nice guy, and she didn't want to hurt his feelings.*

Evie locked herself in the bathroom, leaving the key in the lock as Finn had instructed. The toilet seat was up—a boy was obviously the last to use it—and there were splashes of urine on the rim. At the top of the water line, there was a brown ring lining the bowl. It was disgusting. Evie had never shared a bathroom with a boy—Gentry always had his own bathroom—and she wondered whether most married women had to train their husbands to be less disgusting or if they just put up with it. Finn's mother apparently put up with it. To be fair, though, the poor woman had her hands full with children ranging from two years old up to nineteen, and the toilet was probably the least of her concerns.

Evie leaned against the sink, which was only slightly cleaner than the toilet, trying to think of a plausible excuse to leave. She didn't want to be alone for Thanksgiving, but her sensitive ears were already overstimulated, and she'd been in the house less than five minutes.

Suddenly, as if the cosmos were responding to her thoughts, a hush fell over the house beyond the bathroom door. Evie waited for the pandemonium to resume, but it didn't. Illogically, she felt like she would jinx it if she opened the door, and all hell would break loose again. But she couldn't stay in here forever.

Resigned to her fate, Evie twisted the old key in the lock, but it snapped in half. Stunned, she stared at the broken key in her hand. She tried to turn the doorknob, but it was still locked. Panic started to set in. She was stuck in the bathroom in someone else's house. A nasty bathroom. She could almost picture the germs crawling on her.

What should she do? Knock? Yell for help? How mortifying. Everyone would know that she'd trapped herself in the bathroom. Maybe she could text Finn. Maybe he would be discreet about it. She reached for her phone... but it wasn't in her pocket. Shoot. *She must have left it in the car.*

Evie tried the doorknob again. And again. She pulled on the door. Nothing. And then there was a knock from the other side.

"Evie, you okay in there?" Finn's voice.

"Um... no," Evie admitted. "The key broke. Part of it is still in the lock. I'm... I can't get out."

She heard him chuckle.

"It's not funny," she said through the door. It made her mad that he was laughing at her humiliation, but another part of her felt her own laugh bubbling up. "Finn, get me out of here."

"Okay, hold on," he said. His footsteps walked away from the door and returned a moment later. She heard Finn's voice and another deep male voice conferring quietly, but she couldn't make out any of the words.

A sudden slam against the door made Evie jump, and she yelped.

"Oh, holy crickets," Finn groaned. "Oh, that hurt. That was dumb. I'm not doing that again."

Evie snorted back a laugh, picturing Finn rubbing his sore shoulder.

"That's not how they do it, bro." It must have been one of his brothers. "Here, let me try."

There was another slam against the door, less powerful than Finn's, and then the sound of his brother moaning in pain and Finn laughing.

"Uh-huh. Good work, bro," he ribbed. He raised his voice so Evie could hear him clearly. "I'm gonna go look for something to pry the door open. I'll be back."

"I'll be here," Evie said flatly.

She waited. A few minutes later, Finn returned, joined by several other male voices. Great. It was probably his dad and all his brothers. All of them were there to witness her stupidity.

There was a scratching sound near the doorknob, but Evie couldn't tell what Finn and his dad and brothers were doing. They all spoke over one another, each one declaring with absolute certainty that he knew how to do whatever they were doing better than all the rest.

"Shut up, shut up. I think I got it!" Finn suddenly exclaimed.

The door popped open.

Finn knelt on one knee just outside it, a clarinet reed in his hand, a look of victory on his face. Three of his brothers and his dad huddled around behind him.

"Milady," Finn said gallantly, standing and bowing like a dutiful knight. "Your feast awaits."

Evie felt her cheeks grow hot, but she couldn't stop the smile that tugged at the corners of her mouth. She had a choice: wallow in her embarrassment or embrace the absurdity. She chose to embrace it.

"Thank you for your daring rescue, sir knight," Evie said dramatically. "Who knew the privy was such a dangerous place?"

Finn chuckled and offered his arm as if to escort her. "Shall we, Lady Vincent?"

She took his arm. "We shall, Sir Gallagher."

♫

The memory made Evie grin. They'd called each other *Lady Vincent* and *Sir Gallagher* ever since. Evie had never thought of it as flirtatious, just an inside joke between friends, but she wondered now if she'd subconsciously known all along that Finn was *her* knight and no one else's.

As the sun sank closer to the peaks of the glorious Front Range, Evie pulled onto the street where Finn's parents lived. She hoped she wouldn't be interrupting their dinner. She parked next to the curb and braced herself for the chaos that was sure to meet her at the door.

Evie rang the doorbell and waited, her body tense with nerves. She had so much to discuss with Finn, so much to ask him. Their romance hadn't even properly started yet, and already she was scared of bungling it. What if he decided their relationship wasn't worth it? That *she* wasn't worth it? What if they couldn't agree on what to do? What if…

Regina's voice intruded on Evie's thoughts. *If you're always stuck at 'what if', you are going to end up very lonely.*

Evie wished she had Regina's sense of adventure. Or Sam's boldness. She could use them both tonight.

Finally, the door opened, revealing one of Finn's sisters. Evie couldn't remember the names of all Finn's siblings—two more had been born just since she'd known him—but she remembered this one. Penny. She remembered because the girl had copper hair that matched her name.

Penny did not recognize Evie, though.

"Can I help you?" she asked. Evie guessed she was a freshman or sophomore in high school.

"Um, yes, I'm here to see Finn," Evie said. "I'm Evie. You probably don't remember me, but I came here for Thanksgiving a few years ago."

Penny's eyes went wide. "Oh my gosh, you're Finn's girlfriend! Of course! I'm sorry I didn't recognize you. I was pretty little back then, you know. Come in. Finn's out back with the boys."

The word *girlfriend* was like a dart. A pleasant one. He'd already told his family.

"Thank you." Evie stepped inside.

The house was much quieter than her last memory of it. The small rooms were still over-cluttered, but there were no fights breaking out in the kitchen or kids setting the table.

"How's your dad?" Evie asked Penny as they made their way to the sliding glass door. "He came home yesterday, right?"

"Yeah, he's okay," Penny answered. She didn't provide any further details. "There's Finn." She pointed through the sliding glass door.

Evie watched him for a moment, simply enjoying the sight of him. He and his brothers were playing football. The littlest one—five or six years old—ran with the ball. As one of the older ones was about to tackle the little fella, Finn picked him up and ran with both the kid and the ball in his arms until they reached the imaginary end zone. They did a choreographed dance together in celebration, and all the other boys threw up their arms in frustration.

Evie opened the sliding glass door and walked out. The boys, including Finn, were all too focused on the game to notice her.

One of the boys punted the ball, and it sailed wide—straight toward Evie. She was prepared to catch it, but Finn came barreling toward her, his eyes on the ball and still oblivious to her presence.

"I got it!" he yelled right before he smashed into her, his chest slamming into her face.

Evie stumbled back, but Finn's reflexes were fast enough to grab her arms and keep her upright. Blood poured from her nose, and she cupped a hand over it.

"Holy crickets!" Finn breathed. "Evie!"

She was stunned by the impact and felt a little woozy.

"Sean!" Finn called. "Go get some paper towels." He turned to Evie. "Here, sit down."

He helped her sit on the grass of the lawn and knelt next to her. His brothers hovered nearby, curious, until Finn shooed them away. A moment later, one of them—Sean, Evie presumed—ran up with the requested roll of paper towels. The boy retreated, leaving the two of them alone, as Finn ripped a paper towel from the roll. He handed it to Evie so she could stanch the flow of blood from her nose.

"I can't believe you're here," he said, his blue eyes full of wonder and worry.

"I can't believe you gave me another bloody nose," Evie returned with a chuckle. She closed her eyes, feeling lightheaded. "I think I need to lie down."

"Here." Finn shifted to a sitting position and helped Evie to lie back so that her head rested in his lap.

She could taste blood sliding down the back of her throat and swallowed. Finn gently brushed her hair away from her face. It felt nice.

"Why didn't you tell me you were coming?" Finn asked, gazing down at her.

It had been hard to keep it from him. In the one day since Evie sang *I Could Write A Book* to him, they'd spoken on the phone a few more times and exchanged a million text messages. He'd tried to broach the subject of their future again, but she'd diverted the conversation elsewhere. She hadn't even told him about the job offer from the symphony yet. She desperately wanted to, but she made herself wait until they were face-to-face.

"Surprise," Evie whispered.

Finn chuckled.

Evie reached up with her free hand and tugged on a lock of wild blond hair hanging over his forehead.

"When I was on my way, I thought of Thanksgiving our freshman year," she said. "Your hair was so short then."

"Yeah, and after a semester at college, I couldn't afford that many haircuts," Finn replied.

Evie smiled and chuffed. "I like it the way it is now."

Finn waggled his eyebrows, and she laughed.

"I rode back with Sam and Tobias," Evie said. "I brought your car."

"And… are you here to stay?" Finn asked, hope in his voice.

"I won the audition, Finn," Evie responded. "Principal second violinist with the Des Moines Symphony."

She expected to see disappointment, but instead, he broke into a wide smile. "I knew you would. Didn't I tell you that? Remember? I said I'd bet my life savings you could win any audition in the country, and look at you. You did it."

"You're not… disappointed?" Evie ventured. "I mean… you think I should accept?"

"Of course, you should," Finn replied. "Why wouldn't you?"

"Because if I accept a job in Des Moines, I can't be here," Evie said.

"Would you rather be here?" Finn asked.

"I would rather be with you," Evie said. The words came out before she'd thought them through, but they were truer than anything she might have said otherwise. She *would* rather be with Finn than play for a professional symphony.

"Evie, I'm not going anywhere," Finn said. Then, he rethought his choice of words. "I meant that metaphorically—like, you're not going to lose me either way. Not like, I'm never leaving Colorado and would never move to Iowa for you. I totally would." He paused, a blush on his cheeks. "If that's what you want, I mean."

Evie wanted to kiss him, but her stupid nose was still bleeding. She settled for brushing her knuckles along his cheek, the same one she'd slapped less than a week ago.

"I do want." She let her hand drop. "But I don't want you to if it means you have to give up school. I would never ask you to give up your dream for mine."

Finn sighed. She could see the struggle in his expression. He couldn't afford school if he moved, and they both knew it.

Evie pushed herself to a sitting position and swiveled so that they were sitting side-by-side but facing opposite directions. She looked around. Though they were alone on the lawn, Evie could see several of his siblings watching them curiously through the sliding glass door.

Evie took the paper towel away and sniffed. The blood had stopped. She used another paper towel from the roll to wipe dried blood from her face and hand. As she scrubbed her hand, she took a moment to pray for boldness and a sense of adventure.

"What if you didn't have to pay rent in Iowa?" she said.

Finn's only response was a raised eyebrow. She met his eyes.

"You could move in with me," she suggested, already knowing what his answer would be.

He blushed. "Evie, I know that's kinda the norm these days, but I don't think couples should live together until they're married."

"I agree."

She left it at that, waiting for the implication to sink in. It took a few seconds, but Finn's face was priceless when it finally happened.

He giggled uncontrollably.

"Lady Vincent," he finally said, "am I to understand that you are offering a proposal of marriage?"

Evie pursed her lips. "Lady Evelyn Gallagher has a nice ring to it, don't you think?"

"You're serious," Finn said, his giggles subsiding but a smile lingering on his face.

It was Evie's turn to sigh. "You're my best friend, Finn. If you want to wait, we can wait. I know I can be impulsive, and marriage is way too important to be impulsive about. I just thought... I just wanted you to know… to understand… I want to do whatever it takes to make this work. I love you, Finn. And I trust you. With my whole life."

For a moment, they simply held each other's gaze. The tenderness and longing Evie saw in Finn's blue eyes sent the most curious sensations through her. Then, he lifted a hand. With a featherlight touch, his fingers brushed the side of her neck and wove into the hair at the back of her head. He leaned in and kissed her. Slowly. Tenderly.

Evie had been right on her twenty-first birthday. Finn was a very good kisser. She felt it all the way down to her toes.

29

A Proposal

♫

Evie and Finn spent the weekend batting around ideas and options.

Finn confessed that he felt quite sure Evie was *The One* but insisted that they give themselves time to learn how to be a couple before taking any official steps toward engagement and marriage. His restraint inspired both admiration and frustration in Evie. It was what she needed to keep her impulsive tendencies in check, but the moment he'd kissed her, she knew she never wanted to be kissed by anyone else.

In the end, it was Sam who proposed the perfect solution.

Evie stayed with Sam as she had promised, sharing a bed with her while Tobias slept on the couch in their Uncle Steve's basement. Steve and Kristy had been delighted to meet Evie and assured her she would always have a place to stay at their house. Late at night, with the lights off and the whole house quiet, Sam and Evie stayed up talking and giggling as sisters do.

It amazed Evie how easily she shared her innermost thoughts with Sam and how sympathetically Sam listened. She told her things she'd never even told Regina, things about Liam and Pete and Cassidy and Gemma and Gentry. And Finn, of course. Sam reciprocated, divulging every detail of what their parents had been like and how she grew up, how she ended up living with the Howards and becoming Catholic.

And music—they gushed about music until the wee hours of the morning, and Evie learned that their musical talents were inherited from their father, Robert Rice. Although Sam had never heard him play an instrument, she occasionally caught him singing. Based upon her memories of his voice, she'd later concluded that he must have received formal voice training at some point. Their mother, Renee, had appreciated music, but according to Sam, she couldn't match pitch to save her life. Sam admitted that, as deeply wounded as she was by Robert Rice's abandonment, a part of her still missed going to symphony concerts with him and their mother. They were the only times the three of them ever felt like a family. As much as Evie disliked Robert Rice, she felt a twinge of gratitude that he had given her the gift of music.

On Sunday, the two young couples went to Mass together. It was afterwards, at brunch, that Sam pitched her bold idea.

"So… I talked to Paul and Lydia this morning," Sam started. "About Mom's trust."

Evie had almost forgotten about the inheritance. Even though Sam had insisted she take half of it, Evie doubted it would be easy—or maybe even possible—to actually arrange such a thing. So she'd continued to act as though her budget only included her savings and whatever income she could manage on her own.

In fact, Evie hadn't told Finn about it at all, and she braced for his reaction to hearing about it from Sam.

"I told them how I wanted you to have half of it," Sam continued.

Evie felt Finn glance at her, but she kept her eyes on her food and mumbled, "Mm-hm."

"They said they want to meet you first," Sam said. "They agreed with me in principle—wanting to share with you since you're as much our mother's daughter as I am—but since they are the trustees, they have what they call a *fiduciary duty* to manage the trust the way Mom intended."

Evie looked up at Sam, wondering where she was going with all this. "Okay…"

"But it got me thinking," Sam went on. "There's no question you'll get your half sooner or later. If not now, then for sure when I turn eighteen, because then I can do whatever I want with it. But probably sooner, because I know Lyds and Paul are gonna love you as much as I do."

Evie couldn't help but smile at her sister's optimism.

"Whenever you get it, you can spend it any way you want obviously," Sam said, winding up the pitch. "You could buy a house or invest it or whatever. Or…" She paused dramatically. "You could use the money to help Finn pay for school so he can afford to move to Iowa."

Evie felt Finn stiffen beside her and saw Tobias's eyes widen. She loved the idea. But would Finn accept such an extravagant gift? Would it hurt his pride if she paid for his master's degree? Would it make him feel beholden to her, bound to stay with her and marry her even if he didn't want to?

"Or…" Sam said, cocking her head as if someone had just whispered in her ear. "*I* could use *my* half of the inheritance to set up a scholarship fund for sacred music studies, and only people named Finn Gallagher are allowed to apply." She grinned, pleased with herself.

Finn glanced back and forth between Evie and Sam and huffed.

"There's no way," he said. "I mean, a master's degree isn't cheap. We're talking tens of thousands of dollars."

"You didn't tell him?" Sam asked Evie.

Evie shook her head. "Slipped my mind." She gave Finn a sidelong look. "Our mother left Sam enough money that, if she gives me half, I could pay for your master's degree and still have enough left over to make a cash offer on a house. A house in Iowa anyway. Not here."

Finn stared at her. "Lady Vincent, I had no idea you came with a dowry."

Evie punched him in the shoulder, and he giggled.

"It would be a gift," she said. "No strings attached. No obligations."

He put a hand on her knee and gazed at her with such love in those blue eyes. She curled her fingers around his.

"You said we need to take time to learn how to be a couple," Evie said softly. "We're not going to learn living two states apart."

The corner of Finn's mouth quirked, but he said nothing.

"Come on, Finn," Sam begged. "If it's too weird to take the money from Evie, take it from me. Don't let your pride keep you from being close to your ladylove."

Finn burst with a laugh. "I can't argue with that." He turned to Sam. "I get how Evie can offer to pay for my school—we've known each other for years—"

"And I love you," Evie added, lest he forget.

It distracted him momentarily, and he grinned at Evie, but then he continued his question to Sam. "But *you* have known me less than a week. Why are you so interested in helping me?"

"Because it will make my sister happy," Sam replied without hesitation. She glanced at Tobias with a sweet smile. "I know what it's like to be on the receiving end of a gift that can never be repaid." Tobias planted a kiss on the corner of her brow. She looked back to Finn. "Now I have a chance to be on the giving end."

Finn turned to Evie. "Will it make you happy?"

"Yes," Evie answered honestly. She promised herself she wouldn't hold it against him if he refused the help, but she wouldn't lie to him about what she wanted either. "I don't see any downside. You get to go to school. I get to play for the symphony. And most importantly, we get each other—not long distance, not every once in a while when we can afford to travel, but in the flesh every day—"

Finn kissed her. She hadn't expected it, and she felt her cheeks grow warm knowing Sam and Tobias were watching, but it didn't last long. Finn was a man of knightly chivalry, after all.

"Lady Vincent, Lady Ingram," he said, looking between the two sisters, "I accept your proposal."

Evie kissed him back.

"I have taken you in my arms, and I love you, and I prefer you to my life itself. For the present life is nothing, and my most ardent dream is to spend it with you in such a way that we may be assured of not being separated in the life reserved for us... I place your love above all things, and nothing would be more bitter or painful to me than to be of a different mind than you."

St. John Chrysostom, on what young husbands ought to say to their wives

Christmas

♫

Finn couldn't sleep. In fact, he hadn't slept more than a few fitful minutes at a time since he had returned from midnight Mass to the mother-in-law suite he was subletting from Evie.

Instead of heading straight back to Iowa from Colorado, Evie had made a detour through South Dakota to meet Lydia and Paul—Tobias's parents, Sam's guardians, Renee Ingram's trustees. As Sam had predicted, they fell in love with Evie—Finn couldn't blame them—and agreed to Sam's demand to give her half of the money left by their mother.

Evie made good on her promise. She set aside enough for Finn's tuition and used the rest of her inheritance to buy a house without a mortgage and furnish it, which still left her with several thousand dollars to put into savings. Finn joined her in Iowa as soon as she closed on the house, taking over the mother-in-law suite and starting a job as a director of youth ministry at a small parish just outside Des Moines. It had taken almost two months for all of it to come together—moving the trust fund money around, house hunting, closing on the contract—but Finn settled into his small two-room shack shortly after the semester started.

Now, it was Christmas.

For the first time in his life, Finn wasn't spending Christmas with his parents and siblings. When he'd told them about his plans for the holiday, his mother had sent him on a whale of a guilt trip. He knew his absence was only part of it, the thing that moved his mother from sullen to silent treatment. For some reason, she didn't like Evie, which

257

grieved Finn deeply. He hated disappointing his family, but he loved Evie even more.

And miraculously, she loved him back.

Finn glanced at the clock next to his bed. The sun wouldn't come up for another hour or so, but he couldn't stay in bed any longer. He shoved aside his covers, pulled on a pair of sweatpants, and padded across the bedroom. He peeked out into the main room. Along the wall opposite the bedroom, a stove, sink, and refrigerator made up a small kitchen area. In the middle of the room, there was a sofa and a coffee table.

A long, lanky form occupied the sofa, his feet dangling over the arm at one end.

Could Finn make coffee without waking him?

"What's for breakfast?"

Never mind. He's already awake. Finn grinned and flipped on the light switch, causing Tobias to shield his eyes and groan.

"Rise and shine, Sir Howard," Finn said. "Our fair maidens await."

"It's the shine part that's getting me," Tobias complained. "I was just fine until you turned the light on."

"But you were already awake," Finn said, heading for the coffee maker.

"Yeah," Tobias said, sitting up and rubbing his eyes. "Didn't sleep very well."

"Sorry," Finn said. "I know that sofa's not very comfortable."

"It's not that," Tobias replied. "I'm nervous."

"You too?" Finn asked without thinking.

He paused. He exchanged a look with Tobias. A slow smile spread across Tobias's face in understanding.

"Ohhhhh. That's why Sam's been acting so strange."

"Not a word," Finn warned.

In the two months before he'd moved to Iowa, Finn had become rather good friends with Tobias, and he'd often marveled at—and envied—Tobias's ability to read people.

"Why are *you* nervous?" Finn asked.

"I did it," Tobias said. "I have enough saved to marry Sam. I'm gonna tell my parents today."

"You know, if I didn't know how old you two are—or rather, how young—I wouldn't know."

"That makes no sense."

"What I'm saying is, I think you two are plenty ready," Finn said. He meant it. "And I'll put in a good word with your parents if you need me to."

Tobias smiled.

"Thanks, brother."

♫

Evie couldn't sleep.

What had she been thinking, inviting everyone to her house for Christmas? She had no skill for being a hostess, no instinct for hospitality.

Sam slept peacefully next to her. Pete and Cassidy occupied the guest room across the hall. Gemma and Gentry slept on air mattresses in a room on the main floor that she hadn't yet figured out how to furnish. Tobias was staying with Finn. Lydia and Paul and Catherine had a room at a hotel. Even Bear would be driving down later.

And they'd all celebrate Christmas together in a few short hours.

Evie thought about the food in her fridge. Had she forgotten anything? Overlooked a dish? Would it matter? The grocery store would probably be closed today. Sam and Lydia had promised to help her prepare the food, but their support did little to loosen the knot of nerves in her stomach.

Evie glanced over at Sam's sleeping face. So like her own—except free from anxiety.

All of Evie's fears about not getting along with her sister had proved completely ridiculous. As promised, Sam often drove to Des Moines on weekends when Evie had a concert, and between visits, she called and texted regularly. They grew so close so quickly, Evie struggled to understand how she'd survived without Sam's wit and wisdom for the first twenty-three years of her life.

Sam had protested leaving Colorado and returning to Iowa before July ended, but she obeyed Lydia and Paul. At first, Evie assumed it was because Sam wanted to avoid punishment or emotional blackmail —that's what Pete and Cassidy would have used—but Sam said it was simply because she loved them and respected their judgment. Evie didn't understand until she actually met Lydia and Paul.

Now that she had met them, Evie was more excited to spend Christmas with the Howards than with her own adopted family. Ironically, though, it was Lydia who encouraged her to invite Pete and Cassidy and the twins.

Evie had asked Finn about inviting his family as well. It was their first major fight as a couple. Finn declined to invite them, but he wouldn't tell her why—or rather, he gave her several reasons she knew weren't really true. It infuriated her that he wouldn't tell her the truth after all they'd been through. Only Sam's counsel about assuming Finn's good intentions kept Evie from breaking up with him—which she would have immediately and permanently regretted.

In the end, Finn finally revealed the real reason, and Evie understood what he had been trying to protect her from. His mother didn't like her.

Evie wished that it didn't bother her so much, but it made her worry about her future with Finn. She didn't want to be a wedge driving him and his family apart. She wanted to be part of his family—even if the chaos of their household made her supremely uncomfortable.

"You look worried," Sam whispered.

Evie turned her head and saw Sam blinking the sleep from her eyes. She smiled, shooing away her anxious thoughts. "Merry Christmas, Sam."

"Merry Christmas," Sam responded, stifling a yawn. She grinned sleepily. "This is already the best Christmas ever."

"Why?"

"Mom and Dad never celebrated Christmas, so I never celebrated Christmas until I moved in with Tobias and his family," Sam explained softly. "So this is the first Christmas ever, in my whole life, that I've been able to celebrate with *my* family."

Evie smiled. She loved Sam's indomitable enthusiasm. Her sister saw blessings everywhere and lived every moment with gratitude.

A creak sounded downstairs. Someone else was up.

Evie looked at the ceiling and sighed. "I suppose I should get up and be a good hostess or something."

"Did you sleep at all?" Sam asked.

"Not really."

"Then you stay here and relax," Sam said, rolling away and out of the bed. "Let me play hostess. I gotta practice, you know."

Evie snorted and jumped out of bed, not willing to abdicate her hostessing duties to her sister. "Oh no, you don't. I'm the one who needs the practice."

Sam pulled on a sweatshirt over her pajamas and paused thoughtfully. "I wonder if Finn knows how lucky he is."

Evie snorted as she made her bed. Sam pitched in on the other side.

"To be dating a girl his family disapproves of? I don't call that luck," Evie said.

Sam stopped and gave Evie a horrified look. "What are you talking about?"

"Finn's mom," Evie said. "She doesn't like me. Finn wouldn't even let me *try* to invite his family for Christmas." She paused. "Not that I would have been able to handle it if they did come. I'm overwhelmed as it is. Can you imagine? Adding Finn's parents and ten siblings to the people already squeezing into this house?" She shuddered.

Sam frowned.

Evie sat on the made bed with a sigh. "I don't know, Sam. Sometimes I wonder… maybe his mother is right. Maybe I'm not the right girl for Finn."

"Whoa, whoa, whoa."

Sam rushed around the end of the bed and plopped down next to Evie, clutching her arm with both hands.

"You can't mean that," she said, her eyes wide.

Evie shook her head. "He makes me so happy. But if I put my own happiness above his relationship with his family, that's not love. That's selfish. Isn't it?"

"What about Finn's happiness?" Sam asked.

Evie looked at her.

"He chose to move here to Iowa to be with you, Evie," Sam continued. "He chose to stay here to spend Christmas with you. I think he's made it pretty clear that his happiness lies with *you*, not his family."

Evie sighed. "Okay, but maybe Finn shouldn't have to choose at all. If he were dating someone else, someone his mother actually likes, he could have both. Doesn't he deserve that?"

"No."

"No?"

"You're dating Finn, not Finn's mom," Sam said firmly. "If he dated someone that his mom liked, she probably wouldn't be a girl that Finn likes. Do you think that's what he deserves?"

"And if we get married someday?" Evie asked. "I don't want to join a family that doesn't want me."

"Don't think of it that way," Sam said. "Getting married is about starting a *new* family, not getting absorbed into someone else's family. I mean, yes, we're all supposed to be family in the Catholic sense. But Genesis—and Jesus Himself, I might add—talks about a man *leaving* his mother and father and cleaving to his wife. Right?"

Evie chuffed and smiled. "Which one of us is the older sister here?"

Sam grinned and blushed. "Sorry. I like to pontificate, I guess."

Evie put her arms around Sam's shoulders, forcing her into an awkward side hug. "I like it. And I needed it. Thank you." She let Sam go and jumped up. "Come on. Help me hostess."

♫

Sam waited until Evie left the bedroom to let out a tense breath. Her panic had nearly caused her to blow Finn's secret.

As she stood and followed Evie downstairs, her own advice echoed around her brain. *Getting married is about starting a new family, not getting absorbed into someone else's family.* She wasn't sure where she'd learned such a thing—although she had a prodigious memory, she couldn't recall Lydia or Paul ever saying it. Even more strangely, but for very different reasons than Evie, it was advice Sam realized she needed herself. Being Lydia and Paul's ward, she'd been fully absorbed into the Howard family for years. It only now dawned on her that perhaps that would need to change when she and Tobias finally got married and started their own family. The realization troubled her, but in some deep part of her heart, she felt the truth of it.

Sam shook the thought from her head as she reached the kitchen. Evie's adopted mom, Cassidy, sat on a stool on one side of the island with her hands wrapped around a hot mug of coffee. Her hair and makeup were already perfectly done—a sharp contrast to Sam and Evie, still dressed in their pajamas and strands of hair escaping from their overnight updos.

Evie was just starting to pour herself a cup of coffee.

"I hope you don't mind that I poked around your cupboards and helped myself to the coffee," Cassidy said.

Evie smiled. "Not at all. You want some, Sam?"

"Yes, please," Sam said.

Evie pulled down another cup from the cupboard and filled it. She handed one of the steaming mugs to Sam. The sisters stood across the island from Cassidy.

"What time are the others coming?" Cassidy asked.

Evie shrugged. "Whenever they want."

"You don't have a plan?" Cassidy asked, concern slipping into her voice.

"It's Christmas," Evie said with another shrug. "I didn't want anyone to stress about getting here at a certain time."

"Bear should be here early afternoon," Sam said, trying to be helpful.

Cassidy's brow crinkled. "Bear?"

"My future brother-in-law," Sam said. "He's a seminarian. He had to serve at the early Mass at our home parish this morning."

"Oh, that's right," Cassidy said, her eyes flicking to Sam's left hand. "I forgot you're engaged to that young man."

"His name is Tobias," Evie said.

Sam could tell she was trying—and failing—to keep the edge of annoyance from her voice. She nudged Evie's foot with her own and gave a slight shake of her head. Evie didn't need to be offended on her behalf.

"That's right. Tobias," Cassidy said. She sipped from her mug. "It's an unusual name."

"It's from the Bible," Sam said. "The book of Tobit." Her favorite book in the Bible. It was a love story.

"Oh?" Cassidy looked uncomfortable, and Sam suspected she wasn't familiar with much scripture. She'd probably never even heard of Tobit. Evie had warned her that Pete and Cassidy didn't take their Catholic faith all that seriously. "And does Bear come from the Bible, too?" she asked with a slight smirk.

Sam chuckled. "It's a nickname. His real name is Lawrence." She sighed. "I suppose we'll all have to get used to calling him by his real name after he's ordained. Father Lawrence. That'll be weird." She was glad they still had several years before that happened. It was difficult to imagine calling him anything but *Bear*.

"That's a saint's name, in case you didn't know," Evie said.

Sam kicked her again. She understood Evie's troubled history with Pete and Cassidy, but that was no reason for her to antagonize her adopted mother. Evie kicked her back. It made Sam giggle, which made Evie crack a smile.

"The resemblance between you two certainly is remarkable," Cassidy commented. "Incredible that you found each other after all these years."

Sam thought she seemed wistful. She wondered whether Cassidy resented the fact that Evie had found her biological family—whether she resented *her* for being Evie's natural sister.

"Which of your parents do you take after, Sam?" Cassidy asked.

Sam's stomach clenched. She didn't particularly want to take after either of them.

"We both look like our father," Evie answered on her behalf. "And we both inherited his talent for music, apparently."

Sam looked at Evie and nodded. "We have Mom's build, though. Little." She smiled. "And you have her dimples." It probably wasn't the right thing to say in front of Cassidy, but it made Evie smile. Sam turned back to Cassidy. "But the truth is, beneath the surface stuff, I don't think I'm much like either of them. At least, I hope I'm not. My dad is a sociopath, a criminal, and my mom knew what he was and protected him, even at the expense of her own daughters. Not exactly great role models."

Cassidy seemed to relax. Perhaps Sam had been wrong. Perhaps it wasn't resentment but worry—worry that Evie's biological parents had corrupted the daughter they chose to keep, and that she, in turn, would corrupt Evie.

"Actually, I..." Sam paused, uncertain how the words would sound but convinced she needed to say them. She looked Cassidy in the eye. "I want to thank you, Mrs. Vincent."

"Please, call me Cassidy."

Sam's insides did a little victory dance. It was always a good sign when an adult gave her permission to call them by their first name.

"Cassidy. I want to thank you," Sam repeated. "If it weren't for you and Pete..." she swallowed. "I know my dad pressured my mom to abort Evie. But she didn't do it because she knew there was a family who would take her daughter into their home and love her as their own. You saved my sister's life. So... thank you."

Cassidy's eyes filled with tears, and her hands trembled.

Sam felt Evie staring at her, and it made her cheeks burn. She glanced at her sister and saw tears in her eyes, too.

Evie set down her coffee and rounded the kitchen island. She drew Cassidy off her stool and hugged her. Cassidy returned the embrace.

"Oh, honey," Cassidy said.

"Mom," Evie whispered. "I'm so sorry."

Sam smiled to herself. She'd only ever heard Evie call Cassidy by her first name, having refused to call her *Mom* since the day she found out she was adopted.

This was *definitely* going to be the best Christmas ever.

♫

Tobias and Finn were the last to arrive. Well, other than Bear, of course. When they walked into Evie's house, they found everyone chatting amiably in small groups.

The house had an open-concept layout, with the kitchen, living room, and dining room all bleeding into each other in one giant space. The Christmas tree occupied a spot near the gas fireplace in the living room area. Tobias's dad sat at the dining table talking to Evie's adopted mother. Gentry and his father sat on the sofa sipping what looked like eggnog. Evie and Lydia were deep in conversation as they prepared the meal at the kitchen island, Gemma looking on and jumping in with a comment now and then. Finn joined them, giving Evie a peck on the lips when he reached her.

Tobias smiled when he saw Sam sitting on the floor near the Christmas tree with Catherine. His little sister adored Sam—who wouldn't?—and Sam seemed to interact with the little munchkin so naturally. She would be an amazing mother someday, Tobias had no doubt. He caught her eye, and she raised a mischievous eyebrow. Had she read his mind? He wouldn't doubt it. She knew him better than anyone. Tobias made his way over and knelt next to her. He ruffled Catherine's curly black hair, and she scowled at him, which made him chuckle.

"Merry Christmas, Catherine," he said. "Did Santa leave anything in your stocking this morning?"

The little girl shook her head. "He took my presents to our house. He doesn't like hotels."

Tobias and Sam both laughed.

"Merry Christmas, Sam," he murmured, turning to her and leaning over to kiss her. Her eyes widened a bit—probably unsure whether the *rules* applied here—but she relaxed into his kiss after a moment. He kissed her longer and more deeply than he probably should have with so many people around, but he felt too good to care.

"Merry Christmas," she mumbled when he pulled away. Her cheeks were a lovely shade of pink, and the surprise on her face was adorable.

Tobias grinned. "I'll be right back."

Her brow crinkled with confusion as he left her and approached the dining table. He took a seat next to his father.

"Merry Christmas, Tobias," his father said.

"Merry Christmas," Tobias responded. He nodded politely to Cassidy, and she offered a polite smile in return. He turned to his dad and lowered his voice. "I don't want to interrupt, but can we talk?"

"Go on. I need a refill anyway," Cassidy said, pushing away from the table and taking her empty wine glass with her toward the kitchen.

Tobias's dad smiled. "You did it, didn't you?" he asked softly.

Tobias grinned. He pulled a piece of paper out of his pocket and unfolded it. It was a printout of one of his spreadsheets, the one he used to track his savings progress. He handed it over, and the look of pride on his dad's face made his chest swell. His dad studied the spreadsheet for a moment, his head bobbing.

"Well done," he finally said, handing the paper back to Tobias. "A summer wedding then?"

Tobias smiled broadly. He glanced at Sam across the room and saw that she was watching him. He'd hoped to make it a surprise, but by the look on her face, she'd figured out exactly what he was talking to his dad about.

He cleared his throat. "Sir." He didn't know why, but it seemed right to address his dad formally just then. "I would like to make my engagement to your ward official, and I humbly ask for your blessing."

His dad laid a hand on Tobias's shoulder and squeezed it affectionately.

"You have it, my son."

♫

Sam's insides buzzed with excitement as she watched Tobias and Paul's quiet conversation. Catherine tugged on her hand, recalling her attention.

"What's that one say?" Catherine pointed to one of the presents under the tree.

"That one is for Tobias," Sam said. "From Mom and Dad."

"And that one?" Catherine pointed to another one. Sam had already read all the tags to her once, and they were halfway through naming all of them a second time.

"That one is for Evie," Sam said. "From me."

Tobias plopped down next to her and rubbed her back affectionately. He was grinning like an idiot, and it made Sam grin, too.

"Tobias, will you marry me?" she asked before he could get a word out.

"You!" He pinched her side, and she yelped. "I can't hide anything from you, even for fun."

"You really do need to work on your poker face, my love," Sam said, patting his cheek. He swatted her hand away and planted a quick kiss on her mouth. They both chuckled.

Catherine huffed in annoyance at having Sam's attention stolen away from her. She got up and left, and Sam saw her head toward Lydia.

"Do you want to email Father Bernard or should I?" Tobias asked.

Sam opened her mouth to answer, but her conversation with Evie returned to her. "There's actually something I wanted to talk to you about."

A look of concern flashed across Tobias's face. "Okay."

"We've kind of been operating under the assumption that you would move back to South Dakota once you made enough money," Sam started.

"Yeah…"

"But… maybe you shouldn't," she said. Tobias frowned, and she rushed to continue. "Hear me out. I love your parents so much. You know I do. But I think it would be good for us to live away from them for at least a couple years—and I mean *away*."

"Why?"

"It was something I told Evie this morning. *Getting married is about starting a new family, not getting absorbed into someone else's family.* I love your family, and I love how much they've made me feel like family. But you and I need to figure out what *our* family is going to look like. The Tobias and Samantha Howard family. And I just have a feeling that it will be very hard to do that if we live too close to your parents. If I live too close to Lydia."

Tobias studied her thoughtfully. She could almost see his mind processing her argument.

"It'll mean six more months apart," Tobias said after a few moments.

Sam nodded sadly. "I know."

Tobias hung his head. Sam reached up and brushed her fingers through his hair. "Maybe… maybe since I turn eighteen in a few weeks, they'll let me move to where you are. We still have the option of being fully remote for school. There's no reason I have to stay in Chickenhawk until I graduate. You could get an apartment, and I could live with my Uncle Steve until we're married."

Tobias looked up, and his smile started to reappear.

"I don't really even have to ask permission," Sam said. "They won't be my guardians anymore." The thought made her a little sad. She knew Lydia and Paul would always be there for her, but becoming an adult meant leaving behind childhood—and it struck her that once some things were left behind, they could never be had again.

As if drawn by Sam's thoughts, Lydia appeared next to them at that moment, Catherine trailing along after her. She knelt in front of them and smiled, but Sam could see that she was holding back tears.

Of course she was. Everything made her cry.

"I came over to congratulate you two," she said. "Paul tells me you've held up your end of the deal, so now it's our turn to hold up our end."

Sam and Tobias exchanged a look, and he nodded, giving his assent. Sam turned to Lydia.

"We have another request," she said. Lydia raised a brow. "Instead of Tobias moving back to South Dakota, I would like to move to Colorado."

Lydia looked down, and Sam saw two tears drip to the carpet. But when she looked up again, she was smiling. "My goodness, watching your kids grow up is wonderful and terrible at the same time."

"I don't want to wait to move, Lydia," Sam said, wanting to be sure her intentions were clear. "I can finish high school from Colorado. I *want* to finish high school from Colorado."

Lydia's brow creased in concern.

"We won't be living together, Mom," Tobias assured her. "I'm going to find an apartment to move into, and Sam can take my place at her uncle's house. Until we're married, of course."

Sam reached over and took Lydia's hand. "Please don't be mad."

"I'm not mad, sweetie," Lydia said, shaking her head. "It's just… I've grown kinda used to you. The house is going to feel very… very empty." A few more tears spilled over.

Feeling tears sting her own eyes, Sam got to her knees so she could hug Lydia. She would miss Tobias's parents dearly, but she felt confident that this was the right thing to do.

"I'm so proud of you both," Lydia whispered into Sam's hair. "So, so proud."

Definitely the best Christmas ever.

♫

The meal had been eaten. The presents had all been opened.

Everyone lounged in the living room area in various states of contentment. Pete, Cassidy, and Gemma sat on the sofa. Gentry occupied a plush chair. The Howards had all pulled chairs from the dining table over, but Sam sat on Tobias's lap, apparently enjoying the chance to escape the infamous *rules* at the Howard house. And Catherine knelt on the floor, surrounded by more toys than she knew what to do with.

Evie and Finn sat hip-to-hip on the hearth.

In truth, though, Evie felt a little disappointed in her gift from Finn. She knew his job didn't pay much, and she didn't want or expect anything expensive anyway. But she'd hoped for something thoughtful, at least. Instead, she got a baking dish.

Her disappointment had probably been written all over her face when she opened it, which made her feel bad. She told herself that maybe Finn just wasn't a good gift-giver. But then she remembered past birthdays and Christmases when he'd given her sweet little gifts —she'd assumed then that they were simply gifts from a friend but now knew he had been harboring romantic feelings for her all along. All of which made the baking dish more puzzling. Was it supposed to mean something? Was it a joke?

"Finn, you're always bragging about what a great singer you are," Sam said suddenly over the din of other quiet conversations. "And I've heard stories about how well you and Evie sing together. Maybe you guys should sing some Christmas songs for us."

Finn grinned, and Evie swore she saw him wink at Sam. He turned to her. "How about it, Lady Vincent? Shall we entertain?"

"If that's what everyone else wants..." Evie's adopted family had never cared much about music, but they all looked at her with eager expressions. As she glanced around the room, she found all the Howards nodding as well.

Finn disappeared to retrieve her parlor guitar—he knew where she kept her instruments, and he was one of only two people on the planet besides herself that she trusted to handle them, the other being Sam. Finn brought the guitar back a moment later.

"What do you want to start with?" she asked, reaching for the guitar.

"*Jingle Bells,*" Pete called out with the hint of a smirk.

Evie smiled at him as she tuned the guitar strings, remembering the Christmas he'd discovered her perfect pitch.

"I don't know, Finn, do you know the words to that one?" Evie teased, bumping Finn's shoulder.

"Oh, they'll probably come back to me once you start," he responded. Evie thought she heard a quiver in his voice. Was he nervous about singing in front of her family?

"Verse first," Evie said.

She strummed a couple of chords, fingerpicked the last few notes of the chorus as a lead-in, and then cued Finn to start singing. When he reached the end of the verse, he motioned for everyone to join in for the chorus. Evie harmonized with all of them, but her voice was mostly drowned out—especially by Bear's hideous wailing, which made everyone laugh. For such a simple song, it put the group in a remarkably cheerful mood.

"What next?" Evie asked when things quieted down.

"*Baby, It's Cold Outside,*" Sam requested with a mischievous grin.

Evie gave Finn a sidelong look, and he waggled his eyebrows. She took it as assent, so she began playing. Finn came in with the lyrics a few bars later, taking the part usually sung by a woman—a woman trying to gracefully end a romantic evening—which left Evie with the part usually sung by a man—one persuading the woman to stay longer than would be proper. The back-and-forth duet wasn't truly a Christmas song, but Evie enjoyed the opportunity to sing it with Finn anyway. The lyrics weren't far from reality—on numerous occasions, Evie had tried every excuse she could think of to get Finn to stay at her house just a little bit longer. She had only ever succeeded in delaying him by a few minutes, though.

As the duet ended, everyone applauded politely. Finn leaned down and pecked Evie on the lips, and she smiled, allowing herself to get a little bit lost in his blue eyes.

"I'd kind of like to hear Evie sing with Sam," Bear said.

Sam looked startled. "No!" she said.

"Why not?" Bear said. "I bet your voices would sound great together."

They did, actually. Evie and Sam had spontaneously broken out in song together plenty of times in the short time they'd known each other. The timbre of their voices matched in a way that was only possible because they were sisters and shared so much DNA. Sam's reluctance to sing with her was odd.

"I just… want…" Sam seemed truly flustered, and she glanced at Finn.

"I think Bear's onto something," Finn said. "Go on, you two. I demand to hear *O Holy Night.*" He used his formal, knightly voice.

"All in favor?"

A round of *ayes* went up, and Sam's face changed from confusion to worry. It seemed to Evie that her sister was trying to catch Finn's eye again, but he ignored her.

"There's no reason to be nervous in front of these goons, Sam," Evie said, thinking perhaps Sam had a bit of performance anxiety. She played piano quite well, but she didn't often sing in front of people—not consciously anyway.

"I'm not—" Sam was cut off by a nudge from behind by Tobias. He whispered in her ear, and they shared a long look, as if an entire conversation passed between them without words. Finally, Sam sighed and looked at Evie. "Fine. You take the melody, though. I don't want to mess up that note at the end."

"You got it," Evie said.

As Evie softly played the opening triplets, she suddenly felt nervous. *O Holy Night* was, in her opinion, the most beautiful of all Christmas songs, and she wanted to do it justice, especially singing the melody instead of the harmony as she usually did. But her nerves melted away as she and Sam began to sing, their voices blending in perfect resonance. Sam claimed she didn't have perfect pitch like Evie, but her relative pitch could fool even the best ear.

At the end of the song, no one clapped. No one moved. The moment felt sacred somehow. The first sound to break the silence was Lydia's sniffling, which seemed to give everyone else permission to breathe again.

"It's your turn, Finn," Sam said firmly. She gave him a meaningful look, though Evie couldn't decipher what the meaning might be.

Finn reached over and took the guitar from Evie.

"Mind if I play?" Finn said.

Evie froze. Finn didn't play guitar. As far as she knew, he'd never played guitar. Ever.

"You can still sing the harmony if you want," he said. "I think you'll recognize this one." He played a single chord before he paused and looked at her. "I'm not as good as you, but… I worked really hard on this," he said quietly. "So no judgments."

Evie shook her head. "No judgments."

Finn started a song. It wasn't a Christmas song at all, but Evie recognized it immediately. And it made her grin.

It was a Ray LaMontagne song. *You Are the Best Thing*.

Oh, Finn. Sweet, wonderful, thoughtful Finn! He couldn't afford fancy gifts, so he'd spent weeks—maybe even months—learning how to play her favorite song on guitar. *This* was the real gift.

There wasn't much for Evie to harmonize with. She could've made up a harmony, but the original recording had backup singers echoing Ray LaMontagne's vocals rather than harmonizing with him. So Evie decided to simply listen and enjoy the rich sound of Finn's voice.

When he finished the song, before the final chord had faded, Evie grabbed his face with both hands and kissed him long and hard, not caring that everyone was watching them.

"Thank you," she whispered. "That was my real present, wasn't it?"

"No," Finn said, grinning. "This is."

He set aside the guitar and reached into his pocket. Evie caught her breath when he pulled out a ring. An engagement ring.

"Yes," she blurted before he could speak.

Finn chuckled, and so did everyone around them. "I haven't even asked yet."

Evie clapped a hand over her mouth.

Finn got down on his knee and took her other hand. "You once told me you like the way *Lady Evelyn Gallagher* sounds. I hope that's still true."

She nodded. Finn smiled and cleared his throat, obviously struggling to keep his emotions from stealing his voice.

"Good," he said hoarsely. He took a breath and cleared his throat again. "Lady Evelyn, I think you know that I have loved you for a very long time. You really are the most amazing thing that's ever happened to me. The day you sang Rodgers and Hart to me, you quite literally made my dreams come true."

Evie laughed through the hand over her mouth.

Finn cleared his throat once more. "I am but a humble knight with very little to offer. But all that I have and all that I am, I offer to you, milady." Evie saw tears in his eyes, and his voice dropped to a whisper. "Evie. Will you marry me?"

"Yes!" Evie squealed and threw her arms around his neck so forcefully that she almost knocked him over. They both laughed.

Sam had been right. Best. Christmas. Ever.

As Finn slipped the ring on her finger, Evie was overwhelmed by a surpassing sense of peace. Everything about the moment felt *right*.

Looking back, she recognized with clarity how God had guided every moment of her life, even using her missteps and impulses and worst decisions to accomplish something beautiful. By grace—as Finn had once reminded her—she was a royal princess in the Kingdom of her Heavenly Father. Apart from Him, she could do nothing. With Him, anything was possible.

Like a future with Finn. Evie would never again let *what if* keep her from loving and trusting Finn and letting him love and trust her in return. He was her beloved, and she was his.

Finn stood, pulling Evie to her feet, too. He kissed her briefly and then stepped back to allow the congratulations to roll in.

Pete and Cassidy reached Evie first. Until Sam thanked Cassidy for saving Evie's life, she had thought her relationship with them as reconciled as it would ever be. Sam's words had broken something loose in Evie, a piece of resentment that she'd held onto without realizing it. Now, as Pete and Cassidy embraced her, that broken piece dissolved, finally and totally, leaving only love and gratitude in its place. Though Robert Rice and Renee Ingram were her birth parents, Evie was Pete and Cassidy's daughter and always would be.

Gemma and Gentry stepped in next and then Bear, followed by Paul and Lydia. Lydia gave her an extra good squeeze. Just as Sam had thanked Cassidy, Evie took the opportunity to thank Lydia for giving Sam a home full of love and faith. The Howards hadn't rescued Sam from physical death, perhaps, but they'd saved her life just the same.

Last of all, Tobias and Sam approached. Tobias bent to hug Evie and quickly moved on to congratulate Finn.

Sam threw her arms around Evie, and they hugged for a long time.

"I'm so happy for you," Sam whispered. "He's such a good man."

"You'll be my maid of honor, right?" Evie said as she pulled back to look into Sam's face.

"Only if you beat me to the altar," Sam replied with a look of mischief. "You might have to settle for a matron of honor."

Evie laughed. "I don't care as long as I have my sister by my side."

"Always."

The Official "680 Miles Away" Playlist

Curious about the songs and artists Evie and Finn and Sam sing and talk about and listen to in the novel? Scan the QR code to check out the official playlist on Spotify.

If you don't use Spotify, you can search for the songs on whatever music service you do use. Here's the full song list:

Prologue: The Doppelgänger
Le Nozze di Figaro, K. 492: Sinfonia by Wolfgang Amadeus Mozart

Chapter 1: The Party
Dust in the Wind by Kansas
Blackbird by The Beatles
Trouble by Ray LaMontagne
Falling Slowly by Glen Hansard and Markéta Irglová
Bridge Over Troubled Water by Simon & Garfunkel
Kashmir by Led Zeppelin
Lover by Taylor Swift
Billie Jean by Michael Jackson
Livin' On A Prayer by Bon Jovi
Sweet Caroline by Neil Diamond
Don't Stop Believin' by Journey
La Flor De La Canela by Paco de Lucía and Ramón Algeciras

Woodchopper's Ball by Woody Herman
Little Brown Jug by Glenn Miller
I'm Getting Sentimental Over You by Tommy Dorsey
Tea For Two by Xavier Cugat & His Orchestra
Fly Me To The Moon (In Other Words) by Julie London
Blues In The Night by Ella Fitzgerald
Perhaps, Perhaps, Perhaps by Doris Day
It's Not Unusual by Tom Jones
Man in the Mirror by Michael Jackson
You'll Never Find Another Love Like Mine by Lou Rawls
Get Happy by Judy Garland
I've Got You Under My Skin by Frank Sinatra
Ain't That A Kick In The Head by Dean Martin
You Stepped Out Of A Dream by Nat King Cole
I've Got A Crush On You by Bing Crosby
Magic Moments by Perry Como
(Sittin' On) the Dock of the Bay by Otis Redding
A Sunday Kind of Love by Etta James
Hallelujah, I Love Her So by Ray Charles
Rainy Days and Mondays by Carpenters
Make Your Own Kind of Music by Cass Elliot
Back In Baby's Arms by Patsy Cline
Ring of Fire by Johnny Cash
Coal Miner's Daughter by Loretta Lynn
Hey, Good Lookin' by Hank Williams
Wachet auf, ruft uns die Stimme, Cantata BWV 140: IV. "Zion hört die Wächter singen" by Johann Sebastian Bach
Symphony No. 25 in G Minor, K. 183: I. Allegro con brio by Wolfgang Amadeus Mozart
Symphony No. 7 in A Major, Op. 92: II. Allegretto by Ludwig van Beethoven
Symphony No. 3 in F Major, Op 90: III. Poco allegretto by Johannes Brahms
The Firebird Suite: VII. Finale by Igor Stravinsky
Clarinet Concerto in A Major, K. 622: II. Adagio by Wolfgang Amadeus Mozart

Chapter 24: Audition

Violin Concerto in D Major, Op. 35: I. Allegro moderato by Pyotr Ilyich Tchaikovsky

The Nutcracker, Op. 71: Miniature Overture by Pyotr Ilyich Tchaikovsky

A Midsummer Night's Dream, Incidental Music, Op. 61, MWV M 13: No. 1 Scherzo by Felix Mendelssohn

Die Zauberflöte, K. 620: Overture by Wolfgang Amadeus Mozart

Chapter 25: Sisters

Serenade in C Major, Op. 48: II. Walzer by Pyotr Ilyich Tchaikovsky

Chapter 26: I Could Write a Book

I Could Write A Book by Ella Fitzgerald

Epilogue: Christmas

You Are the Best Thing by Ray LaMontagne

Author's Notes

Well, my characters did it again. I started out writing what I thought would be Evie's story alone, but Sam wanted a piece of the action—a very big piece—and she was awfully convincing. I also had no idea when I started writing that Tobias was going to propose in the second chapter—I had a very different proposal in mind, and it wasn't supposed to happen until the end of the book, if it even happened in this book at all.

Finn and Liam were the biggest surprises, though. Finn didn't exist in my imagination at all until the moment I typed his name, and that's when he introduced himself to my brain and informed me that he would, in fact, be Evie's love interest.

Liam, on the other hand, lived in my brain for a long time before I started writing. For a while, I thought he would be the love interest Evie gets then loses then gets back. And then I thought he would be the rival to another love interest—not Finn, but a completely different character who never ended up in the book at all. Even partway through the first draft of the book you've just finished reading, I still thought Evie might pursue a relationship with Liam until she comes to her senses and realizes that she belongs with Finn. The moment Liam's true role became clear to me was the moment Evie ran away to Iowa— a plot twist even I didn't see coming until the night before Evie made me write it.

I know. I sound like a crazy person. I think perhaps all writers are secretly crazy. But you know something? That's what makes writing so fun.

Even when it's not fun. Truthfully, *680 Miles Away* was much harder and, frankly, more frustrating to write than *6 Blocks Home*. For starters, it's the first time I've ever written a sequel—in novel or screenplay format. I hadn't planned to return to the world of *6 Blocks Home* when it was published in November 2020, but many of my readers expressed hopes that I would. Maybe they were just being polite, but I took their comments to heart and spent the next three years figuring out how to fulfill their hopes. I even took violin lessons for a summer so that I could convincingly write about playing the violin.

It was both satisfying and terrifying to pick up existing characters and tell a different part of their story. I wanted to write a book that could stand on its own—something readers who haven't read *6 Blocks Home* would enjoy—but I also wanted to reward those who did read *6 Blocks Home* with plenty of Easter eggs. I hope I've done justice to this part of Sam and Tobias's story.

680 Miles Away was also difficult because it took me several tries to figure out which part of Evie's story to tell. As soon as I decided to honor my readers' wishes and write a sequel, I knew I wanted to write the story of Sam's long-lost sister. I knew she was a violinist, but I didn't know much more than that.

I started my first attempt at this novel in April 2021 (just five months after *6 Blocks Home* was released). I was seven chapters and almost 14,000 words in when I realized I was telling the wrong part of Evie's story. It took place in the immediate aftermath of Evie finding out she was adopted. I still think it might be interesting ground to tread someday, but nothing about that version was working, so I abandoned it.

My second attempt came more than a year later, starting in June 2022. I put in a ton of work outlining the chapters and figuring out how I could weave Evie and Sam's stories together to make them co-protagonists. I again made it to seven chapters, but this time, I had almost 18,000 words. Once again, I felt that it was the wrong part of Evie's story to write. As I had recently finished my own Camino, I was inspired to make Evie walk the Camino. So this second version took place primarily on the Camino, which I thought would be exciting. It wasn't. It turns out that writing about the Camino is much less interesting than actually walking it. If writing it was boring, I can only imagine how awful it would have been to read. So I abandoned that version, too.

The version that you hold in your hands was my third attempt at telling Evie's story. I started it in September 2023. The only scene that made it into all three versions is the prologue, where Evie sees Sam and Tobias at the concert. I knew very early on that I wanted the book to start that way—that it had to start that way—and it was a notion I could never let go of. I think it works nicely. I hope you agree.

Lastly, *680 Miles Away* was more challenging than *6 Blocks Home* on a practical level. When I wrote *6 Blocks Home*, we were in the first months of the pandemic, and I had nothing to do but write. I wrote a complete draft in record time because that's all I did every single day. With *680 Miles Away*, however, I had a full-time job to work around. The time constraints often made it difficult to remember what I wrote from day to day or writing session to writing session. Maintaining story continuity from beginning to end took far more effort and several more revisions than *6 Blocks Home* ever required.

Still, despite the challenges and moments of frustration, writing is one of the greatest joys of my life. In a way, the difficulties made finishing *680 Miles Away* all the more satisfying. I am proud of this novel—not just because of what it is, but because of how hard it made me work to bring it to fruition. It forced me to grow as a writer and as a human, and for that, I am grateful.

A Note About Quotes and Emojis

In *6 Blocks Home*, I quoted almost exclusively from scripture, the one exception coming from the traditional *Requiem æternam* chant. Here, in addition to scripture, I used several quotes from saints that I've collected over the years.

I keep an ongoing Quote Note in my Apple Notes app that I add to every time I stumble across a quote from a saint that strikes a deep chord in me. Many of them I've collected from a daily email newsletter called "Morning Offering" from The Catholic Company.

Others, like the quote from Saint Gregory Nazianzen on his friendship with Saint Basil the Great, I found while praying the Office of Readings in the Liturgy of the Hours.

The quote from Saint John Chrysostom regarding what husbands ought to tell their wives, believe it or not, comes from paragraph 2365 of the *Catechism of the Catholic Church*.

I used a little prayer book I received from a Miles Christi priest many years ago for the Litany of Humility and the Litany of St. Joseph. You can find these prayers online and in many prayer books. In fact, I encourage you to do just that—depending on the source, some words may have a slightly different translation that speaks to you more powerfully. Find a translation that works for you.

Speaking of translations, all the scripture quotes come from the RSV-

CE translation of the Bible.

Emojis are a weird thing. They've become almost ubiquitous in our day-to-day digital communication, which makes it surprising how complicated it is to use them in print and ebooks. There are copyright issues (end user license agreements regarding the use of proprietary emoji designs) as well as operating system and software compatibility issues (emojis fall outside the unicode range available on Kindles, for example). I could have chosen to lose the emojis in this novel to avoid these issues, but I think their appearance in text messages reveals something important and authentic about the characters. Like the music we listen to, the emojis we use say something about who we are.

I'll spare you the technical details of the solution I came up with. The important thing is to provide appropriate attribution: All emojis you see in this novel were designed by OpenMoji—the open-source emoji and icon project. License: CC BY-SA 4.0.

Acknowledgments

Shortly after I published *6 Blocks Home*, several people asked when my next book was coming out. It made me excited to write the next thing, but both the questions and the excitement wore off fairly quickly. Except for two people, who never stopped asking. To those two people, I owe many, many thanks. If it weren't for their persistence, I might have given up after my first attempt at Evie's story.

Sami B., I promised you I would have this novel finished by the time you graduated from high school. I missed the deadline, but I didn't quit. There were many moments when it was that promise alone that kept me going. This book is a reality because of you. Thank you.

Eileen M., you probably had no idea how much motivation you were giving me every time you asked when my next book would be finished. You, too, are one of the reasons this book exists. Thank you.

Huge thanks to my beta readers, Sarah L. and Denise F. I don't know what I would do without either of you—and not just because you are always the first to raise your hands to beta read for me. Your enthusiasm for my writing blows my mind, but more importantly, your friendship means the world to me. I love you both.

Thank you once again to my incredible cover designer, Bilal Abiyhasa. You are such a joy to work with, Abi, and I'm proud and grateful to have your beautiful cover artwork on all four of my books.

Thank you, as always, to all the family members, friends, and colleagues who have read my stuff, given me notes, and cheered me on over the years. Your generosity and love humble me.

And thank you, readers. I said this in *6 Blocks Home*, and I will say it in every book until I die: A work means nothing without a soul to comprehend it. You, dear reader, give my work meaning.

Above all, I must give all thanks and praise to Christ, my Divine

Spouse. I am nothing without Him: "Whom have I in heaven but Thee? And there is nothing upon earth that I desire besides Thee. My flesh and my heart may fail, but God is the strength of my heart and my portion for ever" (Ps 73:25–26).

About the Author

Tara started writing fiction when she was in first grade, but she didn't discover the thrill of screenwriting until she studied Communications Media at John Paul the Great Catholic University. Screenplays are her favorite way to tell stories, but novels are quickly gaining. She hopes her writing will contribute to a revival of Catholic fiction.

After successfully self-publishing two screenplays as paperbacks and ebooks, she partnered with two of her former film professors to create Story Masters Film Academy, which offers online courses in screenwriting and directing.

Tara resides in Colorado, and in 2016, she became a Consecrated Virgin Living in the World in the Diocese of Colorado Springs. In addition to making things up and writing them down, Tara enjoys praying, hiking (definitely not running), going to the symphony (especially movies at the symphony), discovering new craft brews, and spending time with family and friends.

Follow Tara on Goodreads or join her email newsletter at tarajstonewriter.com.